A LONG BRIDGE HOME

AMISH OF BIG SKY COUNTRY

Kelly Irvin

ZONDERVAN®

ZONDERVAN

A Long Bridge Home

Copyright © 2020 by Kelly Irvin

This title is also available as a Zondervan ebook.

This title is also available as a Zondervan audio book.

Requests for information should be addressed to:
Zondervan, *3900 Sparks Dr. SE, Grand Rapids, Michigan 49546*

ISBN 978-0-310-35673-8 (softcover)
ISBN 978-0-310-35674-5 (ebook)
ISBN 978-0-310-35675-2 (downloadable audio)
ISBN 978-0-310-36619-5 (mass market)

Library of Congress Cataloging-in-Publication Data
CIP data available upon request.

Printed in the United States of America

21 22 23 24 25 CWM 10 9 8 7 6 5 4 3 2 1

To Northwest Hills United Methodist Church,
my church family.
Thank you for standing in the gap for me,
for reminding me that God is good all the time,
and for making me think about what I believe and why.

Jesus answered, "I am the way and the truth and the life. No one comes to the Father except through me."

JOHN 14:6

I urge, then, first of all, that petitions, prayers, intercession and thanksgiving be made for all people—for kings and all those in authority, that we may live peaceful and quiet lives in all godliness and holiness. This is good, and pleases God our Savior, who wants all people to be saved and to come to a knowledge of the truth.

1 TIMOTHY 2:1–4

Deutsch Vocabulary*

ach: oh
aenti: aunt
bopli(n): baby
bruder: brother
daed: father
danki: thank you
dawdy haus: grandparents' house
demut: humility
der fux: the fox
Deutsch: German
dochder: daughter
eck: corner reserved for the wedding party
eepies: cookies
Englischer: English or non-Amish
fraa: wife
freind: friend
gegisch: silly
Gelassenheit: a giving up of self for the greater good of the
    community
Gmay: church district
Gott: God
groossdaadi: grandpa
groossmammi: grandma
guder daag: good day
guder mariye: good morning

gut: good
gut natcht: good night
hochmut: pride
hund: dog
Ich bin gut: I'm good.
jah: yes
kaffi: coffee
kapp: prayer cap
kind: child
kinner: children
mach's gut: goodbye
mammi: grandma
mann: husband
millich: milk
mudder: mother
narrisch: crazy
nee: no
onkel: uncle
Ordnung: written and unwritten rules in an Amish district
rumspringa: period of running around
schweschder: sister
sechndich schpeeder: see you later
suh: son
Wie bischt du: How are you?
wunderbarr: wonderful

*The German dialect spoken by the Amish is not a written language and varies depending on the location and origin of the settlement. These spellings are approximations. Most Amish children learn English after they start school. They also learn High German, which is used in their Sunday services.

Featured Families

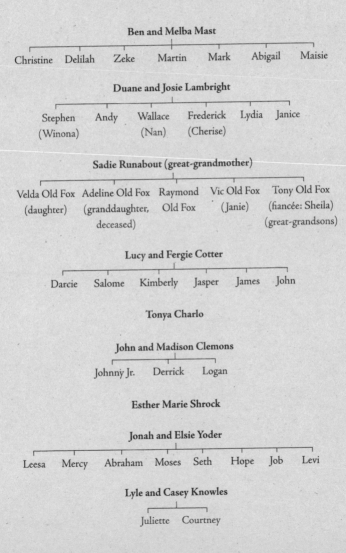

Ben and Melba Mast

Christine   Delilah   Zeke   Martin   Mark   Abigail   Maisie

Duane and Josie Lambright

Stephen   Andy   Wallace   Frederick   Lydia   Janice
(Winona)   (Nan)   (Cherise)

Sadie Runabout (great-grandmother)

Velda Old Fox   Adeline Old Fox   Raymond   Vic Old Fox   Tony Old Fox
(daughter)   (granddaughter,   Old Fox   (Janie)   (fiancée: Sheila)
      deceased)   (great-grandsons)

Lucy and Fergie Cotter

Darcie   Salome   Kimberly   Jasper   James   John

Tonya Charlo

John and Madison Clemons

Johnny Jr.   Derrick   Logan

Esther Marie Shrock

Jonah and Elsie Yoder

Leesa   Mercy   Abraham   Moses   Seth   Hope   Job   Levi

Lyle and Casey Knowles

Juliette   Courtney

CHAPTER 1

Even the fresh scent of bleach couldn't overcome the acrid stench of smoke from the Caribou wildfire that raged in Kootenai National Forest.

Usually Christine Mast approached her work with steely determination to smite every dust particle, ferret out every stain, and banish every germ. It seemed silly to clean a house that might burn to a crisp in the next few days. On the other hand, on Wednesdays she cleaned the Drake house. Period. DeeDee Drake didn't sacrifice cleanliness for anyone or anything. Labor Day weekend might be a time for holiday celebrations, but for Christine, it meant laboring. The Drakes' ranch-style home better be spick-and-span or DeeDee would have plenty to say about it. That's why she and Christine got along so well. Cleanliness was, after all, next to godliness.

The evacuation order could come any second, and yet Christine stood in the Drake living room with her trusty dusting rag in one hand and a Willow Tree figurine of a woman and man holding a newborn baby in the other. These delicate carvings were so sweet. DeeDee had more than a dozen on her mammoth fireplace's wooden mantel.

Christine held the figurine family close to her chest and

closed her eyes. What would it feel like to rock her own baby to sleep on a cold winter night? Her beau, Andy Lambright, talked about marriage, but he never came out and asked her. Sometimes he looked as if he might pop the question any second, and yet, nothing. Wouldn't it be the pinnacle of happiness—cleaning her own house for a husband who appreciated all that hard work?

Neither the man nor the woman holding the baby answered. Their faces remained blandly blissful.

"Christine. You need to go—now!"

DeeDee's voice boomed behind Christine. She jumped. The fragile sculpture slipped from her fingers and hit the pine plank floor. It shattered in a half dozen pieces.

"*Ach!*" Christine sank to the floor. She gathered the pieces of the happy family, their faces a puzzle that couldn't be put together again. "I'm so sorry. Your beautiful figurine—"

"It's okay, sweetheart. It's not the end of the world." DeeDee knelt next to her. "Stop, you'll cut yourself."

Indeed, the end of the world did roar down the mountains, and this tiny bit of beauty seemed too precious to lose. Christine would glue the family back together. No, it would never be the same. Like her serene, orderly life.

A pointed shard pierced Christine's thumb. Blood dripped on her apron. She clutched her hand to her chest, trying to stymie the flow from a small cut. "I'm such a clumsy girl."

"You're not clumsy. It's my fault. I scared you." DeeDee heaved herself to her feet and offered her plump hand. "Let's get you a bandage and get you going. We just got the Code Red Reverse 911 call. It's time to evacuate. The fire's coming."

With one last look at the broken family, Christine scampered after the other woman. A quick fix in the kitchen and she rushed out the door. DeeDee followed. They hugged as if they might never see each other again. Being hugged by DeeDee was like being enveloped in a soft, down-filled comforter that smelled of Dove soap and lavender shampoo. A safe, clean fragrance.

"I didn't finish the bathrooms." A sob caught in Christine's throat. Letting go and leaving this kind woman who had been a neighbor for Christine's entire life seemed impossible. "Alex left a terrible mess in the kids' bathroom."

The oldest Drake son was a teenager sure he needed to shave those three spindly blond hairs on his chin and wear large quantities of a stinky aftershave that made Christine sneeze.

"Honey, God willing, they'll still be here when we come back and you can scrub them extra hard." DeeDee gently tugged free. "We'll see you and yours in Eureka. Don't you worry."

A conversation played in Christine's head. One she wasn't supposed to hear. Mother and Father whispered over glasses of iced tea in the kitchen after the little ones went to bed. Father wanted to go home—to his home. Kansas. Mother argued against it, but if things went as usual, Father would have the final word.

Christine had been two when Father pulled up stakes and moved the family to Montana, drawn by the gorgeous vistas, hunting, fishing, and mountaintops he said brought them closer to the God who created them. Kootenai was their home. Christine had graduated from school here in the eighth grade, cleaned houses for four English families since she was fifteen, and been baptized at eighteen. She went on camping trips with her family to Lake Koocanusa even though tramping around outdoors with the mosquitoes and snakes numbered far down her list of favorite activities. She'd hike in the mountains a hundred times a year to stay here.

All she remembered from trips to visit family was a shimmering asphalt ribbon that cut a straight line through endless flat fields of golden wheat and corn as far as she could see—and dirty convenience store restrooms. Even as a child, she'd rather hold it than relieve herself in such stinky, miserable quarters.

The future heaved in front of her, a winding mountain road that suddenly buckled under the weight of a rock slide. "I'll pay you back for the figurine." Tears choked Christine as she grabbed the bike she'd left leaning against the back porch. "I'm so sorry I broke it. It was so beautiful."

"Knickknacks can be replaced." DeeDee swiped at her dimpled cheeks and then shooed her with both hands. "Go, girl, hurry. Your daddy and mama will be looking for you."

Christine slid onto her mountain bike and pedaled down the gravel road. The thick smoke stung her eyes and hurt her throat. The entire world smelled like a wood-burning stove. The bandaged cut on her palm throbbed.

She glanced back. DeeDee stood on the porch waving as if she had all the time in the world. Behind her, black smoke loomed over the house, a sinister, growing monster lurching closer and closer. The towering pines and spruce that normally guarded the grounds with such stately dignity quivered and shrank as if they could see the seething flames roaring down the mountain, bringing with them the demise of every living creature and plant in their path.

Don't look.

Gritting her teeth, she faced the road and pumped harder. Her muscles complained. Her parched throat ached with each intake of harsh air.

A horn blared. A shiny blue pickup truck loaded down with furniture, boxes, and suitcases swerved around her. She skidded to a stop at the intersection with Wilderness Road. The truck barreled past her. Gene Dickson's wife yelled an apology from the passenger's seat. Her words whirled away on a gust of wind, dust, and smoke.

Christine's legs quaked. She gasped for air and then regretted it. Smoke burned all the way to her belly.

Go, go, go. Gott, *help me.*

A buggy came into view with a familiar chocolate-colored gelding pulling it. The steady *clip-clop* of horse's hooves thudding on packed dirt steadied her.

Andy.

He always showed up when Christine needed him. He showed his love in every way possible—except one.

Now she might never get a chance to hear those words.

CHAPTER 2

Gott knows what's in a person's heart. That's what Christine's dad always said. How surprised would Andy be if Christine hopped from her bike and jumped into his arms? Rather than shocking him half to death, she settled for a sturdy wave. He plowed to a stop in the intersection, hopped from the buggy, and strode toward her with a frown on his tanned face.

"I couldn't believe it when your *daed* said you went to work this morning with the preevacuation notice hanging over us." He punctuated the statement with emotions—anger, worry, fear, love—in that gruff voice that never failed to send goose bumps hiking up Christine's arms. "You should've been on the first wagon out of here."

As usual her heart took a quick vacation from beating as she stared up at his unlined face with his forest-green eyes, high cheekbones, and full lips. His normally crisp, clean blue shirt sported dark sweat stains. His pants were dirty. If only she could do his laundry. He towered over her, but so did most people. He said he liked that she was short, and he never took advantage of her height by treating her as if she were a child because she looked like one. "I was at DeeDee's cleaning when they got the call."

"Get in. My boss got the same call. I'll put your bike in the back."

Andy didn't wait for her to agree. He waggled his fingers at Donut—so named because he'd never met a doughnut he didn't like—and the dog hopped from the front seat into the back with a soft *woof*. Christine slipped from the bike and climbed into the buggy. Donut's snout nudged her arm. She swiveled and petted the gray German shepherd's grizzled head. "*Jah*, it's *gut* to see you too, *hund*."

Andy settled next to her and snapped the reins. "Your daed was headed back to the house. He asked me to come get you."

"Do you think he knows about us?"

"*Nee*. He knows he can trust me with you, that's all." Andy's voice deepened. "He and I are friends despite the age difference. Anyway, he wanted to set up sprinklers to try to protect the house and finish packing the wagon. He wants your *mudder* and the *kinner* out of here. None of us should've been working, I reckon."

Plain folks didn't know how not to work. Sawdust decorated Andy's shirt and homemade denim pants. Fire or not, the Montana Furniture Store had orders to fill for customers from across the country who wanted rustic, log cabin–style furniture. Christine's fingers itched to brush off his shirt. She clutched them in her lap instead. "Daed said we should pray for relief, prepare for the worst, and go about our business, knowing Gott has a plan."

"He's a wise man, but if you were my *dochder*, I would've made you stay home."

"I'm so glad I'm not."

Her dry observation elicited a small chuckle.

Her own laugh skittered away on the smoke-filled wind.

"I heard him say something last night . . ." Should she repeat information she wasn't meant to hear? Christine chewed her lower lip. If she couldn't tell the man she eventually intended to marry, who could she tell? "He and Mudder were talking in the kitchen before bedtime. I went to say *gut natcht*. They're thinking about returning to Haven."

"To Kansas?" He took his gaze from the road long enough to share a look of disbelief with her. "He hasn't said anything to me."

The two worked at the furniture store together. Christine shrugged. "He hasn't even told us."

Andy shook his towhead as he turned onto the dirt road that led to the Mast property. He often did that when mulling over a problem. He likely had no idea how often he peered into space, frowning, his shaggy hair bobbing. "Maybe your parents will allow you to stay. You're a grown woman. You have a special friend. They know that."

Maybe if he'd asked her to marry him, they wouldn't be having this conversation. Why was he holding back? What was he holding back? Since the first time Andy gave her a ride home from a singing, she'd never looked at another man. He said he had to wait until he saved enough money to buy land and build a home for his future family, and that was fine with her.

Only a few months ago a small house had come on the market for rent. A perfect starter home for a newlywed couple. She'd thrown out a comment about it, hoping he'd bite. He nodded and said it would indeed be a good house . . . for some young couple. Nothing more. "Stay where?"

"You could stay with Mercy and the Yoders."

"Maybe. They're staying in Eureka. We could see each other there."

"I won't be in Eureka."

Now Christine shook her head. He couldn't be serious. "Are you staying in Rexford? That's still close. Or Libby?"

Libby would require a car, but it was only an hour away.

Andy didn't answer. His expression was unreadable, as it so often was. They pulled into her front yard. What had been a peaceful mountain country scene at dawn with a sprawling house, chicken coop, horse corral, barn, and swing set for the children was now the scene of furious activity. Christine's dad and her three brothers handled hoses that sprayed water over the house, the nursery, and the sheds. Her sisters and her mother lugged suitcases and boxes to the wagon. They needed her help, but she couldn't let this discussion end with that bombshell.

"Are you going to tell me, or is it a secret?"

"I didn't get a chance to tell you earlier." With a glance around, Andy grabbed her hand, squeezed, and let go. "My daed wants me back home. His health is bad. My *bruders* built on a *dawdy haus* for him and Mudder."

"Lewistown is six and a half hours from Eureka by car." Andy left his family's farm between Moore and Lewistown after a falling out with his older brother—one he never wanted to talk about. "You promised me we would always live in Kootenai. You never wanted to go home."

"It's not forever. Just until he's feeling better. All the *suhs* are at the farm for now."

It must be bad if all the sons were converging on Lewistown. "Whatever you need to do."

"Don't be mad." He hopped down from the buggy and waited while she did the same. "I have to take care of family."

Christine managed a smile. She would do the same, if called upon. "I'll miss you."

His long fingers brushed hers. "Me too. Now go help your mudder. You need to get out of here. Now."

He marched away just like that. No backward glance. No assurances. Men were so hard to understand. "How will we stay in touch?" she called after him.

"It'll work out." He did a backward wave over one shoulder and kept going. "Remember, worry is a sin."

Fine. No worries here. She would let him go and let God sort it out.

. . .

That had not gone well. Leaving such important information until the last second was all wrong. His throat aching, Andy scooped up the hose left on the ground by Christine's brother Zeke and sprayed the log walls in the hope that it would be enough to save the structure when flames surrounded it. He had no choice but to go home. Family came first. Even if it meant leaving behind the woman he loved. Even if it meant dealing with a brother who'd done something nearly impossible to forgive.

Even after four years, the thought of facing Stephen and his wife caused embers hotter than the ones sparked by the fire to burn through Andy. He could be the bigger man. He had no choice. Just when his goal of saving enough money to get his own place and propose to Christine seemed within reach, lightning ignited the mountains above West Kootenai, his father's health failed, and Ben Mast had decided to take his family back to Kansas. If this was God's plan, Andy couldn't fathom it.

Nor question it. An obedient believer did not question. His

father's words the day Andy left the farm rang in his ears. *"It's not your place to question Gott's plan or to run away from it. You're needed here. Forgiveness is one of the most important planks in building a strong faith."*

But he had questioned. Unable to forgive, he ignored the pleading in his mother's eyes and left. And met Christine, for whom his feelings had grown over time despite his stubborn desire to protect his heart. And he'd learned to love this tiny town of just over four hundred people. Sometimes God's plans were more outrageous than a person could imagine. "All's well that ends well," his father would say. But not until Andy learned to forgive.

It would take a stronger man than himself to resist Christine's slightly crooked smile, dimpled cheeks, sky-blue eyes, or the bonfire that raged when her fingers brushed against his or he touched the soft skin on her neck. Or kissed eager lips that melded to his. Or the way she looked when she served him at the supper table when he joined her family for a meal—as if she'd made the cherry pie just for him.

He couldn't tell her that his hesitancy had nothing to do with her and everything to do with his fear that she would be another woman who took his heart and then left him standing at the back of the room while she married another man.

Why would Ben give up and go back to Kansas before the fire touched the home he'd built for his wife and seven children?

Now would not be the time to ask.

"Is everyone packed up and out by your place?" Ben manhandled a wheelbarrow filled with tools toward the wagon already overflowing with boxes, suitcases, two dogs, a cat, and the four girls. Sweat rolled down the older man's face and soaked the collar of his shirt. Christine's father had the build of a giant sequoia tree and a black beard threaded with shiny silver. "If you're not needed there, I can use your help setting up sprinklers around the barn."

"We've done all we can at the cabins. Ian is gone. Henry went to help the Borntragers at the store." Andy turned off the water and unscrewed the hose so he could move to the barn. "I think Caleb is at the Yoders, helping Jonah."

"Gut." Ben swiped at his forehead with his sleeve. "I'll get my *fraa* and kinner moving. Then I'll be back."

Andy connected the hose a second time and grabbed a sprinkler from the pile next to the massive wooden building's double doors. He scooped up a respirator and stuck it over his head. Immediate relief seeped into his burning throat as he watched the tableau of husband and wife saying goodbye. Melba Mast didn't want to leave her husband and sons—that was obvious. Her round face turned red. She gesticulated with both hands. Ben's vigorous shake of his head indicated his reaction to her argument.

The big man stepped into his wife's space and leaned so close it appeared he might hug her or even kiss her. Melba's hands stopped moving. The two seemed to communicate without words. Twenty-five years of marriage shimmered in the space between two human beings more connected than branches of the same cottonwood.

To have that would be the ultimate gift from God. A person had to be worthy of such largess.

Andy averted his eyes. The moment demanded privacy. He concentrated on the spray of warm water that soaked the faded gray barn walls. Drops of water sparkled in the rays of sun that managed to squeeze through thick clouds of smoke like hope in the face of a future that might be consumed by fire.

"*Sechndich schpeeder.*"

Christine's voice held a plaintive, questioning note. God willing, they *would* see each other later. Maybe not today. But later. Andy swiveled and let the hose water grass turned brittle and brown by a long, hot summer with no rain. "*Mach's gut.*"

She smiled and waved. Andy's muscles quivered and begged for the chance to stride over to the wagon and kiss her thoroughly in front of her parents, sisters, brothers, and God. He waved back.

The wagon carrying his hope for a full future jolted down the dirt road and disappeared ahead of a flurry of dust.

Gott, keep them safe, I humbly beg.

He should add, *Thy will be done.*

But God would do what He would do. He didn't need Andy's permission. That was obvious.

Trying not to look toward the mountains, Andy spent the next hour helping Ben move the sprinklers and soak the buildings. Wearing respirators meant little was said, but the set of the man's broad shoulders reflected his desperate need to believe their paltry efforts would make a difference when the fire drove them away from his property.

A siren whooped, a harsh, discordant sound not often heard in these parts. Andy dropped the hose and whirled. A dirt-covered Lincoln County sheriff's SUV swung around the bend in the dirt road leading to the Mast home, leaving a cloud of dust in its wake. Brakes screeched and the SUV halted at a crazy angle a few yards from the shop Ben used for his own creations—benches, tables, and other primitive pieces—from wood he scavenged from the forest floor. Deputy Sheriff Tim

Trudeau, a tall, muscular, red-haired man who normally wore a good-natured smile, emerged.

"It's time to go." Scowling, he waved his paw the size of a catcher's mitt in the general direction of the mountains. "It's coming."

"You said we had four to five hours." Ben coughed as he glanced up at the sunlight leaking through dense smoke. He wiped at his face with a dirty sleeve. "It's not even been two hours since Deputy Quiñones came by."

"We miscalculated." Tim grabbed a can of spray paint from the SUV's front seat. "It didn't slow down when it hit the meadow. The winds picked up. It's moving faster than we figured it would. You gotta go. I'm sorry, Ben. You've done all you can do."

"What are you doing with that?" Careful to keep the hose turned toward the building, Andy moved closer to Christine's father. "Spray painting in the middle of an evacuation?"

"That's how we know who's gone and who's staying."

"We can stay? Isn't the evacuation mandatory—"

"It is mandatory," Tim broke in. "Especially for kids. We have a few thickheaded folks who refuse to leave, but they had to sign a form saying they stay at their own risk. No one will rescue them." His voice grew hoarse. "You don't want to do that, Ben. Get your boys out of here. Please."

"I will. Just give me a little longer . . . I want to set sprinklers around the shop." Ben shook his massive head and turned toward the mountains. Andy did the same. A curtain of hot orange and red flames careened toward them, consuming everything with a voracious appetite that never seemed to be satiated.

"Gott have mercy." Ben whipped toward the house. "Suhs, in the buggy, now."

Gott, help us. Andy turned off the water with hands suddenly all thumbs. He bolted across the yard to his own buggy. Wild-eyed, Cocoa whinnied and shied away from him. "It's okay, boy. You're right. It's time to go."

"No one's in the house?" Tim hollered.

"No one." Ben shooed his youngest boy, Martin, into the buggy. "The women and children went on ahead."

"Thank God for that." Tim shook the can and sprayed a big black zero on the sidewalk leading up to the house. "Now go."

They went. Andy wanted to look back. Surely God wouldn't turn him into a pillar of salt like Lot's wife. The people of West Kootenai had done nothing but live by God's commandments. No iniquity or darkness lived here. Only salt and light.

His new beginning in the heart of God's beautiful mountain oasis far to the west of Eden disappeared behind him, hidden by a dark curtain of black smoke from a fire started by lightning. Not man's doing, but God's.

CHAPTER 3

REXFORD, MONTANA

A few Englishers not put off by fire bans and possible evacuations ate Popsicles, slurped sodas, and took selfies in Rexford's General Store in a last stop before rolling their boats, canoes, kayaks, Jet Skis, and RVs to the shores of Lake Koocanusa.

Christine stuck close to her mother's side as she wove her way between two couples perusing US Forest Service motor-vehicle use maps and discussing how many bags of ice they needed. At the counter Mother found the person she sought. Owner and general manager Terry Dublin.

Terry scratched his shaggy head of silver curls, smiled, and sighed in that order. Which was nothing new. He did that every time the Masts stopped by for a visit to one of their favorite camping spots.

"Sorry you had to evacuate. This fire is a monster." Terry removed his wire-rimmed glasses and replaced them in the exact same spot. "What can I do for you?"

He did not ask the question idly.

"How crowded is it on Rexford Bench?" Mother leaned closer to be heard over the buzz of customers. "We need to set up camp for a day or two."

A day or two. From her lips to God's ears. Christine selected a handful of Bazooka bubble gums and laid a dollar on the counter. The girls would be thrilled with her small gift.

"Everyone here is concerned for your welfare." Terry's kind smile encompassed Christine as he nudged the dollar bill back in her direction. "On the house. Take some Tootsie Pops, too, for the little ones. Don't you worry. With the fire bans and the smoke, people are choosing to camp in other areas. You won't have trouble finding a spot. Did you bring plenty of blankets? When the sun goes down, it'll cool off. You can't make a campfire, of course, but set up your Coleman and the mosquitoes should leave you alone. Also, you'll be close to the facilities. When Ben comes in, I'll tell him where you are."

"That's kind of you."

"What are neighbors for?"

The drive from West Kootenai encompassed the longest bridge in Montana and another seventeen miles north on Highway 37 to get to Rexford, but in Montana they were close neighbors.

Christine thanked him for the candy, and Mother gathered up a few supplies, including more kerosene, hot dogs, buns, pickle relish, extra matches, flashlight batteries, and the ingredients for s'mores.

"S'mores, Mudder?" Christine's mouth watered. Between the Tootsie Pops and the chocolate, the kids would be hopping around like jack-in-the-boxes. "It really does feel like we're camping. Can we go fishing too?"

"I don't know why not. I have a hankering for kokanee, or Kamloops trout would be nice. It's called making lemons from lemonade." Mother tucked wisps of iron-gray hair under her *kapp* as she smiled. In her younger days she and Christine had been as close in looks to twins as mother and daughter could come. Only Mother was taller—like most other adults in the world. "The kinner see this as an adventure. No reason to let them think otherwise. They're getting a vacation from school. They'll work off all that excess energy playing in the water and running around."

"Even if in the meantime our house burns down with everything in it?" The question bullied its way out. Shame immediately raced to catch up. "I keep thinking of *Mammi*'s rocking chair that *Groossdaadi* made for her. And my cedar chest with all those quilts she helped me make."

"It's not like we can take our material possessions with us anyway. You know better than that."

Mother's good-natured expression took the sting from her words.

Truth be told, Christine didn't have many possessions. Her hope chest held quilts Grandma Tabitha helped her make before she passed four years ago. Christine's canvas bag on the wagon held all her clothes, her Bible, a sewing kit, a dozen paperbacks, ranging from a biography of Abraham Lincoln to the story of Corrie ten Boom's time in a Nazi prison camp. Her father found her taste in reading materials odd, but nothing in the *Ordnung* prohibited her from learning more about historical figures.

"What about the other horses?" Pinta, Nina, and Maria were good packhorses for their camping trips into the mountains.

"Daed took them to the Littles' pasture this morning. They'll be safe there."

Aside from the house itself and a few pieces of furniture made by her father and grandfather, the animals were the only possessions that held any importance. The fire could take their home but not their memories, not the lives they'd lived there. *"A house is just a house. It's the family that makes it a home,"* Grandma Tabitha's voice reminded her.

Memories couldn't burn up in a fire. It couldn't take the time spent in front of the fire sewing with Grandma after she came for a visit and decided to stay.

Christine followed Mother out the door and into the parking lot. Maisie and Abigail perched on top of the boxes with Socks and Shoes, their two mismatched mutts, between them. "I'm hungry," Maisie called. "So is Socks."

"You can wait until we get to the campground." At nine Abigail was five years older than her sister, so she liked to think of herself as a little mother to Maisie. "Have some raisins."

She handed Maisie a handful of raisins in a ragged bandanna that had seen better days.

Mother's expression turned suspicious. "Where did those come from?"

"I saved them from church."

"Last week?"

"Hmmm, maybe last month."

Mother chuckled and held out her hand. "Let's wait until we can roast hot dogs, why don't we?"

If it weren't for the pillars of funeral-black smoke cloaking the Purcell Mountains in the distance, Christine could have pretended they were on one of their vacations on the shores of Lake Koocanusa. She climbed into the wagon and grabbed the reins while Mother settled next to her. "So what were you and Mercy hollering about earlier before we crossed the bridge? Something about ASAP? What's that?"

ASAP. Awful Situation Approaching. Usually it involved the men in their lives, but Mother couldn't know that.

"I was hoping I would see her and Nora here." Mercy and Nora had been Christine's best friends since they were all in diapers. There had been no time to compare notes in the race from Kootenai. Mother didn't need to know the details—wouldn't want to know her daughter had accidently eavesdropped on her conversation with Father. "She's been in a funk for a while."

"Because of Caleb."

That her mother knew about Mercy's courting troubles didn't surprise Christine. Her mother had eyes in the back of her head and ears like an elephant. Or so she liked to tell her children. "I suppose. She said it didn't feel right. There aren't a lot of bachelors of marrying age in Kootenai right now, but that doesn't mean she should marry a man just because he asks. Nora, Mercy, and I are all trying to make gut choices."

"Hey, I'm right behind you." Delilah handed Sable, a black tomcat, to Abigail and leaned between her younger sisters. "Leave a man for me."

"You're only eighteen, *kind*. You have plenty of time for such things. Baptism first." Mother guided the horse into the long cement pad that marked their spot next to the sparkling turquoise water lapping along Rexford Bench Campground. Two wooden picnic tables and a barbecue pit that couldn't be used rounded out the amenities. "There's no rush. A fraa and a *mann* are united for life. Picking the right person is far more important than getting there first."

The speech never varied—not in the five years since Christine started her *rumspringa*. Mother and Father never batted an eye, but a fly on the wall probably received an earful when the two talked about having Christine still at home, followed by Delilah and Zeke, seventeen, both in their rumspringas. If they worried about their teenagers' extracurricular activities, they never let on.

Mother never pried, but she surely knew about Andy as well. If only Christine dared to ask more questions. Not now. Not with so much upheaval in their lives. It would be selfish. "We're spreading out from one end of the state to the other because of this fire."

"That's a bit of an exaggeration." Mother's forehead wrinkled. She raised her hand and squinted at the sun sinking into the west. "Some of us will be here. Others will go to Eureka. That's only seven miles from here. You'll see Mercy soon enough."

"Not if we move back to Haven."

No! The words escaped as if they had a mind of their own. Christine gave herself a mental smack on the head.

"We're going back to Kansas?" Delilah hopped from the wagon. "We can't. What about Evan? He likes me. I know he does."

"Will we see *Groossmammi* Ruth?" Abigail shrieked and clapped. "I love Mammi."

"Me too." Maisie was too young to remember her last trip to Kansas, but she liked whatever her big sister liked. "I want to go to Kansas."

Mother's glare singed Christine's eyebrows. "It's wrong to eavesdrop."

"I didn't mean to. I went back upstairs as soon as I heard you arguing."

"Your daed and I do not argue."

"Discuss—"

"So it's true. We're going back to Kansas." Delilah slapped at a fly the size of Christine's thumb. Its angry buzz zoomed up and away. "Why would we do that? Because of the fire?

We don't even know if our house will burn. It could still be there—"

"Hush. Hush!" Mother blotted her damp face with her apron. "This is a conversation for later when your daed is here. Right now we need to set up the tents and get situated before it gets dark."

"Are we living here?" Abigail hopped from the wagon and turned to help Maisie down. Socks and Shoes, one a brown boxer-pit mix and the other a terrier, followed on their own. They raced around in circles, yipping and howling their approval. "What happens if it rains?"

"The tents are waterproof." Mother rummaged through boxes until she found several nylon bags that held their tents. "Pray it does rain. Pray the rain douses the fire and we'll be able to go home. We need to put these up. It'll be fun, like a special camping trip."

Complete with smoke and all the mosquitoes a person could swat.

"Mudder!" Delilah's pout was better than any her four-year-old sister could produce. "Are we living here or are we going to Kansas?"

"I don't know the answer to that question." Mother's tone brooked no argument. "What I do know is that we're having roasted hot dogs and s'mores for supper. We can make them on the Coleman stove. It's not as much fun, but it'll do. In the meantime, why don't you girls play in the water for a little bit, while Christine and I put up the tents. Or take a hike over to the Hoodoos."

The beautiful sandstone formations protruded toward the sky across the inlet from their campsites. A trail made a ribbon along the sandy shores of the lake to their favorite spot.

All the Masts liked to hike, some more than others. Christine managed a smile. "Go on, Delilah, I don't mind putting up the tents."

"Fine." A smile replaced Delilah's pout. "Maybe I'll try to catch us some fish for supper."

"Only if you plan to clean them." Christine couldn't hide her shudder. She liked fish fries, but fish guts stank. "I'll be happy to cook them for you, and I'm better at putting up tents. They're like jigsaw puzzles."

"Be very careful, girls." Mother's smile had ragged edges. "No one gets into the water alone."

When they were out of earshot, Mother dropped a stack of paper plates on the table and turned to Christine. "You understand your daed doesn't make this decision lightly."

"Jah, but I don't understand why he's decided to go now. The fire might not touch our home."

"The fire has nothing to do with his decision."

Christine stopped trying to make two tent poles fit together. She studied her mother's face. Her eyes were red rimmed. From smoke, surely. Mother never cried—except when they buried her parents. Even then she said they were tears of happiness that Grandmother and Grandfather had gone on to be with God. "Why then?"

"When we came here that first time to visit friends, they sang Montana's praises. A beautiful place, close to Gott, and it is. We fell in love with it." Mother's struggle for words to explain etched lines on her face. "But your daed misses farming. The winters are so long and cold here. This is a lovely place to visit, but less so to live. Also, he wants to be close to his parents in their last years."

Every word made sense. To argue seemed selfish. Hers

wasn't the only person's happiness at stake. "His home and yours is in Kansas. But we kinner have grown up here. This is our home. Does Zeke know?" She'd seen him slipping away from the singing with Jane Weaver. "He has a special friend . . . too."

"He's young, barely getting started. So is Delilah. They'll find new friends." Mother threw a tablecloth over the second table and smoothed it with dishwater-rough hands. "Or their love will endure until the time is right. If distance doesn't diminish their feelings, then they'll find a way." She straightened and smiled. "The same is true for you."

She did have eyes in the back of her head and elephant ears. "Andy says he's going to his parents' farm. It's near Lewistown."

Which might as well be London.

"True love will endure until the time is right."

Easy for Mother to say. She had her true love of twenty-five years and seven children. She could live anywhere and be happy as long as she had her family with her.

Shouldn't that be true of Christine?

Gott, I'm sorry. Kootenai has been my home for my whole life. I don't want that to change. I don't like change. At least I don't think I do. Everything has always been the same, which is fine with me.

What if Andy decided to stay in Lewistown? Would their love not only survive but flourish? Would she be willing to live there to be with him? Until today the idea of being separated from her family would have been unthinkable.

Not anymore. Her parents would have to let her stay if their engagement was announced—or better yet, they married.

Was that a good reason to say yes? She cared for Andy. Did

she love him? How did the thrill that tossed her heart around like a tidal wave when he kissed her translate when it came to love?

Too many questions and not enough answers.

CHAPTER 4

With early evening came cooler air, but it still held smoke that stank and irritated the throat. Andy coughed, but nothing could dislodge the taste from his mouth. The shadows from the ponderosa pines that lined Highway 37 grew, giving his buggy much-appreciated shade. He gulped lukewarm water from his canteen. The turnoff to Rexford loomed. Ben would turn there to reunite with his family at one of the campgrounds. Andy should keep going. His ultimate destination was Eureka, another thirteen miles west to Highway 93, where he could spend the night with his friends the Clemonses.

John Clemons delivered furniture for the store and often served as a taxi service for the Kootenai Plain community. Knowing Andy had no family in Kootenai, he'd offered not only safe haven when needed, but his friendship. He'd already agreed to drive Andy to Lewistown when he was ready to return home.

Two more hours on the road, most of it in darkness. Andy could pull in here and spend the night. That would give him time to talk to Christine. Where would he stay? It would be awkward. He couldn't bed down at the Masts' campground. "What do you think, hund?"

Donut's low growl deep in his throat did nothing to assuage Andy's discomfort. "*Danki* for nothing."

The dog raised his head and barked once.

"I don't know about that."

The highway sign with the arrow pointing to a left turn into Rexford appeared, taunting him.

"Fine." He wasn't a coward. Nor did he wish to hurt Christine. She was far too sweet for that. "But you're serving as my pillow, buddy."

No response from Donut.

Andy followed Ben's buggy into Rexford where he pulled into the General Store. Pipe clenched between his lips, Terry sat on a bench out front, his skinny legs propped up on the split-log railing. He had so much fluffy silver beard, it was a wonder he didn't catch it on fire smoking the pipe. He waved and let his boots clomp on the cement beneath him.

"Howdy, neighbors." He stood and stretched. "I figured we'd have some latecomers, so we stayed open past closing time."

Ben slipped from his buggy, as did his three sons, all of whom did their own series of stretches. With sooty faces and blackened clothes, they all looked like refugees from the coal mines. Andy made his way to the impromptu powwow between Ben and Terry, whose scent of cherry tobacco was a welcome respite from the burnt forest stench. The boys headed inside to use the facilities.

"Did my wife stop by?" Fatigue darkened the bags under Ben's eyes. His voice was hoarse and his lips chapped. "I need to find her."

Terry shared information on the women and children's whereabouts. Ben's expression relaxed. "Gut, that's gut. We'll get down there." He turned to Andy. "You'll stay with us, then?"

An invitation made it easier and harder. He couldn't turn it down without some explanation. Nor did he want to share the truth with the father of his special friend.

"I'll bet you all have a powerful thirst." Terry hitched up his baggy jeans and cocked his head toward the door. "What do you say I bring everyone an icy cold root beer on me?"

"That's kind of you. It would be *wunderbarr*." Andy responded before Ben had a chance. "My throat is burning."

"I'll be right back."

Andy waited until Terry disappeared into the store. He turned to Ben. "I was thinking of traveling the rest of the way into Eureka."

"That's another two hours. You have to be tired." Ben shoved his straw hat back on his head. "It'll be dark, and you know there'll be a bunch of *Englisch* tourists on the road who don't know where they're going. They're not used to slow-moving buggies, either."

"John Clemons has a couple of bunk beds in his spare bedroom in Eureka. He offered them to me and Henry."

"So go there tomorrow."

"It's nice of you to offer, but—"

"If you're worried about it being untoward, don't be." A grim smile stole across the older man's face. "I know you respect my dochder—and her parents—too much to take advantage of the situation."

"How do you know about—?"

"I have eyes in my head, don't I?"

So much for their careful avoidance at Sunday services and *Gmay* picnics. "I'm not just headed to Eureka. John will take me to my daed and mudder's place out by Lewistown in a day or two."

"But you'll be back." Ben's bushy eyebrows rose and fell. "I thought you liked it here."

"I thought you did too."

Ben's jaw jutted. A scowl spread across his face. "Who told you otherwise?" The scowl deepened. "Has Christine spoken out of turn?"

"It's true then? You're moving back to Kansas?"

"Jah."

No explanation. Not that he owed anyone—least of all Andy—any such words that would explain how a man could uproot a family after almost twenty years in one of the most beautiful places created by God in the universe. "When?"

"Within the week."

"You won't stay to see what happens to your house?"

"It could be weeks before we get back in there. I want to get my fraa and kinner settled with my family in Haven before winter comes." His face was lined with exhaustion, Ben leaned against his buggy and fanned his face with his hat. "It's better that way. I can return to move whatever's left later."

"And the land?"

"One way or another, I'll sell it."

"No coming back."

"Nee, no coming back."

Andy needed that root beer. He cleared his throat, but he couldn't find the right words. Ben knew about Andy courting Christine. That didn't mean he wanted to talk about it. Plain folks didn't do much of that.

"Kansas isn't a bad place for a fellow to settle." Ben replaced his hat and straightened. "Farmland is plentiful and fertile."

What Andy knew about Kansas would fit on the head of a nail. A good place to farm. Not too crowded. No mountains, no natural lakes. "I'm a mountain man. That's why I moved up here to Kootenai."

"My fraa talked—"

"Here it is. Icy cold as promised." Terry pushed open the double glass door with his elbow.

Zeke came in behind him and held it open while the store owner bounded through with two bottles of root beer. Pop in hand, the boys followed. Mark and Martin, who looked like twins but were actually two years apart, also carried paper bags bulging with unidentified goodies. Knowing Terry, they contained his favorite junk foods—Twinkies, Doritos, and Oreos. How the man stayed so thin remained a mystery.

Andy offered his thanks, even though the man's timing left a great deal to be desired. How he'd love to know who Melba talked to and what was said.

Ben took a long swallow, lowered the bottle, and belched. "You're a gut man, Terry." His smile fleeting, he nodded at Andy. "Do you have a tent?"

"I do."

"You can pitch it at our site. Down by the water."

Translation. Far from Christine. "Danki."

Ben shrugged. "No need for thanks. Let's go, boys."

While his three sons climbed into the buggy, Ben turned back for a second. His stare was long and level. "The kinner don't know. I want to tell them."

"Understood." Andy sucked down half the root beer. The day had been long and difficult.

The hardest conversations were yet to come.

CHAPTER 5

A man should know better than to sneak up on a woman with a flaming marshmallow skewered on her stick. At the sound of Andy's voice, Christine whirled. She came within an ant's tongue of stabbing him with her dessert.

He ducked just in time. "Hey. It's me."

Acutely aware of her mother's observant stare, Christine stumbled back a few steps from the Coleman stove. The roasted hot dogs had been crisp on the outside and juicy on the inside. In other words, perfect. Despite her certainty that this terrible day had left her without an appetite, Christine had managed to eat two on fresh, spongy buns and a large helping of tangy mustard potato salad before they started on the s'mores. "Sorry. I didn't know you were here."

Or maybe she'd closed her ears to the familiar sound of his voice, not wanting to be disappointed by another conversation. The girls had heard him. Maisie and Abigail loved Donut. Socks and Shoes weren't as excited about the German shepherd's appearance, but they tolerated him. Maisie had ridden him like a horse until she grew too big. Now she showered him with hugs and he repaid her with kisses.

Kisses. The word conjured up the first sweet yet fiery kiss

Andy had given her after almost a year of courting. It had taken awhile for him to touch her, but once he had she found herself seeking those intimate moments at every turn. She dreamed about them—during the day and at night. He approached kissing with surprising enthusiasm—surprising because it took him so long to decide to do it at all. She had no experience in this area, but he was good at it. So good her muscles turned to noodles and her brain stopped thinking about anything except when that next kiss would come.

"Your daed invited me to spend the night here." His confident way of speaking sputtered and died for a second. His gaze floundered around her feet. He looked tired and dejected. Christine's heartstrings thrummed. It was impossible to stay mad at him for wanting to do the right thing—even if it meant being apart for a while.

Andy cleared his throat. "It's getting dark. It wouldn't be a gut idea to be on the highway with all these strangers who don't know where they're going."

"Unlike you who's definitely headed to Lewistown."

"Not tonight." A touch of belligerence mingled with a faint bit of hurt in his tone. Could he be as hurt as she was? It didn't seem possible. "A man has to do what a man has to do. For family."

"Indeed."

"Have you eaten?" A package of raw hot dogs in one hand, Mother squeezed between them. "Help yourself. We're stuffed to the gills."

Christine swooped down and grabbed the dogs. "Jah, you look hungry."

It would give them time to talk. Or at least be close.

"I'm beat. I still have to set up my tent." He backed away from the picnic table. The shadows overtook his face so she could no longer see his features. "Tomorrow will be soon enough to figure out what to do next."

A spark of hope leaped over the lake and wafted on the cool September breeze.

"A gut night's sleep will help everyone think more clearly." While Mother's tone was warm, her gaze could pierce skin and bone. "It's time to turn in."

"We didn't get to eat." Martin edged closer to Christine and the hot dogs. "I sure could use a wiener."

"Can we look for frogs first?" Mark asked. "Just for a little bit."

They knew better than to question instructions, but this was a strange night for everyone. Mother took pity on them. "I know Terry filled you up with junk. Hot dogs are pretty much the same thing, but go ahead. Be quick about it, though. The sun will be up before you know it."

She made shooing motions that sent Maisie and Abigail scrambling to their pup tent. Delilah was already in the slightly bigger tent Christine would share with her. The three boys shared the last one, a new green canvas purchased at the beginning of summer. This must be what the Israelites felt like those forty years wandering in the wilderness and living in tents. Dirty and sweaty and no place to clean up.

Surely it wouldn't be that long.

Mother gave Christine a knowing glance—one that said the boys would be nearby serving as chaperones until they finished eating.

No need for worry, that was obvious. Andy unhitched his horse and fed him. From there he grabbed a duffel, a kerosene lamp, and a nylon tent bag from his buggy and ambled several yards from the campsite.

Christine chewed on her thumbnail. Mother and Father disappeared into the biggest beige tent on the outskirts of their site. Their shadows flickered in the lantern's light.

Andy really should eat. A man needed nourishment. Christine settled into her lawn chair. It sank into the loamy soil under her slight weight. The boys stuffed their faces. She stood and went back to the stove where she cooked two more wieners until they had a nice toasty skin. At the picnic table she slid them on buns and added all the toppings. Andy liked his loaded. The image of him devouring one with mustard, catsup, cheese, and relish, a look of delight on his handsome face, floated in her mind's eye. At the volunteer firefighters' fund-raiser. Later he'd kissed her, and the taste of pickle relish lingered on his lips. Sweet and tart. Like him.

She wrapped the dogs in paper napkins and started in the direction he'd taken.

"Where are you going?" Zeke stepped into her path. "It's dark down by the water. We wouldn't want you to fall in."

"I'll deliver these to Andy and be right back." Christine stood toe-to-toe with her younger brother, who, like most men, towered over her. Zeke had his own rumspringa secrets. They'd run into each other a few times in the midnight hour. A teenager couldn't find much trouble in Kootenai, but Zeke had smelled of cigarette smoke and alcohol. "You can keep an eye on the kinner."

Zeke hesitated. He had the same big frame and massive biceps as Father, but in the face he looked like Mother. Especially when peevish. "I think that's your job."

"I'll be right back." She kept her voice soft. The boys didn't need to hear. "How is Jane?"

His expression tightened. "How would I know?"

"Courting is private." She smiled. "So is our rumspringa."

He shrugged. "The hot dogs are getting cold."

"I won't be long."

"Be careful and come right back."

His concern warmed her. They used to have fun together when they both were in school, before they grew up and apart. "I will."

She turned and scurried through calf-high grass and weeds. A breeze rustled the leaves in the trees. The scent of pine mingled with smoke from the mountains wafted in the air. No light sparkled on the normally satiny-smooth water. A strange sense of unreality washed over Christine. The day's events crowded her. Swallowing against a sudden lump in her throat, she approached the clearing where Andy had assembled a two-man nylon tent in royal blue. A book in his lap, he lounged in a lawn chair with a kerosene lantern at his feet.

A low whine in his throat, Donut rose.

"It's me, hund." She spoke softly so as not to startle Andy.

He swiveled. "You came. I was hoping you would."

"I can't stay. I brought you some food. Hot dogs."

"I'm so hungry I could eat my arm." He laid the Bible on the folding stool next to him. "Pull up the other chair."

"I shouldn't."

"Just for a second. I want to talk to you."

Now he wanted to talk. She glanced at her family's row of multicolored, well-used tents arranged in descending sizes. Like a hundred other camping trips over the years. "For a minute."

"I know you think I'm unfeeling or I wouldn't be leaving you right now." He unwrapped the first hot dog. Mustard dripped on his pants. He wiped at it with the napkin, but it smeared more. How long would it be before they could do laundry? He shrugged, took a big bite, and chewed. She waited. He swallowed. "But I'm not. My daed taught me that a man needs to work hard. Gut things come to those who work and wait on Gott's plan. I only want to do what's right and do it the right way."

"I understand that." Christine struggled to find words that didn't make her sound young, selfish, or naive. "I want to do the right thing too. It seemed as if we had all the time in the world. Mammi Tabitha would say that's the curse of the young. We think we'll live forever. Now we know things can happen from one day to the next that change everything. I just wish we'd moved more quickly. If we were married, we wouldn't have to be separated."

"It's not because I don't care for you, if that's what you're thinking."

Even now he avoided the word *love*. "If you care—"

"You aren't at fault for any of this. Please know that." He wiped his face with the napkin. "The fire has made me realize I have to take care of unfinished business at home before I'm ready to settle down."

Once again they were out of step. She wanted to leap off the cliff with his hand in hers. Maybe they weren't supposed to be together. If he really loved her, what kind of unfinished business would keep him from asking her to marry him? "You don't talk much about home. Do you miss it?"

"It's beautiful, like Kootenai, but different. It's a green valley with mountains in the distance." His gaze drifted out to the lake. "I miss my mudder's chokeberry jam. Did you know Lewistown is the chokeberry capital of the world?"

"I didn't." Crickets chirped and frogs croaked in a familiar, comforting concert while Christine mused over his words.

More likely he missed his mother as much as the jam. She would. It was hard to imagine not seeing Mother every day. "Maybe you could bring me some when you come back."

"I miss hunting with my dad. This time of year the elk are bugling and the leaves are changing. My dad likes to fly-fish at Big Spring Creek. We hunt for grouse and pheasant and partridge. Them's some gut eats."

He'd blown right past her suggestion. Hurt chipped away at her determination to be supportive—the way a wife would. Love endured. Distance wouldn't matter if it was truly love. "What about your bruders and *schweschders*? Did you hunt with them?"

"I miss the smell of the alfalfa when we cut it for hay. When I was little I sat with my dad on the wagon that held the propane engine that powered the harvester. Sometimes he let me take the reins and guide the team of horses."

Again, his answer skipped over her question, almost as if he hadn't heard her. He'd been transported to another place and time.

"I thought your daed had a sawmill."

"He does. The farm is only a hundred and sixty acres. It's not nearly big enough to compete with the big two-thousand-acre farms that grow winter wheat, sugar beets, potatoes, and alfalfa and such. Daed had to find other ways to support the family."

"Your bruders work at the sawmill then?"

"The smoke makes the night even darker." His gaze lifted to the looming night. "It blankets the mountains and blots out the stars."

He spoke as if destruction were a foregone conclusion and he didn't want to talk about his brothers. That was apparent, but why? Christine studied his face, letting her gaze trace the familiar contours of his hollow cheeks, perfect nose, and the full lips that gave her so much pleasure. "What is this unfinished business you must take care of?"

"I told you, my father's sick and my bruders want everyone there."

"You said that, but it seems like there's something else bothering you. You don't go home often, even though it's not that far."

"Six and a half hours."

"Less than a day by van."

He scrubbed at catsup on his thumb with the crumpled napkin. His lips twisted. For a moment it seemed as if he would ignore the question. "Family relations can be complicated."

"What happened?"

"It's history. Nothing that needs to be dug up and rehashed."

"But you have to go?"

He raised his head and nodded. "I have to go."

So be it. "They'll put the fire out, you'll take care of your business, and then we'll see where we stand."

His shoulders hunched. His fingers worried the mustard spot. "You're not going home."

Maybe that was the root of his somber stare. Not whatever waited for him in Lewistown. It was her turn to stare at smoke that looked like thunderclouds in the distance. "You talked to Daed?"

"He said the decision is made."

"Mudder said the same." Christine bit her lip. A tiny spiral of pain spurred her on. Now or never. "She also said true love can overcome distance and time apart."

"That's true whether it's Lewistown or Haven, Kansas."

Their gazes held. Breathless, no longer distinct, one from the other. Her heart beat in her ears. Despite the cool evening breeze on her face, heat dampened her skin.

Life could not be this hard. Grandma's tart voice sounded in her head. *"Silly child, of course it can. He's not going off to war like the English husbands. You haven't lost a child to cancer. You haven't been widowed."*

"How far do you think it is to Haven?" She forced her gaze to the lake with its water that shimmered in light but remained hidden and black in the dark.

"I don't know exactly, but it's a couple of days' traveling with kinner and household goods."

Gott, is this Your plan for me? First fire, then desolation, then distance?

God is good.

Grandma said that too. He did what was best for His children, not what was easiest.

The words tripped over Christine's heart and landed somewhere near the pit of her stomach.

Thy will be done.

· · ·

Andy's heart refused to do its job. The hot dogs heaved in his gut. The flickering lantern light illuminated the sadness on Christine's face. That lost look would be forever etched on his conscience. Why did love seem to involve so much discomfort? With Winona it hadn't been true love. It couldn't have been, or they would still be together. Christine's hurt flailed at him, speaking of the fact that she truly cared. She would never do what Winona did. She cared that much.

He'd been mistaken the first time. How could a man be sure? He might not be able to answer that question, but he could try to find a way to assuage Christine's pain. "You have family in St. Ignatius, don't you?"

Her forehead wrinkled the way it always did when she thought hard. "I do. *Aenti* Lucy and *Onkel* Fergie and their kinner. They own the Valley Grocery Store. I'm sure we'll stop to see them on the way to Kansas."

"Don't you see? That's it."

"What's it?"

"What if you stay with them? Don't go to Haven?" Andy's heart began to beat again. "Live with your aenti and onkel. Maybe you can work in their store."

"St. Ignatius is still at least five hours by car from Lewistown." Her hands twisted in her lap. She shook her head. "Not only would I not have you, but I wouldn't have Mudder and Daed and Delilah and Zeke and the kinner."

"I could get to St. Ignatius more often than all the way to Haven." They would have a chance—a much better chance—to finish what they started. He couldn't offer her a full life as his wife until he faced his past and returned to Kootenai to build a home for them. "I don't plan to stay in Lewistown. I want to start my own business in Kootenai."

He almost said it. *With you as my fraa.* Not yet. Not until he faced the past.

Hope flared in her face. "I don't know if Daed and Mudder will agree to let me stay. Let's ask them."

"Right now?" She couldn't know how audacious this sounded in Andy's own ears. She didn't know how his heart threatened to bolt from his chest at the idea. "This minute?" He stood and held out his hand.

She took it. Why keep up the pretense that their courting was a secret? Too much was at stake.

Andy leading the way, they trudged back to the Mast campsite. A cup of hot chocolate in one hand, Zeke sat in a camping chair. He looked as if he had dozed off. Christine reached for the cup. Her brother shifted and raised his head. "You're back." He directed the observation at Andy. "It's getting late."

"It is." Christine cocked her head toward the tents. "You should turn in."

His expression morose, he rose and dumped the rest of his cocoa in the dirt. He set the cup on the picnic table with a thump. "Dawn comes early."

Instead of letting it go, Christine frowned and pointed at the offending cup. "You should rinse that out. It'll draw flies and be a dried-up mess by morning."

Zeke shrugged. His stare said he wouldn't be distracted. Christine didn't give in. "We're just saying good night."

He trod toward the second tent but not without a knowing backward glance.

Christine went to the first tent. "Mudder? Daed?" She whispered, but loud enough to elicit a whine from one of the smaller tents followed by rustling. "It's Christine and Andy."

Two seconds later Melba appeared at the tent flap. She slapped her kapp on her head at a haphazard angle. "Andy?"

"A quick word."

Ben pushed past his wife. He held a kerosene lantern in one hand and reading glasses in the other. "It's time for everyone to turn in. Past time."

"I wanted to ask you something." Christine's voice was soft, but it didn't waver. "Actually *we* wanted to ask you."

Andy took a step forward, but he kept a respectful distance—

from Christine and from her parents. "It's a suggestion. A thought."

"Fine. Be quick about it, then."

"It's okay." Melba tugged her sweater around her ample middle. "I could make us some tea. I'll heat some water on the Coleman stove. It's chilly."

"Nee, Fraa, it's late and it's been a long day." Ben's growl drew a puzzled *woof* from Donut, who'd followed them up the trail at a distance. "I want to get into Eureka tomorrow to the information center at the church first thing."

A gust of mighty wind to carry Andy far, far away would be nice. He shifted from one foot to the other. *Just say it. Onward and upward.* "You have family in St. Ignatius?"

"My sister and her mann." Melba yawned so wide her jaw cracked. "They have the store there."

"I'd like to stay with them instead of going to Haven." Christine stretched to her full height—five two or three at the most—and lifted her chin. "Will you ask them if they'd mind? I could clean their house, help with chores, or even work at the store, I reckon. I can do whatever they need."

Melba's hands went to her throat. She inched closer to Ben. "Not come with us? I don't know, I—"

"We'll think about it." Ben gave them his back. "Come, Fraa. It's time everyone was asleep."

"Gut natcht." Melba didn't move. "See you tomorrow, then."

"Gut natcht." Her gaze bore into the back of his head as he turned and walked toward his campsite. He sneaked a glance at Christine. Her eyebrows rose. She smiled and tossed him a quick wave without raising her arm.

So *"we'll think about it"* was a good sign? He'd known Ben

for four years. Christine had a lifetime of signal reading and translating his words.

Feeling lighter, he picked up his pace. One tiny step forward would surely be the first in a journey toward happiness.

CHAPTER 6

WEST KOOTENAI

So much had changed in only twenty-four hours. Death and destruction had their own peculiar aroma. The stench of burnt wood, rubber, and plastic might never leave Andy's nostrils. Eyes closed, he squatted and fought the urge to hold his breath. He trailed his fingers through the gray ashes, thick as snow, around his worn boots. Maybe his eyes played tricks on him. The cabin had been reduced to a pile of rubble. A cargo trailer had its sides completely melted. Where his cabin and the twin cabin shared by Caleb Hostetler and Ian Byler once blocked his view of the road, nothing stood in the way now.

In fact, Andy could see nothing except row upon row of blackened toothpicks that had once been Douglas fir, ponderosa pine, birch, tamarack, and spruce beyond the land that had been cleared for their humble three-and four-room homes. The insatiable fiery dragon had consumed all three of the cabins inhabited by Kootenai's bachelor men. Leaving Donut with Terry at the store had been a good idea. The dog would have howled in despair at the sight. Andy might have joined him.

So be it. He would rebuild. He and his neighbors would restore what fire had taken.

"I'll miss that western larch in the front yard." Hands on his hips, hat shoved back, Andy's cabinmate, Henry Lufkin, shifted slightly where he stood a few yards from the remains. "The colors were beautiful in the fall. Another month and they would've changed."

"Some foresters say we bring this on ourselves. It's hard to believe it's our own fault." Andy brushed his hands on his pants. If only he could brush away the pain of loss as easily as ashes. "We build too close to the mountains. Fire through lightning has been a way of renewing the forests since the beginning of time."

"I reckon they know what they're talking about." Henry's soft Kentucky drawl hadn't changed in the two years since he arrived in Kootenai. He never had much to say, but he was the best hunter and fisherman in town. He had a knack for it. Something about his ability to be perfectly still. The English tourists often used him as a guide on their hunting trips. His jasper eyes were somber in his tan, acne-scarred face. "Even though we follow all their tips for fireproofing our houses, eventually it catches up with us."

He'd been quiet on the ride over with Lincoln County sheriff's deputy Salvador Quiñones. When the deputy came by the campground to tell them they could get back into Kootenai long enough to carry out a few more of their belongings, he'd stressed it would have to be quick—in and out. That wouldn't be a problem now.

Andy edged away from the smoking remnants of their shared home. He faced his cabinmate. "I need to head back to Lewistown for a while. What's your plan?"

"The taxidermy shop in Eureka is looking for help. Keith Harper said he'd be happy to have me around."

"That's gut. Where will you live?"

"It depends. I could stay at John's until we rebuild here. I know he won't mind." Henry's wince reflected how he hated to nose around in other folks' business. "Are you coming back? It's likely Morris will want to rebuild. We can help him."

Morris Tanner owned the cabins and rented them out as a means of income.

"I hope to."

Sal's Lincoln County SUV rumbled into sight. He pulled off the road and parked. A second later he slid from the truck and strode toward them. "We need to get moving. The wind could shift the fire back this direction anytime."

"How did the Drakes come out?" Andy dusted off his hands and faced the deputy. Christine would want to know. She'd been cleaning that house since she turned fourteen and graduated from school. "Better than this, I hope."

Sal removed his cowboy hat and held it over his heart. He didn't answer for a second or two. Then he slapped the hat back on his head and sighed. "Their house is gone. The fire destroyed everything they had. The outhouses. The garage. Everything. Mike lost it. I wanted to give him a few minutes to pull himself together. That's why I came over here. We'll pick him up on the way out."

"It's a blow, but he'll recover." People who lived in this neck of the woods with long, cold winters and deep snows knew how to survive nature's furies. The Englishers in these parts didn't mind doing without some of the technology and "comforts" valued by city folks. Mike preferred hunting, fishing, and working with his hands at his auto shop. "He's a hard worker. So's DeeDee."

"The governor has declared a state of emergency because of

all the fires." Sal removed his cowboy hat a second time and fanned his face with it. "I told Mike that FEMA will be here as soon as it's safe enough for them to get in. He snorted and said he didn't need no stinkin' FEMA. I reckon he has insurance, though."

Plain folks didn't have insurance, but they did take care of themselves. "Folks around here don't count on government assistance."

To lose a house where a man had raised his family was different. The cabin was just a stop on the road to what every Plain man wanted—a wife and children. Even so, drywall and wood weren't important. Possessions weren't important. Not in the long run called eternity. So why did it still hurt so much? "What about the Masts?"

"They got lucky. The house is still standing." Sal's brown skin was damp with perspiration. He mopped his face and bald head with a bright-red bandanna. "Everything else is gone. The shop. The nursery. The lean-to for the buggies. The barn. Funny thing is, the kids' swing set is still there. And the trampoline. Big as you please."

With a shooing motion, he headed toward the SUV. "We need to roll."

Henry didn't move. Andy met his gaze as he passed him. "Do you need a minute?"

"Nee. Just fixing a picture of this in my mind." Henry's expression was serene. "Whenever I get too comfortable with my stuff, I'll think of this and remember that it's transitory. Like we are."

"I can't help but think it's strange that the Drakes lost everything and Ben still has his house." Andy contemplated the blackened forest that stretched as far as the eye could see on the other side of the road as it wound toward the mountains. "He's loading his family up and taking them back to Kansas. The Yoders lost everything and they're staying. What do you think the plan is in that?"

Together they slogged through the ashes to the SUV. Neither could answer the question. Only God knew His plan, and it was splashed on a canvas so large and so eternal, they couldn't expect to see even a tiny piece of it from their earthly and human perspective.

Henry slid into the back seat. "Christine will be sad to leave."

The closest he would come to asking a question. Andy stared through the bug-spattered windshield, trying to divine a future obscured by smoke and uncertainty. "Ben's moving them back to Kansas. To his parents' place. We talked to him last night about letting her stay with her onkel in St. Ignatius."

"You talked to Ben?"

A gaff in Plain tradition, to be sure. If they planned to marry, they should have talked to the deacon and let him speak with both sets of parents first. "I haven't asked her to marry me. Instead, I asked her to remain close by while I take care of my unfinished business."

"You're engaged?" Sal clapped twice before he pushed the ignition button and the SUV revved. "Congrats."

"Nee, but pretty close." Andy's father once told him that close only counted in horseshoes. Time to change the subject. "What about you? Did you have to evacuate from the Gibraltar Fire or the Three Forks Fire?"

"My wife and the baby girls are in Missoula with her folks, just to be on the safe side." The deputy's tone turned gruff. "I hate being apart from them, but it's better than having to worry about them all the time while I'm trying to work."

"You have three girls. That must be sweet to go home to at night."

"It's the best." Sal turned into the Drakes' property and maneuvered past a deep rut in the gravel road. "Truth be told, I've been lobbying for one more to see if we can get a boy, but Maricela says the factory's closed."

Three would be a start for a Plain family where the rule tended to be the more the merrier. A Plain man would want sons as much as Sal, but every healthy baby was a gift from God.

Sal pulled into the driveway that ended not far from a pit of ashes and melted metal. Mike stood, head down, ball cap in his hands, near the cement steps that had once led to his front porch.

"I'll get him." Sal opened his door. "The longer he stands there, the worse it'll be."

"Let me."

Sal paused, then nodded. "You know how he feels, I suppose."

Not the same, Mike would surely have argued, but closer. Andy took his time approaching. The sheriff would let Sal know if the need to hurry arose. "Hey, Mike."

The man turned. Misery lines etched leathery skin ravaged by years in the sun. His oversized nose was bright red to match the rims of his watery blue eyes. His Adam's apple bobbed. "It's stupid. It's just a house, but I can't seem to leave it."

Tears made his voice raspy.

"It's not stupid. It's human."

"How about your cabin?"

"Gone."

Mike slid his purple Colorado Rockies cap—a flash of color in an otherwise decimated landscape—onto his head. "I was remembering how Kyle chased Alex around the house one night after we'd just put the finishing touches on the kitchen. New cabinetry, new quartz countertops, new pulls, new backsplash. All that stuff women like from watching too much HGTV."

Andy nodded. He'd never watched TV in his life, but he knew about renovating older houses from his work at the furniture store.

"Anyhow, Kyle races through the kitchen in his socks, slides across the floor, and crashes into the cabinets. Crushes the door and busts it into pieces. I wanted to tan his hide, but DeeDee said no. She said it was an accident. Bad judgment. She's one of those time-out people. They all went to their rooms for the rest of the afternoon. I had to special order the new door. I was peeved . . ." His voice trailed off.

Andy stood shoulder to shoulder with the Englisher in silence. No birds chattered. No bees buzzed. No frogs croaked. No crickets chirped. No leaves rustled in the trees. The eerie silence paid tribute to the physical destruction of a close-knit community that practiced the same faith in differing ways.

"We'll rebuild." No words could provide comfort, but Andy tried these on for size. Rebuilding would reflect the resilience of that same community. "We won't let a fire keep us from living the life Gott intended."

"They say God's ways are mysterious." With a loud honk Mike blew his nose in a brilliantly white handkerchief. Its creases suggested it had been ironed by his wife. "But it's the evil one who throws obstacles in our way and tries to tell us it's God. Satan tells us to give up and get out. I won't give him the satisfaction."

"Good for you." Andy offered him a smile. "I have to go up to Lewistown for a bit, but when I come back, I'll help in any way I can. The other men will want to as well. The women too.

They're great at putting together outdoor meals to feed the workers. I reckon men from the other Plain communities will come up too."

"We'll all pull together. I have no doubt about it. I need to get back and tell DeeDee. I have an architect friend who'll draw up some new plans for me. Maybe a little smaller now that the older boys are out of the house." Mike whacked Andy on the back. "Tell that sweet girlfriend of yours not to go too far. We'll need her services as soon as DeeDee starts cooking again and the boys mess up the new bathrooms."

Did everyone in the entire town know Andy and Christine were courting? He didn't dare tell Mike about Ben's plan. "She'll be in St. Ignatius for a time, but I know she wants to come back as soon as possible."

They ran through the list of Kootenai residents as they walked back to the SUV. The dejected, defeated man who'd stood before the ruins of his home had disappeared, replaced by a man filled with anticipation at the possibilities of a new and perhaps better home for his family.

The transformation had been nearly instantaneous. Strong faith renewed hope.

Soaking up the energy of a man much older and wiser, Andy hurried to keep up.

Maybe Ben would see his house standing among the ruins and realize God had wrought a miracle on his behalf. For that reason alone, he and his family should stay.

Christine should stay.

At the truck Andy slid into the back seat and leaned forward to talk to Sal. "Can we run by the Mast property? I'd like to catch Ben if I can."

"Sure, if you make it quick." Sal put the SUV in gear and made a three-point turn. "It's on the way out, but I doubt they're still there."

He was wrong. At the Mast house they found Ben, Zeke, and the two younger boys racing to load more furniture and household goods on the back of Deputy Kimberly LaFortune's Lincoln County pickup truck. The deputy was on the phone, but she waved Sal over while the rest of them rushed to help the Mast men.

Andy strode into the front room after Ben, where Christine's father pointed to the oak table. "Truth be told, Melba will sleep better tonight knowing this wedding gift from her bruder Phillip made it through the fire."

"Praise Gott."

"It's just a table." Ben swept his arm around the room. "I feel convicted for allowing such emotion to swell in my heart at seeing these things still intact while others have lost so much— you included."

"I lost very little. And I praise Gott with you that your home survived." Andy grabbed one end of the table while Ben took the other. Together they hoisted it and squeezed through the front door. Andy took the lead, walking backward, while Ben guided from behind. "I praise Gott, and I wonder if it's a message . . . of sorts."

Ben grunted as Zeke grabbed a side and they hoisted the table onto the truck with Sal pulling from the truck bed. He wiped his forehead with his sleeve. "What do you mean? A message?"

Andy fought the urge to squirm under the older man's level stare. He fell into step next to him as Ben headed back for another load. "Are you sure you should move back to Haven? Your house is still here, waiting for you."

"Your cabin is gone. Is that a message you should leave?"

"Nee." A point well taken. "I just thought—"

"Gott has a plan for you and for me." Ben bent over one of the benches that went with the table. Andy grabbed the other end. "It has nothing to do with buildings surviving or not surviving this firestorm. I've prayed long and hard. Melba prayed. We've talked to the bishop. This is not a decision I make lightly. You're young, and you don't know what it takes to uproot a family and move, but I do. I did it once, and now I do it again. Because I believe it's for the best."

Andy might not have uprooted a family, but he'd moved far from his own. He knew how that felt. It had been for the best—at least it seemed so at the time. "I understand."

"No, but one day you will."

Andy followed him out the door again. The decision had been made. No more discussion. "Do you still plan to sell the property?"

"I reckon. After we get settled in Haven. It'll give us a nest egg to help with the community's medical needs."

Andy nodded. He shoved his end of the bench into the truck and turned to stare at the house. Built log cabin style, it had grown over the years with the Mast family. Bedrooms had been added and the kitchen and living room enlarged. The shop and barn would have to be rebuilt. All in all, it was a beautiful piece of property.

"We have to go." Deputy Kim made a wrap-it-up motion.

Sal trotted to his truck. "Let's head out."

Instead of taking heed, Ben halted and turned to Andy. "I understand this is a hard thing." His hoarse voice deepened. "It's not been easy for any of us."

Andy swallowed his own emotion. Silently, he fought for

control. A deep breath only brought more acrid, smoke-filled air into his aching lungs. "You'll ask your brother-in-law about taking in Christine?"

"Already done. He's agreed."

Relief lightened the burden on Andy's shoulders. "Might you do one more thing for me?" He swept his arm toward the house that had survived when others had not. "When you're ready to sell, give me first option?"

For the first time Ben's grim visage lightened. "It would be nice to know a decent man would be raising his family here."

It could be Ben's family as well, if all went according to plan. His daughter. His grandchildren. "Danki."

"Just don't wait too long to do the asking." Ben clapped him on the shoulder. "Women don't like to be kept waiting."

"I'll do my best."

Ben squeezed onto the back seat in Kimberly's truck alongside his youngest son. "We better get moving."

The deputy wheeled the truck around and took off with a squeal.

"Hey, dude, what'cha waiting for?" Sal beeped his horn. "Let's go."

Andy took one last look at the house. It seemed forlorn and abandoned.

Not for long, if he had his way.

CHAPTER 7

EUREKA, MONTANA

Everybody Christine knew from West Kootenai, Eureka, and Libby was crammed into Eureka High School's auditorium. Plus a bunch of people she didn't know. The community meetings were the fastest way to get news of the fire straight from the horse's mouth—rather, the Lincoln County sheriff's and the US Forest Service's mouths. Rumors ran rampant and emotions ran high now that everyone knew homes had been destroyed in West Kootenai. Sheriff Brody's simple, straightforward responses to sometimes heated questions seemed to have calmed the seas. They couldn't get back into their homes yet, but they trusted the sheriff to get them back to their community as soon as he possibly could.

For Christine, it wouldn't be soon enough. The one person she didn't see was Andy. She stood on her tiptoes and craned her neck, trying to see over the masses of people exiting the auditorium. No Andy. Surely he didn't leave without saying goodbye.

Saying goodbye to so many people all at once stung. Mercy would stay in Eureka. She was already teaching again in the garage attached to the home where her family was staying. Same with their English friend Juliette. She was focused on getting a job and winning over her deputy sheriff boyfriend. But Nora was headed to Libby where she would stay with family. Like Christine, she would be away from home and her special friend for the foreseeable future. And like Christine, she found it unsettling.

Not wanting to say goodbye yet, they lingered next to their seats, watching their neighbors stream by. "I feel so selfish being upset about going to St. Ignatius when Mercy won't have a house to come home to." Christine scraped a chunk of dried gravy from her otherwise clean apron. Supper had been a quick affair in order to get to the meeting. "Same with Juliette's house and the Drakes'. I've been cleaning those houses for four years. I can't believe they're gone."

"My mudder says Jonah and Elsie are rooted in their faith." Nora's tone was matter-of-fact. "They know better than to set too much store by material things. They'll rebuild and move on. So will the Drakes and Knowles. They have their faith too."

"That doesn't mean it doesn't sting." The Knowleses had been the first to hire Christine to clean for them—at their daughter Juliette's insistence no doubt. She and her sister had played softball, been cheerleaders, and played other sports. They were never home to clean. Despite being English, Juliette had been a close friend to all three Plain girls since their toddler days.

"Jah." As much as Nora might like to hide her emotions, she was simply incapable of it. Sadness permeated her round face and normally perky blue eyes. "I wish I could stay around to make them feel better."

"Me too." Father had gathered the children around the picnic table before they left Rexford to confirm his decision to move back to Kansas. They would spend one more night at the campground. Tomorrow she would be in St. Ignatius. Even after returning to Kootenai to find their home still standing, he had no intention of changing his mind.

He'd also called Mother's brother-in-law, Fergie. He and Aunt Lucy would be happy to take Christine in. "I wish . . ." She glanced around. No one paid the least bit of attention to two Plain girls huddled together in the enormous auditorium. "I thought Andy would've asked me to marry him by now. Then we could stay together."

"He wouldn't tell you why he has to go to Lewistown?" All three of Christine's friends had been suitably upset by the news that Andy had made plans to go to his family farm and leave Christine in St. Ignatius, but Nora particularly understood. Her special friend, Levi, would not be with her in Libby. "Why would it be a big secret?"

Christine's question exactly. "I hope to be able to return to Kootenai eventually, but if Mudder and Daed don't come back and Andy doesn't ask me . . . I don't know what will happen."

She might never live in her hometown again. The notion was bewildering. Where was God's plan in that? No one ever accused her of lacking faith. She'd been the first of her friends to be baptized. She never questioned. She never thought of leaving her home and family. She had been content. Now everything she wanted seemed to flee beyond her reach. Even if there had been no fire, she would still be in this predicament. The fire couldn't be blamed for Father's decision or for Andy's. "It's a three-hour drive by car from St. Ignatius. I'm willing to wait as long as it takes, but I'm afraid distance will make it so much harder."

"Still, if he wants you to stay in St. Ignatius, he must plan to ask you eventually." Nora's pudgy cheeks turned pink at the thought. "What a blessing that would be."

Surely she was thinking of her Levi and the distance the fire had created for them. "I hope you're right. He says he's going home because his father has been sick, but there's more to it—more that he won't share with me."

"Men are so hard to understand."

Nora's sage words almost made Christine smile—almost. As friends they'd spent years trying to unravel the mystery of boys. And shared every tidbit of information as they learned it.

"What does Levi say about you leaving? Is he afraid you'll end up evangelical?" The Libby Amish were different. They'd left Kootenai to worship the way they saw fit. She didn't know much about it—her parents saw to that—but many of Nora's extended family members embraced the new way of thinking while still calling themselves Amish. Christine didn't understand how that worked. "We never go down there. I think my daed is afraid it's contagious."

"Levi says not to worry. Libby's only an hour away. He'll come visit as often as he can. And it's not for long. He's sure we'll get the all clear to go home soon. He even joked that I shouldn't let Groossdaadi teach me how to drive while I'm there. He knows Mammi would never allow it. She clings to the old ways, even when he strays."

"It must be so hard for her—"

"Look, there's Henry." Nora squeezed her plump body past Christine and waved frantically at Andy's cabinmate. "Hi, Henry, how are you doing?"

The smile on his face slid away. His pace slowed. After a moment he edged into the row of seats where Christine and Nora stood. "Hey, Nora, Christine."

It would be forward to ask about Andy, but these were difficult, unusual times. They all had a right to be concerned about their neighbors. Nora's nudge with her elbow indicated what she thought of the situation. Christine took a breath. "I'm sorry about your cabin. Andy told us about it. Is he here with you?"

Henry ducked his head and studied a scab on his knuckle. "He's not here."

"I'm surprised. Everyone's here." Her cheeks bright pink now, Nora motioned with both hands as if to encompass the entire auditorium. "I would think he'd want to help with the rebuilding."

"He does." Henry shifted his gaze to his dirty, scuffed work boots. "He will. After he gets back from Lewistown."

"Back? He left?"

Finally, Henry's gaze lifted and met Christine's. "I thought you knew. John Clemons picked him up yesterday after they returned from Kootenai. Didn't you see him at the campground?"

"We came into Eureka to buy some basics that we didn't have time to gather at the house." Christine steadied her voice. *"Find your backbone, child,"* Grandma's voice reminded her. *"Masts don't bawl."* "I guess we missed him."

That squeeze of her hand before Andy went back to his tent the first night at the campground had been goodbye.

Not enough. Not nearly enough.

"He didn't say goodbye." Nora's eyebrows rose. So did her voice. "That's just—"

"It's okay. We knew he was going." Christine lifted her chin. Her situation with Andy was private. He wouldn't be happy to have it hashed out in front of Henry or anyone else. "He'll be in touch soon."

The question was when?

CHAPTER 8

LEWISTOWN, MONTANA

The squeal of brakes and sudden quiet that followed rousted Andy from a dream-ridden sleep that featured him dousing flames around his cabin with a water hose. The flames had flared and chased him into the woods where deer, rabbit, elk, mountain lions, and even grizzlies joined him in a downhill race. He leaped with the grace of an antelope, but the deer and the elk were faster. They kept glancing back at him in dismay as they left him behind.

He rubbed his eyes and sat up. His seat belt tightened against his chest. The scent of coffee, artificial pine, Donut's scruffy fur, and John's spicy aftershave mingled in the lukewarm air generated by the old Suburban's failing air conditioner. Donut slumped over the middle seats as if he owned the SUV. As usual John hummed along with the country music singer on the radio. The big man had a deep bass, and he'd been known to burst out in song on occasion when the highway attempted to lull him into sleep while at the wheel.

Andy stretched and cleared his throat. "Where are we?"

"You're home."

Andy peered through his window. Sure enough. The two-story wood-and-stucco house where his family had lived outside

Lewistown for the past twelve years still stood. Frederick and his brothers-in-law, along with some neighbors, had expanded the right side to include three new rooms—a bedroom, a galley-style kitchen/breakfast nook, and a bathroom for Mom and Dad. Their own adjoining dawdy haus. The men did a nice job. It didn't look like an add-on but a natural extension of a gracefully aging home built in the nineties.

The willows, cottonwoods, and single aspen in the front yard were a little taller. The chokecherry bushes were heavy with fruit. Someone—probably Mother or his brother Frederick's wife, Cherise—had planted a flower garden now fading away in the shorter fall days. "Sorry I fell asleep. I hope I didn't snore."

"I don't mind. Sometimes a man likes to be alone with his machine and the road." John patted the wheel. "Besides, you seemed pretty tuckered out. A nap was in order."

Could a person classify three hours of deep slumber as a nap? "Thanks. Like I said before, I'm not sure how long I'll be here." Andy fingered the handle, but he didn't open the door. "I'll be in touch when it's time for me to go home—back to Kootenai."

"I'll be here a few days visiting with family. Call my cell phone if you need anything." John unscrewed the cap of his thermos and poured a few ounces of steaming coffee as if he planned to kick back and stay for a while. "I'm headed to my sister's off Highway 89, right there by Eddie's Corner."

Andy knew the spot. The Sky Country Grocery Store, owned by a local Plain family, the Grubers, sat at Eddie's Corner, the junction of Highways 89 and 191. "If you decide to do some hunting, let me know."

John's free thumb beat a soft rhythm on the wheel. "For a

guy hell-bent on getting home, you don't seem too anxious to get out of the truck. You know you have to open the door."

"I know." Andy studied the wind-worn building where he'd lived from the age of eleven to the age of twenty. Many good memories elbowed a few bad ones in his head. "To be truthful I wasn't all that excited to come home. It was more a necessity than a blessing."

"You won't know that until you actually dive in. Blessings come from the strangest circumstances. Good or bad, family is family. Gotta love 'em." Enthusiasm buoyed John's words. He sipped the coffee and *m-m-m*-ed his approval. "Madison makes a fine cup of coffee. Among other things. I don't know what I'd do without my wife and sons. They're my life."

Love them or leave them. The image of Winona's face as she turned and placed her hand in Stephen's on their wedding day assailed Andy. Her face glowed. Her smile engulfed the room. She'd never looked happier. Certainly not when Andy had kissed her or hugged her or held her hand.

"My dad's been sick. He's retiring." Andy unbuckled his seat belt and swiveled so he could see John better. "If my brothers agree, I might move his portable sawmill operation to Kootenai. What do you think of that idea?"

"Not a bad idea at all. It's another source of income and jobs for the community. Having a source of lumber right there is convenient, too, especially when we start rebuilding the homes lost to the fire." His forehead wrinkled under thinning dark-brown hair, and John scratched the salt-and-pepper five o'clock shadow that spread across his square jaw. "Are you looking for business partners? I'd be interested. I like taking you folks hither and yon because it takes up some of my spare time, but being a retired vet on a military pension can get boring. I can only hunt and fish with my boys when they're not in school. Madison's up to her eyeballs in papers to grade and parent-teacher conferences these days. I could use another job."

John had served in the US Marines for twenty-five years, doing more than his share in faraway places that Andy wouldn't be able to find on a map. John didn't talk about it much. A medical ailment forced his retirement. He puttered around the house while his wife taught school in Eureka.

"I like the sound of that." The elders liked John. He was a reliable taxi service. He didn't smoke or swear. If he drank, he didn't do it while driving his sturdy ten-year-old Suburban. He attended the Baptist church in Eureka regularly and could be seen shoveling the sidewalks at the church on icy winter days with subzero wind chills. "It's still only a thought, but I'll let you know if anything comes of it."

"I can rent a trailer for the equipment. If you decide to stay here a few weeks, don't worry about it. I plan to go down to Missoula to look for a new SUV at some point. This baby's odometer just rolled over a hundred thousand." His chestnut eyes somber, John smoothed his rugged hand over the steering wheel with a loving glance. "Madison says it's time. If I'm going to make a business of carting folks up and down the road, I'd better get something with all the latest safety bells and whistles, which means a trip to the big city. And then I want to take the boys hunting to get our elk during bow season. But I can always come back for you. You've got my cell phone number."

"Safety is good. Your wife is right." Big John might seem like the head of his family, but his wife ran the show. Everyone knew that. John was crazy about her. "I'll try to give you advance notice, and maybe you can swing by on one of those trips. I wouldn't mind doing some hunting myself."

John was more family than Andy's own flesh and blood. His sons were like Andy's younger brothers but closer.

John held out his hand. Andy shook it. John grinned and started the engine. "Get going. Your mother will be over the moon to see you. That alone will be a blessing. Go on!"

Andy shoved from the Suburban, let Donut out, grabbed his duffel bag, and ran up the steps. The third one still creaked the way it did the day they moved in after that never-ending three-day drive from Berne, Indiana—a place his father could no longer stomach because of the influx of "Amish" tourism. This house had belonged to his father's childhood best friend, Amos Hitly. Amos sold it for a song and moved to Libby to join their charismatic church.

A person could count on change, if nothing else. Might as well expect that. With a deep breath Andy tugged open the screen door and entered. The spicy aroma of elk chili hit him first, and his mouth watered. He sniffed. Baking bread. And cinnamon rolls. The smells took him back years. He was no longer the wayfaring brother and son. Together, all ten of them would sit at the table, heads bowed. His father would say amen, and they'd dig in. His mother always made enough for two or three helpings for her growing boys.

The living room hadn't changed much. Pine plank floors. Stone fireplace with a huge chunk of native wood for a mantel. Two hickory rocking chairs. An old, lumpy sofa with a knitted blanket thrown over the back. A table covered with mail, seed catalogs, greeting cards for card showers, and a gas lamp.

On second thought it had changed in small ways. Gone were his father's wire-rimmed reading glasses and the worn German

Bible that always lay on a small wooden table next to his rocking chair closest to the fireplace. His feet were always cold.

A bowl of assorted hard candies always sat next to them.

Dad's sweet tooth was legendary. He and Christine would have that in common if they ever met. Christine preferred chocolate, but she'd never met a piece of candy she didn't like. Not true. She did reject licorice on no uncertain terms. She and his father had that in common too.

When they met. They would get on famously. So would Christine and his mother. His mother loved cleaning as much as Christine did. She preferred knitting to hunting and baking to fishing—just like Christine. So why hadn't he introduced them yet?

Focus.

No candy bowl in sight. Even if Mom and Dad had their own rooms, it seemed odd that their touches would disappear from this place—the center of family life for so many years.

A sense of uneasiness pricked the skin on the back of his neck. Donut, ever attuned to his owner's moods, whined softly. Andy scratched the mutt between his ears. "Mudder, are you here? It's me, Andy."

Steps sounded in the hallway. A child wailed. "Hush, hush, little one," a soft, soothing, familiar voice cooed. "You're fine. You're fine."

That voice still came to him in his dreams, whispering sweet nothings, giggling over yellow wildflower petals floating in the breeze. *He loves me. He loves me not. He loves me. He loves me not.*

When it was all said and done, she loved him not.

Or she loved another more.

Winona slipped on bare feet into the room as quietly as she'd slipped from Andy's life. Her peaches-and-cream complexion had turned rosy. Her enormous belly preceded her. Her gaze didn't falter. She simply smiled as if no time had passed since their last conversation so long ago. "*Guder daag*, Andy."

The way she said his name sent a shiver down his spine, just as it had done the first time he met her at a Sunday service a few weeks after her family moved to a farm down the road. He'd been sixteen and just beginning his rumspringa. Same for her.

A moment made in heaven. Or so he thought.

He stared. How could he not? She balanced a dark-haired, wiggling toddler on one hip. Her own chestnut hair escaped her kapp in fine spiral curls on her forehead. Her dimples deepened round cheeks. Being in a family way only increased her God-given beauty.

"Andy?"

He started. "Guder daag." He managed to tear his gaze from her face. It fell to the floor somewhere between her feet and his dirty boots. "The kind is unhappy?"

"Teething. Little Will is not a happy camper. Isn't that right, kind?" She patted his back. William responded with a loud burp. She chuckled. "Not exactly the answer I wanted, but it might make him feel better."

Of all the scenarios he'd imagined, seeing Winona first and being alone with her—the boy, who looked about two, didn't count—had not been one of them. Andy dropped his duffel bag on the floor and crossed his arms. "Where are my mudder and daed?"

"In the dawdy haus. Duane is taking a nap. Your mudder likes to do her sewing while he sleeps. It's quiet there. This *bopli* makes a lot of racket."

Sudden vertigo caused the room to rock. His father never napped during the day. "Is he that ill?"

"The doctors haven't been able to figure out why he's feelin' so bad. They do tests and more tests. In the meantime he's tired and weak. He goes back to Missoula tomorrow to see the doctor for some results."

Not knowing the cause of the problem would aggravate anybody. On the phone Frederick had been sure they would have an answer soon. Apparently he'd been wrong. Andy brushed aside his anxious fears. They wouldn't help anyone, least of all his father. "Where's everybody else?"

"Stephen is helping Frederick cut the last of the hay. Cherise is teaching. Wallace and Nan will get here tomorrow."

"And everyone else?"

"The kinner are outside playing. Or working. Your other schweschders are on their way. *Wie bischt du?*" Her words were soft, her expression questioning. "Well, I hope."

He let his arms drop. He straightened. *"Gut. Ich bin gut."*

He *was* good. Regardless of what she might think, the world did not revolve around her. He had moved on. He'd fallen in love with another.

"Gut." She turned away. "Let me get you a glass of tea. Or would you rather have a cup of *kaffi*? It's chilly today."

He had no choice but to follow her into the kitchen. Donut trotted alongside him, his toenails going *clickity-clack* on the pine. She plopped Will in a playpen nestled between the table and shelves laden with home-canned fruits and vegetables and baking goods. The child had her hair and fair skin but Stephen's features. Much like Andy's. What would their children have looked like? Not much different. He brushed off the thoughts like annoying gnats. "Kaffi would be gut."

"It's been a long time since we talked." Winona poured the coffee and brought it to the table. Despite her size, she moved with light feet. "You look tired and thin."

She shouldn't be commenting on his looks. Andy worked to control his unreasonable irritation. No matter what happened in the past, he should not only forgive but forget. He needed to sweep the memories from his brain. Permanently. "My cabin burned. My neighbors lost their homes or outbuildings. Those aren't the sort of circumstances that bring sleep."

"I'm sorry."

These were familiar words she'd spoken to him before. They didn't help the first time and they didn't help now. "Gott has a plan." A plan that hadn't included her. Andy still had no idea why. He also had no room in his heart for small talk. The words threatened to choke him. "You're happy then?"

With Stephen. With his older brother who looked so similar and acted so differently.

"I am." Her cheeks bloomed red. She picked up a glass of water, sipped, and swallowed. "I know you can't understand."

"Nee, but it doesn't matter. You chose another. It doesn't matter who."

"It does matter. You know that and I know that." With a small groan she sank into the farthest chair and began to knead her hands. They were chapped and red. Donut plopped down next to her feet and laid his head on his paws. *Traitor.* "Who knows why two hearts call out to each other in such a way that can't be ignored?"

"No one does. That's true." The words stuck like sharp chunks of gravel in his throat. He sipped the coffee. The hot liquid burned all the way to his belly. Memories floated on the air like feathers drifting by, made insubstantial by the passage of time. And by the hard work of sweeping them from his heart and mind over and over again through the years. "That doesn't release a person from doing what's right or honest or kind or decent—"

"I tried, please believe me, Andy, I tried to ignore the feelings. I never wanted to hurt you." Fussing emanated from the playpen. William wailed. Winona picked him up and brought him back to the table. She sat him on her lap and handed him a wooden horse. His fussing subsided. "You and Stephen may look alike, but you are two very different men—"

"I know. I grew up with him. But you found him . . . preferable."

"A spark ignited between us—"

"I don't want to know—"

"What's going on here?" Stephen tromped through the back door. His gaze bouncing from Winona to Andy and back, he halted and stuck his fists on his hips. "So you decided to show up after all this time, Bruder?"

CHAPTER 9

Three years packed with missed picnics, Christmas programs, weddings, the births of nieces and nephews, and the simple moments spent drinking iced tea on the front porch—those were the missed memories that comprised the threads woven together to make family. A family to which Andy no longer felt close.

He arose from the chair in his mother's kitchen and faced Stephen. His brother was responsible for those precious lost days. While Winona offered apologies on more than one occasion, Stephen never had. Not that it would matter. "What do you mean? I came as soon as I could, given what's going on in Kootenai."

Stephen removed his straw hat and hung it on a hook near the door. His movements were slow and deliberate, belying his cool expression. He swiveled and tromped to the table where he took his son from Winona's lap. He planted a kiss on Will's cheek. Crowing with delight, the boy patted his father's beard with chubby fingers. "After three years away. That's what I meant. You didn't move to China. All you had to do was hire a driver and come for a visit. Do you know what that would've meant to Mudder? To Daed?"

The highway traveled in both directions. Not long after his move, Mother and Father had visited—more to make sure Andy lacked for nothing than for their enjoyment. As had Frederick and Cherise, Wallace, and his sisters. The only one who hadn't visited stood across the room from Andy. But the visits tapered off over time. They all worked hard and had little time or money to spare. While 385 miles—or six and a half hours—was nothing to Englishers, it could be an enormous chasm for Plain folks.

Andy fixed his gaze on the window over the kitchen sink to his brother's left and slowly, carefully, breathed in and out. Tree branches swayed and dipped in an autumn breeze that spoke of the changing seasons. Forgiveness served as a fundamental building block of their Christian faith. Everyone in the room—minus an innocent babe—knew that. Did Stephen count on forgiveness when he did the unforgivable and stole Andy's beloved?

Over the years they'd had their share of spats, like all brothers only two years apart did. Baseball games won and lost. Who got the last piece of fried chicken. Whose turn it was to clean the chicken coop. Or slaughter the old hens. But they always came back together. They worked at the sawmill, farmed, fished, hunted, and played as brothers. Until the night Andy had come upon Stephen inexplicably driving away from Winona's parents' home late one spring night three years ago.

"You've no answer then." Stephen shifted Will to his hip. His son laid his head on his father's chest and stared at Andy with big owlish eyes. Stephen's eyes. His brother, on the other hand, had trouble meeting his gaze. "You said you were fine. We thought you were gut with . . . everything."

For the first time Stephen faltered. His gruff voice deepened. "We know it's not an easy situation—"

"I did my best to be fine." Andy tore his gaze from the window and studied the canned goods instead. Cherries, peaches, beets, green beans, pickles, tomatoes, to name a few. His mother and sister-in-law had outdone themselves this past summer. "That doesn't mean I wanted to stay around and watch. I told Daed and Mudder I needed a fresh start. They didn't like it, but they understood."

They didn't like it, but they at least attempted to see it through Andy's eyes. Father's words had rung in Andy's ears as he packed, said his goodbyes, and jumped into the van that would take him to his new life. *"Forgiving small acts of transgression is easy. The true testing of faith is when the transgressions are enormous and painful. That's when a person must set aside his smallness, his humanness."*

And then Mother's contribution. *"It's better to know now than to be yoked for life to someone who realizes you're not the one for her. That you're not right for each other. It's a blessing, really."*

Not right for each other. Winona had him fooled. Her ardent kisses. Her sweet hugs. The way she laughed at his jokes. At what point had she stopped feeling those sparks that threatened to burst into flames? Why had he not noticed? Why didn't she say something sooner?

So many whys. Not a single one answered.

Andy had tried, but the words *I forgive you* stuck in his craw. They choked him. They tasted more sour than grapefruit peel on his tongue. They weighed heavier on his shoulders than the logs they turned into planks at the sawmill. He'd carried this load for so long he couldn't remember how it felt to be free of it.

"They need their suhs and dochders all together now."

Stephen's tone was half challenge, half plea. "What they don't need is the digging up of old hurts and dissension among their kinner."

"There will be none of that on my part." Finally, Andy found neutral words, if not those of reconciliation so needed. "I came to see my daed, and then I'll be on my way."

He forced himself to stand. Donut did the same. Taking his time, his dog at his side, Andy stalked from the kitchen, through the living room, and down the hallway. His lungs sucked air greedily. His hands shook. He managed to unclench his aching jaw.

Humming greeted him at the first door. His mother's soft, sweet tones beckoned memories of her cool hand on his fever-ish forehead when he had the flu. She always hummed while she took his temperature and fed him her homemade chicken noodle soup. Tension dissipated around him as if the sun had cleared away an ugly fog.

"Mudder?"

She glanced up from darning a sock and smiled. With her finger to her lips, she laid the sock aside and rose from the rock-ing chair that sat next to a huge oak bed. Father slept on his back, mouth open, arms flung out. A gentle snore ruffled his gray beard. Even asleep, he looked the same as always. Sturdy, indestructible. At peace.

Mother scampered from the room and tugged the door closed behind her. "Suh, you're here." Her delight burst forth in the form of a squeal and a hug that squeezed the air from his lungs. "I can't believe it. You're here."

"Believe it. How is he?"

"The same. Who knows what ails him? The doctors surely don't." She held Andy at arm's length and scrutinized him from head to toe. "You are skinny as a rail. That's what happens when a man lives on his own."

She stopped. Her lined face turned tomato red. She sighed. "Will this falling out with your bruder always be the wild boar in the room?" She stomped her sneaker-clad foot. "It will not. Time to let bygones be bygones. You're here. You came. That's your version of a peace offering."

"I'm trying."

"I know you are. Stephen will, too, if you give him a chance. I know he feels horrible about what happened, even if he doesn't say the words. He's like your daed. He doesn't talk much, but he feels it."

The same thing she'd said three years ago. Shouldn't Stephen have to say the words? "So as the oldest son, he's the head of the family now?"

"Your daed is retired. Frederick is running the farm, but Stephen handles the sawmill." She bustled past Andy. He followed her into the living room where she settled onto the couch and patted the seat next to her. "Sit, sit. Tell me everything. The fire? Is it past? How did Kootenai fare?"

"My cabin burned. So did the other cabins. About thirty buildings altogether but only one Plain house." He eased onto the couch next to her and leaned back. His body ached with exhaustion. "It's not done yet. No one is allowed to return. About twenty thousand acres have burned. It's a sight I won't soon forget."

He poured out the story, leaving out no small detail. Tut-tutting now and then, his mother soaked it up. She was like that, full of concern for others. What could she do? How soon could they go to help rebuild? The women would feed the workers. The men would provide the elbow grease. The three-hundred-plus miles meant nothing to her when other Plain families were hurting.

"Everyone from districts across the state will help, Mudder." He smiled at her expression. "I'm sure a load of men will go from here, but I reckon you have your hands full with Daed."

"I go with him to his appointments. I cook for him. He eats. He sleeps." She smoothed her wrinkled apron. "But truth be told, there's little more I can do for him except watch and wait."

"He hasn't had any more fainting spells?"

"Nee, just the two on back-to-back days. He was on a ladder, replacing siding, the first time. He hit his head, knocked himself out, and got a concussion. The second time he was helping Frederick with a break in the fence." Mother recounted these events even though she knew Andy had been told about them. She seemed to need to talk about them, to relive them until she could understand them. "Your bruder was right there, thanks be to Gott. Mostly, he's tired and weak. They've tested him for every disease known to man, it seems."

"Nothing?"

"Not all the test results have come back yet. His white blood cell count is low and his platelets too." That she knew about such things spoke to how much time she now spent with doctors. "We'll know more when the remaining results come in."

"Could it be old age?"

"Your daed is fifty-five. Not so old." She shoved her bronze-rimmed glasses up her nose and frowned, but her green eyes were suddenly bright with laughter. "I worry that it's my cooking. I've never been a good cook. Maybe it's too much fried food clogging his arteries. Or maybe he has the diabetes from too many of my pies and cakes."

"The doctors would test for that right away." She never

cooked anything fancy, but what Plain wife did? Her cooking satisfied her husband and her eight children. Andy had no complaints in that department. "He always worked hard. He's never been fat."

"I think what he really wants is for his kinner to be close to home. He wants you all to work together. With him."

There it was. The true reason for Frederick's call. The message behind the message. *"Come home where you belong."*

"I'm here now, but I can't stay."

"Can't or won't?" Mother's thin eyebrows rose and leaned toward each other in distaste for what her ears had heard. "Maybe you should speak with the bishop. Gideon might be able to help you work through your refusal to not only forgive but forget."

The words were made so much harsher by Andy's surprise at her attitude. "And Stephen? Has he spoken with Gideon about his sin of coveting what belonged to his bruder?"

"Has he not asked for forgiveness?"

"Nee, he hasn't, actually."

"Maybe you didn't give him a chance. Either way, it doesn't matter. Your job is to forgive."

"All of this is my fault, then." Andy heaved himself to his feet. "I shouldn't have come."

"But you did. That is gut."

His father shuffled into the room and dropped into the closest rocking chair. "My family is back together. The way it should be."

The jut of his jaw suggested that now wasn't the time to argue. Upsetting him would be wrong. Despite the nap, his father had dark circles under his eyes. His frame was gaunt, and knobby wrists stuck out from the rolled-up sleeves of his faded cotton shirt. He looked like an old man. But he was still the head of the house and Andy's father.

"I've made a life for myself in West Kootenai. They're gut folks. I like being in the mountains."

"The mountains are close here as well."

"True. They are. But in Kootenai, they're on my doorstep."

"Which is why the cabin burned to the ground."

Father didn't mince words. Mother tugged at Andy's arm, forcing him to sit. "Nothing has to be decided now. Let's enjoy this time, all of us together."

"I've been courting."

Mother's look of worry disappeared. She clapped as if applauding a great performance. "I'm so glad. Your heart has healed. You've no reason to hang on to the past."

"It's not that easy."

"No one said it was easy." Father still hadn't smiled. "Only expected and what's right. You've found your way to another. Let the past go."

"This special friend lives in Kootenai. That's where I intend to make our home."

"She could live in Lewistown just as easily." Father stroked his unruly beard. "Unless you haven't told her of the troubles you've had here."

"She doesn't need to know."

Mother and Father exchanged troubled glances.

Father fixed Andy with that fiery stare that made him quake in his boots as a child. "To enter into a union with secrets doesn't bode well for the future of that union."

"That's between Christine and me."

"You need to talk to the deacon or the bishop. You need advice."

The rest of the thought hung in the air. *And you won't take it from me.*

How could he when his own parents had refused to counsel Stephen for his transgressions? They'd played favorites in the interest of keeping the peace. And let Stephen take over their business.

They couldn't turn around now and expect Andy to live here. He rose again, stretched, and edged toward the door. "It's getting late. We'll talk about this later. I'll go help with the chores."

"Andy."

He stopped at the door and turned. His father held his gaze. "One way or the other, you do need to tell her. Our past affects who we are in the future. There's no getting around that. Even if we want to. Even if we try our hardest. We are shaped by our past. Stop fighting it and come home."

The hard knot in his throat kept Andy from answering. He managed a curt nod and escaped before he did something unmanly like cry.

Only one day here and he missed Christine.

He missed her and he needed her.

CHAPTER 10

St. Ignatius, Montana

The pain of saying goodbye dwarfed even the beautiful Mission Mountains that climbed high in the sky beyond the tranquil Mission Valley. Christine swallowed against a lump the size of a bitter lemon. The weekend had been filled with making a few last-minute memories. Eating hamburgers dripping with melted cheese, mustard, and catsup around the picnic table. Visiting with friends. Singing together. Telling Maisie stories before she slipped off to sleep. Eating Mudder's fry pies. Memorizing the lines on Father's face. Now the time had come to let them go. Like it or not.

Mother shooed Maisie and Abigail into the van. She instructed Zeke to make sure their seat belts were tight. Then she turned to Christine. Her eyes reddened, but her smile stayed firmly in place. She brushed imaginary crumbs from Christine's apron. Her gaze bounced to the Valley Grocery Store's porch where a hodgepodge of outdoor furniture, firewood, and plants beckoned to shoppers. She scooped up a huge canvas bag of gifts for family back home in Kansas and snacks that she'd purchased at the store and held it against her chest like she would a baby.

"You don't have to stay. Lucy and Fergie will understand if

you change your mind." A rare look of hesitancy on her face, Mother shifted her sneaker-clad feet. "How is it possible that you're old enough to be out in the world on your own?"

"You're not leaving her in the middle of New York City, Schweschder." Aunt Lucy chuckled and gave Mother a gentle nudge toward the van. "She'll be snug as a bug with her cousins here. I'll keep her busy and I'll make sure she behaves herself with that young man you mentioned."

"Mudder!" Christine couldn't contain the wail. Nothing was private in this family. "He's not even in St. Ignatius."

"I might have spilled the beans about your . . . situation." Mother's sadness turned into an impish grin reminiscent of Maisie when she stole a cinnamon roll from Abigail's plate. "I'm sorry if you think such conversations are untoward, but it is the reason you're staying behind."

Delilah chose that moment to hop from the van and administer a third medicinal hug to Christine. Which meant Abigail and Maisie had to do the same. Which caused the dogs to bark and the cat to meow.

"Enough! Everyone in the van who's going to Kansas or you'll get left behind. We need to get moving or we'll be driving half the night." His voice gruff, Father tugged at Mother's hand. He had yet to look Christine in the face or say goodbye. Even now. "We'll call the store phone when we get to Haven to let you know we arrived safe."

"You do that. Now run along. Take care. Be safe." Aunt Lucy waved at the children, who took time from arguing over which seat they'd occupy to whoop and holler. "Don't be driving too fast either."

That was directed at the driver from St. Ignatius Uncle Fergie had recommended.

Father climbed into the passenger seat next to the driver and leaned his elbow on the open window. "Be gut, Dochder." He cleared his throat. "Do what your onkel and aenti ask of you."

Not trusting her voice to speak, Christine nodded.

"You'll come visit for Thanksgiving." Mudder stuck her arm out the window and waved like a crazed person. "And for Christmas."

Holidays that seemed a hundred years away.

Christine waved back.

That was it. They drove away.

She whirled, jerked open the door to the Valley Grocery Store, and went inside without looking back. As much as her heart begged for one last peek at the twelve-passenger van that would carry her family to Haven, it was better to let it go. No doubt Maisie would have her chubby face scrunched up against the window glass. Socks and Shoes would crowd her, licking her tear-streaked cheeks. Abigail would hug her. Delilah would start telling her a story, and Zeke would tell all three of them to imagine how wonderful life would be in Kansas with Grandma and Grandpa Mast and all their aunts and uncles and cousins.

Don't cry.

"We're so glad to have your help, my sweet girl." Huffing and puffing, Aunt Lucy bustled past Christine and headed toward the twin checkout stands that stood at the front of the store she and Uncle Fergie had opened fifteen years earlier. "Since Darcie had her bopli in July, we've been shorthanded. Salome and Kimberly filled in, but now they're back in school."

Don't you dare cry.

"Danki for letting me stay with you. I'm happy to help." Having never worked in a store before likely meant she would be more of a hindrance than a help. Talking to strangers. Making change. Knowing the price of hundreds of items available in the store with its bulk and discounted foods as well as fabrics, sewing supplies, quilting supplies, cookbooks, church hats, suspenders, furniture, and prepared foods from the deli. "I could clean for you—sweep, mop, wash the windows, whatever you need."

Aunt Lucy kept a somewhat clean house, but Christine could do better. She could scrub the stains from the bathroom sink and use bleach on the toilet. She knew several tricks for getting mud and grass stains from clothes. Chores would keep her mind from the homesickness that already permeated every bone in her body.

Her expression thoughtful, Aunt Lucy waved at a couple pushing a cart down the cereal and bread aisle, dispensed hugs to two small English children begging their mother for candy, and stopped to straighten the jars of homemade jams and jellies by the registers.

"Nee, nee. Kimberly and Salome will clean when they come in after school." She slid her arm around Christine and squeezed. Together they traipsed to the back of the store where the full-service deli did a booming business in everything from sandwiches to ice cream to a wide array of cheeses. "Why don't we start with the deli? I know you can make sandwiches and dish out macaroni salad. The prices are marked on the containers. The scales are easy to use. You punch in the number, and it'll print out the weight and the price tag."

"Sounds easy enough." Not as easy as scrubbing toilets, dusting curio cabinets, and washing dishes. However, there'd been a time when Christine didn't know how to use a vacuum cleaner or start a dishwasher, either. "I'm sure I can learn."

"The important thing is to clean up as you go. Keep

everything—from the slicing machines to the countertops— pristine. We want to make the health inspector proud."

Keeping a kitchen clean. Christine would excel at this job. She eyed the refrigerated coolers with their neat rows of meats— roast beef, honey ham, salami, chicken, turkey, and at least a dozen more. Then every kind of cheese imaginable. Five kinds of potato salad, coleslaw, macaroni salad, pickles, olives, four kinds of mustard. Tomatoes, lettuce, jalapeños. That didn't even cover the myriad of breads. Who knew making a sand- wich could be so complicated?

Four customers crowded the glass cases, but the Plain woman behind the counter didn't seem the least bit flustered. She looked to be in her midtwenties, with acne-scarred cheeks, cornflower-blue eyes, wheat-colored hair, and a frame so thin a brisk wind would blow her away.

"That's Esther Marie Shrock." Aunt Lucy leaned closer and lowered her voice. "She's worked here for going on three years. Her father is a friend of Fergie's. She knows the deli inside and out. She'll be the one to train you."

Esther Marie didn't look up. She worked her way through three sandwiches of roast beef, swiss, lettuce, tomato, spicy mustard, pickles, and mayo on whole wheat submarine rolls without the slightest waste of energy or motion. Not only that, she made it seem easy as she asked questions of the Englisher, who wanted three bags of chips—one barbecue, one sour cream, and one plain—and three chocolate chip and six peanut butter cookies to go with the order.

"She used to be shy—because of the way she talks—but she got over it." Lucy rearranged the chip display so all the pack- ages were even in each row. "Her stutter has actually improved the longer she's been here. Her parents thought it would never work, but when I suggested she take the job, she didn't even flinch. The tourists get a kick out of talking to Plain people, and they find her charming."

If a woman with a stutter could be brave enough to do this job, so could Christine. "I never thought of myself as shy . . ."

"It can be overwhelming if you're not used to dealing with the public. St. Ignatius is small, and our store is on the outskirts of town, but everyone and his uncle comes here. Kootenai is so much more secluded. And cleaning houses means you never deal with strangers. I promised my schweschder I would take care of you."

"I'm all grown up." Christine tamped down the words. No need to be defensive. Aunt Lucy was right. She'd lived a sheltered life. One she loved. That didn't mean she couldn't learn new skills. The fire, her father's decision to move, and Andy's trek to Lewistown converged in a place in time that resulted in her chance to live a different life—if only for a short while. She could do this. "Show me what to do, and I'll jump right in."

The quiver in her voice betrayed her.

"Ach, sweetie, there's no rush." Aunt Lucy wrapped Christine in a hug. Her round body was warm and soft. She smelled like fresh soap. Between her stout body and the crinkly laugh lines around her eyes, she was a Plain version of DeeDee Drake. Christine's heart dropped another foot. Lucy squeezed harder. "This has been a big day for you. You left home. Your family moved. There's no need to start a new job too."

"I'm gut. I'm ready to go." Christine heaved a deep breath. "I'm fine."

"Tell me about this special friend of yours. How soon will he return to Kootenai?"

"I don't know. He couldn't say." The words were like shards

of broken glass in Christine's throat. More goodbyes. More loss. "He has family matters to take care of. He didn't know how long it would take."

"But he's worth waiting for."

Absolutely. She'd lost all interest in other men the second she laid eyes on Andy. "He is."

"When patience and perseverance are required, we appreciate the fruits of our labor more."

Another version of her mother's platitudes. "I'd like to get to work, if I may." Work would take her mind off the wait and the homesickness that engulfed her like a dust storm. "I want to make myself useful."

Taking a step back, Lucy pursed her lips and cocked her head. "Why don't you dip your toe in the water today for about an hour? The girls will be here then, and I'll give you a ride back to the house."

"An hour, two hours, whatever you need." Lifting her chin, Christine offered her a smile. "I can stay until closing time if needed."

Lucy's baby-blue eyes contemplated Christine's face for several seconds. She nodded, made the introductions, and then rushed off to sign for a shipment of fabrics for the sewing section.

Her stomach twisted in knots, Christine washed her sweaty hands and donned a store apron, all the while watching Esther Marie's quick work at filling an order for two pounds of mustard potato salad, three pounds of baked beans, and three pounds of tapioca pudding. The woman never missed a beat when the elderly English woman decided to add three pounds each of roast beef, salami, and spicy roasted chicken—each sliced differently.

A young man behind Esther Marie's customer fidgeted. His phone dinged. He thumbed something on the screen, then stuck it in his back pocket. He caught Christine's gaze. "Are you on the clock?" The question came with a diffident smile. "If you're not, it's okay. I can wait."

"Me?" Her hands fluttered to her neck. Of course her. To whom else could he be talking? Christine's nervous giggle only served to make her feel sillier. "I mean, jah, I can try to help you."

His smile grew. His teeth were slightly uneven. His almond skin glowed with health. His ochre eyes behind dark-rimmed glasses were warm. "Are you new? I haven't seen you behind the counter here before."

"Jah—yes. You're my first customer." Another high-pitched giggle escaped her mouth. *Lord, have mercy on me. I sound like a silly duck. Quack, quack.* "What would you like?"

Instead of giving her his order, he stuck out his hand. "I'm Raymond Old Fox. It's nice to meet you. I stop here on my way home to Arlee from my job in Pablo."

Did all the customers introduce themselves? Christine stared at his hand. He had stubby fingers that matched his burly body. They weren't the hands of a man who worked outdoors. "Is that really your name?"

Raymond laughed. So did Esther Marie and her elderly customer.

Embarrassment roared through her quicker than the Caribou fire currently decimating her beloved Kootenai. "I'm sorry. I didn't mean to be rude."

Raymond's hand dropped, but his smile didn't fade. "Don't apologize. It's a good quality to speak what's on your mind instead of hiding it behind good manners. Old Fox is my real name. It was my mother's name and her father's name before her. We're native Kootenai."

In her family's infrequent visits to Uncle Fergie's, Christine had spent little time outside their tight circle of Plain family and friends. The families knew their properties were on the Flathead Indian Reservation, but no one thought of it as a topic of conversation. "You're Native American Indian?"

"Native."

"Native." She filed his response away for later review. Her knowledge of Indians was confined to the historical Westerns she'd read. "What can I get you? A sandwich for lunch?"

He didn't answer for a long moment. Maybe he was still deciding. "Did you just move to St. Ignatius then?"

"I'm from West Kootenai. We were evacuated because of the fire." No sense in going into all the gory details with a stranger. "Lucy and Fergie are my aenti and onkel."

"Ah." He seemed to take in that information, mull it over, and accept it. A careful, slow process. "I'm sorry you are uprooted."

His gentle sincerity brought Christine's tears dangerously close to the surface. He had no way of knowing just how uprooted she felt with her family trekking to Kansas as she stood here conversing with him, but his sadness at her loss seemed genuine. For a second she chose to forget about the deli and sandwiches and her state of limbo between homes and families and even with Andy. "You're kind."

He smiled. Such a sweet smile from a stranger. "I try."

Esther Marie coughed. Christine jumped. "What did you need? Lunch?"

"Actually, I'm here for my great-grandmother." Raymond looked to be in his midtwenties. He wore faded blue jeans

and a T-shirt that had a number sign followed by the words
Computer Geek run together as one word. His shiny, straight,
obsidian hair was parted in the middle and hung long enough
to brush his collar. Nothing about him seemed the sort who
did shopping for a family member. "She's been sick, and I'm
trying to tempt her to eat. This store is off the beaten track,
but it has some of her favorite snacks. I can't get them anywhere else."

"The tapioca is good. Does she like pudding?"

He laughed again. He had a deep, hoarse laugh like her
father's. "She's more into smoked horseradish cheddar. I'll get
some sausage, a loaf of dark rye, and peach salsa. She also likes
the scorpion cheddar cheese and fresh butter. At her age, she
doesn't worry about too much fat or cholesterol."

Scorpion cheddar was made with some of the spiciest chili
peppers available. "Are you pulling my leg?"

A perplexed look on his clean-shaven face, he glanced at his
hands and then at her. "I don't think so. She's ninety-four. She
says her taste buds stopped working somewhere in her eighties.
Food tastes like sawdust. She's wasting away from old age but
not for lack of attitude. In her head she's twenty and eats whatever she wants."

"I'm sorry she's wasting away."

"You need not apologize. I promise."

She didn't mind at all. His soft, sweet tone and his concern
for his great-grandmother were touching. He'd driven out of
his way to a dirt road that led to St. Ignatius's tiny airport
in hopes of finding something that would entice his great-
grandmother to eat. Her first customer was a kind man and a
good grandson.

Christine grabbed a huge chunk of the cheese and went to

work. Slicing cheese was more difficult than it looked. Her first efforts were ragged and torn. The next slice was thicker than a piece of toast. "Sorry."

"Let-t-t-t me." Esther Marie wiped her hands on her apron and held them out. "There's a tr-r-i-cccck to it."

"Nee, danki, I can do this."

"I believe you." Raymond's tone said he did indeed believe her. "A person can't learn skills without practice."

With an encouraging nod Esther Marie turned to a new customer who needed a "quick" order for half a dozen sandwiches and all the fixings.

Finally, Christine handed over the package with a flourish. "I did it. I mean, here's your cheese. Can I ask you another question?"

"Sure." With an oddly formal bow he accepted her offering. "What would you like to know?"

"What does your shirt mean? Number sign and Computer-Geek?"

Again, he laughed. He had the unrestrained laugh of a man who used those muscles a lot. "It's hashtag ComputerGeek. Have you not heard of Twitter?"

"No."

"It's okay. I'm giving you a hard time. I know Amish people don't use computers. I'm a computer nut. I live and breathe computers. People think I'm a nerd, but I'm really more of a techie."

"They have computers where my father works, and I looked up a book at the library on a computer once." Acutely aware of Esther Marie's curious stare, Christine chose her words carefully. Plain people had good reason to avoid technology. It connected people to a world filled with vices and took them away from the important people who were right in front of them—their families. At least that's what the bishop said. And her father. And he knew everything. "I mean the librarian searched it for me. I looked over her shoulder."

Why was she going on and on? This sudden lull in customers left her no excuse to get back to work.

Raymond Old Fox didn't seem to mind. Nor did he seem in a hurry now. "You never told me your name."

"Christine."

"Welcome to the Flathead Indian Reservation, Christine."

Something about the way he said the words made her look closer into his eyes. Even with the glasses as a shield of sorts, they were full of life and a touch of humor. They held a note of mystery, of the unknown, and yet invitation. She took a breath. He strode away before she could say more.

A gray-haired woman in a purple broom skirt and white western-style shirt harrumphed as she picked up the sandwiches Esther Marie had made for her. "Uppity Indians."

Christine opened her mouth. Esther Marie shook her head. Christine pressed her lips together, grabbed a washcloth, and wiped down the counter.

"They act like we stole our land from them. My great-grandparents bought our property in the early nineteen hundreds way before that kid was born. It was surplus left over after the Dawes Act gave the Indians their allotments." Her long nose wrinkled as if she smelled something bad. "Everybody knows the white people around here bought their land fair and square. Anybody who says different is just a sore loser."

With a vague smile Esther Marie handed the woman a huge container of macaroni salad. "Is there anyth-th-ii–nn–g else I-I-I can g-g-get you?"

"No thanks." The lady nodded at Christine. "Welcome to *St. Ignatius.*"

The final word, apparently.

After the woman pushed her cart in the direction of the fresh produce, Christine turned to Esther Marie. "What was that about?"

"Don't worr-r-r-ry about it." Esther Marie stowed the remaining roast beef back in the cooler as she talked. "Most folks around-d-d-d here g-g-g-et along well. We share this b-b-b-eautif-f-ful place made by Gott-t-t for all his kinn-n-n-ner. But there's a few who hang on to old diff-f-f-ferences like their first loves. We find it's best-t-t-t to ignore them. Outside of our jobs, we keep to ourselves and let it roll off us like water-r-r-r off a d-d-d-uck's b-b-b-ack."

The words slipped from Esther Marie's tongue with more ease than any had previously. Almost as if she'd heard them oft repeated. Nodding in agreement, Christine stared at the Englisher's retreating back. A new home, a new job, a new world.

A Native man with eyes the color of volcanic rock who invited her to take a road to no place she'd ever been.

If all her customers were like Raymond Old Fox, she might like it here in her new world.

CHAPTER 11

Gramma's formidable stare from the couch where she lay propped up on a pile of oversized pillows on the sofa in her tiny cabin's only room meant she was having a good day. Good days were to be celebrated. Raymond set the Valley Grocery Store bag on the skinny pine table with its hanging leaves squeezed against the wall next to a mini refrigerator and small gas stove that served as Gramma's kitchen.

Ignoring her scowl, he stowed the food, set up his laptop on the coffee table in front of the couch, and then added a straw to the cherry milkshake he picked up at The Huckleberry Patch on his way down Arlee's main drag and took it to her. "*Ki'su'k kyukyit*. What's new, Gramma?"

She peered over the thick black rims of glasses that needed to be cleaned and frowned. Her deeply wrinkled, sun-leathered skin mapped the geography of her face like so many hills and valleys. Those wrinkles told her story if a person only knew how to read them. "*Ki'su'k kyukyit*, Raymond. An obedient and loyal great-grandson visits his elders regularly. That is new."

"It's only been three days since my last visit." He handed her the shake without adding that his three great-aunts—her sisters—had visited during that time. And his Grandma Velda, who was his true gramma. Never a day went by that some-one did not visit with his great-grandma Sadie Runabout. She might be old, but she still had much to say, and they wanted to listen for as long as they could. "I see that you've eaten nothing of the groceries your sisters brought you. How do you expect to maintain your strength if you don't eat?"

"I am as strong as a bull moose. I eat plenty. One little runner my size and age does not need to gorge on meat and bread and potatoes. You want to feed me like I work building bridges." She leaned back on her pillows, her frown replaced by her trademark impish grin. "I am only teasing you. I know you go to work. You volunteer at The People's Center. You volunteer at the grade school, teaching Kootenai. You have a full life. That is good."

The rest of her thought hung in the air between them. Words not spoken could still be heard. She wanted a good, honorable life for her great-grandson. If that included a wife and children, it would happen in its own time. Not necessarily on her time. Neither of them controlled its passage. The desire to have his children sit at Gramma's feet and learn the ways of their people grew strong roots that wrapped themselves around Raymond's heart and squeezed with greater ferocity each day. Yet the woman who could prune and shape those desires, freeing his heart, had yet to appear.

His phone dinged. An email from his boss about a difficult project they'd tackled earlier in the week. He tapped out a response before he reengaged. "You won't be strong as a bull moose for long if you don't eat."

"You work too much."

He shoved his glasses up his nose and rubbed his forehead. Work filled his life like dirt in a series of holes. Working at

S&K didn't fill a hole in his soul, but it did take his time. And what he chose to do, he did with determined enthusiasm. A man gave his all or stayed home. "I took today off, as a matter of fact, to use up some leave before I lost it. But I do what the job requires. Otherwise, how can I accept the paycheck?"

"When I'm gone, will you still fill up your days with work instead of people?"

"You wanted this for me, Gramma. You told me to stay here, to go to school here. And you're not going anywhere."

"When I go, I go."

Knowing this to be true didn't make it easier. Gramma Sadie had raised Raymond and his two brothers when their mother died in a car accident while working as a tribal cop. Grandma Velda continued to work, so Sadie had no choice but to be mother to her great-grandchildren. Memories of his mom were hazy. A warm, soft hand on his cheek at bedtime. A laugh. The jangle of beads when she dressed for a powwow. Her smell of sun and sweat after an afternoon of picking chokeberries.

Her face escaped him. Photos existed, but Grandma Velda never displayed them. Adeline had been her only child with Grandpa Evan Old Fox, who drowned in the Kootenai River when his daughter was a toddler. That Gramma Sadie had foreseen these deaths in visions didn't diminish the impact on their family's life.

"I'm hungry. How does a grilled cheese sandwich sound?"

"Men hunt and fish. Women cook."

An old argument born of Kootenai cultural heritage that had men hunting while women gathered. If she could stand long enough on the hip she'd broken last fall, Raymond would have bowed to her desire to honor their culture. Or she would have insisted. Just as she had held out against an indoor bathroom until she could no longer make the trek to the out-house. *"A Kootenai does not poop where he eats."* One of her many pronouncements that as boys made Raymond and his brothers snicker behind their hands. "I bought your favorite cheese. The smoked horseradish cheddar."

"A grilled cheese is good. Not moose steak, but good."

Gramma's teeth were bad, making it hard for her to chew meat. Besides, she liked the Amish cheese from the Valley Grocery Store. That truth brought Raymond full circle back to the thoughts that had chased him like hungry grizzlies along Highway 93 the sixteen miles from St. Ignatius to Arlee. Christine of the demur pale-lilac ankle-length dress and white prayer covering. Her inquisitive expression and eyes the color of blue flax flowers that bloomed throughout Montana summers.

Women of all shapes, sizes, and colors appealed to Raymond. Despite being a student of his tribe's history, his heart and his nature held no room for bitter dismissal of an entire race because of what their ancestors had done. All were created equal at the time of their conception. Under their skins, painted a multitude of colors, lay blood, muscle, and sinew fashioned from the same materials.

Raymond's head, however, chose to limit his choices to Native women. He chose to honor them and to do right by them. As a sign of his passion for the history and culture of the continent's indigenous peoples. They were profoundly affected—and nearly decimated—by contact with non-Natives throughout history. He also wanted to do better than his mother had. She had made a baby with a white man who then abandoned them both.

Grandma had been punished by St. Ursuline nuns for speak-ing her native tongue at a school to which her parents had been forced by the Bureau of Indian Affairs agent to send her and her siblings. She didn't need to hear his thoughts on his mother's mistakes. Raymond busied himself making the sandwiches.

"What has happened that you don't share your day with your *ka'titi*?"

"I'm just tired."

"Did you forget who you are talking to?"

Never. Gramma Sadie was also a medicine woman. Her knowledge of herbs and roots coupled with her visions meant many from the reservation still came to see her when illness struck or family problems boiled over. "I talked to someone today—a woman—who remains in my thoughts unexpectedly. That's all."

"A white woman."

Her body might be old, but Gramma's mind made leaps that mountain goats could never accomplish. "An Amish woman who has started working at the Valley Grocery Store."

"The Amish are a new kind of interlopers on the reservation."

The first Amish moved onto the reservation in 1997 when they bought property near St. Ignatius, which by Kootenai elders' standards made them newcomers. Compared to the white people who bought allotments after the Flathead Allotment Act in the early nineteen hundreds, they were. Raymond had given them little thought, one way or another, until now. "She is searching for something."

"Most people are. Although the Amish search within the confines of their own beliefs, for the most part. They don't mix with outsiders." Gramma's tone sounded as if she might admire this attribute, however grudgingly. "You would think they would have a better understanding of our need to reclaim the allotments taken by non-Natives on the reservation."

"From what I've read, their education is confined to what they need to know in order to maintain their way of life." Raymond had first become aware of their presence on the reservation as a teenager. He looked them up online, trying to understand the buggies, the head coverings, and their choice to fund and build their own schools. "It's weird to think they came to this continent from Europe to escape religious persecution while we ended up being persecuted by European settlers who thought we should adopt their religion."

"It is true they did not come out west with the intent of converting the heathens who had peopled the earth here since before the age of the big ice." Gramma snorted. Raymond swiveled from the stove long enough to make sure she hadn't choked on the milkshake. She made a face.

He turned back to flip the sandwiches and smash them down with the spatula in a cast-iron skillet as old as he was. Gramma's harrumph didn't tempt him to turn again.

"It is also true they have fought for the right to educate their children in their traditions and their faith. They have braved the white justice system in more than one battle."

She sounded almost impressed. As impressed as a woman could be who'd served on the tribal council and worked with other leaders to set up an education committee and eventually the tribal college, Salish Kootenai College, where Raymond earned his degree. She knew what it took not only to survive but to thrive in a place where the majority held all the power. Treaties and legislative acts had allowed Native lands to be overrun by outsiders, but the tribal leaders were now buying back the allotments as they came up for sale. Paying to recapture their birthright.

"They also mate for life." He dropped the sentence into the

lake of silence to see if the words would sink or swim. "They believe in love only in the confines of marriage. And they don't believe in divorce."

"In theory, I believe the same thing." Her quick retort was as tart as an unripe lemon. "But our human resolve often crumbles in the face of desire and circumstance and the evils of this world."

Did that make his mother and father evil? Or simply human?

"You have mixed with Amish people before." Gramma wouldn't be diverted by a historical-philosophical discussion of the differences between Native peoples and the Amish. Nor would she take the bait regarding the circumstances of his birth. Who was his father, and why didn't he stay or make himself known? She chose not to share those facts that were missing puzzle pieces in her great-grandson's life. "Why does this one occupy your thoughts now?"

"She asked me a question, when most would've only wondered." Spoken aloud the words didn't begin to explain why her presence behind a deli counter made such an impression on Raymond. English words often seemed inadequate to him. Gramma, whose first language had been Kootenai, had insisted that her daughter, granddaughter, and great-grandchildren learn it. A rarity even in those days. Kootenai was an isolated language, spoken by no other people in the world. Only a few hundred at most spoke it now. "The outside didn't match the inside. The incongruity struck me."

"They teach you all those big words at the college."

"She's a mystery to me."

"A mystery best left unsolved."

There it was. The elder had replaced the great-grandmother. Raymond laid the sandwiches on her favorite blue china plates, added grapes, and carried them to the couch. He settled on a footstool across from her. "I'm just naturally curious."

"Curiosity can have consequences." Her expression fierce, she tugged absently at the two long, white doubled-up braids that lay on her chest. "Remember when you stuck your hand in the crevice of the rocks and the snake bit you?"

"Don't you always say it's important to learn for learning's sake? Isn't that why you insisted we go to college?" To SK College, of course. When he'd argued for his dream of archaeology at the University of Montana in Missoula, she'd put down her high-arched bare foot and said no. Simply no. He would never go against her will. Now he was twenty-three. A man. A man whose heart held a void left by a white father who didn't stick around and a Native mother who died too soon. "She had life questions written on her face. I recognized them because I have those same questions all my own. I'm not thinking of marrying her or even dating her, simply knowing her."

"All this across a deli counter?"

"Those moments are available for all who seek them. You yourself say that. Be present in the moment. Listen to what the wind says. Listen when the rain speaks."

"Now I say watch out. The snake will sting you again." Gramma took a big bite of her sandwich. "*Mmm*, good. For a man you cook good."

End of discussion.

Raymond laid his half-eaten sandwich on his plate and set it on the coffee table. He gently tugged her glasses from her wizened face and cleaned them with the cloth he kept in his jean pocket for his own glasses. Her eyes, made colorless by age, remained hooded. "Thank you, *ka'titi*. It is an honor to cook for you."

She looked like a vulnerable old lady without her spectacles. But he knew better. The heart of a mountain lion resided in her body. He replaced the glasses. She smiled at him and patted his cheek. "You good boy."

She wasn't one for empty compliments. Her words warmed him. Others might have missed having a mother and father, but he and his brothers had both in Gramma.

He would keep her words close, but as a man he had to navigate his own destiny, a tiny canoe on dangerous rapids. He would take care not to upend it on the falls and crash into the rocks below. The strange restlessness that followed him, a reluctant shadow that didn't dissipate in the dark, must be dealt with.

Raymond ate his sandwich with gusto and finished Gramma's when she didn't. Soon they would need more cheese from Valley Grocery Store. Even if he had to eat it all himself.

CHAPTER 12

LEWISTOWN, MONTANA

Even blindfolded and plopped down in the middle of the night, Andy would have known exactly where he stood. The fresh, piney aroma of Douglas fir and the high-pitched whine of the head rig band-saw blade slicing into the logs were unmistakable. Wood chips flew. Sawdust floated in the air. His father's sawmill smelled and sounded like home, sweet home.

He trudged along the conveyor belt toward Stephen who stood at the end watching the best opening-face cants. They still had to go through a second run to become secondary cants that would be roughly the right size for finished lumber products. The waste would be recycled as chips or mulch.

Andy touched his brother's shoulder. Stephen glanced up. He moved to turn off the machine and remove the headsets that protected his hearing. The sudden silence roared in Andy's ears. Stephen didn't immediately speak. Instead, he wrote something on a clipboard, stuck the pencil behind his ear, and laid his paperwork aside. Finally, he faced Andy. "What brings you here, Bruder?"

"Guder daag to you too."

"I didn't think we were in need of pleasantries."

"Maybe not." Peace, calm, patience. Brotherly love. Fruit of the Spirit. Andy counted off the important qualities needed to repair his relationship with his brother—whether he liked it or not. A mended relationship would be best for everyone involved but especially for their parents. Father didn't need the dissension. "I came to talk to you about all this."

He waved his hand at the sawmill operation that filled a metal warehouse building he and his brothers had helped Father erect so many years ago. The high ceilings and loading dock doors allowed for plenty of light and ventilation for operating the diesel-powered equipment. A huge open space at the far end provided room to air-dry the softwood lumber that could be used for houses and commercial construction from framing to boards used in sheathing buildings and planking floors to beams and posts. All these materials would be needed to rebuild Kootenai's lost homes.

"I'm keeping it going as best I can." Stephen repositioned one of the large-cut cants to begin the resawing that created smaller-sized sections or cants. "Daed had orders that need to be filled, and these logs needed to be processed."

"It's gut that you and Frederick have been keeping up with it."

"Frederick is a farmer." Stephen wiped at bits of sawdust caught in the light sheen of perspiration on his face. "I'd rather be at the dairy working, but we do whatever's necessary to help Daed."

"What if I took the sawmill off his hands—your hands?"

"You mean run it? You're willing to move back to Lewistown?" Surprise mixed with pleasure lightened Stephen's face. From one second to the next, he looked younger and less harried. "That would make Daed very happy. It would be a load off my mind and our bruder's too."

His misunderstanding only made the situation harder. That his brother found this situation so difficult plucked at Andy's heart. It also stirred guilt and shame. He lived far away. He didn't have to face their father's decline day after day. Or be responsible for the work he could no longer do. "I'm sorry. That's not exactly what I meant. I—"

"You want the sawmill but not here." Lines furrowed Stephen's forehead as understanding rushed in. Of the brothers, he looked the most like Daed, but he and Andy also looked alike. "Like stairsteps," their mother had once said. All part of a matching set. She also remarked just as often on how different in temperament they were. "You want to run back to Kootenai and take the earnings with you."

"Kootenai can use the jobs, and they'll need the finished wood for rebuilding when we finally get back in." Andy ignored the word *run* and its implications. *Don't bite. Be the peacemaker. The meek shall inherit the earth.* He didn't want to inherit the earth. He only wanted to make his own small place in it with Christine and, someday, their children. "You said yourself you don't want the job, and neither does Wallace or Frederick. I can make this work in Kootenai."

"Why ask me? Why not Daed?"

"I wanted to talk to you first. He'll ask me if I have. He'll say jah if you agree."

"Think about what it would mean to him if you stayed. Mudder too."

"I have. You'll be here, and Frederick and the girls." Andy inhaled the heavenly scent of fresh-cut wood. "The woman I want to marry longs to settle in her home. In Kootenai. I promised her we would. Mudder and Daed understand that."

Stephen shoved his straw hat back and wiped sweat from

his forehead. He cleared his throat. "You need to do what you need to do . . . to be happy. You have a right to that, I suppose."

The closest Stephen could come to admitting the role he played in Andy's situation. "Then you won't fight me over moving the sawmill?"

"Nee." Stephen threw the switch, and the head rigger sprang to life. The conversation was over.

Andy used the thirty-minute drive from the outskirts of Lewistown to his father's farm halfway to Moore to gather his wits. Stephen carried a heavy load. *Be a peacemaker for your father's sake.*

Which father? His heavenly Father expected even more than his earthly father.

He parked the buggy and stomped up the steps. Father sat in a hickory rocker on the porch while Mother sat in the other, pitting a bowl of cherries.

"That's one sour expression." Father removed his reading glasses and folded the newspaper on his lap. "You've been talking to Stephen."

"How did you know?"

"It's the only time you look like you've bitten the rear end of a skunk."

"Ha, ha." Andy plopped into a nearby lawn chair. The seat sank under him as low as his spirits. "I did talk to him, and now I need to talk to you."

"So talk."

"I'd like to take the sawmill off your hands."

"You're always welcome to work at the sawmill. Stephen could use your help. He'd like to get back to the dairy. He prefers cattle to machinery and all the noise it makes. Did he say something different?"

"I want to move the equipment to Kootenai."

"Ach." Mother stopped rocking. She tossed a pit at Andy. It pinged against his shirt, leaving a tiny purple mark before it fell away. "You're determined to go away again."

"It's just down the road."

"It doesn't seem that way." She sniffed and went back to pitting. "I thought you were over the tiff with your bruder."

"It wasn't a tiff." He stopped and closed his eyes for a second. *Peacemaker.* "I'm fine with Stephen, but Kootenai could use a sawmill. It would be a source of jobs, and the finished wood will be needed when we start rebuilding."

Plus it allowed him to have his own business and an income with which to support his wife and future children.

"I never thought I'd give up the sawmill. I spent many good years there." Father leaned into the late-afternoon sun that graced the porch. His eyes closed. He murmured something Andy didn't catch. Mother set her bowl aside and stood. His eyes opened, and he waved her back. She sat. "Did you talk to your friend?"

Andy had no need to play coy and pretend he didn't know what Father meant. "Nee."

"Talk to her, Suh. Marry. Have children. Gott has a plan for you. I want to see how it unfolds. I hope to see how it unfolds. You're welcome to the sawmill, but I would like you to keep it here. Your fraa will go where you go and stay where you stay."

The words scented the air with sweet fatherly love. How could he go against his father's wishes? "I'll think about it. I promised Christine we would stay in Kootenai, but that was when her family was there."

"Talk to her. Don't wait. It would be nice to have a wedding to look forward to."

It would be nice for all of them. "I'll do it soon. I promise."

"I think I'll go in." Father rose. Mother popped up from her seat and held out her hand. "I'm not an invalid, woman. You don't need to follow me around."

Mother's hand dropped, but she smiled. "You like it. Admit it. Your fraa takes care of your every need."

"I'm not a doddering old man yet."

"I know that. I'm just going in to make a cobbler with these cherries."

Still bickering, they slipped into the house, leaving Andy to ponder a tightly knit union that had become more so with each passing year.

He would beg for Christine's forgiveness. He wanted what his parents had, and he wanted it with her. It remained to be seen if she wanted it too.

CHAPTER 13

The key made a satisfying clicking sound when Christine unlocked the Valley Grocery Store doors. Only three days on the job and her aunt already trusted her to get the store ready to open. With a smile that no one but the tabby cat curled atop a display bench could see this cool September morning, she slipped the key into her canvas bag and went inside. There she turned on the propane-powered lights and began checking the shelves to see what needed to be restocked. They'd swept and mopped the night before. She'd cleaned the restrooms—twice. The store smelled like fresh-baked bread, pickles, and potpourri. Homey.

The quiet pleased her. Living with big families meant quiet could be rare. It turned out she liked working in a store. She liked talking to customers. Her new job might even be called fun. Cleaning house was fun, but here she met new people. To her surprise, she liked it.

The *ding-a-ling-ling* of the bell that hung over the front door broke the silence. She hadn't locked the door behind her. Maybe Aunt Lucy had been wrong to trust her. "We're not open yet," she called out. "Sorry. Please come back at eight."

"I'm looking for Christine. Is she here?"

It took only a second for the slightly familiar voice to register. The man with the unusual name Raymond Old Fox had returned. Christine's hands fluttered in time with her heart. What was he doing here before the store even opened? And why was he looking for her?

It didn't matter. She was in charge of the store at the moment, and Raymond was a customer. She happened to be the only employee in the store. She sucked in a long breath and marched to the front. "Good morning, Mr. Old Fox." Christine arranged her face in a welcoming smile. "We're not open yet. Could you come back at eight, by any chance?"

"Just Raymond, please." Hands stuffed in khaki pants, he stood on the welcome mat next to the front doors. "I'm sorry. I took a chance that you would be here. I'm on my way to work, and I can't be late."

His blue polo shirt pocket bore the embroidered words S&K Technology. A computer techie, he'd said. Christine managed what she hoped would be an understanding nod. Why did he take a chance that she would be here? "It's okay. Are you picking up refreshments for a meeting?" Sometimes folks did that. Baked goods. Cinnamon rolls. Cookies. Coffee cake. "I can get it for you. I'm still learning how to use the cash register, but you can leave the money and get your receipt on your way home, if that's okay."

"That wasn't it, but thanks." He ran his hands through his dark, silky hair. "I wondered if you might want to learn more about the Natives who first lived on this land."

He spoke with no hesitancy, but his uncertain smile suggested he wasn't as confident as he sounded. Why seek her out? Did he see something in her even she didn't see?

A shiver ran through her—the kind she felt as a kid when they climbed the huge tree that had branches that spilled out over the pond. The branches swayed in the breeze and threatened to dump them in the water. They screamed with laughter. The slight hint of danger delighted her. "You want to teach me Native Indian history?"

"History, culture, customs."

"Why?"

"Because you seemed interested the other day." He gestured toward the back as if recalling their encounter. "I don't know. Did you not feel it?"

The feeling had been real, then, and not just hers. How could an Amish woman admit to such a strange feeling as if she suddenly stood on a precipice looking down at an adventure? She moved to the closest end cap and began to straighten a display of cookbooks. "Feel what?"

His smile melted into a disappointed frown. "I'm sorry I bothered you."

He turned to go.

"Wait."

He turned back. Hope once again peeked through his dark-rimmed glasses.

"How would you do this teaching?" She picked up a cookbook and held it against her chest like a shield. "Where would I go? To a class?"

Shaking his head, Raymond grinned. "No way. There are places you need to see to understand why we feel so strongly about our land and what happened to it. We know what some people say. They forget we were here first. We are not Native *American* Indians. We were here before this was America. We have a long history forever changed by white men who came to convert us so they could take our land and make it theirs."

Breathless, he stopped.

"Okay."

"Okay?" His smile grew. "When?"

Good question. How would she explain it to Aunt Lucy and Uncle Fergie? She couldn't any more than she could explain her rumspringa forays to see a movie in Kalispell or making up her face and trying on necklaces in front of a mirror in a department store in Missoula with Juliette Knowles as her guide.

She didn't understand herself. She had no intention of abandoning her faith any more than she had then. Her baptism had been a sincere commitment to their beliefs. But this was a chance to stretch her life experiences to the very edges of the boundaries set by her faith. With the fire and all that had happened after it, the rules had changed. Her family left her. She had to find her own way. "Tomorrow's Saturday. I have the day off because my cousins are out of school and will work my shift. I'll meet you outside The Malt Shop at nine o'clock."

"Just like that?"

Lucy and Fergie would be at the store. She had been looking forward to a day on her own. For the first time in her life, no one would shake a finger at her. No one would look over her shoulder. Adventure beckoned. "Just like that."

His grin widened. "Nine o'clock at The Malt Shop."

Then he was gone.

The rest of the day passed in a blur of steady customers, mostly from the area. The flow of tourists had decreased with the end of summer and the beginning of the school year. The fires didn't help either. The smoke from half a dozen fires floated even as far as the Mission Valley. The inhabitants would never again take fresh air for granted.

Christine floated from one task to the next. Slicing meat, making milkshakes, bagging rolls, stocking fabrics, inventorying canned goods, even running the register while Lucy took her lunch break—whatever her aunt needed. The job itself stretched Christine so much more than cleaning houses. Her brain received a workout, and she could talk to people.

She missed Nora, Mercy, and Juliette. She missed her family, but they weren't in West Kootenai. It wouldn't be the same without them. St. Ignatius held family and a job she liked. Christine stopped counting bolts of fabric in midcount. Enough to stay here?

When she agreed to meet Raymond, she hadn't given a single moment's thought to Andy. Andy, who hadn't said goodbye when he left Eureka. Andy, who hadn't called or written. Christine's heart jolted like someone had poked it with a sharp stick. Andy had suggested she stay here so they would be closer. This was his solution.

Would he even regret it if she met another man? Not that Raymond fell in that category. He wasn't Plain. She wasn't even sure if Native Indians worshiped the same God.

Or any God at all.

"What have I gotten myself into?" She spoke the words aloud. The teddy bears on the bolt of pajama flannel didn't answer. "I know, I know. I have no one to blame but myself."

"Who are you t-t-t-alking to?"

Christine whirled. Esther Marie stood at the end of the aisle, a perplexed look on her face. She had a banana box of slightly dented cans in her arms. Christine rolled her eyes.

"Sometimes I talk to myself. I used to do that when I was cleaning house because no one else was around to talk to."

"That's pret-t-t-t-ty *gegisch*." Esther Marie giggled. "And it makes you sound *n-n-n-narrisch*."

"Silly and crazy, that's me."

"Be sure to tell your friend Andy that."

"What? How do you know I have a friend named Andy?"

"He's on the phone."

"Why didn't you say so?" Christine dropped the bolt of flannel and shot past the other woman. "You're the one who's *narrisch*."

Esther Marie's giggle followed Christine down the aisle, past the deli, and into the office at the back of the store. To her relief, no one sat behind Fergie's desk. The receiver lay on its side next to a stack of spreadsheets. Christine snatched it up and plopped into Fergie's chair. "Andy?"

"Christine? Why do you sound breathless?"

"Never mind that. Why haven't you called? Where are you? I've been on pins and needles, wondering how things are going for you and when you'll be back—go back to West Kootenai. Have you heard anything? Or are they letting—?"

"Slow down, slow down." Andy didn't sound like himself. Christine couldn't put her finger on it. He sounded . . . deflated. "I'm at John Clemons's sister's house in Lewistown. He let me borrow his phone."

"Why do you sound so serious? Is something wrong? How's your father? What do the doctors say?"

"He's weak and tired. He sleeps a lot." Andy's voice deepened and grew hoarse. "The doctors are still trying to figure out the problem. He's at the doctor today getting some test results."

"I'm sorry. I hope they figure it out soon. It's gut that you've been there to help out." She hesitated. Being so far apart was hard, but she didn't want him to feel guilty or think she was mad at him. She wasn't. Only at the situation. "I was hoping you would call sooner."

"It's only been a few days."

"It seems like a lifetime. Everything's changed. I love my job at the grocery store. Onkel Fergie and Aenti Lucy treat me like an adult in a way Mudder and Daed never did. I feel so independent. Is that bad? To like that feeling?" It felt so good to talk to him. He would understand her mixed-up emotions. Maybe not like Mercy or Nora, but he had known her for three years. They'd talked about all sorts of things. Feelings, even. Like a husband and a wife must talk, surely.

Silence filled the line. One beat, two beats, three beats. No response. "Andy?"

"Tread carefully, Christine. It's your first time away from home. Freedom and independence can be costly for a Plain person. We are part of a community. Family and community come first. Don't get too connected to the world. Don't forget where you come from."

"Now you sound like Daed." Disappointment blew through her. Andy had moved from Lewistown to West Kootenai to gain that freedom. Plain women rarely had that opportunity— nor did they seek it. They were taught to be content in their small, safe world. Christine didn't relish being alone, but she could enjoy a tiny taste of the world, couldn't she? Was it really wrong? "I'm living with a Plain family and working in a Plain-owned store and going to our church every two weeks, just like at home. Besides, my coming to St. Ignatius was your idea."

"I know."

More silence.

"Andy, what's wrong?"

"It's hard being here and not seeing you all the time."

"I miss you too." The silence lingered. "Andy, are you there?"

"There's something I need to tell you."

"You can tell me anything. We're friends." More than friends. "You're worrying me."

"I never told you why I really left home."

"It doesn't matter. You said you needed a fresh start. A lot of people move west for that reason. I think Daed—"

"I needed a fresh start because my brother Stephen stole the woman I loved. My special friend Winona. We planned to be married. Before I could ask her, she broke up with me to marry Stephen. The day after they married, I moved away from home."

Christina took her turn at being silent. Hurt squeezed the air from her lungs. She couldn't decipher his words. They were a foreign language. Andy once had another special friend. He'd planned to marry her.

He loved another before he met Christine.

In three years of courting, he kept his past a secret from her.

"Christine, are you there?" His voice held panic. "I'm sorry I didn't tell you before."

"Me too." The words escaped in a mere whisper. She cleared her throat. "Not that it matters."

"It doesn't?"

Of course it did. If he'd courted another woman, he'd hugged her. And worse, kissed her. His first kiss had not been reserved for Christine. He dreamed of having children with a woman named Winona and growing old with her. "Nee."

"Your words say one thing, but your voice says another."

"I'm trying to understand, to imagine. You loved a woman named Winona, and now she's married to your bruder. That must be very hard. No wonder you didn't want to go home."

"I'm glad you can put yourself in my shoes."

"I hope you can put yourself in my shoes."

"I'm trying."

"It does hurt." She swallowed hard and pressed her free hand against her closed eyes. *Gott, don't let me cry, please.* "To know you . . . cared for another. And that you didn't tell me. It's gut that we have this time to think it over."

"I don't want to think it over. I don't want anything to change."

"When are you returning to Kootenai?"

"I don't know. My daed wants me to stay here."

"Permanently?"

"Jah."

"And you're considering it?"

"I thought I would take his sawmill business to Kootenai, but Daed wants his kinner close. He says a fraa goes where her mann goes. I'm having a hard time figuring it all out. That's why I came over to John's sister's house."

"Let me know when you figure it out." With great care Christine laid the receiver on the base.

The silence hummed around her. She put her hands to her ears and closed her eyes. On the other side of a much-desired phone call, her delight with her new life ebbed. Her body ached for the familiar. For DeeDee's hardy laugh and the snickerdoodles she liked to feed Christine with iced tea after she finished cleaning. For Delilah's endless questions about courting and rumspringa, for Abigail's knock-knock jokes, for Nora and Mercy's well-meaning advice. For Juliette's sarcastic observations about life and love. For Socks and Shoes and their rough-tongued kisses on her fingers and the way they warmed her feet on cold winter nights. Even the way they stank of wet doggie fur. For the everyday, familiar life that had been hers for nineteen years.

Adventure might not be so exciting after all.

CHAPTER 14

That went well. Silence hummed in Andy's ears. He laid John's cell phone on the coffee table in Lois's living room in the ranch-style home where she lived with her husband and two kids. John and his sister had been kind enough to disappear into the kitchen for cherry pie and coffee while Andy made his call.

He leaned back against the crocheted afghan that blanketed the back of the plaid couch, and closed his eyes. His head throbbed and his jaw ached. Did Christine have a right to be angry or hurt about something that was in his past? What happened had nothing to do with her. His time with Winona was long over when he began to court Christine. Her sweet company helped him recover from an awful period in his life that he simply wanted to forget. Did she really need to know about it?

The questions ping-ponged in his head. No answers joined them. Or maybe the guilt that washed over him like a case of the flu provided an answer he didn't want to accept.

Something wet nudged his fingers. He jerked them back and opened his eyes. Lois's shih tzu whined and nudged his thigh. Misty was one of those dogs who wanted attention from whomever might be willing to give it. Donut, who lay sprawled in front of the fireplace, raised his head, yawned, and went back to snoozing. "You aren't exactly a faithful hund, are you?"

Andy patted the little dog with ribbons in her hair and a flowered bandanna around her neck. She huffed in pleasure. Dogs offered a surprising friendship he rarely found with people. Ben and Henry were his only Plain male friends. He would miss working with Ben, despite the fact that he mixed belches with farts on alternate days. It wouldn't be the same without him.

"You look like you could use a piece of Lois's cherry pie and a cup of hot coffee with an extra tablespoon of sugar." John set both offerings on the table in front of Andy and settled in the brown leather La-Z-Boy recliner. "I'm thinking it didn't go so well."

Andy postponed answering by taking a large bite of pie. The sweet-tartness of the cherry filling and the flaky crust melted in his mouth. Good. Not as good as Mother's but still memorable. He concentrated on a second bite. Then a third. Pretty soon there would be no pie to take his mind from the pain in Christine's voice when he dumped his past on her. He took a sip of sweet, hot coffee. Maybe it could burn away the bitter lump that clogged his throat. "Her feelings were hurt."

He'd explained his predicament to John on the ride from his parents' home to Lois's.

"That comes as no surprise."

"It happened before I even knew her."

"No girl wants to be second choice."

"It's not like that."

"In my world it wouldn't be a blip on the screen. English folks date around, sometimes having many partners before selecting one. Some even sleep around—if you'll excuse the expression. It's not right, but it happens all the time in this modern world we live in." John took out his pipe, looked at it longingly, and then stuck it back in the pocket of the leather vest he wore over a blue plaid flannel shirt. "It surely is different for a Plain man and woman who pledge to one another for life. A Plain woman may kiss only one man in her entire life. Do you know how unusual that is these days?"

"I reckon I do." Never in his life could Andy imagine having this conversation with an English man—or any man. "I didn't plan it this way."

"Nope. Life threw you a big old curveball."

"Now my father, whose health is poor, wants me to come back here to live and work with my bruders."

"Another curveball."

"Christine can't go back to Kootenai on her own. She has no family there now. She'd have to stay in St. Ignatius or go to her parents in Kansas."

"Or you two get hitched and she comes to Lewistown."

"I didn't get the impression she would consider that option right now."

"She needs time to adjust. She had a picture of you and of the two of you together. The picture shifted." John popped the recliner back so his feet were up, and patted the armrest. Misty hopped from the couch and raced to join him. "Right now you need to figure out what you want. What's best for you. Get your life in order before you try to fix things with Christine."

Good advice, but easier said than done. Rather than respond, Andy sipped his coffee and studied the trees blowing outside Lois's floor-to-ceiling living room windows. The branches bent low to the ground in a blustery north wind. If only it would rain. Rain would extinguish the forest fires.

If he looked closely at his heart, would he find that he wanted to go to Kootenai because it was his home now, or was he simply escaping his past? Would a better son ignore his own desires—and those of the woman he loved—and stay in his hometown for his father's sake?

"Sorry to ask, but do you mind taking me to my father's?"

"No worries, but you should stay for dinner. Lois is making my favorite beef-spinach-mushroom lasagna." John flipped the lever and sat upright in the chair. Misty whined, but John stood anyway, the dog under one arm. "It's my last night here. I want to get back to Eureka. I promised the boys I'd take them hunting next weekend. My wife needs a girls' weekend with her sisters. Besides, I hate spending too much time away from her. She's my girl."

John and his wife had one of those time-and-tragedy-tested marriages that seemed to grow stouter every year. John didn't talk about it much, but enough to know there had been a little girl who died of a birth defect before the boys were born. Andy had attended their thirtieth anniversary celebration the previous year. Madison claimed John's trademark humor was the reason they managed to stay together. That green snake envy threatened to wind itself around Andy's neck and slither down his lonely body.

"That sounds fun. I'll catch a ride with another driver when I'm ready to return to Kootenai—if I do."

"No way. I brought you here. Call me when you're ready."

"We'll see."

He stopped by the kitchen to thank Lois for her hospitality and then followed John to his SUV. A few minutes later they were on the road. John didn't try to make conversation, which suited Andy just fine. His friend turned up the radio and sang along with a country song about sitting on a pier drinking a beer. Despite the words, it sounded sad. John had a nice tenor, and he lifted his voice as they turned onto the street that led to Highway 87 south toward Moore where most of the Plain families had their properties.

He stopped at the light, and the music gave way to a commercial. John grimaced. "My sons say I should make music lists on Spotify or some such thing. Then I wouldn't have to listen to commercials or songs I don't like. Of course I have no idea what they're talking about."

"Don't ask me." Andy leaned forward to reach the volume knob. "I like it quiet. The birds singing is enough music for me."

The light turned green, and John took off into the intersection. A big, black fume-spewing truck barreled toward them from the left, running the red light. "John, look out!"

John slammed on the brakes.

The brakes squealed. Rubber burned.

Too late. No way to brace for it. Nowhere to go. Nothing to be done.

The mammoth truck slammed head-on into the Suburban's driver's side.

Metal screeched against metal.

The world spun at a dizzying speed. The landscape whirled.

An air bag blew up. It whipped Andy back against the seat. His neck snapped.

A fleeting image of a county fair carnival ride danced in Andy's head.

I don't like it.

Gott, help us. Gott, stop it. You have control. Not me. Only You.

Andy's seat belt strangled his body. Ribs popped. His head slammed against the door. Lights exploded inside his brain.

The air bag deflated, sending puffs of white powder dancing in the air.

As suddenly as it began, the sickening ride ceased.

His body, which seemed to have a mind independent of his brain, wanted to slump forward, but the seat belt held with bruising intent.

Open your eyes. Open them. See if you're alive.

To have died wouldn't be so bad. No more trying to figure this life out.

Pain. Pain. There would be no pain if he were dead.

His eyes didn't want to open. *Open. Come on. You're no coward. Look. John might need your help.*

Propelled by that thought, Andy sat up. Pain pulsated through his body. Blood dripped from his nose.

Definitely alive. Danki, Gott. I think.

Hoping to clear the fog, he shook his head. Bad move. Pain ricocheted from his gut to his chest to his head and back. His stomach lurched. The cherry pie and coffee threatened to spill out.

"John? John." Andy meant to shout, but only a puny whisper emerged. He coughed and cleared his throat. "John? Are you all right?"

No answer.

Sirens sounded in the distance. An ugly high-pitched shriek that never meant anything good filled the air.

Strangers' faces appeared in the smoky air that surrounded the mangled SUV. They jabbered and pointed. One took pictures with his phone. Another paced with a phone to his ear. A guy pulled on his door, but it didn't open.

Andy closed his eyes and swallowed the bile that burned his tongue. The metallic taste of blood from his tongue made him gag.

Get up. Get out. Move.

Andy tried to shift in his seat. His shaking hands couldn't connect with his seat belt. A great weight seemed to hold him there. He forced his eyes open and cocked his head to one side.

Need to see. Where is John? Donut?

The driver's side door had caved in with the force of the crash. The SUV's frame crumpled and smashed inward so that the front seat no longer had space for two. The weight against Andy shifted. His neck and shoulder complained. He looked down.

John.

He lay almost prone, his head near Andy's lap. Blood and tissue muddied the side of his face. His head looked swollen and misshapen.

The truck's front end had crushed him. His head rolled back. His eyes were wide open, his expression frozen in surprise. Blood trickled from his nose and mouth.

"Ach, John."

His throat clogged with tears, Andy gritted his teeth to hold back sobs. Ignoring a stranger who ripped open his door and reached for him, Andy hugged John to his aching chest. He patted his friend's still warm, bruised cheek. "I'm sorry, *freind*." A sob escaped. Andy tried to wrangle it back. "You go on ahead."

A keening howl from the back seat told Andy that Donut joined in his mourning.

John's days in this world were done.

CHAPTER 15

Puke or pass out? Andy stuck his head between his knees and fought to breathe. The hospital air reeked of antiseptic and cleansers. Neither odor helped. The Montana Medical Center emergency room doctor said the light-headedness would ebb after his blood pressure receded from the stratosphere. The doctor looked like a young kid, but he talked like a walking dictionary. After expressing his disapproval of Andy's refusal to submit to X-rays or scans, he'd completed his exam with quick efficiency followed by the pronouncement, "You were lucky. Abrasions and contusions. You'll be stiff and sore for a few days, but you'll be fine."

Lucky didn't belong in any scenario involving a fatal traffic accident caused by a man who glanced down at a text message while driving. A penitent man who kept telling Andy over and over how sorry he was at the crash scene as medics forced Andy to lie on a gurney and be shoved into an ambulance he didn't need.

What would happen to the driver now? He ran a red light. John died as a result. The driver didn't mean to do it. Accidents were accidents. The proper thing to do now was forgive.

The bruises on Andy's body were tiny compared to the

one that turned his heart into one massive ache. *Give me the strength, the fortitude, to forgive, Gott. I can't do it on my own.*

Andy needed forgiveness. For John's death. If Andy hadn't asked him for a ride, the man would be alive now. He needed to be forgiven for his inability to forgive others. The plank in his eye made it impossible for him to see.

Who would tell John's beloved wife, Madison? Who would tell his three sons that there would be no hunting trip with their father next weekend or ever again?

A Fergus County sheriff's deputy stepped into the tiny exam room with the belt around his substantial girth weighted down with his gun and other equipment Andy had no desire to identify. A hefty man with heavy jowls and red cheeks, he filled a space already claustrophobic in size. All the air seemed to whoosh from the room, replaced by this gargantuan man with a kind face and a handlebar mustache. He held a pen and pad dwarfed by his hand and his cowboy hat in the other. "Excuse me, sir. The doctor said I could have a word now that he's looked you over."

"I'm Andy. No need to 'sir' me. Can you tell me where my dog is? Is he okay?"

"He's fine. He's making the rounds in the parking lot out back with one of my buddies. Everyone wants to pet him." That was Donut. Making friends wherever he went. "I need to ask you some questions."

"Go ahead."

Even if Andy had no answers. A split-second recognition that pain barreled toward them. Dawning horror. No time. No time to do anything. A vague recollection that an enormous, brutal, black truck with a shiny chrome bumper and bright lights hurtled toward them. The foggy, dim memory of an apologetic man dressed in camo from head to foot who tried to talk to him afterward. His beard bobbed and his lips moved, but no sound penetrated the ringing in Andy's ears.

"Your account matches that of several witnesses at the scene." The deputy scribbled in his notebook. He didn't look up. "The driver admits he was distracted. He was arguing with his wife via text about a hunting trip she didn't want him to take."

"I guess she got her way now." The words sounded cold in Andy's ears.

The deputy nodded. "Where were you and the victim going?"

"John was taking me home—to my father's home between Lewistown and Moore."

"What were you doing before he gave you a lift?"

"Drinking coffee. Eating cherry pie." Andy's stomach heaved. Acid burned the back of his throat. He swallowed and reached for the blue barf bag the nurse had given him when he first arrived. "Talking."

"No alcohol? Hot toddy? Bailey's?"

"No." A red tide of anger roared through Andy. He gritted his teeth against it. John did not drink and drive. He took his job as a driver seriously. "John wasn't at fault."

"I have to ask these questions as part of my investigation. I'm sorry for your loss." The deputy slapped the notebook shut and stuck it in his pants pocket. "Your family's out there waiting to see you."

How had they known? The deputy didn't give Andy time to ask questions. He disappeared through the curtains, leaving Andy to try out his legs. He slid from the exam table, stood, wobbled, and plopped onto a nearby stool.

He dressed quickly and then took a moment to practice breathing. *In, out, in, out.* Like a toddler just learning to walk, he stood again. This time his legs obeyed. He put one foot in front of the other. *Step, step, step.* Past other exam rooms filled with an elderly man with a breathing mask over his face, a crying child whose mother tried to shush him, and a man who'd sliced off his finger in a cross saw.

Mother saw him first. She rushed across the waiting room and crashed into him. Her hug nearly knocked him from his unsteady feet. "How did you know?"

"John's brother-in-law came to our door." She hugged him again and then leaned back to inspect him. His brothers stood shoulder to shoulder watching. "He said the sheriff came to their door with terrible news."

"Is John's fraa here? I need to tell her how sorry I am." Andy tugged free of her grip. "It's my fault. If I hadn't asked John for a ride, he'd still be here."

"It's not your fault." Stephen's Adam's apple bobbed. Tethered emotion made his voice hoarse. "The deputy told us. The other driver ran the light. He smashed into John's Suburban. It was his time."

"It's not your fault." Lois's voice sounded wispy, not like the snappy voice of the woman who'd offered him cherry pie what seemed like years earlier. Stephen and Wallace parted to allow her to approach Andy. Her husband had a tight grip on her arm. "We had to stop here to make sure you're okay. I had to see for myself."

Grief made her seem tiny and frail. Her shoulders stooped and she staggered. Her eyes and nose were red and snot trickled from her nostrils. She looked how Andy felt. He grasped the shaking hand she held out. "I don't know what to say. I've never experienced something like this." To be with a man who was alive and singing sad country music songs one minute and dead the next boggled the mind. Death was part of life. But to have it occur so close, within inches of his own body, shook him to the core. "*Sorry* is a stupid, inadequate word."

"John wouldn't want us to grieve." Her voice quivered. "He's in heaven now, grilling sweet Jesus on everything from how He came up with the cocoon-to-butterfly thing to why He doesn't hurry up and return."

Her faith made his seem puny. "Does Madison know?"

"The sheriff in Lincoln County and their preacher went over to the house and delivered the news." This time her voice broke. She swiped at her nose with a crumpled, sodden tissue. "Her parents are with her and the kids. Greg and I are headed there from here. The whole family will descend. Don't you worry. They'll be swaddled in love."

Her swift hug took him by surprise. The knot in his throat grew. "Tell her . . . tell her I'm sorry."

"She knows, Andy, she knows."

Her husband put his arm around her shoulder and guided her toward the exit.

It would be nice to follow them out, to return home. The desire overwhelmed him. The fir-scented mountain air, the chatter of the birds, the heat of the sun on his face—those were the medicines he needed in order to heal. In nature he felt closest to God. As had John. His friend didn't talk about his faith much, but he'd said once that he loved to camp and hike because nature reminded him of how carefully and artfully God had created it.

Nowhere in the world was that more evident than in the mountains of northwest Montana.

"Let's go home." Mother squeezed his hand and let it drop. "You need to rest."

"I need to get my dog, and I need to go home—to my home." The hurt look on Mother's face made him wince. "Not now, but soon. As soon as they let us back into Kootenai, I need to rebuild and get on with my life."

Mother couldn't understand. No one could who hadn't seen a man so alive leave his body so abruptly and with such violent force.

God numbered their days on earth. Andy was simply passing through. In the meantime he meant to make the most of his days.

He would rebuild. He would ask Christine to marry him. *Thy will be done, Gott. Thy will be done.*

CHAPTER 16

St. Ignatius / Polson, Montana

If this were a date—and it wasn't—the awkwardness would be understandable. Raymond rushed around to the passenger side of his ancient fern-green Volvo station wagon and jerked open the door for Christine. It tended to stick. She ducked her head, murmured her thanks, and slid in. He shut the door.

Of course now it decided not to stay shut. He slammed it a second time. *Stay. Stay.* The door cooperated. He whipped back to his side, stumbled over a rock, righted himself, and jumped in. *Deep breath.* Despite a cool northerly breeze, his hands were sweaty and his long-sleeved henley shirt stuck to his back.

This was ridiculous. He heaved another breath and offered Christine his best smile. "I wasn't sure you would come."

"I said I would." Her forehead wrinkled, but she returned the smile. Her azure eyes were made bluer by the matching color of her ankle-length dress. "I always try to follow through when I say I'll do something. Don't you?"

"An idea might seem good in the moment, but after careful thought, its foolhardiness becomes apparent." Gramma's words sounded odd spoken in his deep bass. "You don't know me, and you're hopping in my car to take a ride. If I were your brother or father, I'd scold you."

"So would mine, but they're in Kansas now."

"Why are you not with them?"

She studied her hands clasped in her lap for a few seconds. "I asked to be allowed to stay with my aunt and uncle here in St. Ignatius for personal reasons. Now it seems I may have made a mistake."

Her gaze lifted to his. It seemed she would say more, but the seconds ticked by and she remained silent. Raymond jumped in to ease her obvious discomfort. "Are you sure you want to spend your day off with me?"

"It depends on what that means." Her beautiful eyes studied him intently. "I prayed last night that I wouldn't regret a rash decision."

"I promise you won't." Such innocence should be preserved and honored. "Put on your seat belt."

He waited while she fumbled with the clasp, buckled up, and leaned back in her seat. "Where are we going?"

"We're taking a trip down memory lane." His memories or those of his ancestors to be more precise. He pointed the car toward Highway 93 and Pablo. Traffic shouldn't be too bad on a Saturday now that the tourist season was over. He scrambled for a conversation starter. "What do you know about the Kootenai tribe?"

"The what?"

So that's where he started. In the half-hour drive from St. Ignatius to Pablo, he gave her an abbreviated version of the Kootenai's history as nomadic hunters who lived in teepees, hunted buffalo, moose, and elk, and gathered berries and roots in the spring and summer that were preserved to last through the frigid winters. Together with the Salish and Pend d'Oreille tribes, their aboriginal territories covered twenty million acres in Montana, northern Idaho, and parts of the southern Canada provinces.

They were known for being avid canoeists, trappers, and anglers. They built light craft and devices to help with fishing and hunting, like fish weirs and bird traps. Then came the years when horses, guns, traders, and Jesuit priests changed the fundamental way the Kootenai lived their lives. More changes, these devastating to the Kootenai, followed with the Hellgate Treaty in 1855 and their confinement to the reservation where they were expected to understand the concept of land ownership and to become farmers. Not able to follow their food sources, they began to starve. Even as they were forced to worship the white man's God. Today the reservation covered 1.3 million acres with 790,000 owned by the tribes and their members.

An occasional glance at Christine's face assured him that she not only listened but understood the gravity of his words. Emotions flitted across her open features that hid nothing. Interest, surprise, sorrow, and obvious perplexity. When he hit tiny Pablo's city limits, he paused in his storytelling. "Do you have questions?"

"Your people's God is different from the 'white man's'?"

The Amish were devout. It seemed natural that she would start there. Raymond grappled for words that could be understood by someone who grew up with spiritual beliefs in a completely different context. "We believe the Sun and the Moon were brothers, and they produced the powerful life force for all creations. The Sun and Moon transformed all who chose to live on this earth into physical forms and assigned them with a domain and tools. We work to maintain that delicate balance in the natural world. Spirits inhabit everything in nature."

"Who do you pray to then?"

"I don't think we pray in the way that you mean. We co-exist with Mother Earth's creations. We show respect for all elements of the natural world. Life has no value if you don't appreciate the earth and have regard for all that is sacred."

"Could our God encompass your Mother Earth? He made the earth from the void and the sun, moon, and stars. He made the animals and He made man. From man, He made woman."

"The difference is we don't believe man is greater than the animals."

"But you hunt."

"To eat. We never hunt for sport. We never waste a single scrap of the bison."

She was quiet for a few minutes. "Our people do understand persecution. We have a book called *The Martyrs' Mirror* that reminds us of the religious persecution our ancestors experienced in Europe when they left the Church of England and later when they decided they wanted adult baptism instead of the baptism of babies."

"The white people who took over our land didn't just want us to worship the way they did. They wanted us to forget our language, our customs, and our way of life. My forefathers didn't know how to survive when they couldn't follow their food sources, so their families starved." The injustice could never be forgotten. Natives from the mountains to the plains to the seas had similar experiences. They were bound by those experiences, whatever their battles had been in the past. "We had to get a signed piece of paper to leave the reservation for any reason. When the Bureau of Indian Affairs gathered up our children and sent them away to schools, the families thought it was for the best. At least there they would be fed."

"You don't sound as if it was for the best."

"Our children worked at the schools before and after classes, doing the cooking, cleaning, and laundry. They were punished if they spoke their language. They were separated from their families for the first time in their lives. Our daughters bore children fathered by priests. The babies were thrown away."

Those dark days were in the distant past, but still they hurt.

Her face filled with a tender sadness, Christine leaned forward to stare at the building beyond the parking lot where he pulled into a space and turned off his car's sputtering engine. "We were blessed. Our forefathers went to court for the right to keep their children home and teach them our values and our ways. They knew our lifestyle would not be preserved if we were in constant contact with the world. It was considered our right to end our formal education at eighth grade. We have a right to teach our children as we see fit."

"We weren't given that right. Instead, we have to fight tooth and nail, lot by lot, to get our land back. We've started our own schools and eventually opened Salish and Kootenai College. We have cultural classes like beading, quilling, the cooking of roots, drying of medicinal herbs, and language classes. Slowly but surely, we are able to reintroduce our culture to our people."

"In some ways our people are alike." She stared at the round columns of the stone building. "In that we're different than those who seem to have all the power."

"What was your first language?"

"*Deutsch.*"

"Mine was Kootenai only because my great-grandmother is one of the few remaining Kootenai who speaks the language. She taught her children, her grandchildren, and then she taught her great-grandchildren, including me. Now I teach it to children at the grade school."

"Teach me a word."

"Natanik."

"Natanik."

"It means 'moon.' It also means 'sun.' Only the pitch changes." He demonstrated. Then he pointed at her. "You are *pahiki*— 'woman.'"

"Now my turn." She pointed at Raymond. *"Der fux."*

"What does that mean?"

"'The fox.'"

"Very funny."

She grinned. "You do look a little like a fox. Very sly."

He pretended to stare at himself in the rearview mirror. "I look more like a deer. Fleet of foot."

"And tender in a pot of chili."

"Nice."

She laughed with him. She had a nice laugh. Tinkly. "So my town is called Kootenai. What does it mean?"

"The word *Kootenai* doesn't exist in our language." That she wanted to know was amazing. Many of his own people didn't care enough to ask. "We were originally known as the Ksunka or People of the Standing Arrow. The French called us Kootenai. It either means 'deer robes' or 'water people.' We're not sure which."

"It's funny. I've never really thought about it, but knowing two languages makes a person's life richer, doesn't it?"

"I think so." Learning made life richer. That a woman with

an eighth-grade education understood that was equally amazing. "I feel like I've talked your head off."

She patted her head. "Nee. That means 'no.' It's still here."

Her sense of humor reminded him of his own. The ability to laugh bound people together in friendship. "Have you had enough of me blabbing, or can you take a little more?"

"You haven't told me anything about yourself."

"These are my people we're talking about."

"Dead people." She put her hand to her mouth for a second. "That came out wrong. I mean, who are you now?"

"I have two brothers who live in other places. My mother died and my father was never in the picture. Gramma and my grandma Velda, who makes jewelry and sells it at craft shows around the state, are my closest family."

"I'm sorry about your mother."

"It was a long time ago."

"What do you do?"

"I'm a tiny cog in a big machine called S&K Global Solutions in Polson. It's one of five subsidiaries of S&K Technologies. We do information technology support, research, and software development for customers like NASA and Boeing."

Her blank expression was normal. Most people, even those who were somewhat computer savvy, had glazed eyes when he finished describing what he did for a living.

"Does it have something to do with computers?" She pointed to the laptop that sat on the seat between them.

"I won't bore you with the details, but yes. I have a bachelor's degree in information technology from Salish and Kootenai College."

A perplexed look on her face, she shook her head. "Information technology?"

"It doesn't matter. Enough about me. What about you? What do you do? Tell me about your family."

"I clean houses, and I like it." Her cheeks turned pink as she swiveled in her seat and let her gaze encompass his car. "I could do a lot of good in here."

Stacks of reports and papers from work. Fast-food bags. Dirty sneakers. Empty Styrofoam coffee cups. The detritus of his life. When had he last run the beast through a carwash? The date escaped him. "Family."

She ran through the statistics.

"That's a big family." Compared to his, with two brothers and two grandparents and some great aunts and their families. "I bet you never get lonely."

"Do you?" Her compassion enveloped the words. "I can't imagine not having a big family."

"I'm good." Hanging on by the hair on his chinny-chin-chin. "We should get moving if we plan to get you home by five."

Her aunt and uncle would come home from the store early on Saturday to prepare for Sunday's services and visiting.

She nodded, but the knowing look remained.

He led her to the front door of The People's Center, where he dug out the key from his jean pocket. "This is where we teach people—visitors and our own kind—about our past."

"You come and go here as you please?"

"I'm a volunteer. This time of year, it's closed on the weekends. We'll have it to ourselves."

A strange expression flitted across her face. Embarrassment, maybe even a touch of fear or guilt, appeared. The reason hit him full force. "Have you ever been alone with a man?"

"Of course." The words came out in a stutter. Her cheeks

turned bright red, making her even prettier. "My brothers. A friend."

The stutter worsened over the word *friend*. "You mean like a date."

"Something like that."

"You don't know me, but I promise you can trust me." Heat toasted his own cheeks. The keys jangled in his hand. "What I mean to say is, I respect women—all women. I have no ulterior motives for bringing you here other than to try to know you and let you know me."

"Okay."

The earlier hesitation disappeared. A smile bloomed in its place like an early spring.

He unlocked the door and held it for her. She murmured her thanks and trotted ahead of him into the foyer. They turned right into the exhibit area. Raymond took a breath. He'd told these stories hundreds of times to hundreds of visitors, but it never felt like it did this day, this place in time and space. Her inquisitive gaze sharp, her questions thoughtful, Christine wandered from exhibit to exhibit. She wanted him to teach her how to make moccasins from deer skin and explain what it must've been like to live in teepees in the cold Montana winter.

"Our women could use those papoose carriers." She touched the glass that separated them from the exhibit with the fingertips of both hands. "We have so many children and not enough hands. How are they made?"

"The women made them using deerskins." The division of labor wouldn't sound odd to her. The Amish also held strong beliefs about the work men and women should do. "My grammas would know how. They've studied the crafts of our ancestors."

"I'd love to meet them and learn from them."

If only that were possible. Raymond hesitated. The last thing he wanted to do on this first outing was hurt Christine's feelings. Gramma wouldn't want him to bring a non-Native girl around. She didn't want him spending time with her at all. Grandma Velda seldom said much about anything. The grief of losing her husband and her only child had dried up all her words. After she retired from her position as a secretary at the high school, she took up crafting jewelry from deer bone and bird feathers. She did well selling her wares. They saw less of her than ever.

"Do they know about . . . this . . . about me?" Christine's hands fluttered to her chest and rested there. She had sturdy but small hands. Hot water and cleansers left them chapped and dry. She wore no rings or other adornments. "Or are they like my folks—wary of mixing with those who are different?"

"Gramma knows enough about the Amish to know your family won't welcome my attention to you. She prefers I focus my attention on Native women. Grandma Velda traveled to Bonner Ferry this week."

Christine cocked her head and stared up at him. After a few seconds, she turned back to the display. "Tell me more."

Tears wet her eyes when he explained that smallpox decimated his tribe not once but twice. The first time it cut the tribe's number in half. Thousands died. Twenty years later the disease hit again and the tribe died down to a third of its original size. He told her the story of the grizzly bear who took care of a little boy after everyone in his family and his community died of the disease. He took him to another tribe that adopted him.

"You believe these stories?"

He examined her face and saw no judgment there. "We believe animals are as smart as we are."

She rested her forehead against the glass that separated her from the artifacts for a few seconds. She stared at them, then turned to Raymond. "Sometimes they're smarter. Humans kill for pleasure. They're mean to each other. They lie and cheat. They take what doesn't belong to them."

"No one knows that better than the Natives."

"A woman in the store said the Indians think they're better than the whites. She said her family has been here just as long. They bought their allotments around nineteen hundred."

"Archaeologists have found evidence that Natives were here during the first Ice Age. We were here when Columbus 'discovered' this continent."

"A few years earlier." She chuckled softly. "I reckon that's why you object to being called Native American Indians."

"Indian isn't so bad. The explorers were saying *en dios.* 'In God.' Indians. But there was no America when aboriginal peoples freely roamed the land."

With silent agreement they moved to the next exhibit. At this rate it would take days to cover everything in the room. He pointed out the next display. "This is bitterroot. It's really a wild herb, but it's also Montana's state flower. Long before it was adopted in 1893, it was very important to Native tribes. The women would dig up the roots, and the whole tribe would pray. When the Salish people were starving, a grandma had children and grandchildren who were starving. She prayed and cried. Her tears hit the ground and became bitterroot. It is very bitter. It was mixed with meat or berries."

"What about this?" Christine pointed to the camas roots.

"The women do a camas bake in June. They gather the roots and cook them in the ground for three days. It's a long process."

"One the women are responsible for?"

"Men do the hunting and guarding. Women take care of the children and the teepee and gather the plants and roots."

"It's the same for us."

"Except your women hunt and fish."

"They do, but I've never liked it. I'd rather cook and clean." She sighed. "I'm the only one in my family who doesn't like to camp or hike. Delilah, my sister, makes fun of me because I hate sleeping on the ground in tents. I don't like getting dirty when we go hiking. I don't like cleaning fish."

"Are you fussy, then?"

"No, but I like things clean and neat. The outdoors is so . . . messy. I'd rather be indoors where I can keep things in their place."

"Maybe you need the right guide to help you see nature through a different lens, from the vantage point that my ancestors saw it. Our Creator made every animal, every plant, every tree with the same care that He made you. Only when you see in them what the Creator saw will you truly appreciate nature."

Her forehead wrinkled, she studied his face with an intensity that held him completely still. As if she sought something— something important. "I never thought of it that way."

He breathed again. "I could be that guide."

"I'd like that." She ducked her head. "I feel like I'm on an adventure."

One didn't normally think of a trip to a museum as an adventure, but her words held a kernel of truth. Seeking out those who were different and getting to know them was an adventure every person should have.

"So do I."

CHAPTER 17

ST. IGNATIUS, MONTANA

So much learning in one day caused a person's head to feel stuffed and heavy. What to think about first? Christine rode her bicycle back to Uncle Fergie's after Raymond dropped her off at The Malt Shop. It gave her time to try to figure out what it all meant. She'd never seen a man so full of learning and so passionate about a past that's ink had long dried on the pages of history books.

Her father and the district elders had passion for the history that brought their ancestors from Europe to America, but it was different. More stoic. More forgiving. Because they had a forgiving faith.

The Kootenai didn't forgive or forget. Raymond didn't forgive or forget. She propped her bike against the porch and clomped up the steps. He didn't even believe in Jesus.

How did that feel? How did she feel about it? Myriad emotions tumbled around in her head, like clothes in a wringer washing machine. Jesus said, "I am the way and the truth and the life. No one comes to the Father except through me."

Jesus Himself said it, so it had to be true. Every word of the Bible was God-inspired, God-breathed. That's what the bishop said in his sermons. The apostle Peter said salvation was only possible through Jesus.

So where did that leave people like Raymond whose people had been treated badly in the name of religion?

Her heart ached for him and for his ancestors, even though he didn't want or need her pity. He didn't know what he was missing.

Should she try to tell him? Her people didn't evangelize like the Jesuits. They witnessed by the living of their lives.

For some reason Raymond Old Fox found it important for her to understand that she now lived on a reservation that belonged to his people. Every non-Native person should know, understand, and appreciate the enforced sacrifices that had led to this arrangement. Even West Kootenai didn't really belong to its residents, according to Raymond. It belonged to the mountains and the creatures who lived there.

She stopped on the porch, just short of the door. The realization spun her around. She'd lived in the shadows of those mountains her whole life. She had no appreciation of them beyond an occasional glance their way as she made venison stew or sausage from elk meat or grilled salmon. She enjoyed the bounty they were able to eat because of these creatures, but she didn't truly appreciate them the way Raymond did.

Peering through the lenses of his people, she caught a glimpse of nature's beauty and grace. Her infinite abundance when mankind didn't abuse her or fritter away her bounty.

Another thought sent her reeling a second time. This entire day had passed without any thought of Andy. Andy and his first special friend. A friend he kissed and hugged and hoped to marry. When she chose another, then he set his sights on Christine.

Second choice. It didn't hurt as much now that she'd spent an entire day talking to another man. She hadn't paused to compare Andy's tow hair and fair skin or his tall, lean build to Raymond's black hair and dark eyes or his compact, burly build. Nor had she paused to consider what Andy would think of Raymond's storytelling. The two men were from different worlds, and only in her did the far margins of those worlds touch.

Andy's voice from the first time they kissed sounded in her head. *"Your lips are so sweet. I'd like to kiss them every day."*

A delightful idea indeed. Had he said the same to his first love?

A bitter taste burned the back of her throat.

Conflicting feelings stumbled around in her head, bumping into each other. Drunk on emotion and uncertainty and strange new ideas.

Too much to think about. Better to think about starting supper for Aunt Lucy. She would be tired after a long day at the store. Christine tugged open the door and slipped inside.

"So there you are."

Aunt Lucy sat in the hickory rocker in front of a dark fireplace. She held a basket of sewing in her lap. Uncle Fergie sat at the old oak desk shoved against a wall next to an open window that overlooked their garden. He had a spreadsheet book open. Both of them had the same disappointed, disapproving expression on their plump faces.

"You're home early." Without bending over, she used one black sneaker to nudge off the other and then her bare toes to remove the second one. "I was about to start supper. I thought pork chops and fried potatoes sounded good."

"Where have you been?"

"I went to a museum in Pablo."

Uncle Fergie's woolly silver eyebrows rose and fell. "Your cousin was at the ice cream shop this morning getting a gallon of vanilla for his fraa's birthday supper. He saw you get into a car with the Indian man who comes into the store sometimes. Raymond."

"Jah. He took me to The People's Center in Pablo. It was closed. We were the only ones there. No one saw us."

The significance of her words spoken in haste made even Christine wince. She'd been alone with this virtual stranger the entire day. And she knew she shouldn't be or she wouldn't be assuring her aunt and uncle that no one saw them.

"What were you thinking—"

"Let me." Uncle Fergie cut into Aunt Lucy's horrified shriek. "You are here because your daed and mudder trusted us to watch over you. You are a young woman now. Old enough to know what's right and wrong. Old enough to know better. You've violated our trust in you."

His somber pronouncement cut far deeper than Aunt Lucy's emotional outburst.

Christine fought to keep from hanging her head like a repentant child. "Nothing untoward happened. He simply wanted to teach me about his people so I would understand why this land we live on is so important to them."

"Did you stop to wonder why he picked you out to tell this story to?"

She couldn't explain the connection. Raymond had been right when he asked her if she felt it that day in the deli. "He's kind and welcoming to a stranger who is away from her family for the first time because of a fire burning around the only home she's ever known."

Aunt Lucy's harrumph lingered in the air along with Uncle Fergie's stare that could slice meat from bone without moving.

"You are with family. Me and your aenti." Uncle Fergie's words followed a low growl in the back of his throat. "You're not to see him again."

Ach, Raymond. He had so much to share and she had so much to learn. Christine edged toward the kitchen door.

"Did you hear me?"

She managed a jerky nod.

She almost made it to the kitchen door when he spoke again. "We came home from the store because we thought you should know your friend Andy was in a car accident yesterday. His driver, John Clemons, died."

Guilt and shame buffeted Christine from all sides. She hadn't given Andy a thought until she arrived here, when a tragedy had changed his life forever. "Is he all right?" She whirled and stumbled back into the living room. "How badly was he hurt?"

"His mudder called the store and left a message with Esther Marie." Aunt Lucy stood and picked up her coffee mug. "She said he's bruised and banged up, but he's at home resting. She thought you would want to know. Like me, she thought there was something between you and Andy."

Something real and tangible did exist between her and Andy, but she didn't dare speak of it to her aunt and uncle. That something kept her awake at night, thinking of his lips on hers and the sound of his voice as he carved toys from chunks of wood he brought home from the store. The way his eyes lit up when he saw her. The way his hand gripped hers when he helped her into the buggy. A day with a dark-haired stranger didn't change any of that.

"I feel terrible about Mr. Clemons. He was a nice man."

Lucy's shoulders slumped and her eyes filled with tears. "She sounded pretty shaken up herself. I don't know your friend Andy or even the English man who died, but it sounds so very sad."

"Gott's ways are a mystery to us, but He can use even this for our gut." Uncle Fergie's stern gaze bounced from Aunt Lucy to Christine. "Never lose sight of that."

"May I call him?"

Aunt Lucy seemed on the verge of nodding, but Uncle Fergie's "nee" sealed her lips. "You can't be trusted to go to the store by yourself. It's almost suppertime. Help your aenti in the kitchen."

She deserved his distrust. Andy wouldn't know of her sorrow because of it.

Adventures took their toll on everyone, it seemed.

Were they worth it?

CHAPTER 18

St. Ignatius, Montana

L ack of planning never paid off. Raymond threw back his shoulders and marched through Valley Grocery Store to the deli. Lucy Cotter's perturbed stare from her perch on a stool behind the cash register did nothing to improve his mood. She didn't offer her usual cheery salutation. In fact, she frowned and looked as if she might say something else. But she changed her mind.

He should have asked Christine to go to Kootenai Falls with him when he dropped her off on Saturday. He'd been living in the moment. Given his background as a kid, that wasn't surprising. A person never knew what might happen next, so he should simply enjoy the here and now.

No Christine behind the counter in the deli.

He sighed and turned back. Fergie Cotter stepped into his path. "Could I have a word?"

Raymond knew Fergie by sight, but they'd never spoken beyond a simple "Morning." Raymond nodded.

"Not here. Outside."

Raymond followed the rotund man whose homemade dark-blue denim pants made a rubbing sound between his thighs when he lumbered through the aisle out to the store's front porch. The man was built like Humpty Dumpty. Fergie pointed to the lawn chairs for sale next to a pile of fireplace wood. "Have a seat."

"I think I'll stand."

Fergie shrugged. He removed a toothpick from his mouth and rolled it between chubby fingers. "Were you looking for my niece Christine?"

No point in denying it. She was a grown woman. "Yes."

"You don't know much about Amish folks, do you?"

"Actually, I've done my research." After their outing on Saturday, he'd powered up his Mac and learned everything he could. He wanted nothing of white man's religion for himself, but he thrived on understanding what others believed. "You have concerns."

"Christine has lived a quiet life among her own people in West Kootenai." Fergie drilled Raymond with a frown. "We choose that for our children."

"She's a grown woman."

A grown white woman. To get to the why required more time. More conversation. Raymond studied people.

"Who has chosen to live her faith. Which means keeping herself apart from the world and its worldly ways."

"Sometimes learning about the ways of other people reinforces your own beliefs."

"I understand why you might think that. I don't expect you to understand why we choose to live apart from the world—"

"No, I do understand. My people were not given that option."

"I know enough about your history to have great compassion for the Native American Indians—all the many tribes. The Anabaptists were also persecuted."

Raymond started to interrupt. Fergie held up his hand. "But

that's neither here nor there. Right now I'm only concerned for Christine's well-being. I'm asking you to leave her be."

If Raymond could he would. He wanted to leave her alone. A Native man like himself—albeit one who had white man's blood running through him—wanted nothing to do with a white woman in his head. Why this particular white woman demanded his attention, he simply couldn't say yet. "That's for her to decide."

"Do you feel an obligation to honor your elders' wishes?"

"I do."

"Then why would you make it hard for her to do the same?"

A Native man didn't put these feelings into words—especially not to the woman's elder. "I understand your concerns, and I promise you I mean her no harm and have no disrespect for your beliefs or culture."

"I know you believe that." His pudgy jowls turning a bright red, Fergie chewed on his toothpick for a few seconds. "If she continues to disrespect our wishes, she'll be sent to her family in Kansas. Did she tell you she stayed with us in St. Ignatius because she has a special friend who intends to marry her?"

She had not. In fact, she'd said little about herself. She had a way of being still and listening as if every pore of her being absorbed his words. As if she thirsted to know. Raymond didn't find that quality often in his colleagues at work. His relationships with women had been sweet sometimes, but always short, because of him, not them. It had been a long dry spell since a falling out with the one woman who'd matched him stride for stride in thought and deed. Tonya's face flitted across his mind's eye and disappeared into a mist filled with what-ifs.

"No, and I didn't ask. We don't know each other well enough to share that sort of thing."

"But you wish to." Fergie punctuated every word with a huff. Lines deepened around his eyes and mouth. "You've thought of it."

As much as Raymond desired to relieve the man of his discomfort, he couldn't lie. "I haven't traveled that far yet. I'm trying to discover what it is that keeps bringing me back to this store." He pointed to the sign. "It's not the horseradish cheddar cheese."

"And I'm asking you not to go down that road. Honor my request."

Christine had what her people so quaintly referred to as a special friend. He should leave it alone. She'd separated from her family in order to keep that man in her life. The honorable thing to do would be to respect it. "I'll do my best."

"That's all I ask." Fergie pushed the door open for a mother and the toddler who held her hand. He smiled and nodded at her. When he looked back at Raymond, the smile disappeared. "Take care."

"You too."

Fergie went inside. Raymond stood on the porch, staring at the Mission Mountains beyond the valley. They were purple and white today. Clothed in majesty, according to the white songwriter. He breathed the cool autumn air and let the fraught feelings of the previous moments leave his body on the stream. What happened next would not be up to him or to Fergie Cotter.

Christine had a say in her life, however small it might be in the Plain world.

He dug his car keys from his jean pocket and stomped down the stairs.

"Psssst, pssst."

He turned at the persistent sound emanating from somewhere behind the piles of fireplace wood at the far corner of the store's front porch. Esther Marie stuck out her head. "Excuse me, R-r-r-raymond Old F-f-fox." She waved a white folded piece of paper in his direction. "Chris-t-t-ttine asked me to-to-to-to give this to-to you."

She disappeared around the corner. Raymond followed. Her bike was propped against the wall. The homely girl's cheeks were pink. Her prayer covering lay askew on her head, and strands of her dishwater-blonde hair had escaped. He held out his hand, and she laid the note on his palm as if giving him a great gift. "Thank you."

She ducked her head. "I have to go t-t-t-to work. I'mmmm late."

"You are a kind person and a good friend, Esther Marie."

She didn't answer, but her cheeks went scarlet. She rushed around the corner. A second later the door banged.

Raymond waited until he sat behind the Volvo's wheel before he unfolded the note. Christine's handwriting proved to be neat and painstaking. Like that of a fourth grader taking a test.

Raymond,

I can only hope you come to the store to buy fresh cheese and bread for your gramma. If you do, Esther Marie can give you this note. Otherwise, I don't know when I'll see or talk to you again. My aunt and uncle have decided I should stay at home. I'm to clean their house, do laundry, cook, and tend the garden. It's like being back in West Kootenai. They're not wrong. I know that. But my heart hurts. I like working at the store. I like talking to customers. I like talking to you.

You never said what came next. You said you would teach me. I still want to learn. I don't think God finds learning bad. Do you?

If you get this note, meet me at the Amish school at seven o'clock next Saturday morning. My aunt and uncle will go to Libby to visit his mother for the weekend. It's our Sunday off from services. If you don't come, I will understand.

Sincerely,

Christine

No mention of the special friend. No mention of feeling guilty about going behind her family's back to see him.

How did he feel about that? He read the words again and then a third time. Running his fingers over the paper didn't help to ferret out the feeling behind them. A hawk caught his gaze. It soared overhead, dipped a wing, then flew from sight, seeking food in another place behind the horizon.

Christine was a smaller version of that hawk. More of a sparrow longing to soar higher and faster than her flock permitted. To see more of the world before being confined to a cage gilded with beautiful mountains and towering conifer forests.

He would give her that and then send her back to where she belonged. However hard it might be, it was the honorable thing to do.

CHAPTER 19

KOOTENAI FALLS, MONTANA

The rushing water of the Kootenai River played musical notes that rose and rose in a crescendo that lifted Christine's heart as she followed Raymond along the trail that led to their destination—Kootenai Falls. Much of the three-hour drive along Highway 2 from St. Ignatius to this beautiful spot downstream from Libby had been spent in comfortable silence. Raymond didn't seem to mind it. He didn't turn on the radio. Nor did he ask her about her decision to meet him today. He simply drove.

The time to contemplate served Christine well. Without going to the store, she couldn't call Andy. She had to take Aunt Lucy's word for it that he had survived the accident with only bumps and bruises. That didn't cover how he must have felt at the loss of his friend John. Genial, hearty, kind John.

In some ways it was better that she couldn't call. She still didn't know what to say to him about his revelation that he'd loved another woman first. It would be nice to simply say it was okay, no harm done, and offer a fresh start. *"Seventy times seven, child."* That's what Mammi would say. *"Seventy times seven. Are you perfect? Dare you cast the first stone?"*

Mammi Tabitha was full of one-liners.

What would she say about Raymond?

"Are you planning to go fishing, child? Because you just opened a can of worms."

One-sided letters were easier. She could offer her condolences without addressing the other issue. She asked Esther Marie to mail it for her. Esther Marie had turned into a good friend. She agreed to the favor, no questions asked, just as she had done with the note to Raymond. Christine's words in the letter to Andy were engraved on her brain. They seemed puny in light of what he'd experienced.

Andy,

Aenti Lucy told me about the accident. I am grieving with you the loss of a friend. John carried my family on many outings. He liked to tell us knock-knock jokes. He asked us about school and always remembered when our birthdays were. He sent Maisie a card when her kitten got run over by Mr. Knowles's truck. I am happy that you are all right. I know our last conversation didn't go well. I'm not sure what to say about it. I wish I could talk to you in person. I think it's the only way we can talk about such hard things. I'm trying to understand. I'm trying to understand why you didn't tell me before. It's hard, but I reckon it's hard for you too. I am not working at the store right now, so you can't call me there. Take care.

Christine

She hadn't mentioned why she no longer worked at the store. She wasn't ready to go fishing with that can of worms. Not yet.

"What does that tell you, child?"

That she shouldn't be in this car with this man?

Too late.

"We're here." Raymond stopped at the entrance to a swing-ing bridge.

Below them the Kootenai River dropped into a series of glo-rious, rushing waterfalls. He had to raise his voice to be heard over the frothing water. He started out on the bridge. Christine hesitated. He looked back. "It's safe, I promise. This bridge was first built during the Great Depression. After it was destroyed by flooding, the Forest Service rebuilt it with concrete piles. It's twenty-one hundred feet in the air, so it's the best place to see the falls."

Very impressive, but it didn't make Christine any more convinced that stepping onto the bridge was a smart idea. Grinning, Raymond held out his hand. Christine took it. His fingers were warm and his grip firm. He tugged. She followed.

Raymond stopped in the middle of the bridge and placed her hand on one of the wooden posts to which the metal net-ting attached. "You're okay." His reassuring tone and amused gaze made it hard for her to look away even as the roar of the water below called her name. "Hang on and look down. The water drops ninety feet in less than a mile. It's breathtaking."

Indeed it was. Her head swam every time she peeked over the railing. The sound of the water invited her to relax and to trust. She tried again. "It's so beautiful."

"You can feel Earth's blood pulsing through her veins here. You can hear her heart beat."

Christine closed her eyes. The pulse pounded in her ears. The water roared through her own veins. Her breathing accel-erated to match its rhythm. The post's wood felt rough under her fingers. Every part of her body vibrated. She opened her eyes.

"You felt it, didn't you?"

"What is it?"

"The spirit that lives in this place, that tells us we came from the earth and will return to the earth. Our bones and muscles will turn to dust and be swept up in the wind and scattered to the four corners of the earth."

"I feel clean here."

"That's a start." He nodded. "Do you want to find a bench and sit down?"

She allowed him to take her hand again. Her legs weakened. They couldn't be trusted to carry her to solid ground. Raymond settled on a spot where the cottonwood trees didn't obscure their view of the spectacular falls. Christine eased down on a spot a reasonable distance from his solid presence. "Why did you bring me here?"

"To try to help you understand our spirituality—what you call religion."

"Here?"

"This is where the aboriginal tribes came to prepare spiritually before hunting. My aboriginal tribe covered part of Idaho, Montana, and Canada, but this was the center point. We came here to harvest salmon, whitefish, and trout. We hunted bighorn sheep; Rocky Mountain goats; grizzly, brown, and black bear; moose; elk; whitetail, blacktail, and mule deer; and woodland caribou." He stared at the water, shadows from the surrounding tree branches making dappled patterns on his face.

He looked as if he could see his ancestors in their deerskin clothes and moccasins traipsing along the trails he said they'd marked with cairns, or piles of rocks, along the steep mountains split by the gorge that held the river captive. "Before they did anything they undertook spiritual preparation."

"What does that mean?"

"We are dependent on nature. The spiritual guides who protected us and instructed us could be found here. We sought them out in visions."

Visions. Like the angel who came to Mary and then to Joseph before baby Jesus was born. Like the God who walked with Adam and Eve in the garden and made a covenant with Abraham and then gave the Ten Commandments to Moses? "I don't understand."

"We have spirit guides who we still respect and contact regularly through vision quests and ceremonies conducted by our religious leaders. Can you understand that?"

"My father says we should always respect the beliefs of others, even when they are different than our own."

"He is a wise man."

"How do you contact these spirits?"

"Those ceremonies are private. This place is a tourist attraction now. People come and leave their pop cans and chip bags on the ground next to the trash cans."

"So where do you go?"

"We have areas on the reservation that are kept primitive. Only tribe members are allowed there. No development occurs. It's quiet and the spirits come to us."

"Do you have visions?"

Raymond leaned forward, elbows on his knees, and watched the burbling, white water below. "Not yet. I hope to, one day. My gramma, she is the visionary. She is a shaman, a medicine woman. She saw death before my grandpa died and before my mother died." He squinted in the sunlight, his expression glum. "You don't believe me?"

"I believe with God all things are possible. He spoke to

Abraham. He spoke to Moses. He spoke to the prophets of the Old Testament. Moses and Abraham appeared to Jesus during the Transfiguration. The disciples saw them. They saw Jesus after He was dead and buried."

"So you understand."

"Not exactly, but I know nothing is too hard for my Lord. The Word tells me so."

He studied his hands. "Do you ever have doubts about your God?"

"He is your God too."

"Don't try to convert me." For the first time his voice acquired a sharp edge. "The Jesuits spoiled any chance that many of our people would worship the white man's God."

"You don't believe in forgiveness?"

His face relaxed. "I try, but not because of your God's requirements, but because it is good and honorable. Men make mistakes."

"All men are sinners and fall short of the glory of God."

He sighed.

"What happened to your mother?"

He snatched a twig from the ground and began to peel away its bark with nimble fingers. "She was a tribal police officer. One night when I was ten, she went after a car that was speeding outside Arlee. A Native she knew was driving. He'd been drinking and refused to stop. She drove too fast in the pursuit, swerved to avoid another car, crashed, and died."

"Because of another person's poor mistakes."

"For many reasons, most of which I cannot understand."

"And your father?"

The pause lasted long enough that it seemed he wouldn't answer. She reached over and stilled his fidgeting hands. "It's all right. If you don't want to talk about it, I understand. It's none of my business."

"He was—is—white. He was out of the picture before I was old enough to remember him. Grandma Velda doesn't talk about it and neither does Gramma. I'm not sure if it's because he was white or because Mom didn't marry him. Probably both. She didn't marry the fathers of my two brothers, but they were Natives." He glanced her way, his gaze tentative. "That's not uncommon on the rez. Or in the rest of the world. Your people probably don't see it that way. You have a book where you get your beliefs. Ours have been handed down orally."

"Why do you think she didn't marry any of them?"

"Some might say she was a free spirit. Gramma said she had the rebellious soul of a wild mustang. She couldn't be tamed. She refused to be ruled by a man." Raymond tossed the twig back in the grass and leaned back to contemplate the sky. "It's smoky here. The fires near Libby are causing more evacuations. Soon even this area might be off-limits. It's nature's way of refurbishing her lands. It inconveniences those who didn't understand her. They built too close to the mountains and messed with the natural rhythm of the land."

He was changing the subject. She should let him. "Are you blaming us for the fires?"

"Not you specifically. Our people did the same thing. When they had to buy allotments of land, they chose the ones closest to the mountains and to water sources. That was the life they knew. They didn't understand farming instead of hunting and gathering."

Christine couldn't let it go. "I can't imagine not knowing my father."

Pain flittered across his smooth face. "There is a hole where my father's name belongs in my heart, but I adapted. Children do. My brothers did too."

"But they shouldn't have to. They are gifts from God meant for a husband and wife."

"Maybe in your world."

"Do you ever think of venturing outside the reservation and seeing the white man's world from another place? Maybe you could see a perspective that isn't so narrow."

He laughed.

"Why is that funny?"

"I'm not laughing at you. We are like two sides of the same coin. It is strange that our paths would cross now, in this time, when you are at a crossroads and I know my life is about to change in ways I don't relish." He shook his head, his expression perplexed. "I wanted to go to the University of Montana in Missoula to study archaeology. I filled out the application my senior year of high school and all the financial-aid papers. I got accepted. When I showed Gramma, she said no."

"Why?"

"She said I needed to stay with my kind. She said the college in Pablo was there for me to learn my tribe's ways and pass them on to my children. That's why she worked so hard with the other tribal elders to establish the college."

"My aunt and uncle said I shouldn't see you anymore. We are to keep ourselves apart from the world."

"So both of us were schooled to keep the world at bay. Yet, here we are, the edges of our worlds touching. It's not so bad, is it? What are they so afraid of, I wonder?"

The silence stretched for several minutes. Lulled by the water and the comfort of his presence, she closed her eyes.

"Look, a red-tailed hawk. He's hunting."

She opened her eyes in time to see the raptor soar over the falls, zoom to the ground, then flee upward again, a tiny mouse flailing in its talons. "He's quite the hunter."

"He knows how to survive. Strong, unafraid. All things Native men aspire to be."

"Is he one of your gods?"

"We don't have gods. There's a kingfisher." Raymond pointed to a cottonwood below them. "See how he has a wide white stripe around his neck and his body's blue-gray? He's called a belted kingfisher."

"How do you know so much about birds?"

"Everything I know I learned from Gramma."

"She sounds special."

"She is. I can't imagine how life will be when she's gone."

"Is she dying?"

"We all are—eventually."

"You know what I mean."

"I want to take her to the medicine tree in Bitterroot Valley." He leaned forward, elbows on his knees, and tucked his chin on his palm. He seemed to be contemplating joining the rushing water below. "She says it's been spoiled by nonbelievers who take the coins others have left there."

"You leave coins for your god?"

"Let's just sit here and think."

"I can do that." Her thoughts refused to be still. They wanted to soar like the red hawks and the eagles and break free from the earth. Healing trees, shamans, and lithe foxes whirled inside her brain.

The sun slipped behind a cloud, taking with it the day's warmth. She shivered and crossed her arms. Her folks didn't evangelize. And Raymond had no desire to be converted. What did God intend to accomplish by putting them together? "Maybe you should take your gramma anyway. It's enough that she believes. It doesn't matter what others do or don't believe. There's healing power in believing."

He straightened and smiled. "You're very wise for so young a woman."

"I don't think so. I think I'm just beginning to figure things out."

"I know that feeling." He stood and held out his hand. "Let's go home."

Home. More and more, the true meaning of that word escaped Christine. She stood as well but didn't take his hand. "Whether you like it or not, I will pray to my God for your gramma. It's what we do. That His will be done. If she is to stay a little longer, praise God, if it's her time to pass on, that she go peacefully, praise God."

"Your faith in your God is like our faith in the medicine tree. Because you believe, it helps you."

"It's different."

"We'll have to agree to disagree on that."

They walked single file across the swinging bridge. Only a few feet separated them, but they remained worlds apart.

CHAPTER 20

LEWISTOWN, MONTANA

The phone rang and rang. Maybe no one would answer. Andy rubbed his aching neck. He leaned his forehead on the edge of the desk in his father's sawmill office. It smelled of sawdust. He stared at his boots.

He sat up straight and turned Christine's letter facedown. Her words had been conciliatory. Forgiving, even. She was right. They needed to speak in person. Soon.

Please, someone, anyone, answer. He needed to hear Christine's voice. To see her. To know she still wanted what he wanted.

He had to return to Eureka for John's funeral. That would give him an opportunity to find out what was happening with the evacuation. The fire and its devastation seemed a million miles away right now.

"Hello. I mean, Valley Gro—ccee—rry St-st-ore."

"Jah, this is Andy. I need to talk to Christine."

"She's not-t-t-t here."

Andy gritted his teeth. This woman was not to blame for her speech impediment. His lack of patience was his fault. It made him petty and sinful. He breathed. "I know she doesn't work there anymore, but I hoped you could get a message to her to call me. I have a letter from her that says she doesn't work there anymore. Why is that?"

"Because of Raymond Old F-f-f-f-ox."

Andy leaned back and removed the receiver from his ear. He stared at it. Had he heard right?

He returned the receiver to his ear. "Who is—?"

A rustling sound filled the line.

"Andy? It's Fergie."

Christine's uncle sounded different on the phone. More commanding. Andy's family's vacation travels had sometimes meant a stop at the St. Ignatius store where the owners were everywhere, welcoming and chatting with shoppers. In person he was a roly-poly guy with big glasses. He looked like a hard-boiled egg wearing suspenders, glasses, and a beard. It would be easier to talk to him—and harder. Andy took a long breath. "Jah, it's me. Is Christine all right? Who is Raymond Old Fox?"

"She is gut." Fergie's tone belied his words. "Are you recovered from the accident? I am sorry about John Clemons. He was well spoken of in these parts. He brought folks to the store a few times."

"I'm gut. Sore but gut. Christine wrote me a letter. She said she no longer works in the store. Is it because of this Raymond Old Fox?"

"It is."

Normally, Fergie was a talker, a storyteller, a joker. Today he barely had two syllables to rub together.

"I have to go to Eureka for the funeral. I think she would want to go."

"It would be gut for her to go. To remind her of who she is and where she comes from."

Had she forgotten all this in such a short time? "What's going on?"

"Nothing that Lucy and I can't handle."

"I plan to rebuild in West Kootenai. While I'm there I'll see when we are allowed back in."

"Christine will come back here—for now."

Fergie's tone was sharp as the knife Andy used for whittling. "I will bring her back—for now."

"I'll tell her you are coming for her. My fraa and I cannot get away. The store needs us. My son Jasper can go with you to Eureka. He has friends there."

A chaperone. Fine. "I'll be there in the morning."

Andy needed to talk to Christine. Something had changed. Something that had easygoing Fergie worried.

CHAPTER 21

The seating arrangement didn't bode well for conversations of a personal nature. Nor did Andy's frame of mind. He swiveled in the van's front passenger seat to look at Christine. She smiled and raised two fingers in her lap in a tiny half wave. She had to know about his phone conversation with her uncle Fergie. Bewilderment dogged Andy. Less than two weeks out in the world and she'd been drawn to someone outside her Plain community. Someone besides Andy. It didn't seem possible, but Fergie's angry tirade had left no doubt. Christine had strayed.

The thought socked Andy in the gut. *Not again. Please, Gott, not again.* The pain and the humiliation—yes, pride did play a role, as much as he longed to rise above it—and visions of long, lonely days ahead taunted him.

Please, Gott, I can't bear to go through this again.

She had said little when he came to her uncle's front door. She simply grabbed her duffel bag and scurried to the van while her cousin Jasper took his time saying goodbye to his family. Jasper insisted Andy take the front seat. He had no way of knowing the intensity of the nausea that rocked Andy's gut when he contemplated getting into a motor vehicle so soon after the accident that killed his friend.

Andy returned Christine's small salute and faced the bug-spattered windshield. The white-knuckled ride from Lewistown to St. Ignatius had lasted for days it seemed, despite driver Chuck Larson's attempts to reassure Andy that he was a safe, defensive driver. "Never had an accident yet, not even a parking ticket."

Neither had John. Until the day he died. The 140-mile drive from St. Ignatius to Eureka would take two and a half hours. Despite the cool autumn air that wafted through the open window, sweat trickled down Andy's temples. His throat tightened. The bitter taste of bile burned the back of his tongue. The pit of his stomach heaved. The roar of the engine filled his ears.

Glass shattered. Brakes shrieked. The acrid smell of the air bags filled his nostrils.

He closed his eyes and opened them. He gritted his teeth against the vomit that rose in his throat.

"You know, it might work better if you sat in the back seat." Chuck's concerned expression bounced from Andy to Jasper. "You don't mind, do you, son? This man's got a case of PTSD, sure as shootin'. I don't want him hurling in my van."

Jasper's frown said he did mind, but the driver ruled on these trips. Everyone knew that. He had no choice but to switch with Andy, but not before he offered him a hard warning stare. Still in his early twenties, Fergie's son had his father's brownish-red hair, receding hairline, and dark-rimmed glasses. He even had the start of a paunch. And the same severe frown. To look at him must remind Lucy of what Fergie looked like in the early years of their marriage.

"I know my place," Andy murmured the words as he passed Jasper. "Don't you worry."

He gulped fresh air and forced himself into the seat next to Christine. Donut stuck his head between the seats from the cargo compartment and barked. "Hush. You can't come up here."

Donut huffed and pulled back. Christine's hand crept across the vinyl seat and grasped Andy's. "How are you?"

Her sweet concern warmed him. He drew his first easy breath since the predawn darkness. The nausea abated. "Better." Acutely aware of Chuck and Jasper in the front seat, Andy kept his voice soft, barely above a whisper. Maybe the road noise would rob the two men of the ability to eavesdrop. "Wondering how you are and what you've been doing."

Her cheeks turned pink. She squeezed his hand and let go. "I've been learning."

Her penchant for reading books about historical figures and faraway places had made buggy rides interesting. She regaled him with little-known—or necessary—facts about those people and places. The way her mind worked intrigued him. Trying not to note the rising speed of the van and the whiz of oncoming traffic at the intersection that would take them to Highway 93, Andy focused on the soft, instrumental music that floated from the speakers over their heads. "Learning is always gut, as long as you're sure what you're learning is fact, not fiction. I thought you liked working at the store. You said you did. I was surprised when I got your letter. What changed?"

Would she tell him about the man with the strange last name? They had nothing if they couldn't be honest with each other.

"I did. I still want to work there, but Onkel Fergie didn't

approve of how I was learning. A friend took me to The People's Center in Pablo. Onkel said it was wrong for me to go."

"It was wrong," Jasper piped up. Obviously the road noise wasn't enough. "You went in a car with a stranger, an Englischer, without telling Mudder or Daed. You sneaked around, which means you knew it was wrong."

"He's not English. He's a Native Indian." Her tone remained respectful, but something sparked in her deep-blue eyes. Raymond Old Fox was important to her. Andy's chest tightened. He grabbed the door handle and held on. Christine scooted around in her seat so she faced him. As if to make it clear her words were for him and not Jasper. "Did you know the store and the school and Onkel Fergie's farm are all on the Flathead Indian Reservation?"

Andy wracked his brain, trying to remember what he knew of Montana history. Very little. His early years were spent in Berne, Indiana. After his family moved to the countryside a couple of miles from Lewistown, he only had a few years of school left. He learned some US history and a little of Montana, like the Lewis and Clark expedition, the gold rush, and such. Not much of it stuck. A sawmill worker and furniture maker had little need for US history. "I don't think I did. Why is that important to you?"

"Our ancestors came to the United States to escape persecution. So did many of the first settlers from England. Later on they spread out and claimed land that belonged to the original people who lived here. The Native Indians." Her words were slow and deliberate. "It seems important to me to know that our people bought land from folks who had no right to own it in the first place. I try to put myself in their shoes . . ." Her voice trailed off.

Andy shifted in his seat and forced his gaze from her face. Christine glowed. Fergie was right to be concerned about this Raymond Old Fox. Not for any physical attributes or attractions. The man had done something far more dangerous than capturing her heart. He had her mind in the palm of his hand.

"I'm not a scholar." He stopped and scrubbed at his face with both hands. These words had to be chosen with care or she would be driven closer to something far from her Plain beliefs and values. And to this man.

Pain beat in his chest where his heart should be. "We do need to respect the history and culture of others, while clinging to our own. It's important not to lose sight of why we came to the new world."

"It was new to us, but old—very old—to the aboriginal tribes who peopled this land since before the Ice Age."

How did a simple man such as himself answer such a learned statement?

"You've been talking to one of the Kootenai or Salish people who live on the rez." Chuck chimed in just in time. "Those of us who get along with them—which is most of us in Mission Valley—feel for them and the way they were treated. But that don't make us the bad guys. We weren't around when they were driven onto the rez or when their land was sold off after the Allotment Act. We benefited from it, granted, but we had no ill intent. The main thing we try to do now is take good care of the land we have and get along with everyone around us."

That sounded like a good plan. A way of being good neighbors in an awkward situation. But it didn't address the more personal question that pestered Andy like a pesky bee buzzing around his ears. He leaned toward Christine, but she turned her head away from him. She seemed entranced by the passing scenery.

"What else did you learn from Raymond?" He lowered his voice to a soft whisper. "Anything that . . . involves us?"

Nothing. It seemed she wouldn't answer him.

Fine. He leaned his head against the headrest and tried not to look out the window. He closed his eyes and focused on the wordless music piped in over his head. *Breathe. In and out. In and out. Gott, help me understand what is going on in her head. Why does she care about ancient history that isn't even our history?*

"You moved to West Kootenai when you were grown." Her voice, barely audible over the music and the van's rumbling engine, sounded strained. "You spread your wings. Is it so strange that a woman might want to do that too?"

Plain women didn't have wings. They longed to marry and have children and grow old with their husbands. He eased his head so he could see her without lifting it. "You said you wanted to grow old in West Kootenai."

"West Kootenai was the only place I knew. I liked my life because everything was clean and neat and orderly. Cleaning houses was perfect for me." She tugged at her seat belt as if the restraint bothered her. "Then the fire made a mess of it. It doesn't matter how many times you clean a house, it gets dirty again. Raymond says life is messy. It's meant to be that way. I worked a new job. I met new people—"

"Like this Raymond."

"Like Raymond. But it's not just him." She shook her head and frowned. "I wish I could explain it. I walked a trail high on the mountain with a deep river below me. If the rocks and stones crumbled below my feet, I would fall into the river and drown. That's how my life feels right now. There's nothing orderly about it."

"I would catch you."

Her frown grew. "You say that now, but you kept secrets from me." She pressed her hands together in her lap. Her voice dropped to a mere whisper. "It hurts me to know that. How can I trust that you don't have other secrets?"

"I don't. I promise I don't." Her words cut Andy like a hook on the end of a fishing line that flailed in a strong wind. He couldn't be sure where the next cut would appear. Nor could he capture the line. "How do I know you're not traipsing around the countryside with this man for reasons other than the ones you speak aloud?"

"It's not what you think. I'm not the one who can't be trusted. My life suddenly changed. I realized I've lived my whole life in the most beautiful place in the world and I never appreciated it. I could lose it all to fire or to my parents moving to Kansas. I didn't do justice to the time I had in Kootenai." Her gaze went to the window, but her expression said she saw something far, far away. "I didn't recognize the connection we have to nature. We take that for granted. The Natives don't. They see themselves as part of nature. Their spirituality—what we would call faith—is intertwined with animals and trees and plants and birds. It made me see all those things differently. We're knitted together with nature, but we don't acknowledge it or give nature her due."

She drew a long breath. Her cheeks had turned pink. Her face shone as if she'd received a precious gift. She trod precariously close to sacrilege. All this natural beauty came from God the Father. She was blinded by light that came from Raymond and his so-called spirituality. Words had to be chosen carefully or they would drive her farther into this stranger's world. "The fire made all of us stop and think." He should not take her words personally. Something bigger was at stake. "It's important to do that, but we must never lose sight of the hand of Gott in all this. He is sovereign. He is the Creator. But I'll not rush you to draw these conclusions. I have my own crumbling trail to walk."

"Winona." Bitterness soaked the name.

"I'm sorry I didn't tell you about her." Andy raised his head a fraction. Jasper's head drooped, his chin touching his chest. The man slept. Chuck peered at the highway. "It's in the past. It didn't seem necessary to drag it into our present."

"You loved another before me. That influences how you treat me. It influences what you believe about women and about what I may or may not do."

She was too smart for her own good. Maybe too smart for a simple man like himself. Maybe this man Raymond interested her because of his learnedness. Maybe he had book learning. Maybe that's why cleaning house didn't appeal to Christine as much anymore. "I'm sorry I disappointed you. I only wanted to leave it behind."

"But you couldn't. Which is why you returned home. Not because of your daed's health."

"It was both." His protest sounded weak in his ears. "Even now nothing is resolved."

"So you can imagine yourself living there, close to your bruder and Winona?" Christine stared at him. "Because your father insists? Even though you'd made up your mind to make Kootenai your home?"

With me. The rest of the sentence wrote itself on the space between them.

"I'm still considering what to do. My father is ill. I want to honor his wishes."

Sorrow replaced her frown. "That's understandable. I just wish . . ."

"I know."

"So you have your trail to forge and I have mine."

"Do you think our trails will cross in the future?"

"Daed would say Gott has a plan." She ducked her head and shrugged. "I hope so."

Despite the sentiment of her words, her tone suggested she leaned toward a future where their trails ran parallel, never touching.

Andy would do more than hope she was wrong. He would pray.

Not only for their future, but for her salvation, which now seemed in peril.

CHAPTER 22

St. Ignatius, Montana

Stalkers end up in jail. Raymond slumped against the seat in his Volvo and pounded a rhythm on the wheel to the rap song on the radio. What was he doing here? When Christine hadn't shown up at their meeting place the previous day, he'd chalked it up to a change in her aunt or uncle's schedules at the store. Not to their conversation at the falls. His unbelief in her God bothered her, no doubt, but she hadn't let it deter her from the conversation. She didn't dump on his people's beliefs.

So where was she now? Both Lucy and Fergie were at the store today. No sign of Christine at the school or at Fergie's house. Life would be so much simpler if she had a cell phone.

Raymond snorted. He might be a technophile, but he also recognized the beauty of being disconnected from the world. The immense quiet and the relief when the constant chatter and the resulting cognitive dissonance disappeared came each time he went to the primitive area with his brothers and great-uncles and the elders. The sweats brought a freshness, a freeness he could not experience in front of a computer screen, a TV screen, or a phone screen. Plain folks had the right idea, even if it inconvenienced him.

As much as a relationship with such a woman remained beyond the realm of possibility, Christine still managed to burrow under his skin with her burning desire to know. To understand. A rare quality in people her age—or his age. She had a grip on his mind, if not his heart. A white woman in an apron and prayer covering.

A prayer covering, for crying out loud.

Was it the white man's blood in his veins that surged like a tidal wave when she drew near?

A desire to explore his white man's heritage?

No.

He had no white man's heritage. The white man abandoned him. His Native mother didn't leave of her own accord, but she also abandoned him.

A sharp rap on the window broke the silence. He jumped and glared into the brilliant sun that made it hard to see his attacker. He squinted and put his hand to his forehead.

Lucy glared back at him.

He rolled down the window. Which meant shoving it down the last two or three inches. "Hey, Lucy, how are you?"

"Gut." She held out a chunk of cheese wrapped in plastic wrap. Horseradish cheddar. "Take this."

"What's *this*?"

"Take it. Cheese for your great-grandma."

He accepted her offering.

Silence for two, three, four beats. He sucked it up and entered the fray. "You know that's not why I'm sitting out here."

"I was hoping you were taking a phone call. You'd finish up, get out of your car, do your shopping, and then go about your business." Gazing at the Mission Mountains in the distance, Lucy pushed her glasses up her nose with one finger. She looked down on him. "When you didn't come in, I figured I'd come out. She's not in there."

"I know."

"She's gone to Eureka."

His chest tightened. He cleared his throat. "For good?"

"As far as you're concerned, that would be for the best, but no, she'll be back in a few days."

His lungs inflated again. "Okay. I should get to my gramma's. How much do I owe you for the cheese?"

"It's on the house this time." Glancing at her store, Lucy crossed her arms. Her ample chest heaved. "The gift of the cheese comes with the right to give you some free advice. I've seen enough of you over the past two years to know you're a decent young man. You take care of your great-grandma. You're kind and polite and plainspoken. I know my husband asked you to leave Christine alone. There's a reason for that. You're young and you can't see the trials that lie ahead. Us older folks have been there and done that. You need to find someone more suited—"

"You mean someone like me. An Indian."

"We're not racists. Not any more than your people are racists when it comes to the way you think about all white folks and lump them all into the same covered wagon they rode in on."

He'd have to give her that one. "I've only ever dated Native girls my whole life."

"Those two decades or so you've been around?" Lucy chuckled, but she sounded more perturbed than amused. "You can't date my niece. Not because you're an Indian but because she's Amish. We don't marry outside our faith. Her eternal salvation is at stake or I wouldn't be out here talking to you.

Amish women don't do this." She pointed at herself, then at him. "I have no idea what you believe in, but I do know what we believe. Did she tell you she'll have to leave her family and friends if she marries outside her faith? She'll never be able to see them again."

"Whoa, whoa, hold your horses." Heat scorched his face despite the fall breeze that floated through his car. "Who said anything about marriage? We visited a museum. We hiked at Kootenai Falls—"

"You took her all the way to Kootenai Falls?" Lucy's hands went to her red cheeks. "You say you're not interested in marrying her, but you're spending hours alone with her. Where I come from that's serious courting."

"I'm sorry. I know you don't understand my ways any more than I understand yours. I mean no harm."

"Then stay away."

Still mumbling under her breath, her arms flailing, Lucy whirled and marched back to the store.

The entire twenty-minute drive back to Arlee, Raymond chewed himself out. That conversation couldn't have gone worse. Antagonizing Lucy Cotter only made life more difficult for Christine. What had he been thinking? Not thinking with his brain, that was the problem. This situation resulted from thinking with his heart instead of his brain.

He would never allow either to get in the way of his basic tenet that Native men should date and marry Native women. Just as Amish men and women should marry among themselves.

Christine hadn't mentioned the punishment she would receive for not following the rules. Probably because marriage hadn't been on her mind. It certainly wasn't on his. The frequent but fragmented image of his children sitting at

Gramma's feet, listening to her stories, barreled its way into his imagination. Yes, he wanted his children to know her. The clock ticked so loud it boomed. Yet the fragment told him nothing of the woman with whom he would have these children.

Native children who would still be one-quarter white.

He pulled onto the cracked, oil-stained cement pad that served as a parking space next to his gramma's cabin. An old—but still muscle-bound—powder-blue Impala took up half the space. Who did that belong to? He smacked his hand on the wheel. *Keep calm. Breathe. Life happens.* What other clichés could he come up with on short notice?

At least Gramma wouldn't be able to pelt him with questions about his job or how he spent his free time. She had plenty of spare time to contemplate her questions and their answers.

He grabbed the cheese and headed to the door. It opened before he laid his hand on the knob. Tonya Charlo offered him a smile. She had a bag of Gramma's favorite mini chocolate-covered donuts in her free hand. "Hey."

"Hey."

"Son, you remember Tonya?" Her grin gleeful, Gramma shouted from where she sat on the sofa, a faded green and blue knitted shawl around her shoulders, donut crumbs on her chin. "She is Tilly and Sal's oldest granddaughter."

Sal Charlo had served on the tribal council with Gramma.

Of course Raymond remembered Tonya. That would be called an understatement. Now a medical assistant at the Tribal Health Department Medical Clinic in Pablo, she'd been one of a handful of girls he dated in high school. They reconnected at S&K College where she earned an associate's degree in medical assisting. Their on-again, off-again relationship had been smoldering in the off phase for about a year. "I didn't realize you two knew each other."

"Mom asked her to teach me beading." Tonya had the silky voice of a songbird and the body of a dancer. In fact, she'd performed at the Arlee powwow with her family since before she started school. Her dark hair hung to her waist in a shiny, rippling black sheet that touched the top of her tight, faded Levi's. "She's also helping me with my Kootenai."

"That's good. You know they have classes at The People's Center." He moved past her and stuck the cheese in the refrigerator. "I can get the schedule for you."

"Thanks, but I'm recording Little Runner's stories for a paper I'm writing."

"You're back in school?"

"Online classes for now. I like helping people at the clinic, but it's not enough. Taking temperatures and blood pressure, asking a few questions, helping schedule procedures—it's all superficial." Tonya went to the counter and settled the donuts next to a bag of pistachios and a can of Folgers coffee.

Raymond took the opportunity to mouth, "*I'll get you for this*," at his great-grandmother. She shot a wicked grin back at him.

Tonya didn't notice. She just kept talking. "I plan to get a bachelor's degree. Public administration. Maybe I'll run for office someday. Did you see two indigenous women got elected to Congress? One Laguna Pueblo and the other Ho-Chunk? They're the first Native women to serve in the US House of Representatives."

Natives only became citizens in 1924, and some states didn't give them the right to vote until 1948. Progress came slowly. If this could be called progress. "I wonder if it's worth becoming entangled in the white man's political machine. Look how it worked out for your Salish ancestors."

They refused to sign the treaty that would move them to the Flathead Reservation—then known as the Jocko Reservation. When the document was published, it had Small Grizzly Bear Claws's *X*. A forgery. He refused to move from Bitterroot Valley. The military forcibly moved his ragtag remnant band in 1891.

"I don't need to be reminded of my tribe's history. I'll never forget it, and I won't let those white guys forget it either."

The fierce look on her face punctuated the words. Raymond couldn't suppress a grin. They didn't know what they were in for. "Are you transferring to Missoula?"

"Yes, if I can get the money together. Right now I'm barbecuing moose steaks out back." She picked up a platter of raw meat and pointed at a basket of spices and cooking utensils. "Help me out. Bring that for me."

"Right behind you."

She left the scent of sandalwood in her wake. He waited until the screen door slammed and then turned to Gramma. "You shouldn't meddle in people's lives. It's not right. You don't know what's going on in my head." He touched his chest. "Or my heart."

"Neither do you." Gramma's blithe words made Raymond's blood pressure shoot up. "Any Native man who decides to chase an Amish girl wearing a bonnet has lost his bearings."

Two women on the same day who thought they knew his business better than he did. "I like to learn about people who live differently than we do. Nothing more. Nothing less."

"Much more. Much, much more." She coughed, and her grin disappeared. He patted her back and removed a donut from her clawed grip.

"Hey."

"You're supposed to take it easy on the sweets, remember?"

"Sweets for the sweet."

More coughing, but her cackle followed him out the door where he found Tonya stoking the wood-burning grill. "Chocolate donuts as appetizers. Moose steak and baked potatoes for the entrée. She's in heaven."

"Wait until she tastes the chunky monkey caramel coffee– flavored ice cream I brought for dessert."

No use in arguing about the sugar-laden treats. Gramma would eat what she wanted to eat. "What's the occasion?"

Tonya flipped her hair over her shoulder and bundled it into a quick ponytail. She grabbed the plastic bags and wrestled three steaks from the Italian dressing they'd been marinating in. With an expert twist of the wrist, she plopped them on the grill and seasoned them with paprika and salt.

Finally, she turned and handed him the tongs. "Nothing. She invited me to join her for dinner. I told her I would come as long as I could bring the dinner."

"She has trouble chewing steak, and she doesn't digest it very well. Her body is weak."

"I'll cut it up small for her. At her age she deserves a treat now and then." Tonya stuck her hands on her hips and looked Raymond over, head to toe. "What's eating you? You didn't used to be so cranky."

"You know Gramma doesn't do anything without an ulterior motive. She's messing in my life and she's messing in yours."

"And I'm willing to let her think she's messing in my life if it gives an old woman pleasure. She has so little to amuse her. Besides, she's a shaman. She knows more than she's telling you or me." Tonya motioned to two sun-faded lawn chairs with frayed woven bottoms that were sunken with use by big behinds. "Sit down. Take a load off. Relax."

She plopped into her chair and crossed her legs. She wore scuffed hiking boots. She'd always been an outdoorsy girl. More into hunting and football than dresses and makeup. She and her family had one of the best stick-game teams around. Second only to Gramma's in her younger days.

Forcing his gaze from her long, jean-clad legs, Raymond followed suit. Beyond the thicket of silver sagebrush, rabbitbrush, and mock orange shrubs with their citrus scent, ponderosa pine, mountain ash, and burr oak spread across the open fields. The sun hovered on the horizon. Dusk approached, made hazier than usual by smoke drifting over the valley from the mountains. Raymond took a long breath. He hadn't barbecued in ages. The mouth-watering aroma of the steaks made his stomach rumble. He hadn't eaten lunch or breakfast.

"What's going on with you? What's got Little Runner so anxious?" Tonya studied him like a scientist peering through a microscope lens. "She told me she had a vision. Something about a man killed in a car accident. The last time that happened she lost your mother."

Gramma hadn't mentioned this latest vision to him. His chest muscles seized. Shadowy memories of the tribal police at the door. Grandma Velda's keening. Those were dark days. "How do you know so much about my life?"

"Not from you. You were into the big, silent-man thing when we dated. Did you ever try to find your dad?"

Never. In kindergarten or first grade, he'd asked his mother why the other kids had fathers and he didn't. She said he was special. He had a mother who could do both. One of his few memories of her. It wasn't a happy one. Her sad expression belied her words. He never asked again. "No."

"Look, if you don't want to talk about this, it's fine." Tonya got up and turned the steaks. Grease dripped. The fire flared and smoked. The aroma filled the air. "But getting to know my dad was one of the best things that ever happened to me. My parents divorced when I was three. I didn't spend time with him until I was fourteen and old enough to demand it. It's like finding an arm or a leg that you've been missing all your life. Suddenly you're whole for the first time. You can imagine doing things you've never done before."

"Good for you."

"Back to the big, silent Indian again."

"Your dad is Native. Mine isn't. There was a white man at her funeral. I didn't recognize him. He kept staring at me. I asked Gramma about him." His mother's funeral had been the only time he'd ever seen Gramma cry. "She said she didn't know, but her eyes said she did. She looked mad."

"Maybe you should ask her again."

Tonya had changed in the last year. Grown more self-assured. But she'd always spoken her mind. That would never change. She had no way of knowing she poked in crevices where rattlers coiled ready to strike if disturbed.

"Why are you so interested in poking around in my life? Seems like you've got enough on your plate."

"Because you were always full of dreams in high school. That's one of the things I liked about you. Then you shut down in college. You were voted most likely to climb high mountains, not stare at computer screens for a living."

The assessment stung like a horde of wasps. "I'm not shut down."

"You wanted Missoula and archaeology? Why didn't you fight for it?"

"Gramma needed me here."

"Little Runner has plenty of people taking care of her."

"You sure are nosy."

"You sure are prickly."

"One of the things you liked about me in high school? I didn't notice you liking me all that much. You dropped me like a fresh-roasted camas root when Kevin Birdsbill came along."

"I was sixteen, for Pete's sake. He had a car. A Thunderbird."

It was an old argument, one he dug up whenever they started arguing, which they did often. Two strong-willed people with flames for hearts. The Volvo was Raymond's first car. He'd been eighteen when he finally had enough cash from his first job at the Arlee grocery store to buy it off Dusty Tapia who ran an auto shop and wrecker service out on Old Person's Road. "I like that Impala you're driving now."

"It was Jordan's."

Bad subject. Tonya's older brother enlisted in the Army after high school graduation. His first tour in Afghanistan, an IED took out him and two buddies. He came home in a body bag.

"Gramma likes her steak raw. Like the moose is still bugling."

Tonya stood and picked up the tongs. "You should talk to her again about your dad."

"Maybe you're right." He stood. "Or maybe I should let sleeping bison lie."

She snorted and plopped a sizzling steak on a platter. "I could use a friendly face in Missoula."

"You make friends fast." He held the platter while she added the other two steaks. "I'm sure that hasn't changed."

She brushed past him. "Apparently so do you. Watch out or we'll change your name to Man Who Chases Woman in Bonnet."

"Gramma has a big mouth."

"And a big heart to go with it." Tonya held the door for him. "Follow your dreams. Not someone else's."

What if a guy couldn't tell the difference?

CHAPTER 23

All of West Kootenai, Rexford, and Eureka had turned out for John Clemons's funeral. Andy squeezed into a pew toward the back. Madison and the boys sat on the front row with Lois and her husband. The three boys' heaving shoulders and surreptitious swipes of their noses made his own throat ache. The Baptist church had a big sanctuary nearing capacity. Folks poured through the doors in a steady stream. Many stopped to pat him on the back or shake his hand.

Everyone wanted to tell him it wasn't his fault. Every time a person said that, another wave of guilt swallowed him, leaving him gasping for air. A texting driver had been at fault, but John would have been at Lois's eating a second piece of cherry pie if Andy hadn't asked for a ride back to the farm. He lowered his head and stared at the hat in his hands in hopes that people wouldn't notice his red eyes and the dark circles around them. Nightmares involving car crashes kept his sleep company every night.

Knowing that Christine was nearby at Jasper's uncle's house didn't help. Their conversation on the drive to Eureka hadn't resolved much.

"Can we sit by you?"

As if his thoughts had crossed with hers in midair. He turned. Looking uncertain, Christine stood in the aisle, Jasper right behind her. Her confusion made sense. In Plain services, women sat on one side, men on the other. Here families sat together.

Christine looked back at Jasper. He shrugged. She slipped closer and sat, leaving a goodly space between them. Jasper swiveled to talk to some folks who'd come from Libby and sat in the row behind them. Christine's eyes were red rimmed. She held a sodden tissue in one hand.

"I know I should rejoice for John. He was a devout believer." She dabbed at her nose. It matched her red cheeks. "I'm really sad for his sons more than him. They'll miss him so much."

"So will I." To his dismay Andy's voice cracked. Embarrassment sent heat barreling through him. He cleared his throat. "He was a gut friend."

Her gaze softened. Her hand moved from her lap to the space between them, close but not too close. "I'm sorry for your loss too. We're to take joy when a bruder in Christ goes ahead of us. But that doesn't mean we can't mourn the hole that's left behind."

"Where do you get the words?" Strangled by emotion, he stopped and forced himself to breathe evenly. *In, out, in, out, in, out.* "It's not the words. It's the ability to know what to say. I don't know what to say to his sons, Derrick, Logan, and Johnny Junior. Derrick's only twelve. Johnny is the oldest at sixteen."

"Don't give him the man-of-the-house speech." Christine sighed, a kind sound that soothed the pain in Andy's heart without any physical touch. "Someone surely already has done that. Offer to take them fishing or hunting. They'd like that, I reckon."

The desire to touch her blew through him, a hard, south

wind, warm and full of the heady vanilla scent of clematis and sweet gumbo lilies. Intertwining his fingers tightly in front of him, he begged them to behave themselves. *This is a church*, he scolded his thoughts. *Have respect.*

Christine might not welcome his touch. She might prefer the touch of a man named Raymond Old Fox.

He gritted his teeth and swatted the thoughts away. They didn't belong at John's funeral.

"They would." He uttered the two syllables without letting the other, less acceptable words escape. *Don't do this to me. I need you. I want you to need me. I want you to love me. I want to marry you.* "I could do that, if Madison will let me."

"She will."

"She doesn't blame me. I'm grateful for that."

"No one blames you, except you." Her hands fluttered. So close. So close to touching him. They inched back to her lap. Her blue eyes simmered with August-like heat. "The bruises are starting to fade, but you still look tired. Are you still having pain from the accident?"

"My neck and back are sore. But nothing worth talking about."

Jasper leaned forward, turned toward Andy, and stared. "You look like a horse someone rode hard and put up wet."

"I'm fine." He drew another long breath. "Will you stay a few more days after the funeral?"

"We're to return to St. Ignatius tomorrow." Jasper leaned back on the cushioned pew and crossed his arms. "I have to get back to work, and Mudder needs Christine at the house."

Christine's look said, *Sorry for his attitude.* "When will you go back to Lewistown?"

"It depends. I was hoping the evacuation would be lifted

soon. I want to help with the rebuilding even if I don't . . ." He floundered for a second in the face of her inquiring stare. "Sheriff Brody says the end isn't in sight yet."

"When it is lifted, Onkel Fergie will come with a load of men from St. Ignatius to help with the rebuilding. Aenti Lucy will want to cook."

"You could stay with Mercy or Nora."

"Nora is in Libby still, although she may come with the Libby folks when construction starts. I heard Mercy got herself in a pickle by passing the time with a smoke jumper, or maybe he's a firefighter. I'm not sure which."

"We'll start building her house first. Jonah says he'll borrow an RV for him and the boys to stay in out there. Maybe Mercy, too, if she's to teach school."

"She's teaching in Grandma Knowles's garage right now. I'm sure she'll be glad to get back to Kootenai when the time comes." Christine craned her neck and glanced around. "I'd hoped to see her here, but she's probably teaching today. I miss her and Nora and Juliette so much. We need an ASAP."

He'd forgotten about their silly name for getting together to compare notes on life, and especially on men. Awful Situation Approaching. It seemed a lifetime ago that any of them had been that young and carefree. He and Christine stood at the same bridge. They could cross over it together or go their separate ways. In the distance he could see their life together. Behind him stood their old lives.

Christine's stare didn't waver. What was she thinking? Jasper was only inches away. He turned to talk to Henry, who slid into the pew just as the pastor moved to the pulpit.

"Don't give up on us." Andy made the words the barest whisper.

Christine turned so Jasper couldn't see her face if he glanced their way. Regret chased sadness in her face. "I haven't. Have you?"

"I'm not throwing away what we have for a person who has no faith. You'll leave me, your family, and your faith for him?"

"It's not about Raymond. It's about having time to see a little bit of what's out there. And to figure out some things. Like whether I want to be with someone who wasn't truthful with me and live in a place where he can't be happy because of his past."

"I could be happy anywhere if we were together." The truth of those words struck him hard. "That's why it's so hurtful to think of you spending time with another man. Especially one who could lead you away from your faith."

"Are you worried about my salvation or your heart?"

"Both. I can't go through this again."

"I'm not to blame for what your bruder and that other woman did to you."

True, but she was finding a new way to destroy his hope for happiness. He'd worked hard to move past his anger and start fresh, only to have a new obstacle careen toward him out of the blue. "I can't do this again. I won't—"

The pastor began to speak. The soft murmur of conversations died away. Pastor Dave knew John well. He spoke of the man's love of nature, country music, hunting, fishing, and most of all, family. The congregation laughed at stories told by John's brother in the eulogy and cried while his niece sang "I Can Only Imagine."

Andy couldn't imagine. Only by God's sovereign grace would he stand before the throne. He was too humble to assume his salvation was secure.

With John's blood still fresh and bright red in his mind's eye, Andy could be sure of a few things. One, he loved Christine. Nothing she had done thus far could change that. Two, he needed forgiveness for his own stubborn inability to forgive. Three, life was too short to dally. A person had to come to grips with mortality and stop acting like he had all the time in the world.

He would set aside his own discomfort and offer to spend time with John's boys. He owed his friend that and more. He needed to go back to Lewistown and set his world right. From there he'd find a way to cross that bridge with the woman he loved.

. . .

Andy looked so angry. And forlorn. So abandoned. Christine didn't intend to abandon him. Her heart wouldn't allow it. Despite everything that had happened, despite the secret he kept, her heart refused to relinquish its love for him. Why hadn't he told her the truth? Was it wrong for her to hold him to his promise to live in Kootenai?

Far from the mess he'd left in Lewistown. She'd left her own mess in St. Ignatius. Now who had unfinished business? She'd left town without saying goodbye to Raymond. He still had lessons to teach her. And it seemed she might have something to teach him as well.

Confusion weighed her down as she settled into the buggy Jasper had borrowed from his uncle. To her surprise he'd offered her a hand up before going around to the other side.

"What were you and Andy talking about?" He pulled into the line of buggies and cars that snaked from the parking lot and along the street toward Highway 2. "You did an awful lot of whispering before the service started."

"He's still sore and stiff after the accident." Christine chose her words with care. Jasper's effort to unbend toward her boded well for the long drive back to St. Ignatius tomorrow. "Losing his friend like that was traumatic."

"Gott's ways aren't our ways."

If only Nora or Juliette or Mercy were here. Christine could share an eye roll with them over Jasper's attempt to sound old and wise. "I know I'm not smart enough to figure out why these things happen."

"You're not even smart enough to know you shouldn't mix with the Indians."

His acidic tone burned. Christine counted the cars in front of them. Eight before the intersection. It would be a long, slow ride to his uncle's house. "I like learning new things. I don't think Gott minds."

"I don't think we know what Gott minds beyond what the Word tells us. We don't need more than that. To be safe you should probably stick to learning new dishes to make for supper or new quilt patterns. Being the woman your family expects you to be." He snapped the reins and the buggy jolted forward a few yards. "A Plain woman shouldn't be flitting about in public with a heathen. Native American Indians don't believe in Gott."

"I'm not planning on becoming an Indian." Not that such a transformation was possible. Explaining the thirst to see more and know more before she settled down in a tiny nook in the mountains was impossible. Especially to a man with a closed mind and flapping gums. "Or giving up my faith. Kootenai

Indians believe in Gott. He's manifested differently—as spirits in everything we see."

"No wonder Mudder and Daed are worried. You're spewing sacrilegious rigmarole." He shot a scowl in her direction. In that second he looked like Fergie's twin, but with hair on his head instead of his chin. "Daed should send you home to Kansas."

"Kansas isn't my home. Kootenai is."

"You can't have it both ways. Is it the Indian or the Plain man?"

Christine clamped her mouth shut before furious words escaped. Heat burned her cheeks. She wrapped her fingers together in her lap, squeezing them until it hurt. Jasper had no right to question her, give her advice, or tell her what to do. Jasper wasn't much older than she or Andy. "Haven't you ever been in love?"

The scowl faded. Red suffused his fair skin. His gaze returned to the road. "That's a private matter."

"If you had, you'd know that all these wonderful, scary, strange, new feelings get all tangled up inside you until you don't know what's up and what's down."

"I'd know."

"It's not something you can study and decipher like arithmetic problems in school."

"I was gut at school." Jasper's voice dropped to a low growl. "Not so gut with people."

Jasper wasn't a jolly man like his father, who gave lollipops to the children who visited the store with tourist parents whom he gave detailed directions for finding Glacier National Park and the Road to the Sun. Christine corralled her ire. "Is that why you don't work in the store?"

"I like farming." He snapped the reins. "Giddyup. I'll be glad to get back to work."

Subject closed. Still, she'd learned something about her cousin. His distaste for her adventures might well be envy because he wouldn't dare leave his own well-worn place hidden behind Plain walls. He was afraid.

With all the upheaval of the past few weeks, the pain and heartache, one thing remained certain. To feel—truly feel—made life worthwhile. Living in a tiny, protective bubble was nice but not always possible. A person had to get used to that idea.

The rest of the ride passed in silence. Christine hopped from the buggy, scurried up the steps, and went to the room she shared with Jasper's uncle's two youngest daughters. She packed her bag and set it by the door.

Tomorrow they would return to St. Ignatius. She would get her answers. Then Aunt Lucy and Uncle Fergie could stop worrying.

And so could she.

CHAPTER 24

St. Ignatius / Elmer, Montana

Fog mingled with smoke made the predawn hour seem much more like dusk. Adrenaline left a metallic taste in the back of Christine's throat. Despite her woolen sweater, she shivered in the September early morning air. Her empty stomach pitched. Escaping from Uncle Fergie's house for the day might be the transgression that broke his hospitality's back.

She gripped Raymond's note in one sweaty palm and jogged in black sneakers down the dirt road toward the school. The note, delivered by Esther Marie who wore a worried face, read: *You were right. Taking Gramma to medicine tree. Come with us. Be at school by five a.m.*

Any later and Lucy and Fergie would be up, getting ready for their day.

The old green Volvo idled on the road in front of the school. Black smoke puffed from the tailpipe. The brake lights flickered. Raymond jumped from the car and approached before she could get any closer. "I'm so glad you could come." He looked as if he might hug her. Instead, he stuck his hands in the pockets of his Lees. "Gramma had a bad day yesterday, so don't expect her to be chatty. She didn't sleep much last night, and she'll probably doze most of the way."

"She isn't mad that I'm coming along?"

"Here's the thing." He slowed his step. "She agreed to let you come on one condition."

"And what was that?"

The front passenger-side door popped open. A slim, beautiful woman with long hair caught back in a single braid exited the car. "Hi. I'm Tonya. Nice to meet you."

"Tonya is an old friend of mine—"

Tonya snorted. Raymond glowered at her. "Gramma is teaching her beading, Kootenai, and some of our ancient ways. She asked her to come with us."

An old friend. The air fairly crackled with the sparks between them. Christine couldn't help but smile at the look on Tonya's face. She liked giving Raymond a hard time, that was obvious. And Raymond didn't know how to handle it, also obvious.

"It's nice to meet you, Tonya."

"Jump in." Tonya grinned. "Little Runner can't wait to meet you." She slid back in the front seat and closed the door with a definitive bang.

"Sorry about this. When Gramma makes up her mind about something, there's no changing it." He spoke fast, as if trying to get it all in before he opened the car door for her. "Take anything Tonya says about me with a grain of salt. Gramma appears to be prepared to do battle with the White Woman, but she'll warm up."

"Plain folks don't believe in war or battles. We don't fight."

"She knows that. She also knows you don't believe that trees have spirits that can heal."

"That's not going to change."

"I know." Finally, he opened the door, waited for her to get in, then closed it for her—twice.

Gramma sat on the other side of the seat. At least she appeared to be there somewhere under a pile of faded plaid flannel blankets wrapped around her in layer upon layer. Her sun-leathered skin was so wrinkled, her mouth and eyes could get lost in the crevices. Dirty dark-rimmed glasses sat on a wide nose. She wore a blue bandanna over her head, but long white braids, doubled up, hung past her shoulders. One skinny arm with a knobby wrist stuck out from the blankets, and her knotted fingers rested on the top blanket. Her head was back and her mouth opened. A snort might have been a snore.

"It's rude to stare."

Or not. Heat singeing her cheeks, Christine faced front and the back of Raymond's head.

"At least introduce yourself."

"You know who I am. Christine Mast."

"It is rude not to face a person when you talk to her."

Christine sucked in air and swiveled again.

"That is better." Gramma had faded eyes that might once have been brown. She squinted as if her head hurt. "I like to tease a girl to her face."

"Be nice, Gramma." Raymond turned the key in the ignition. "You promised. You both did."

"I had my fingers crossed."

The two women spoke in unison and then chortled. They were like twins born seventy years apart.

The engine coughed and sputtered. So did Gramma.

Christine smiled. Though she returned the smile, the old woman wiped spittle from her chin with a ragged tissue and sniffed.

It would be a long ride.

Sadie and Tonya took turns peppering Christine with questions the entire hour and twenty minutes on Highway 93 to Hamilton. Where was she born? Her parents? How many brothers and sisters? Why didn't she drive a car, and why was it okay for her to ride in someone else's car, and what was the problem with electricity? And why did she wear a prayer covering all the time? Which brought Gramma around to the true topic of the day—Christine's religious beliefs.

"Why you want to see the medicine tree?"

"I'm interested in what other people believe."

Tonya sniffed.

"You promised." Raymond growled deep in his throat. "I'll slow down to fifty and drop you off in a ditch."

"Sorry." Tonya pivoted in the seat so her sharp gaze drilled Christine. She didn't look sorry. "Your people do not care what others believe. You cling to your beliefs like ants on a log in the middle of the raging rapids of a mighty, angry river."

"We keep ourselves apart from the world." Which seemed like a good idea now that Christine was under fire from two women—one old in years and the other old in spirit—with fiery attitudes and tongues as sharp as Father's ax. "The Bible says, 'Be not conformed to this world: but be ye transformed by the renewing of your mind, that ye may prove what is that good, and acceptable, and perfect, will of God.' Romans 12:2."

"Yes. The *Good Book*." Gramma's disdain brought another warning growl from Raymond. "We know it by reputation."

"Your words say one thing but your tone another."

"Forgive them." Raymond shot Christine an apologetic smile in the rearview mirror. "Gramma's experience with the Good Book wasn't so good."

"Do not apologize for me, Son." Sadie tossed off the blankets. She wore a blue plaid man's shirt over a darker blue dress that hung over the emaciated body that could've belonged to a boy—if he were ancient and exceptionally wrinkled. "You believe God made His son come down in the form of a man. Why could He not have sent Him in the form of a bear or a hawk or in a tamarack?"

"The apostles recorded Jesus' history soon after His death. They don't say anything about Him being a hawk or a bear." Christine should have paid more attention during baptism classes instead of staring at Micah Borntrager. He ended up marrying Missy Hawkins anyway. "The Bible says we're made in His image, so He must've been a man."

"And the Jesuits said it was wrong for us to wander our land, hunting and fishing and providing for our families. That we had to become farmers. Because that is what God intended. Where does it say that in your Good Book?"

"I don't know. They might have had good intentions but gotten it wrong."

"Very wrong."

"My mammi always said to forgive seventy times seven." Christine leaned toward the old woman. "She always said what she thought even though Plain women are expected to keep their thoughts to themselves."

"Forgiveness is in your book." Still, Gramma looked pleased at something. "Is your grandma still alive?"

"Nee. She passed four years ago."

"So she skipped through the pearly gates and has been running around on streets of gold for the last four years." Tonya didn't laugh. She wasn't making fun, but the words carried a certain bitterness. "Does she have angel wings?"

"People don't become angels. I hope she is in heaven, though."

"I do not believe what you believe." Sadie's voice had gone soft. "But I, too, hope to see loved ones on the other side of the great divide."

Who was she missing? Raymond's mother?

Before Christine could probe further, Gramma leaned forward and put both clawed hands on the front seat. "Are we there yet, Son?"

"Does it look like it?"

"Do not get smart with me."

"You know the way better than I do. You tell me."

One hand in the air, she listed toward the window to her right like a slowly deflating balloon. "Bitterroot Valley, the most beautiful place in the world."

"Says the woman who's never been more than two hundred miles from here in her entire ninety-plus years of life."

"I do not have to go anywhere if I am where I should be to start with."

"May I know about the medicine tree—what makes it special?" Christine interceded. They were more like squabbling brother and sister than two generations apart. "How did you find it?"

"I did not find it. Our ancestors have always known it." Gramma leaned back and gathered up her blankets around her once again. "A big mountain sheep was chasing Coyote. Coyote ran for his life. He came to the tree and hid behind it. The sheep charged the tree, rammed one of his horns into it, and got stuck. Coyote made it a medicine tree after that."

"With magical powers?" Christine studied the beautiful red-and-orange-leaved trees that dotted the fields as they passed through a seemingly endless valley. Houses were few and far apart. The sun warmed the car, undaunted by wispy clouds that floated by on their way to unknown destinations. The Bible called magic or sorcery sinful. "Or is it like the wishing wells where the Englischers throw in their coins, hoping the wish will come true?"

"This is not Disneyland we are talking about." Tonya rolled her eyes. "It's not unlike lighting candles in a church."

"She's trying to understand, Tonya. She has no context for this conversation."

Gramma joined Tonya in the eye rolling. "Again with the big college statements."

"She may live a few miles down the road from us in Kootenai, but she grew up in a different world."

"Same world." Gramma raised her knotted index finger and shook it back and forth, slowly. "There are holes in the trunk and people used to leave their coins, but now people steal the coins because they are old."

"Nothing is sacred anymore." Raymond slowed as they entered Hamilton city limits. The tiny town, population 4,738, was the county seat of Ravalli County according to the sign they passed. The town was clean, neat, and sparse. Like most towns in this part of Montana. "People don't believe in anything, and they make fun of people who do."

Were spirits in trees and talking coyotes any stranger than the virgin birth of her Savior to an unmarried young girl who spoke to an angel who assured her she was carrying the Messiah? Miracles happened. Her mother said so. Her father said so. The bishop said so. Who was an ignorant house cleaner like Christine to argue?

By the same token, how could she argue with taking presents

to a medicine tree in exchange for health? Plain people didn't judge others. They simply lived their lives according to the gospel.

Whatever Gramma thought of Raymond's statement, she wasn't sharing. Christine glanced at her. Gramma's head lolled back, her mouth open. The snoring resumed.

Christine smiled. Tonya smiled back at her, then turned to face the front. "She does that a lot now." Sadness tempered her words. "She's a wild woman one minute, an old lady sleeping the next."

"She asks a lot of questions."

"She never stops being interested in everything and everyone." Raymond's words held the same sadness. "It's all her business."

This trip was more than an outing for an old lady. They were saying goodbye to a woman they loved. With each mile, her destination on the other side of eternity came closer. Christine had just met Sadie Runabout, yet the same sadness overwhelmed her.

"She makes your life interesting."

Raymond and Tonya laughed and shared a look, but neither spoke.

Christine chose another, less volatile topic. "It's so beautiful here. The fall colors are so bright."

"She was right when she said it is the most beautiful place in the world." Raymond hunched over the wheel and pointed to the right and then the left. "Sapphire Mountains are to the west, Bitterroot Mountains to the east. The trees you see out there are ponderosa pine, alpine larch, and white western cedar."

"I wish I knew as much about trees and plants as you do."

"It helps to have Gramma."

"My family pays attention to vegetables, mostly, but my mother does plant some flowers in the spring."

"It's apple season. We could get some cider."

"The medicine tree first."

"You know you can't actually go to it with us." Tonya glanced back. She looked almost apologetic. "You'll have to wait in the car."

Disappointment welled in Christine. "I understand."

"Do you?"

They entered Bitterroot National Forest. The colors blossomed around her. Reds, oranges, yellows, and greens so vivid she couldn't take it all in. "The land of your ancestors."

"Yes." Raymond pulled to the side of the road near a visitor station. "We'll be back. You could sit here and enjoy the view."

"Is the tree real?"

"It is. We believe. If you don't, it's just a tree."

"Faith is believing in something you can't see."

Raymond turned off the engine He glanced at Tonya. She shrugged and got out of the car, then leaned down and looked at him. "You're the amateur philosopher. Ball's in your court, big guy."

She shut her door. Raymond scooted around in his seat. He removed his glasses and rubbed his eyes. Finally, he spoke. "'Now faith is confidence in what we hope for and assurance about what we do not see.'"

"Hebrews 11:1. For a man who doesn't believe, you know a lot about my religion."

"There's a difference between knowing and believing." He returned his glasses to his nose as if they would help him to envision more clearly what neither of them could see. "I took a world religion course in college. I wanted to understand what people believe and why."

"Me too."

"I wish—"

"Are we getting out or what?" Gramma popped forward so her bandanna-covered head came between them. "I'm not getting any younger."

"We'll be back." Raymond smiled at Christine. "This may take a bit, so feel free to sit on a bench and soak up the scenery."

. . .

The scent of pine and fresh air, and the feel of warm sunshine above and soft leaves and grass underfoot like clouds ushered a traveler into a world where humans were small and nature an unending, peaceful space. Raymond inhaled. Nature put her arm around him. She welcomed him like a long-lost son. *Be at rest. Be still. Be at home.*

Gramma took the lead, followed by Tonya who had said nothing when he got out of the car and left Christine sitting there alone, contemplating a world so different from her own. Raymond took up the rear, contemplating the same topic.

Gramma's steps grew lighter. She leaned into a wooden walking stick taller than she was. Her smile grew while her breathing quieted. They didn't speak. No words were needed as they surged deeper into the forest away from the relentless cacophony found even in a state as sparsely populated as Montana. Their pace slowed to allow Gramma the space to commune with the spirits that greeted her in the same way.

She began to hum a tuneless song. They entered a small open area surrounded by yellow larch and screaming red and orange maple trees dwarfed by their friends the ponderosa pines farther up the mountain. A gentle breeze greeted them as a parent welcoming wayward children returning home after running away.

Gramma's tune evolved into mumbled Kootenai words. Some were unintelligible, but a few stood out. *Present. Thankful. Offering. Peace. Health. Giving.*

Raymond leaned against a tree and rested his hands on the gnarly bark, rough under his soft fingers unfamiliar with manual labor.

Tonya knelt a few feet from the old woman and lowered her head. Her eyes were closed, her fingers splayed across her thighs. A stillness came over her. A peace. A woman who never stopped moving or talking rested.

She had never looked more beautiful.

Tsk-tsk. Gramma shook her head. She peered at the sky and then at the ground. Finally, she dug three quarters from the pocket of her shirt and tucked them in the crook of the tree's lowest bough.

She stood not moving for so long it seemed she might have nodded off on her feet.

Still, no one in his right mind would have interrupted her.

"You have nothing to say?" She didn't turn, but her tone left no doubt that the words were directed at Raymond. "Do you laugh like the others? Do you think it is a joke?"

"No, Gramma. It's no joke." He straightened and let his hands fall to his sides. "Your medicine is strong enough for both of us."

"The tree is dying."

"I know."

"People come and dig the coins out of the trunk and leave holes."

"The world has changed."

"People do not care anymore. They do not reap the roots or dry berries. They do not make medicine."

Raymond moved to her side. "But you believe, Gramma. That's what is important."

"No, Son." She raised her face to the sun. "Those of us who are old are dying off. With us goes all the strong medicine. The ways of our ancestors will be gone."

"No." Tonya opened her eyes. "Never. There will always be those of us who carry on. Believe that, Little Runner."

"That's why I volunteer at The People's Center and drum at the powwows." Raymond memorized her wizened face, her hooded eyes, her bony body. This woman was his mother in every way but one. She needed assurance now, close to her end. "I play the stick game. I teach the language to the children. No worries."

Gramma sank to her knees in the grass. "You should not have brought her here."

"Christine is not the problem. My thoughts are my own."

"If you have questions, you should ask them. My time is coming."

"Don't say that."

"No matter what others say, time is finite. I long to run with the mustangs, free of this body. When the time comes, stick me in the ground and go about your business. Do not mourn. Be happy. I will be."

He dared not argue. She was right. Time wafted across the sky with the smoke. It spread across the universe unencumbered by the past. "Who is my father?"

"It is about time." She patted the grass. "Sit here with me. Both of you."

Tonya crawled across the grass to be closer. She sat cross-legged within arm's reach of Raymond. Her scent of sandalwood and earth steadied him. Somehow she knew and she would make it all right.

The story had ugly fangs. Once told, it could not be untold. Nor could Raymond be a coward, afraid of the shadows that followed him.

Oliver "Cap" Dawson came and went from his mother's life like a parcel delivery man. Here one minute, gone the next. But always back with that next package. Until Raymond's birth. Gramma plucked a piece of grass and held it to her lips. She blew. The faint whistle came and went in the same way.

"Cap was drawn to your mother like a man dying of thirst who finds a water hole in the desert. He thought it would quench his thirst, but it turned out to be a mirage."

"My mother wasn't a mirage. Her touch was real. Her milk fed me. Her voice sang to me at night."

"She was not who he needed her to be. To him she was exotic and beautiful. He wanted to capture her and stick her in his cage. He didn't understand that caging her would be the end of her. She would no longer be the woman he desired." Gramma tossed the blade of grass aside. Her expression contorted. "Your mother saw her future in his eyes. She saw your future and let him go."

"Because he was white. She chose to ignore that I, too, am half white. Just as you do."

"I see nothing of him in you. Not one trace of his lack of gumption, of his whine, of his empty laugh. Look in the mirror and you will see the face of Adeline."

"You see what you want to see."

"Every action has consequences. Your mother learned that.

The spark that drew her to this man died a quick death, but she could never be free of him."

"Because of me."

"She never regretted you, only that you would have no father."

"Yet she learned nothing. She had two more sons who grew up without fathers."

"Some horses cannot be tamed. She sought something she couldn't find. A restlessness filled her like an infection that couldn't be cured."

As a child Raymond loved his mother as children do. Now a fierce anger assailed him. She had not been as perfect as he remembered her. Nor his father the bad guy Gramma had made him out to be.

Tonya's hand crept across his thigh and captured his. Her touch was soft but sure. He swallowed his anger, a dry, bitter pill. "Maybe I should seek out this white man."

"He became involved in a church that believed in the supremacy of the white race."

The words came at him like an arrow shot from a finely tuned bow. Tonya's hand let go of his and began to rub calming, comforting circles on his back. He leaned into her touch. "How is that possible if he loved a Native woman?"

"Who said anything about love?"

"I can't understand it."

"Because you have a sweet, clean heart. There is a difference between love and lust."

Grandma could never know how often Raymond had settled for the second while longing for the first. Like his father? "So then he left for good?"

"He did. Your mother kept seeking happiness in men. She

never learned that a man could not give the kind of contentment she needed."

"And she died without finding her contentment?"

"Yes."

She couldn't find it in raising and loving her sons. She
couldn't find it in other people. Contentment came from understanding her place in the universe. He swallowed unmanly
tears and cleared his throat. "You don't find her story sad?"

"It is her story. Period. Much like the story of many men and
women. Especially Natives who drift away from the beliefs of
their ancestors. They look for something they think they will
find in a white man's world."

"But this Cap, this father of mine, came back. I saw him at
the funeral."

"Velda sent him away. As she should have."

"Why do you think he came? Had he changed his mind
about the supremacy of his race?"

"I do not know. Does it matter?"

"To me, it does."

"A boy thinks he needs a father."

"A boy needs a father. White or Native."

"A boy needs a man who guides him in the right direction.
Cap Dawson would take you on a road that leads to a world that
will forsake you. Is this why there is a white woman waiting in
the car for you? You think you are white inside because of this
man?"

Tonya's hand stopped rubbing for a second. He hazarded
a glance in her direction. Fierce emotion flashed in her eyes,
then disappeared. Her hand began to rub again. He breathed.

"No." He couldn't be sure. Nothing in this world was sure.
"You can't know that he will lead me down a bad road." Maybe

she could. Maybe she'd seen something in those strange visions that visited her in the middle of a bright sun-drenched day. "Is he dead?"

"I do not know the answer to that question. Only to your other question."

"What question?"

"Should you seek him out?"

"Should I?"

"Yes. It is the only way to quiet the naysayers in your head."

"Even if it takes me away from you?"

Or from the woman who sat next to him, rubbing his back, offering him comfort despite the white woman in the car.

"Nothing will take you away from me. I am stitched by love and time into every muscle, every sinewy tendon, every drop of your blood. I am you and you are me."

The drumming of his heart slowed. His breathing did the same. "I find peace in that fact."

"Me also."

They stopped talking then and listened to the music played by the wind and the tree branches and the trickling water of a nearby stream.

The concert soothed Raymond. It settled the thoughts that wanted to do battle in a boxing ring inside his head. Those that would fight chose instead to sit around a table and mull over this new information. They nodded and rocked and hummed to the tunes played by leaves rustling in boughs overhead.

"I will go to the university in Missoula after you're gone." The words spoke themselves. He had no knowledge of them until they fell into the air and made themselves heard.

Tonya's intake of breath offered her thoughts on this plan. Her hand found his.

"You should go now."

"I want this time with you. I want to soak up your thoughts so I can take them with me. Once you are gone, so are they."

"You have learned enough from me." Gramma held out her hand to an orange-and-brown butterfly. It fluttered as if waving but flew on. "Stop loitering around an old woman, and get on with it."

"Make up your mind. You told me to stay and go to S&K. Now you want me to go. Which is it?"

"Bitterroot Valley was the home of the Salish."

"I know."

"Their women are beautiful."

Tonya giggled.

Even now Gramma had the need to meddle.

"I'm not a meddler."

"Stop reading my mind."

"Stop being so predictable."

"You didn't answer my question."

Her eyes closed. She lifted her face to the sun. "I'm tired. Let me rest for a few moments."

She curled up in the grass like a child, jacket rolled up under her head.

Raymond's love for her made his bones ache. What would his life look like—feel like—when she was gone? No matter what religion a person espoused, the suffering was for those who were left behind, not those who moved to the lands beyond eternity's gate.

"Why do you think you and I come and go from each other's lives?" Tonya unfurled her long legs and slipped around so she knelt facing Raymond. "Have you given that any thought during this time when our relationship has laid fallow?"

An interesting choice of words. What he deemed irretrievable she saw as simply dormant, waiting for the right time to be reseeded. "I know that I missed you when you were gone, but I could never put my finger on why you left."

"I didn't leave." Her smile tinged with bittersweet, she shook her head. "You did."

"You let me go."

"You always go. I won't try to catch the wind and wrap my arms around the air. You weren't ready. You still aren't."

"Ready for what?"

She traced the line of his jaw, touched his lips, leaned in and kissed his cheek, a quick kiss that somehow lingered when her lips moved away. "For the rest of your life."

"How do you know?"

She cocked her head toward the trail. "Have you forgotten you have a guest patiently waiting in the car? You invited her here, knowing she couldn't come to the tree. Why did you do that?"

"She seeks answers."

"And so do you." She scrambled to her feet. "Time to go find them."

A sweet sadness like a light seen through lacy curtains on a cold, dark night permeated her face. She squatted next to Gramma and helped her struggle to her feet.

Together the two women, one shortening her stride for the other, started for the path. Neither looked back.

A cloud passed over the sun, creating sudden shadows. Panic curled up in a ball in Raymond's gut. If he didn't move quickly, he would be left behind.

He might never find his way home.

CHAPTER 25

The faint scent of dish soap tickled Andy's nose. He leaned away as Winona set a huge bowl of mashed potatoes on the table in front of him. He averted his eyes to the pork chop on his plate. His entire body still ached in the aftermath of the accident, but the dull throb in his heart bothered him more. This warm, raucous gathering of children and adults breaking bread around the table served as a reminder that not every family sat down together tonight. John's boys would sit at a table with an empty chair at its head. Everyone, even Father, sat around these two tables, one for adults and one for kids, such was the size of their combined broods. Such a blessing. One for which he had not shown true appreciation.

Danki, Gott. I am a sore loser. An ungrateful wretch. I have found love with another, yet I still begrudge Stephen his happiness. Gott, forgive me. Show me the way You would have me go. Give Daed peace, whatever that path is. And me also.

"Ach."

Hand on her belly, Winona hunched her shoulders and bent over. Pain furrowed her forehead. She rubbed her stomach with both hands. "Just indigestion," she murmured as she turned to go back to the kitchen.

"Ach."

Andy swiveled as did Stephen and the others. His brother scooted back his chair. "Are you okay, Fraa?"

"Nee." Winona straightened. She stared at a small puddle on the floor. "The bopli is coming."

"I'll go for the midwife." Stephen shoveled another bite of corn into his mouth. He grabbed a pork chop and stood. "I'll be back. Try not to have the bopli before I get here."

He started toward the door, did an about-face, and strode to his wife. With his back to the others at the table, he leaned down and whispered in her ear. Despite the pain etched on her face, Winona smiled. "Me too."

Grinning, pork chop still in hand, Stephen whirled and sped out the door.

He had the look of a happy man. It matched the look on his wife's face.

A look every married person should have.

Mother hopped up from her seat. The other women followed suit. "Let's get you settled." She patted Winona's back. "I reckon you're just getting started."

Winona chuckled. "If he's anything like Will, he'll refuse to come out for days."

The other women laughed. "Do you think it's a boy?" Wallace's wife, Nan, asked as she bent to clean up the floor. "You keep saying 'he.'"

"We'll know soon enough."

Their voices faded as they moved into the hallway toward the bedrooms. Even the little girls traipsed after them like children to the pied piper.

The men kept eating. Except Andy's father. He dropped a napkin over a plate Mother had loaded with food. "I'm tired. I think I'll take a nap. Josie will call me when the bopli comes."

"You didn't eat." Andy held out the potatoes. "At least finish your food."

"The medicine takes away my appetite."

"What did you find out at your appointment?" In the aftermath of the car accident and his trip to the funeral, Andy had missed the news. Little had been said on his return. Everyone went about life as usual, it seemed. "Did the doctor tell you anything?"

Father sipped his iced tea. The boys' laughter filled the space. Wallace shot them a glare. "Time to finish the chores, boys." He tossed his napkin on the table and strode from the room. Frederick did the same. The boys followed, pushing and shoving.

That left Andy at the table, alone with his father. "Well?"

"I have leukemia."

Foreboding wrapped its tentacles around Andy's heart. He knew enough of this disease to know it wasn't good. "But it can be treated?"

"Jah. I have to go to Billings. Chemotherapy."

"Okay."

"Don't look so sad. It's in Gott's hands. I'm gut with that."

"I know." Andy did know, but that didn't mean he had to like it. Their faith dictated that they were simply passing through this broken world. They would be better off with God. His head understood all that. But his heart secretly struggled. A tiny voice grew louder at night, keeping him awake. *Malarkey*, it yelled in his ear. No wonder he had trouble sleeping. "Your faith is strong."

"Yours is not?" The lines around Father's mouth deepened as he frowned. His age-spotted hand raked his beard. "Have you changed so much since you moved to Kootenai?"

"Nee, it is. I try. It's been a hard season, that's all. The wildfires burning our homes. John's sudden death. Christine . . ." He stopped. "Life lessons."

"The Holy Bible says in this life there will be trouble, but not to worry. He has overcome the world."

"I know."

"Then you should act like it." Father picked at a roll and tossed the crumbs on his plate. "Go to Kootenai. Rebuild. Make your life."

"You wanted me to stay." Surprise ran through him like a flash fire. "You told me to stay here and run the sawmill."

"This life will have trouble, but that doesn't mean we shouldn't seek joy in it as well." Father smiled for the first time. "This sickness has taken much from me. I won't let it take life from you as well. If Kootenai makes you happy, it makes me happy. You're no longer running from your home. You're returning to a place you love."

"Danki, Daed." Staying held no angst. "I'm not sure if Christine will still have me, but I plan to try."

"Gut. Have you settled things with Stephen regarding the sawmill?"

"He knows what I want to do." Suddenly hungry, Andy helped himself to creamed corn and potatoes and gravy. He nodded and dug into his food. A man had to keep his strength up in the midst of so much upheaval. "But we haven't talked about it again. I thought you wanted me to stay, so I didn't pursue it. With John's death and the funeral and your doctoring, there's been a lot going on."

"Don't blame others for your failure to act."

"I'm not—"

"Frederick is a farmer. Wallace makes log cabin kits with his father-in-law. Stephen works on his father-in-law's dairy farm. Not one of them is interested in the sawmill. If you want it, take it. Ask that girl to marry you."

"Are you sure you want to let it go? Your disease will be treated. Gott willing, you'll go back to work."

"I'm retired. I'll let you young whippersnappers do the heavy lifting now."

He even sounded like an old codger now. "If you want me to stay while you're doctoring, I will."

"I'm a grown man. Your bruders and schweschders are here. Your mudder is here."

"You're my family."

"It's time you start your own family."

An angry wail cut the air. It emanated from the playpen in the corner of the room.

"Ach, Will is awake." Father stood, swayed, and sat back down. "Bring him to me. I'll hold him for a minute. He'll want his mudder. He's in for a big surprise. A new bruder or schweschder isn't so welcome at his age."

The toddler, with his curly dark hair gone wild and cheeks rosy with sleep, popped up. He wailed again and then stuck his thumb in his mouth. His eyes searched the room. His face scrunched up. The thumb came out. More wailing.

"I've got him." Andy headed to the playpen. He raised his voice over the mournful cry. "You take your nap. Don't worry about the sawmill. I'll take it. I'll work hard. I'll build a new life in Kootenai. But I'll come back more often now."

"See to it that you do." Shuffling steps told Andy his father had taken his advice.

Andy lifted Will from the playpen. The boy's sobs abated, but his frown said he wasn't sure about this new development. Andy settled the child's warm body against his chest. "It's okay, *kind*. I'm your *onkel* Andy. Remember me? Your mudder is busy having a *bopli*. A *bruder* or *schweschder*. You'll like that, won't you? Someone to play with."

He kept up the steady patter as he moved to the rocking chair near the tall windows that looked out over the backyard toward the fall garden, the apple trees, cottonwoods, and spruces. Will's tiny nose wrinkled and his lower lip bulged, but he didn't cry. "How about I rock you? I'm not much of a singer. Not like your mudder. She has a beautiful singing voice. That's where I met her—at a singing. But that's another story." Not one that he would ever tell Will. Andy began to rock and sing "Jesus Loves the Little Children," the only song that came to mind at that moment.

Will clapped in approval—at least it seemed like approval. He wiggled. "*Millich*."

Andy stopped rocking. "So you talk. What else do you say?" "Millich."

Milk. Naturally. Andy stood and hoisted Will onto his hip. "Mama."

"She's busy right now." That was an understatement. "Millich."

"*Eepies*."

Milk and cookies. Not a bad combination. "Don't get greedy, *kind*."

He went back to singing as he hustled to the kitchen. Maybe that would take the child's mind off Winona's absence. He found a sippy cup on the counter, settled Will on the floor, and rustled up some milk from the propane-powered refrigerator. All the while singing.

"You have a terrible voice."

"You were never much of a singer yourself." Andy handed the sippy cup to Will and held out a cookie to Stephen. "You didn't get to finish eating."

"I'm gut." He waved away Andy's offering. "The midwife is with Winona. How did you end up with Will?"

"Everyone was so surprised about Winona, I guess they forgot about him."

"Mudder will send one of the other fraas out for him in a minute."

"No worries."

Stephen leaned against the counter and waved at his son. Will transferred the cup to his other hand and waved back. He giggled. So did Stephen. His smile disappeared. "I'm sorry. It must be hard for you to see all this."

"I'm happy for you."

"Are you?" The words held no animosity, only wonder. "How is that possible?"

"I'm growing up, I guess."

"I hope you don't blame her. It was my fault. I saw it coming, and I did nothing to stop it." Will threw his cup. It landed at Stephen's feet and splattered milk on his work boots. He scooped it up and laid it in the sink with a chuckle. "I guess he's done with that. I wanted what I wanted. A better man would've left to be removed from temptation."

"It is better that she be with you than yoked to the wrong man for the rest of her life."

"If I could've spared you this, I would've."

"Danki."

The kitchen grew quiet except for Will's tuneless humming as he crawled to his father's feet. He tugged at Stephen's bootlaces. Laughing, Stephen picked him up. "You are a busy bopli, aren't you?"

Will pulled Stephen's beard and giggled. "Dadadada."

No pain ricocheted behind Andy's ribs. No angry words threatened to burst from his lips. Peace captured his heart instead. "Daed is fine with me taking the sawmill to Kootenai. He's decided I should go back and live my life there. In fact, he wants me to go."

Stephen's eyebrows lifted, but his smile looked forced. "Gut." The single syllable expressed more gusto than it warranted. "You can start your own family. It's time."

"That's what he said. You still find all this awkward, don't you?"

"I can't help but think of those moments that must've occurred before she realized she had feelings for me." Red crept across Stephen's tanned face, darkening his skin. He ducked his head and landed a kiss on Will's curly locks. "It must be the same for you."

The heated cool evenings spent under a full harvest moon. Stars cast light on their embraces under the vast Montana sky. Her laughter tinkled like the leaves on the breeze. Her warm breath tickled his cheek. "Let's not go there."

Stephen shifted his weight and tucked Will on his hip. "Right."

"You'll help Frederick care for Mudder and Daed." It wasn't a question. It was a given.

"He told you of his diagnosis."

"Only because I asked."

"He is close-lipped about it." Stephen patted Will's back, but his expression left doubt he realized he was doing it. "Mudder is worried and trying not to show it. She doesn't want to disappoint him."

"They want to set the example for us."

"They always have. When will you go then?"

"Soon. I want to greet my new nephew or niece first. Then I have to go to St. Ignatius."

Time to fight for the woman he loved.

Mother appeared in the doorway. She held a tiny, red-faced mite with wild shocks of black hair wrapped in a faded crib quilt. "Your dochder is here." Mother offered her bundle to Stephen. "She was in a hurry to see what all the fuss was about around here. She's perfectly formed. Winona is fine. She says she feels like making a batch of brownies. I told her to take a nap first."

She nattered to hide her emotion. That was Mother. Andy took Will so his brother could meet his new daughter. Stephen's face filled with a tenderness so profound Andy had to look away. His murmured sweet nothings were a private conversation between a father and his child.

Not wanting to intrude further, Andy handed Will to his mother. "I should go to the sawmill. I need to start making arrangements to move the equipment."

"Wait." Stephen took a step toward him. "You wanted to meet your new niece. Don't you want to hold her?"

"I couldn't. This is your time."

"I have the rest of my life—however long that is—to get to know her." He held out the wiggling bundle of red, wrinkled skin and black hair. "She looks like her mother, don't you think?"

Only a curmudgeon could reject such a beautiful peace offering. Andy took her. She gurgled and sucked on her hand. "She's smart. She already found her fingers." He studied her tiny nose and rosebud lips. "She looks like you, Mudder."

"Awww." Mother beamed. "Don't say that, poor thing."

"Hello, little girl. I'm your onkel Andy." He held her close so she could feel his heart beating in his chest. "You are blessed, bopli. You have a mudder and daed who love you."

So sweet. So tiny. So loved. The lump in Andy's throat threatened to explode. He drew a deep breath and expelled it. "Have you decided on a name?"

"She'll be called Joy."

Nothing could give parents more joy than a new baby. Andy wanted that joy, and he wanted it with Christine. He would fight for her. "I have to go."

"You'll be back?" The entreaty in Mother's words made it more of a statement than a question. "Soon?"

He kissed Joy's forehead and handed her to her father. "Soon. But right now there's someone I need to see."

CHAPTER 26

The trip to the medicine tree seemed to have broken the stubborn mule's back. Christine studied her hands in her lap. Aunt Lucy and Uncle Fergie had been waiting in the living room when she returned home after a long, dusty walk from the school to their house. She was so engrossed in trying to grasp all she'd learned about this new world from Raymond, Gramma, and even Tonya, that she didn't see them at first. Until Aunt Lucy cleared her throat. Uncle Fergie started talking, and he hadn't stopped yet. His voice rose and fell. His words pricked her skin like tiny knife wounds. *Rebellious. Stubborn. Disrespectful. Consorting with pagans. With heathens. Ungodly.*

Ungodly? She looked up and opened her mouth.

Aunt Lucy shook her head vigorously.

Christine clamped her mouth shut.

"I'm sending you to Haven. Jasper will take you."

Jasper, who sat at the desk by the front window, ostensibly studying a seed catalog, turned around. "But I—"

"I can't go to Haven. Please, Onkel Fergie, I want to go home. To my home. To Kootenai."

"They haven't allowed anyone back into the town yet. And

when they do it'll be for your daed to decide. I'll call and leave a message at the phone shack tonight."

Her father would be so disappointed in her. Mother might understand a little better—but only a little. Were Raymond, Tonya, and his grandma heathens? They believed in taking care of the earth, in treating it with respect. Plain folks believed that.

They didn't believe in Jesus. They didn't pray to the same God she did. She should pray for them. She liked them. They were sweet, kind, good people.

Being a good person was not enough. That's what the bishop said during the baptism classes. *"Remember, you can never be good enough to get into heaven. Entrance comes through salvation made possible by Gott's sacrifice of His only begotten Son."*

The memory battered her. More sharp words pricking her skin.

I don't understand, Gott.

"Are you listening to me?" Fergie's face turned red and his eyes bulged. He would either explode or have a stroke. Or both. "Do you understand how wrong it is for you to go traipsing around the countryside with an Indian—or any man not related to you? I know you do. Did you act like this before—with your parents?"

"We weren't alone. We were with his great-grandmother and his friend Tonya. There is nothing unseemly about this trip. I simply wanted to know more. I've read a lot of books, but it's not the same as learning firsthand about people. I never had a chance before."

The truth of the matter. She'd lived in a tiny bubble called Kootenai. And she'd been happy there. Now she knew the world was bigger and more complicated. Threads of many colors made up the fabric of this world. Its brilliance drew her in. She wanted to touch this bright, worldly shawl and wear it around her shoulders. If only for a short while. Then she'd come back and settle down and be the woman she promised to be when she was baptized.

"So you decided to turn your back on your baptismal vows while under my roof instead?"

"Nee. I didn't decide anything."

"I blame that boy Raymond." Aunt Lucy fanned herself with a horse auction flier. Her face was as red as Uncle Fergie's. "He's a bad influence, and he's pursued her even after both of us told him not to. That's why you have to go to Kansas. It's the only way to break the hold he has on you."

"He doesn't have a hold on me. He's not a boy. And he's not a bad influence." Could studying history and the culture of another people be wrong? It wasn't the same as leaping into a fallen, modern world. It simply helped students understand how this world had been shaped by past events. "I've learned history from him. I've learned to think for myself."

"Such pride. Have you forgotten *Gelassenheit*? *Demut*, not *hochmut*. Plain women do not gallivant across the countryside with men who are not family members. It's not done. You know that. You know better."

"I haven't forgotten anything. I'm unmarried. Until I find a mann, I have more latitude—"

"A rumspringa that never ends? Even then you don't rub your family's nose in it. Much latitude is given, but once you're baptized, you've joined the church. You're held to a higher standard."

"I don't mean to disrespect anyone." How could she explain her desire to know—really know—Raymond Old Fox? It had nothing to do with man-woman things. Words weren't big enough to describe the feeling she had when he introduced her to the falls under the swinging bridge, when he pointed out the red hawk or simply sat without speaking, letting the sound of the roaring falls inundate their senses. "The respect they have for the land and the plants and animals is similar to ours. They have fought against the Englisch for the right to their culture, religion, and even their language."

"They have no religion—"

"That's not true—"

A sharp rap on the screen door stopped Christine from pouring out all she'd learned of the Kootenai beliefs. They would never understand. She didn't even understand. She didn't defend their beliefs, only their right to have them. Did that make her a heathen?

Would God smite her?

Jasper went to the door. A minute later he returned with Bishop David Hershberger in tow.

Fergie's fierce frown said it all. *Now look what you've done.* He hopped up from the couch. "David, gut to see you. What brings you by?"

David nodded at Lucy, who offered him her seat in the straight-back chair near Christine's. "Sit, sit. I'll get kaffi. There's a chill in the air today. You remember my niece Christine, don't you? How's Diana? Are the kinner over their colds yet?"

She flitted around the room like a butterfly, not giving him time to answer any of her questions, and then flitted right out the door to the kitchen.

His expression amused, David said nothing until Fergie settled back on the couch and Jasper stomped up the stairs. "I'm glad you're here. I wasn't sure if you'd still be at the store."

"We had business here at home."

"I thought as much." David had drawn the lot at the young age of thirty-one, according to Aunt Lucy. He was well respected for his even temperament and insistence on prayer before action. He never raised his voice and seemed content with his wife and six children under the age of ten.

Now he stroked his blond beard and openly studied Christine's face. "You're not a member of this district, Christine, but you're living here with Fergie and Lucy, so what you do reflects on them and on us as a Gmay."

"I was just telling her—"

"I heard what you were telling her all the way out at the road." David removed his straw hat and settled it in his lap. His brownish-blond hair lay flat on his scalp. He had a big head for a rather slight man. It made him look top-heavy. "Loud words spoken in anger are rarely heard by the recipient."

With one sentence he'd put Fergie in his place. Fergie's pudgy jowls shook. His vigorous nod acknowledged the critique, but he said nothing.

"This isn't about how it looks to others." David's stern gaze returned to Christine. She fought the urge to squirm. His eyes were a pale brown. "My concern is for you. All of us must be concerned for you rather than ourselves and the discomfort your actions may cause us."

"I don't mean to cause trouble."

"Nee, you don't. Yet your actions reflect a troubled heart and mind." He studied her so hard she felt like a math problem he couldn't solve. He sighed. "What troubles you so much that you seek fellowship with an Indian? Is it the wildfires that upended your world in Kootenai? Or your daed's decision to move back to Haven? Why did you choose to stay here?"

A bundle of questions, none easy to answer. Especially in front of Fergie. "Private matters made me ask for permission to stay here."

"With the understanding that you would abide by your onkel's rules while living in his house?"

"Jah."

"Yet here we are. Again, I ask what troubles you so much? Or is it simply the lure of the unknown or that which is different? A desire to experience the world? A desire that should've died when you were baptized."

The soft delivery of his damning words was far harder to take than Fergie's blustering. The lump in Christine's throat didn't help. Nor the voice in her head that screamed repeatedly, *He's right, he's right. What's wrong with you?*

"I don't know," she whispered. "Restlessness beset me like a bad case of the flu."

"A person can recover from the flu, although a few die from it. The same is true of spiritual malaise." David leaned forward, elbows on his knees, his expression intense. "You may not belong to our Gmay, but you are a member of Gott's family, a child of Gott. I pray for your soul. I pray for Gott to remove the veil from your eyes so you can see the hope and the joy and the contentment you will find if you only lean on Him. We talk about obedience and humility and dying unto self often, and all are necessary, fundamental building blocks of our faith, but that doesn't mean we can't also experience joy in the Lord and contentment, knowing our hope is in Him. Do you understand that?"

"I do. I do." That didn't mean she couldn't imagine finding all those things outside the Amish faith. The thought made Christine's heart race. Her hands went to her throat.

She had chosen to be baptized at eighteen—early by some standards. She'd never considered any other option. To leave her family and friends and never see them again was unfathomable. Not the fire in Kootenai, her father's decision to move her family back to Kansas, not even Andy's admission that'd he once loved another woman changed her bedrock—her faith.

This faith shaped how she saw the world. Not until she met Raymond Old Fox had she given any thought to what others believed or why. She'd simply gone along with her parents and the deacon who taught her class, never questioning their words.

It had been a safe, secure place. In a few short weeks, everything had changed.

"I can see the struggle in your face." Sadness a halo around his head, David gently shook his finger at her. "Don't give up the struggle. Fight through it. If you must study the ways of another people, do it within the confines of your family and faith. Don't run away. Face the restlessness. Persevere through the flu that afflicts you."

He stood and placed his hat on his head. "I expect you at my house two days hence for counseling. Our deacon, Matthew Miller, will sit with us. Gott expects us to fight for the souls of our children. Fight, we will."

"Wouldn't it be best to send her to her parents in Kansas?" Fergie shuffled to his feet. "Let them fight the fight, so to speak."

"Sending her away won't abate the temptations set in front of her. She needs to confront them."

Her life in a nutshell. Two men arguing over what was best for her. At least she didn't have to go to Haven. Mother and Father would be horrified and angry. And she would likely never see her friends in Kootenai again. Or Andy. Or Raymond and Gramma and Tonya.

"You know best." Fergie's tone didn't agree with his words. David simply smiled and nodded.

A tray filled with coffee mugs and cookies in her hands, Aenti Lucy trotted into the room. "Sorry, I had to make a fresh pot of kaffi . . ." Her gaze went from David to Fergie and back. "I brought lemon bars. Aren't those your favorite, David?"

Nodding, David snagged a lemon bar and trotted past Christine toward the door. "I can't stay, I'm afraid. Diana is waiting supper for me. She doesn't ask much, only that I be home for supper." He tugged the door open and then looked back at Christine. "Remember, Thursday, around nine o'clock. Matthew is an eager beaver. He doesn't like to be kept waiting."

"I understand." Christine managed a smile. Her stomach rocked and bile burned the back of her throat, but she still smiled. "I don't like to be late either."

David tucked the entire lemon bar in his mouth and opened the screen door. The muffled words that followed could've been hello or goodbye or neither.

Before the screen door could close, Andy walked in.

CHAPTER 27

St. Ignatius, Montana

Autumn might be cool in Montana, but the temperature in the Cotter house was more winter-like, as in subfreezing and falling fast. Andy waved hello from behind the Plain man who'd been on his way out but turned around and led Andy into the house. He had curiosity written all over his face.

Andy ignored it and focused on the Cotters. "It's me again." Whatever caused the hullabaloo had died down. Lucy and Fergie were all smiles. Christine retreated to the rocking chair by the fireplace, even though it was dark and empty on this fall day. She looked like a rabbit caught between two hungry foxes. No telling what was going on.

Arguing over an old fox, perhaps.

Christine's eyes and nose were red. She wrung her hands and said nothing. This was not a good sign. The urge to go to her warred with the sense that any move right now would be a wrong one. He planted his feet and directed his smile to Lucy. She held a tray of coffee mugs and cookies, for which there appeared to be no takers. "Is everything all right?"

The stranger introduced himself. He had powdered sugar

and crumbs in his beard, and his smile was apologetic. Andy offered up his own name when Fergie failed to complete the introductions. "I'm from Kootenai, but I've been staying near Lewistown awhile because of the wildfires."

A knowing look—mixed with a major dose of pity—transformed David's face. "Then you know Christine."

"Jah." Very well. Or so he had thought. She had changed in the last few weeks, but so had he. He would forgive her transgressions and hope she could do the same. She studied the pine floor as if the answer to all her questions resided in the wood. "I worked with her daed at the furniture store."

"Gut to meet you. I must go before my fraa feeds my supper to the goats."

Quiet reigned for several seconds after the bishop left for a second time. Maybe he had the right idea. "I wanted to stop by to . . . let you know I'm back in town." Andy directed the statement to the space between Fergie and Christine. "I'm waiting for word that we can return to Kootenai. Then I'll move my daed's sawmill operation down there."

"He agreed then." The look of shame and despair on Christine's face dissipated, replaced with a smile. Her delight was encouraging. She cared. Notwithstanding a certain man named Raymond. "He's retiring, is he?"

"He has leukemia. He's being treated at a hospital in Billings."

"I'm so sorry." This time Christine beat her uncle to the words. She didn't look contrite, either. "Do the doctors think he can be cured?"

"They say his prognosis is gut, according to Mudder. Daed doesn't say much of anything about it."

"He is a man." Fergie scowled at Christine. Definitely not in the man's good graces. "We don't complain about our lot in life. The will of Gott be done."

Christine began to rock. The chair squeaked on the floorboards.

"I called our bishop, Noah, in Eureka. He says we are being allowed back into Kootenai in a few days."

"Gott is gut."

"He is." How best to approach this? Fergie wasn't Christine's father, but he was responsible for her while she lived in his house. "I'm staying here until he calls me to say we can get in."

"Why not stay with your family while your daed receives his treatment?"

"I have business here." He didn't look at Christine. He didn't dare. He did have business here, didn't he? It all depended on her. "I also need Ben's telephone number in Haven. He said he would sell his house to me. My parents are helping me with the funds."

"Gut for you." Fergie's expansive smile encompassed Christine. Perhaps he did see where Andy was going with this. He glanced at the clock on the wall. "It's suppertime. Why don't you stay and eat with us?"

"Where are you staying? We have an extra bed in the boys' room," Lucy added. "We can squeeze you in."

"I have a room at the bed-and-breakfast." It might be easier to get a word alone with Christine if he stayed here, but it wouldn't be right. And if she chose to keep her distance still, it would be horribly awkward. "No need to squeeze. But I will accept the supper invitation."

Maybe he'd get a chance to talk to Christine after supper. Or at least let her know he would come by later for a buggy ride. They could court like before. Those days seemed a hundred years ago. They were burned up by the fire, wrecked by the accident, and blotted out by a man as different from Andy as day from night.

Lucy put on a good spread that included chicken-fried steak, baked potatoes, green beans, pickled beets, and hot rolls, followed by apple pie. Conversation around the table centered on the hunting season. Christine's cousin Jasper had bagged his moose, but the others had not.

"I want to go after a black bear now." His gaze on his empty plate, Jasper laid his knife across it and fiddled with the spoon. "Have you hunted bear?"

"Nee. I like elk and moose for the meat."

"You shouldn't hunt anything you can't eat." Christine spoke for the first time. "It's disrespectful to the animal."

Jasper groaned. His brothers giggled.

"Animals don't have feelings." Kimberly, the youngest of the cousins, pursed her lips. "Do they, Daed?"

"Nee." Fergie took a drink of water, but his gaze remained on Christine. His thick eyebrows looked like scraps of gray yarn. "But that doesn't mean we should let them suffer or shoot them for sport. They are creatures of Gott too."

Christine's expression lightened. "Can I get you another piece of pie, Onkel?"

He patted his rotund middle and seemed to examine the question with care. "I believe you can."

"I'll be right back with it." She disappeared into the kitchen.

"Kinner, go finish your chores."

Without a word they pushed in their chairs and tramped out the back door.

Lucy took her cue from her husband. She rose and shooed the girls into the kitchen.

Fergie leaned back and curled his fingers around his suspenders. "I know you're chomping at the bit to ask me something, so ask."

"It's really Christine I need to ask, but I don't want to be a bother to you and your fraa."

"Ah. You're not. Believe me, you're the medicine the doctor ordered or my name's not Fergie." Sighing deeply, he shook a toothpick from a holder on the table and chewed on it. "I should keep my nose out of it. Courting being private and all."

"I appreciate that."

"I'd appreciate it if you'd get a move on before it's too late." He threw the toothpick onto his plate. "I wouldn't say anything, but her eternal salvation is at stake while you hem and haw."

"I'm not hemming and—"

"Here it is. With a scoop of vanilla ice cream." Christine returned with the pie. Two slices in fact. Another one for Andy. His stomach protested but he smiled. She smiled back. Her eyes begged him to understand. "To celebrate you being here."

"Go help your aenti with the dishes." Fergie picked up his fork. "Tell her to wait on the kaffi."

Not even his wife was welcome to this conversation. Andy forced himself to take a bite of the ice cream. The cool creaminess slaked the dry thirst in his throat. "Danki."

"No need to get fancy." Fergie demolished half his pie in one big bite. "The girl is too full of herself as it is."

"I never noticed it."

"Maybe she's changed since coming to St. Ignatius. She's developed a stubborn, rebellious streak."

"That doesn't sound like the Christine I know."

"She needs a gut, strong mann to set her straight."

"Has something happened since we dropped her off after the funeral?"

Fergie snapped his suspenders so hard he must've felt the pain down to his oversized feet. "I'm afraid to tell you for fear you'll want nothing to do with her."

"You've come this far." If he had no desire to scare Andy off, why bring it up at all? "It takes a lot to run me off."

"She's still gallivanting across the countryside with Raymond Old Fox, visiting his people's sacred grounds and such."

"Does it bother you that he's an Indian, or is it because he's a man?"

"I'm not a bigot. No man should call himself a Christian if he harbors feelings of superiority over others who believe differently." Fergie's sudden fervor was impressive. The man might seem all bluster, but he had substance to him after all. "She seems taken with his people's view of the world. Even their lack of faith."

Maybe he'd come too late. Maybe she'd gone too far. "Is that why your bishop was here?"

"Jah. I wanted to send her home to Kansas, but he said no. He wants to counsel her. It's generous of him, considering she isn't from this Gmay."

"I could take her to Eureka, to our bishop."

"We could take her, but she has no family up there."

"She has friends. We—you can be sure they'll be glad to have her stay awhile, just until . . ."

"You've plans to ask her to marry—"

"That's between her and me."

"You're right."

If he hadn't left it for too late.

. . .

If only Andy and Uncle Fergie would speak a little louder. Christine didn't dare edge any closer. Eavesdropping was not a pretty habit. She'd made the excuse of going to the bathroom to leave the kitchen, but she needed to get back. Aunt Lucy might not mind doing the dishes without her, but her cousins did. Work shared was work done quickly.

Andy's tenor was a mere whisper at this distance. She slid back toward the dining room.

One step, two steps.

A hand grasped her shoulder. She jumped, clapped her hands to her mouth, and turned. Aunt Lucy frowned at her. Her gray eyebrows raised over the top of her glasses. "I reckon you forgot about returning to the kitchen to help with the cleanup."

"Nee, I just wanted—"

"I know what you wanted." Aunt Lucy tugged her toward the kitchen. "The girls finished their part. They left you the pots and pans to wash, dry, and put away."

Christine followed her into the kitchen. "I just want to know why he's here."

"I suspect you know why."

"He's been so back and forth, and I don't mean from Lewistown to Eureka and back."

"He's here now." Aunt Lucy plunked two mugs on the counter and poured coffee. "He didn't come to St. Ignatius for the fishing at Flathead Lake."

Christine sank a large saucepan into the plastic bucket of hot, sudsy water that filled the sink. A bubble floated in the air and tickled her nose. "He looks so thin and tired. He's been through a terrible time, what with the accident and his dad's sickness."

And she hadn't made it any easier. She'd failed to be forgiving about a situation that had hurt him terribly. The pain caused by Winona's choice of his brother was so agonizing, he chose to move away from home. To start a new life. No wonder he didn't want to talk about it. Then Christine had reacted just as he had feared she would. "Will you tell him about Raymond?" Aunt Lucy's tart tone left no doubt what she thought Christine should do.

"He knows I've spent time with Raymond. Besides, Andy has nothing to fear from Raymond."

If there had been the tiniest possibility of her feelings growing into something more than friendship and respect, it had dissipated when she saw Tonya. Raymond might not know it yet—or maybe he did—but Tonya had staked her claim. The air around them crackled with the power of an electrical storm about to break overhead on a hot, humid August night.

"Does he really?" The words reeked with skepticism. Aunt Lucy added milk and sugar to the coffee. She offered a mug to Christine. "Does he know you have feelings for another man?"

Christine wiped her hands on her apron and took the mug. She set it on the counter. "Is it not possible for women and men to be friends? To be like brothers and sisters, even if they're not related?"

Lucy's snort clearly expressed what she thought of that sentiment.

In the Plain community the lines were clearly drawn. Husbands, fathers, brothers, uncles, cousins—family, in other words.

So why did Raymond fascinate her? She squinted at the

setting sun that shone through the small window over the sink. His beliefs challenged her to think about her own—something she'd never done before. His view of the world bumped against hers and sent it spinning out of control. For the first time she had to justify—in her own mind—what she believed. Christians had done terrible things to Raymond's people. How could they still be called God's children?

She wasn't supposed to judge them. She should, however, do better. That's what Father would say. She should live her life as an example to others, but it wasn't her job to convert them.

Even if they were headed to hell?

She shook her head.

"Then what is it like?" Lucy sipped her coffee, but her frown had nothing to do with its flavor. "You're shaking your head. What are you thinking?"

Christine added another cookie to the pile as if to sweeten her response. "I wish I knew. I'm confused. I can't unlearn the things I've learned. I don't want to unlearn them. I worry about those who don't know Gott. Is that wrong?"

"It's not your place to worry about them. Gott will deal with them." The frown turned to a scowl. "It is prideful to think you have control over other people's salvation. All we have is the living hope that Gott will deal kindly with us, knowing we have followed Him in all things."

"I know. I know." Christine whispered the words. God must laugh at her hubris. "What have I done?"

"You've let your head—if not your heart—run wild. Time to return to your roots." Her expression kind, Aunt Lucy picked up the saucepan from the counter and dried it. "Do you still have feelings for that man out there, sitting at our table? If you don't, you must tell him. Don't string him along. Men might be big and strong in their bodies, but their hearts are delicate and easily fractured."

Aunt Lucy and Uncle Fergie had been married forever. They had six kids. They were plump and gray. It was hard to imagine them breaking anyone's heart. "How do you know so much about matters of the heart?"

She smiled, but her gaze moved beyond Christine's shoulder to some far, far away place. "We haven't always been old."

"Andy had a special friend before." The words stuck in her throat like week-old biscuits. "One he failed to tell me about."

"Life is like that. None of us is perfect."

If she quoted Scripture, Christine might fall to her knees and throw a tantrum like a toddler. Or not. Time to grow up. "Would it be possible for me to use the phone at the store?"

"Why?"

"I need to talk to Nora and Mercy." Her friends still walked this unfamiliar road on which there were no signposts, no stoplights, no solid stripes. Their parents thought it wrong to speak of such things, but letting them bump around in the dark would surely lead to crashes like the one Christine had experienced in the last few weeks. "They understand. They know how it feels."

"You think your parents don't understand? You think I don't understand? Or the bishop? We do, but you've been raised to know what is right and what is wrong. You have all the words of wisdom you need to hear. Simply do the proper thing."

Aunt Lucy was right. That didn't make it easy. *"No one said it would be easy."* Mammi's sharp voice grazed her ear. Christine stuck her hands in the water and scrubbed a skillet harder than necessary.

"I think it's clean." Lucy tugged the skillet from her. "Scrubbing it won't make you clean. Repent, ask forgiveness, and start fresh while there's still time."

What exactly was she repenting? She hadn't been unfaithful to the man she loved. He, on the other hand, had loved another. Had she been unfaithful to God?

Christine gave up the skillet. She leaned on the counter and inhaled the scent of dish soap. Once nothing had made her happier than washing dishes. Now she needed to clean up her own mess.

If only it were as easy.

CHAPTER 28

ARLEE, MONTANA

R aymond dropped another log on the crackling fire that filled the small cabin with more heat than necessary, but Gramma's wasted, shivering body couldn't be warmed. Nor could the flames burn away the sense of impending grief. The dry wood popped and crackled. It spit anger at him. Only a sense of decorum kept him from spitting back. He rose from a squat and dusted off his hands. He shed the long-sleeved shirt he wore over a white T-shirt.

Across the room, Grandma Velda tugged another blanket over Gramma Sadie. Her ropey skin hung from her underarms as she tucked the faded blue-gray flannel around her mother's chin. She murmured words meant only for the old woman whose deep slumber that bordered on unconsciousness meant she heard nothing.

Raymond turned back to the flames. They leaped and danced. He leaned into the heat and the smell of burning wood, seeking the peace that came from letting go. He must let nature take her course, whether he liked it or not.

"You're so quiet." Velda crept to his side and held out her knotted, arthritic fingers above the fire. "No need to be sad, my son. She's ready to go. Her body is weak. Her spirit longs to be free of it."

"I know."

"Knowing and accepting are two different animals."

"She raised me."

The words weren't intended to cause his grandmother pain. Her smile said she took no umbrage. "She was a force all her own. A good mother to me. A good mother to you. Her work is done."

"You'll feel no sadness?"

"I didn't say that. We mourn for ourselves because we're selfish that way." She shoved skinny wire-rimmed glasses up her hooked nose. "I don't think I have a single bad memory of my mother. Not many can say that. She lived well. She mothered well. She loved well."

"Is that why she never remarried after Great-Grandpa died?"

"Her heart remained full in her love for me and for you and your brothers. She told me she had no room for another man or a need for one."

"And you? You never married again either."

"For me it was different. I never came across the right man after your grandpa died."

"He wasn't the love of your life?"

"He was a hard man. I loved him but he didn't make it easy."

It seemed to run in the family. The women made poor choices when it came to love. "Why didn't you ever tell me about my father?"

"Nothing to tell. Biology doesn't make a man a father."

"Do you know who fathered Vic and Tony?"

"I do."

"Will you ever tell them?"

"If they ask. They seem happy in their ignorance."

Vic joined the Army immediately after high school and married one of the soldiers in his unit. They were stationed in Fort Riley, Kansas. Tony went to trade school and became an electrician. He had a steady girl who trained horses outside of Butte where they lived. Raymond's brothers never rocked the boat. They didn't come home much either. Nor did they express an interest in their heritage.

"You think I should be equally content?"

"I think you are your mother's son. She took after her grandmother."

"And you?"

Grandma Velda peeked over her shoulder at Gramma. "I loved your mother. She was my only child. But I didn't understand her. She was a wild girl. She loved to run like the antelope on the trails and ride horses up the steep inclines. She drove cars the way she rode horses. I always knew . . ."

Her voice choked. She turned away and went to the minuscule kitchen where she dumped coffee grounds in the trash and added fresh coffee to the old metal pot.

Raymond eased into a chair with a ripped vinyl covering on the seat that allowed the stuffing to peek out, and leaned his elbows on the narrow table. "That's the most you've ever said about her to me."

Velda lit a match and held it to the gas burner. The smell of phosphorus mingled with the coffee. It fanned a faint memory. The taste of coffee melded with milk, sugar, and cinnamon. A cigarette burning in a heavy stone ashtray sent smoke signals into the wooden rafters above. His mother held a handful of cards. He sat on her lap. She nuzzled his head with her chin. She had an ace, a spade, and a ten of hearts. The vague remnants of a man's face appeared. White with a dark mustache and beard. He tapped a yellow BIC lighter on the table and laughed.

Mom laughed, too, and slapped the cards facedown on the table. "I fold, you lucky devil."

"*You lucky devil.*"

"She liked to play cards."

"And the stick game. She liked to gamble. She liked to live hard and fast."

"Why?"

"Because her daddy died young and she knew she would too."

"Do you know where my father is?"

Velda reached for a mug on the open shelf over the sink. She froze, her hand in the air. Her face contorted with pain.

"Grandma?"

Without answering she shuffled in fuzzy gray slippers that made a flip-flop sound on the hardwood floor to Gramma's bed. Her hand touched the old woman's cheek. She stroked her neatly braided hair. She kissed her forehead. "Little Runner is no longer here."

A shriek rose in Raymond's belly. It filled his lungs and his heart and his throat. The shriek left no room for air. No room to breathe. No room for his heart to swell and beat. His mouth went dry. He swallowed again and again. He gritted his teeth until his jaw ached.

Without rushing he crossed the room. He kissed Gramma's still-warm forehead. "Until we meet again."

He settled on a stool next to Velda. Her back straight, head up, gaze forward, she began to rock and keen.

Raymond closed his eyes and let her wail be his song.

Time passed. The coffee percolated. The smell, at first aromatic, turned sour and burnt. Finally, Raymond rose. He turned off the gas. The fireplace glowed with embers. He let them die.

"Call your brothers." Velda spoke through stiff lips. Tears stained her wrinkled cheeks, but her eyes were clear. "I'll call the others."

Nodding, he tugged on his shirt and his windbreaker. Anything to escape the heavy grief that pinned his feet to the floor and his spirit to the wall. He shoved through the door into the chilly late-September night where he put both hands on his knees and sucked in cold air until his lungs ached.

Where was Christine tonight? What would she say about Gramma's death? That her days in this world were done? That she wandered through pearly gates and walked streets of gold with a man who once turned water into wine and raised the dead to life?

No. Her spirit swirled and danced with the coyotes on the range. She leaped over gorges with mountain goats. She prowled along streams, pausing to lap up the icy water, a mountain lion on either side of her. She sat on the bough of a larch and gazed at the moon through the snowy owl's sleepy eyes.

The animals gathered around her and howled their welcome.

He straightened and stumbled to the driveway.

The powder-blue Impala sat next to his Volvo, its engine a low rumble. White smoke puffed from the tailpipe. Headlights blinded him.

He hesitated. To speak to anyone at this moment seemed beyond impossible.

The door opened. Tonya's dark head appeared. "She's gone then?"

He nodded.

"I had a feeling." She inclined her head for a second. "Can I give you a ride somewhere?"

"I have my car."

"I know, but you don't want to drive."

Raymond didn't bother to ask how she knew any of this. He grabbed his laptop from his car, climbed into the Impala, and closed the door. Tonya shut hers. For a second neither of them moved. He stared out the bug-spattered windshield at the big orangey moon. How could it continue to welcome the night when Gramma no longer breathed the same air as Raymond?

"She runs faster than the mountain lion now." Tonya zipped up her black leather jacket and whipped her long hair into a quick ponytail. Preparing for something. "She shimmers on Flathead Lake."

"She tastes the stars." He forced the words around the lump in his throat. "She's laughing at my silly tears."

"She was never mean."

"She was always right."

Tonya put the car in gear. "Where to?"

"I don't know yet."

She backed from the driveway, turned onto Highway 93, and drove toward Arlee.

He called Vic first. His middle brother took the news with his usual stoicism. Vic would seek bereavement leave and come when he could. They would stay at Velda's house. Then Tony. His younger brother's voice cracked. He hiccupped a sob. After a murmured conversation somewhere beyond the phone, he returned to say he and his girlfriend would get on the road first thing in the morning.

The task completed, Raymond turned his cell phone into a hotspot and searched his laptop for churches with white supremacist ties in Montana. To think of anything but Gramma's sightless eyes and slackened mouth. The results were scary. They weren't really churches. They didn't worship a deity but their own race. They deified racism and bigotry.

He closed the laptop and tried to breathe normally.

Tonya glanced his way and back at the highway. "What if I feed you?"

He shook his head.

"Do you need to talk to her?"

"Who?"

"Christine."

"No."

"You were thinking of her when you left Sadie's house."

Again, no point in asking how Tonya knew. In the old days she would have been a shaman with Gramma. Together they would have been members of the Crazy Owl Society that warded off epidemics with dances that took them round and round the teepees until their feet left the ground and they ran in the air. "I wondered what words of wisdom she would offer about Gramma's death."

"To them we are heathens." Tonya spat the last word. The car accelerated as if it felt her anger. "Pagans."

"Yet they still pray for us. They long for us to be saved, as they put it."

"So did the Jesuits."

"I don't need to be reminded of our history."

"Would you want to go back to a time when we had no choice but to accept assimilation?"

"Resistance is futile? No."

"Good. Velda will arrange the burial with the elders. We'll look for your father in the meantime."

"Stop doing that."

"Doing what?"

"Reading my mind."

"Well?"

"Stop at a McDonald's. We'll get coffee and I can use their Wi-Fi."

Being a computer nerd had its advantages. Two cups of coffee, an apple pie, and an order of fries later, he'd found Oliver "Cap" Dawson, former boxer, former motorcycle gang member, and former Army MP who spent time in Germany while in the Army. He worked on the railroad, built roads, and hauled lumber. A jack-of-all-trades, master of none. A nomad.

Now he lived between Flathead Lake and Glacier Park in a place called Swan Lake. Strange place for a racist to live—in the midst of all those Indians.

"You found him?" Tonya's sleepy eyes surveyed him. Her words were softened by exhaustion. During his search she'd drunk coffee and filled pages of a journal with a purple ink pen. She wrote in cramped cursive that couldn't be read upside down. "You don't look happy."

"He's close."

"So close we might have crossed paths at the convenience store?"

"Yes."

Tonya scooped up her leather binder and stood. "Let's go."

"It's late."

"No rest for the weary."

"Take me back to my car."

She sighed. Her fingers traced the hummingbird that hovered on the cover of the binder. "You don't know what you want, do you?"

"No."

She leaned down. Her scent of sandalwood enveloped him. Her lips brushed his forehead. "Let me know when you do."

Every nerve in his body vibrated. He cleared his throat. "I will."

"No you won't." Her soft, tender lips deserved better than that sad smile. "I'll have to do all the work, as usual. It's a good thing you're worth it. Come on. You need sleep, and I have to go to work in the morning."

If she said so, it must be true. Whether this half-breed was worth it remained to be seen.

She left him at the Volvo and drove away without further adieux.

Raymond slid into his car. He slammed the door. Slammed it a second time. He laid the laptop on the seat. The tears refused to be ignored. They pounded against the dam in his throat.

He glanced around. No one would see. No one would know. The stars and moon would keep his secret. He rested his head on the wheel and wept.

CHAPTER 29

St. Ignatius, Montana

The thud of the horse's hooves on the dirt road, the soft, cool breeze, and the scent of fresh-cut grass as dusk crept into night created a hazy world that was half memory, half dream. Christine breathed in the late-September air and stared at the stars splashed across a deep-navy night. Could this be real? After everything that had happened. The wildfires. Her parents leaving her to go to Kansas. Andy's revelations about his past love. Raymond's unnerving critique of her faith and the faith of those who ravaged his ancestors.

As if he read her thoughts, Andy pulled up on the reins and steered the buggy into a clearing that overlooked a small pond on her uncle's property. Bullfrogs serenaded them. An owl hooted. Crickets chirped. A perfect night for a romantic ride.

Only this wasn't that.

She cast a surreptitious glance at her companion. He'd said little since the insistent tapping on her window three nights after his unexpected arrival in St. Ignatius had forced her to peek through the curtains and find him waving at her. Like two teenagers new to their rumspringas, they'd slipped away while everyone in the house slept. New lines etched themselves around Andy's eyes and mouth. Dark patches bruised the soft skin under his eyes. A painful twinge in the vicinity of her heart made her wince. "How are you?"

He wrapped the reins around the handle and leaned back in the seat. "Gut. You?"

So it was like that. "Nee. You're not. We can pretend nothing's happened and we're out for a drive on a Thursday evening, no cares in the world. Or we can act like we know each other in a way that others don't."

"It's hard to know what to say. I know my head isn't on straight and the words are all mixed up." He straightened and hopped from the buggy. "If I sit for very long, I'll nod off."

"I'm that boring, then?" She tried out a giggle. He responded with a smile. She jumped down and met him in front of the horse he'd borrowed from his friends at the B&B. "I'm glad you came."

"You're never boring."

"I'm sure after all you've been through you could use a little boring." Shivering in the cool night air, she slid her hand through the crook of his arm and tugged him toward the water that shimmered in the starlight. "I'm sorry I haven't made it easy for you."

"What did the bishop say?"

Her session with David and Matthew had lasted almost an hour—fifty-five minutes too long. In her entire life Christine had avoided trouble. She always toed the line. She always obeyed. A girl didn't get into much trouble cleaning house, washing clothes, and baking bread. Until now when it meant talking to two strangers about something wholly personal and beyond even her own understanding. "David is a kind man. So is Matthew, their deacon. They went over passages from the Holy Bible regarding obedience and humility. 'Blessed are the meek for they shall inherit the earth.' 'Children, obey your parents.' They reminded me of my baptism and my commitment to my faith."

"And what did you say?"

"That I have not forgotten any of this." They had the same perplexed looks on their faces that Andy had now. David suggested Fergie was right to send her home to her parents before her transgressions grew bigger. Trying to hang on to a shred of dignity, she came very close to begging him to reconsider. "I'm not trying to be disobedient. I'm trying to see the world through different lenses while I still have a chance. It was easy to be baptized when I'd only heard one version of the truth."

"There are no versions of the truth. There's what's true and what's not."

"I need time."

"How much?"

"I don't know."

"Because of Raymond?"

"Nee . . . not exactly. Because of what he represents."

"You're in trouble with your onkel and with the bishop because of this man, and yet you persist." In the light cast by the moon, she caught a glimpse of his troubled, wondering expression. "What hold does he have over you?"

She tucked her hands under her arms to warm them. Despite the flush of guilt mixed with bravado, the night chilled her. "It's not him, exactly. For the first time ever, I was on my own, away from family and friends. I was startled by the world."

"Ensnared by it, more likely."

"I'm only a woman, I know, but I'm not stupid."

"No one who knows you would say that." Andy squatted and picked up a handful of rocks on the pond's edge. He stood and tossed the first one into the darkness over the lapping water. "But you used to be more . . . more—"

"Obedient?"

"More as Gott would have women."

Perfectly aimed missiles, the words sliced to the bone. "You think Gott is upset with me for overstepping my place, for no longer being happy with my toilet brush and my mop and my wringer washing machine?"

"I don't know what Gott thinks. My pea brain hurts just trying to understand my own situation. I know keeping my past from you was wrong. I feel that this has somehow added to your determination to strike out on your own."

He felt responsible for her transgressions. Guilt and remorse washed over Christine. "I was hurt. I am hurt, knowing you cared for another woman. But one has nothing to do with the other. Raymond's people are connected to nature. They respect it. I never noticed the plants and trees and mountains the way they do. I'm ashamed to have taken it for granted." She struggled to capture the essence of this new perspective. It was as if she were blind before and could see for the first time. The colors of the sky, the grass, the water, the sun shone so bright she had a perpetual squint. "They love animals and plants. They hunt and fish, but with respect for the animals and fish that they kill and eat. I have never felt . . . whole before. I liked scrubbing toilets and mopping floors because I could do it all on my own with no help. That's prideful, isn't it? Being clean is gut. Dirty is bad. It's so simple and clear. Life isn't like that. It no longer is . . . fulfilling."

"It's not about fulfilling you. The point is to make yourself small and Gott big. Faith, then family, then self."

"I'm not putting myself first." Christine cast about for

something Andy could understand. "Their ancestors were introduced to our Gott by men who used religion for their own selfish, worldly use. That history still follows them. They reject it because it was forced upon them in an ugly way."

"That is sad, but it's not for us to try to right a wrong that is more than a century old."

"Shouldn't we be concerned for their souls?"

"We live our faith by example." He tossed another rock into the void. Harder this time. "Don't try to convince me that your interest is in converting this man to a Christian faith, let alone our faith."

Not convert him but save him. To imagine Raymond consumed in hellfire scared Christine. He was good and kind. Did God not find that appealing? Father would say hard work and kindness propelled no one through the gates to heaven. Only the blood of Jesus did that. However, kindness and industriousness were the fruit of their faith. These values kept them from straying into a world less and less known for either.

It seemed so uncomplicated when the bishop explained it. Now in this world peopled by men like Raymond, suddenly the twists and turns kept Christine off balance. She wanted good people to go to heaven. She wanted them to be saved.

As if she had a hand in it. *Gott, forgive me for being so prideful. So arrogant. So human.*

"I don't want him to go to hell. He's good and kind. I'm trying to understand how it can be right for him and his people to be condemned for something that wasn't their fault."

"Scripture says, 'Enter ye in at the strait gate: for wide is the gate, and broad is the way, that leadeth to destruction, and many there be which go in thereat. Because strait is the gate, and narrow is the way, which leadeth unto life, and few there be that find it.'" Andy's voice softened despite the hardness of the words. He sounded so weary. "The explorers came here and tried to force a life in Christ on the Indians. Maybe their methods were wrong, but their desire to save souls was right. They gave up their homes and their families, like the apostles did, to travel to the wilderness to bring the gospel to people who were in need of salvation."

"It was in the way the message was delivered."

"It happens all the time in this fallen world. You only have to read an English newspaper to see it. Corrupted churches. Preachers who claim faith will give believers wealth and happiness. Preachers who preach hate against those who are different than they are. Churches where pastors have abused children. There's no shortage of stories like the one your friend Raymond tells. Despicable human behavior persists to this day."

"Raymond's ancestors weren't given a choice. They were forced into the church."

"The Jesuits and nuns didn't give them a choice about how they worship. Gott always gave them a choice about what they believed. He invites us all to be a part of His family." This time the rock Andy threw against the water smacked so hard it sounded like glass breaking. "It's up to us to accept or reject His invitation. That's what we do when we're baptized."

Andy had far more answers than David or Matthew, who hadn't given her the chance to frame the questions. They simply assumed her heart had strayed. "How do you know all of this?"

"I've had a lot of time to think about what I believe. What happened with Winona was the start of it. Then John's death. When something like that happens, you either cling to your beliefs or you toss them in the trash. When I was in Eureka,

I stopped to talk to Noah. He, too, has given these questions thought."

Andy let the remainder of the rocks seep through his hands to the ground. He turned to her. "I chose to believe. Trouble has a way of forcing us to keep our eyes on the one true God. I'm praying you'll see that too."

"I want to." She smoothed damp palms against her apron and tried to discern that place where the water met land. Darkness prevailed. "But I'll never stop praying for Raymond and Tonya and Gramma. They are good people. They don't deserve to burn in hell."

Andy's sigh rippled in sync with the breeze that rippled across the pond. "Just when I want to be angry with you, I can't. You have a soft, kind heart. No one will ever tell you—least of all me—not to pray for someone. We are called to pray for non-believers. Scripture says so."

His hand sought hers. His fingers entwined with hers. He bent down, his lips seeking hers. She leaned into his warm body and let go. All the distrust, the uncertainty, and the pain subsided. Thinking of anything but his soft yet demanding lips seemed impossible. She leaned up on tiptoes, wanting more of him. *Don't stop, please don't stop.*

The kiss deepened. He let go of her hands. His fingers moved up her arms, trailed across her neck, and touched her cheeks. She slid her arms around his waist, certain she would sink to the ground if he moved away.

Finally, when breathing no longer seemed possible, he straightened.

Breathless, she opened her eyes and stared at his face in the moonlight. "What was that for?"

"For being you. What happened with Winona would never

happen with you. You think things through. You say what's on your mind. You want to do the right thing, even if it's the hard thing." Andy's calloused fingers brushed tears she hadn't known she'd shed from her face. "I know Fergie and Lucy don't understand. Your daed and mudder won't understand. But I'm trying to understand because I love you."

More tears threatened to spill over. She willed them to stay put. "What happens now? Fergie called my daed."

"What happens now depends on you." He let her hand drop and backed away. "Are you done with Raymond? Are you done seeing the world?"

She put her hands to her warm cheeks. The memory of Gramma's impish grin peeking from the pile of blankets in the back seat of Raymond's car held her captive. "Is it wrong to want to try to share the message of salvation with a woman who will die soon?"

"It's not wrong, but it's not your place."

Wasn't it every Christian's place to win the lost? "She's lived a good life, been a good mother, grandmother, and great-grandmother."

"Being good doesn't guarantee a spot in Gott's house." He climbed into the buggy and grabbed the reins. "Let's go."

She scrambled up the incline. Mud and twigs clung to her dress. Her hands were icy and her head ached. "Please don't be mad at me."

"I'm not mad." His voice cracked. "I'm trying to understand how you can be so ensnared by these people you hardly know. There's a reason we keep ourselves apart."

Christine crawled onto the seat next to him. "I'm sorry."

"Me too."

Fair enough. "What will you do?"

"I received a call from Henry today. He says word is we will be able to return to Kootenai tomorrow or the next to start rebuilding."

"Please take me with you."

"I can't."

"Because you don't want to?"

"Of course I want to." He glanced her way. The battle waging in his eyes made her heart hurt. His gaze returned to the road. "Because Fergie likely won't allow it."

"Jasper can go with me."

"Poor Jasper."

"I know."

His gravelly chuckle held a sliver of humor. He pulled up in front of Fergie's, but he didn't get down. "Finish your business in the world soon."

"Andy, I—"

"You cannot have your feet in two different worlds." He met her gaze head-on. "We both have unfinished business. I need to see John's boys. We need to get our heads on straight. Maybe then we can meet in the middle."

The hope that infused the words stayed with Christine as he drove away. They could still find their way back to each other.

Now she just had to convince Fergie and her father to let her stay.

CHAPTER 30

Using Gramma's death as a reason to miss work seemed wrong when Raymond had no part in preparing for her burial. He need only be present. Vic would arrive toward afternoon, Tony not until later in the evening. They wouldn't need him. Velda would feed them and regale them with stories of Gramma's last days. So Raymond told his boss at S&K the truth. He needed a day off to look for his father. His boss didn't hesitate. Raymond hadn't missed a day's work in two years. Twice he showed up with a fever and had to be sent home. "Do what you need to do. Come back when you're ready."

Such was the advantage of working at a Native-run business. Raymond grabbed more coffee at a McDonald's drive-through in Polson and pushed through to Swan Lake where his research said Cap Dawson rented a duplex half a block from the lake's shore.

The prune-faced Native lady with wrinkles that looked like mountain ridges on a geography map kept digging up weeds in her flower garden while she talked to Raymond. Yes, she'd seen Cap Dawson walking toward the lake an hour or two earlier. He probably went fishing. He liked to fish when he didn't have to lead a bunch of tourists on a hunting or fishing trip.

The tourist season was over. They could all be thankful for that. Blankety-blank tourists driving like idiots, throwing their trash on the grounds and carousing all day and all night.

She kept talking, cursing, and digging, even after Raymond thanked her and started walking away. He trudged across the asphalt road that separated the strip of duplexes from the wedge of bait shops, canoe rentals, outfitters, and other businesses that lived off Swan Lake toward the closest dock. A middle-aged man with the leathery skin of someone who spent most of his life outdoors sat on the weathered planks over the lake, but he had no fishing pole. Instead, he sat with bare feet swinging just above the lapping water, hands empty, expression vacant.

No one sat with him. In fact, only gulls yammering overhead broke the midmorning silence. And the sporadic hum of an engine as a car passed by. No boats cut through the lake's smooth glass surface. The turquoise water shone so brightly it hurt Raymond's eyes.

He hesitated at the top of the dock. Nothing about the stranger seemed familiar. The man coughed, cleared his throat, and spat into the water. He wiped his mouth with his Led Zeppelin T-shirt sleeve and took a swig of a bottle wrapped in a brown paper bag.

Raymond's stomach clenched. He breathed in and out, trying to loosen his jaw. *What am I doing here? Stepping outside my circle.* Doing what Christine had done with him. Opening himself up to the possibility that life could be different. He could be different. He wasn't Native. He was biracial. The blood of a white man ran through him, whether Gramma liked it or not. Whether Velda liked it. The reality could no longer be ignored.

"You gonna say something or just stand there and stare? Didn't your mama teach you that it's rude to stare?"

"Are you Cap Dawson, by any chance?"

The man's face held little interest in the stranger he saw standing a few feet away. Dawson had curiously pale-yellowish-brown eyes and a gray five o'clock shadow that matched bits of hair that stuck out from a red Kansas City Chiefs cap. "As good a chance as any." He chuckled, a sound as abrasive as sandpaper. "Who wants to know?"

"Raymond Old Fox."

No sign of recognition in his face, Dawson turned back to the water. For a long moment he kicked his bony feet back and forth, back and forth.

Raymond shifted his Nikes. Maybe this was a fool's errand. Maybe he should have stayed by Gramma's side as they prepared to put her in the ground. Maybe he was stupid to think he'd find something in this man that he lacked after all these years. Maybe the Native blood ran stronger for a reason.

He turned to go.

"You look like her."

The muscles in Raymond's shoulders tensed. Pain ping-ponged through his brain. He did an about-face. "I'm surprised you remember what she looked like."

"Ouch." Dawson licked his forefinger and sketched a one in the air. "Point for you, Son."

"I don't think you get to call me that."

Dawson leaned to one side of his flat butt and tugged a worn leather billfold from the back pocket of his faded cargo-style camo shorts. With calloused fingers he dug through it and plucked out a faded photo. He held it out.

Raymond hesitated.

"You traveled this far, dude." Dawson stretched his arm up and out. "I don't bite."

"Whatever." What made him act like a rebellious teenager around this stranger? Was it because he never had the chance in those days when Gramma had been the only person who stood between him and juvenile delinquency? He stomped across the dock and snatched the photo from Dawson without touching his grimy fingers. "A photo doesn't change anything."

"Depends on how you look at it. Depends on what the photo is and who took it. Photos have history."

The man might be white, but he was channeling Gramma.

The picture had been taken when Raymond was eight or nine, not long before Mom died. They leaned against her 1999 midnight-blue Dodge Ram. Her long raven hair hung down around her shoulders. Her head thrown back, she smiled as if she hadn't a care in the world. She wore a red embroidered blouse open at the neck so her turquoise-and-silver necklace glinted in the sun.

She was beautiful. He'd forgotten that about her. An equally huge grin on his face, he leaned against her, his head almost to her chest. Her arms were around his neck. His hair hung in his chubby face. His pudgy hands grasped her wrists. He'd been a fat kid who grew into a husky man made into solid muscle by years of playing football and baseball. He looked so young and so happy.

So innocent.

Raymond touched the base of his throat with his free hand. Her fingers had been soft on his skin. The sun shone warm on his face. The breeze picked up and rustled the leaves in the cottonwoods. Just like it had that day. They'd been to the July Fourth powwow in Arlee. She loved the powwow. She loved to dance and play the stick game and eat grilled moose on a stick. They set up tents and slept there three nights. He and his brothers in one. Velda and Mom in another. Gramma insisted on her own because Velda snored. Velda claimed it was Gramma who snored.

Those days were some of the most uninterrupted time they'd spent together as a family. Vic and Tony were there, but only on the periphery of his memory. Who took the photo? Velda? Gramma?

One of the men she dated but never brought home after Tony's dad faded from their lives?

"She sent that to me." Faint surprise scented Dawson's words. "A long time ago. Look at the back."

On the back his mother's loose cursive writing read, "Do you really regret making this boy with an Indian?"

"Did you regret it?"

"Not at the time of conception, no. The only reason she sent it was because she heard through the grapevine about me and the Church of the Creator."

An ugly chill crept up Raymond's spine. "Why would she try to contact you after learning something like that?"

Dawson patted the dock. "Take a load off. I'm getting a crick in my neck."

"Are you sure you want to be seen with a subhuman species such as myself?"

"Hey, man, I disconnected from that garbage a long time ago."

"Because she reminded you that you had a kid with an Indian?"

"No, because I got unstupid. A guy does all kinds of stupid stuff before he gets his sh—his act together."

Why he would choose not to swear in front of Raymond was a small mystery in the midst of many bigger ones. "I know about that." Raymond plopped down on the dock but kept a reasonable amount of space between himself and this stranger who'd given him life.

He handed the photo back. "Why that stupid thing? You had a relationship with a Native. Then you went white supremacist on her. That's a huge leap."

"Is that why you showed up now, after all these years? To find out why your old man was so stupid?"

"She never talked about you. Neither did Gramma. I didn't know until a few days ago how stupid you were—other than doing the disappearing act instead of hanging around with my mom and being a dad to me."

"Thank God for small favors—about the stupid part." Dawson patted his pockets and produced a pack of Marlboro 100s. He took his time lighting one with a silver butane lighter. The stench wafted over Raymond. "I had a motorcycle. I was hanging out with a bunch of bikers. I listened to the wrong people. I was looking for something and I thought I'd found it. Nobody's ever called me a genius."

"I don't understand."

"Neither do I." He shrugged skinny shoulders and took a sip from the bottle. "So what are you doing here? What do you want from me?"

"Nothing."

Anger burned through him. No *How are you?* or *What have you been doing with your life?* No *I'm sorry I wasn't around to give you advice or wop you upside the head when you needed it.* No nothing.

"Spit it out, kid."

"I'm not a kid." Not anymore. "You missed that part."

"You here to bust my chops for being an absentee father? Go ahead. Get it out of your system. I'm tough. I can take it."

The words fizzled like firecrackers, wicks lit, that failed to blow up. Raymond studied the muddied water below their feet. "Like I said before, whatever."

"You drove all the way from Arlee for that? Come on, kid, take your best shot."

"Why didn't you stay?"

"I was about your age when I met your mom." He sucked on the cigarette and let the smoke rush from his nose in a long, steady stream. "I was drinking beer and playing pool in a bar in Polson. She came in with some girlfriends, but I never even saw them. I couldn't take my eyes off her. Legs up to her waist. Tight jeans. *Touch me and I'll break your arm* look on her face."

"I get it. You liked the way she looked."

"She was the only woman I ever loved." He swiveled and leveled his gaze at Raymond. "I tried to forget her. I dated a lot of women over the years. Bedded a lot of women. But your mother was like alcohol and nicotine and weed all bundled into one addictive drug for me."

"Not so it was noticeable."

"She never told you anything about me?"

"Nope. But I was a kid when she died."

"I didn't leave her. She kicked me to the curb."

Just like Gramma remembered it. The puzzle pieces of his life pushed and shoved until they created a painful new picture. "Why?"

"She said we had nothing in common. That hooking up with a white guy was a big mistake. The only good thing to come out of it, according to your mother, was you."

It was Raymond's turn to be silent.

Dawson flicked his cigarette butt into the water. It hissed and sank. Irked, Raymond rubbed his eyes. He should leave. This was a mistake. True, he knew more than he had when he arrived, but at what cost? This man didn't fit any of the images he'd held close to his heart of an imaginary father. Clad in a superhero cap or riding a palomino bareback or saving the world from cancer. A white man, true, but one who appreciated indigenous people enough to fall in love with his mother. And then ran like the wind as far to the other end of the spectrum as he could go.

His mother, on the other hand, didn't see Raymond as a mistake. Half white but all Native at heart. "So you gave up."

"Not without a fight. But between Sadie and Velda, I couldn't get a word in edgewise. I had to seek your mother out on her lunch hour after she went back to work. Or speed in a school zone so she'd pull me over."

His expression pensive, he picked at a scab on the back of his hand. "We hooked up a few more times over the years—in between the guys who fathered your brothers. She always came flitting back to me and then flew away. It was like trying to catch and hold a lightning bug."

"Vic and Tony aren't yours, then?"

"Nope. All Indian."

"So you became a white supremacist?"

"Your mother hurt me like no one else could. I was looking for a way to fill that hole. I got messed up."

Raymond needed to fill a hole too. Did an Amish girl with sapphire eyes and rosebud lips serve as his new church? No, he wouldn't mess with her tender heart like that. "Did you ever find someone else?"

"I tried." His gaze meandered across the lake to the Swan Mountain range. "I tried hard. Tall women. Short women. Chubby women. Skinny women. Married women. Old, young, everything in between. Nothing worked. Adeline was it for me. Then she died and left me with nothing."

"I'm not nothing."

"Adeline didn't want me to have nothing to do with you."

"Because you're white?"

"Because I never grew up. I never amounted to nothing. She wanted better for you."

"What *do* you do?"

"I work for one of the outfitter companies doing guided hunting and fishing trips and horseback-based pack trips into Bob Marshall Wilderness." For the first time his face grew animated. His pale eyes lit up. His smile looked hauntingly like the one Raymond saw in the mirror when he brushed his teeth. "We do two-, three-, even six-day horseback pack trips. People can hike, see wildlife, and do a little roughing it. My favorite is the fishing trips, though. Rainbow, bull, brooks, native cutthroat trout at Swan River."

"Sounds like you found your groove. Your place to be."

"Took me long enough. I can't believe they pay me to do it. It's not actually work. At least it don't seem that way."

Connected to nature, to the animals, and the fish. Maybe a little of Raymond's mom rubbed off on this white man. "So you're happy."

"Content might be a better word. I've stopped beating my head against the wall since your mom died. I realized I lost her a long time ago and I was never gonna get her back."

He didn't sound sad but rather resigned.

"Do you have any other kids?"

"Not that I know of."

Not the same thing, but given his roaming lifestyle, likely accurate. That left Raymond, his half-breed son. "Why did you come to the funeral?"

"I wanted to pay my respects. I wanted to talk to you."

"Velda said no and you just gave up."

"She said to do you a favor and let you grow up in your mama's world. She said a boy like you shouldn't have to straddle two worlds."

"A boy shouldn't grow up without a father."

"I think we can agree on that."

A tiny sliver of light peeked through the darkness that had descended on Raymond when Gramma took her last breath. "I like to fish."

"Yeah?" Dawson's sideways glance was assessing. "I got a boat."

"Yeah?"

"It's not much, but it ain't sunk yet. You could come back sometime, if you want."

"I could." Raymond hoisted himself to his feet. "Right now, I have to go see my brothers. They're coming in for Gramma's burial."

"The old biddy—I mean Sadie—died?"

"She raised me after Mom died."

"Sorry for your loss, kid."

"I'm not a kid."

"Last time I saw you was at the funeral. You were nine or ten."

"Nine."

"You're frozen in time for me."

"I grew up the hard way without my mom or my dad. I'm lucky I had Gramma Sadie and Grandma Velda."

"I know. I'm sorry. I tried to talk to you that day, but Velda wasn't having any of that."

"I know. I saw her shoo you out."

"Chew me out and then shoo me out. She practically shoved me out the door."

"She is strong-minded."

"Other words come to mind."

"I gotta go."

"You'll come back?"

"I'll think about it."

Dawson dug another cigarette from its package. The cellophane crackled. "I'll be here."

"If those cigarettes don't kill you first."

"Worried about my health?" He grinned for the first time. He had a gap between his two front teeth, the way Raymond had before the tribal dentist fitted him with braces that Gramma claimed cost more than her first house. "Now I know you're hooked."

"Whatever."

His father's cackle followed him up the dock and across the street.

CHAPTER 31

EUREKA, MONTANA

Facing an angry grizzly empty-handed would have been easier than this. Despite a cool morning breeze, sweat dampened the armpits of Andy's shirt. He wiped his boots on the welcome mat a second time, inhaled, and blew out air. John's wife and sons lived in a neat two-story, redbrick house on a quiet street near downtown Eureka.

His decision to return here to see them seemed a rash one in the light of day. His unfinished business meant forging a relationship with John's family now that John was gone. His sons would need men in their lives. Madison would think that he showed up because he needed a place to stay while in Eureka.

Caleb Hostetler had offered him a bunk bed in the RV he'd borrowed. *Danki, Gott, for provision.* Maybe Henry would be there. He'd been staying at the Clemson house since the evacuation. More likely, his cabin roomie was at work at the taxidermy shop.

Stop procrastinating. Get it over with. Best to rip the bandage off. Don't be a coward.

Some pep talk.

He'd told Christine he had unfinished business. Just as she did. He had to be there for John's boys. She had to talk to Raymond Old Fox. Only then could their journey continue. Andy closed his eyes. Heat flooded his body. The feel of her lips on his was as real as the cool morning air on his cheeks. Could they meet in the middle? She couldn't be the simple Plain girl who cleaned houses. The experiences in St. Ignatius had changed her. John's death had changed him. The question was whether the changes had been for good or for bad. Was he a better man for his suffering? Was she a better woman for having known a man named Old Fox?

The memory of Christine's anguished face as she spoke of her concern for the woman she called Gramma flooded him. She had a soft heart for others. A loving heart. Andy loved her more for that, not less.

Could she feel the same for him?

Thy will be done, Gott.

"Andy? What are you doing standing out here?"

Startled, he jerked back a step and opened his eyes. Madison peeked through the half-opened door. "I thought I saw a van pull up and drop you off, but you never knocked."

"I was thinking."

"I see." Her tone said she didn't really. "Would you like to come in?"

"I don't want to intrude."

"Please do. I'm going crazy in here. I should be boxing up John's things for the Goodwill Store, but I keep stopping to reminiscence over each rip and every stain and when I bought that black bomber jacket for him for Christmas or when he wore that gray suit to my sister's wedding. The Colorado

Rockies T-shirt he refused to throw away because he wore it when I was in labor with Derrick."

She put her hand to her mouth as if to staunch the flow of words. Her eyes filled with tears.

Andy understood a little. Plain folks' clothes were all the same and, as such, held little sentimental value. Still it hurt when they gave away their dead loved ones' possessions to those who could get some use out of them. No sense in keeping them when they could be put to practical use. It felt like losing those loved ones all over again. "Is Henry around?"

"You came to see him?"

"No, no, I just wondered." Wondered if his presence would ease this awkward, painful encounter. "I haven't talked to him since the funeral."

"He's at work. Having him around has been nice, though. The house doesn't seem so empty." She motioned Andy in and closed the door behind him. "He's handy. He helps out with things I always counted on John to do." Her voice quivered. She stopped talking.

Andy followed her into the dining room where three closed boxes sat on the floor. A fourth one sat open on a chair. Madison ran her hand through silver-streaked brown hair that curled around the collar of her long-sleeved blue turtleneck. "Sorry for the mess. I thought it would help not to have so many reminders around."

Never mind that she had three boys who were the spitting image of her husband to remind her each day of what she'd lost. Andy focused on the woman in front of him and not the room where he'd eaten many hot, home-cooked meals with his English friend. "It's okay. I wondered if there was some way I could help." Searching for the words he'd practiced on the long drive from St. Ignatius, he found only bits and pieces of the speech remained within reach. "I don't think I told you how sorry I am."

"Thank you." She sank into a padded chair at the slick cherry dining room table. She snatched a tissue from a box that sat between them and wiped her eyes with almost angry swipes. "Sit down, please. I actually wanted to talk to you."

Unease tickled his spine. He pulled the chair out but couldn't make himself sit. He gripped the back with both hands and hung on as if the chair served as a raft on stormy lake waters. "If there's anything I can do to help, I want to do it."

"I wondered . . . did John say anything . . . about me or the kids? I mean, was he conscious?"

"I'm sorry." Andy's legs wobbled. Better to sit than sink to his knees. He slid onto the chair and laid both hands, palms down, flat on the table. "He went quickly. By the time I understood what had happened to us, he was already gone. Praise God, he didn't suffer."

Madison nodded once, hard. She crumpled up the tissue and tossed it into a growing pile. "John never said much to people about his faith, but he was a solid believer. I take comfort in that."

She tucked her hair behind her ears. Tears trickled down her smooth peaches-and-cream skin. "Sorry. I keep thinking I'm done with the tears, but the spigot won't turn off."

"I'm sorry too."

"It wasn't your fault. I know you think it was, but John would've laughed at that. He did a lot of driving. He said the odds would catch up with him sooner or later. I wanted it to be later, that's all."

"We all did."

"Let me get the boys. They'll want to say hi."

Andy sucked in air and held it. During the many suppers he'd eaten at the Clemons table, the boys had plied him with questions about the Amish way of life. They played pranks on each other, burped the alphabet, and argued over the last biscuit. John egged them on to Madison's pretend disgust. She said she prayed for patience and God gave her four boys, including a husband who never grew up.

Would they remember those good times or only that moment when Madison gathered them—probably in this very room—to tell them their father had died in a car wreck while driving Andy to some unknown destination?

Madison returned a few minutes later with Johnny Junior, Logan, and Derrick. None looked happy to see him. Johnny's truculent stare showed no sign of recognition before he returned to the cell phone in his hand. Logan didn't make eye contract. Derrick had a laptop under one arm and a can of Coke in his other hand. He couldn't seem to decide whether to drink or open the computer.

"Hi, boys."

"Hey." Derrick, at least, responded.

"Boys!" Madison's stern stare elicited grunts from the two older boys. "Johnny, put the phone away or I'll take it. Get Andy a cup of coffee. Logan, bring out a plate of those cookies I brought home yesterday. Then I want all three of you to sit down and have a civilized conversation with our friend."

"He *was* dad's friend."

There was no denying the past-tense emphasis. Logan jammed his hands in his pockets and glowered at the gleaming wood laminate beneath his Nikes.

"He's our friend, and he's come to see how we're doing."

Johnny's head snapped up. His chestnut eyes, so like his father's, pinned Andy to the wall. "How do you think we're doing?"

"Bad."

"Yeah." Johnny spun around and headed for the kitchen. Logan and Derrick trudged after him.

"Forgive them. It's been rough. They idolized their dad."

"He was my friend." Andy cleared his throat. He couldn't tell even John's wife that he felt closer to her husband than to his own father. "We talked about going into business together when he drove me to Lewistown after the evacuation. He took me to your sister-in-law's house when things weren't going so good at my parents'. I can imagine how much worse it is for them."

"Thank you for being so understanding."

"You're the one who's understanding."

Johnny and his brothers returned with the coffee and cookies. They served them in silence, but Derrick's gaze kept sliding across the table to Andy's and then back to his can of pop.

Andy accepted the steaming cup of coffee with a generous splash of milk and two store-bought chunky chocolate chip cookies served on a paper napkin. His heart churned painfully inside his chest. The memory of John's bass singing a country song about driving his brother's truck banged around in his head. He sipped the coffee in hopes that it would drown the lump in his throat.

He forced himself to level his gaze on Derrick, who settled into the closest chair with three cookies in front of him. "Your dad was thinking about taking you boys fishing when he got back to Eureka."

Johnny snorted. Madison glared. "No amount of grief excuses bad manners. Let Andy talk."

"People show they care in different ways, I reckon." Talking about this stuff landed on Andy's worst nightmare list. "John liked to fish with you guys because spending time with you made him happy."

"Hunting, fishing, camping, horseback pack rides with his boys." Madison smiled despite eyes wet with tears.

"And his girl."

"Being with his family made your dad very happy." She grabbed another tissue and wiped her nose. "He went through some bad stuff in the Marines. He never talked about it, but it changed him. He needed to be out in the open. He didn't like being in small spaces. Sleeping under the stars was his dream life."

Johnny crumbled up his cookie and picked out the chunks of chocolate. He didn't eat them. "My favorite time was the two weeks we spent backpacking in Yellowstone."

"I liked riding the rapids on the Colorado River," Logan added. "Remember when we went over that really bad patch and I fell out of the raft and Dad jumped in? He grabbed me and dragged me to shore."

"Good times." Johnny grinned for a second. "Mom said she got all her gray hair from that one trip."

"I like fishing at Lake Koocanusa," Derek offered. "It's close and we could do it anytime. It didn't have to be a special occasion. We could pick up and go any weekend."

"That's what I was thinking." Andy waded into deep water. "I was thinking maybe we could go fishing in your dad's honor."

"When?" Derrick and Logan asked at the same time. Johnny's morose expression had returned, but he didn't say no.

"Today. This afternoon."

Madison tapped the table with nervous fingers. Her eyes welled with tears. "We haven't been apart since the funeral. I haven't even made them go back to school."

"You could come with us."

Shaking her head, she pointed at the boxes. "I promised myself I would finish this today. I can't take much more looking at these boxes and knowing what's in them."

"Then let me take the boys off your hands for a few hours. We'll bring you home some fresh trout."

"A memorial fishing trip?" She rubbed her hands over a green cardigan with a hole in one sleeve as she murmured the words. "John would like that. What do you boys think?"

"I like it." Derrick gobbled down the last of his cookies and swallowed. "Dad would like it."

"Johnny?"

Johnny pushed the chocolate chunks around the napkin in a circle. His head lifted. He stared at Andy. "It's better than sitting around here."

Logan burped so loud Andy jumped. All three boys laughed. Johnny fist-bumped his younger brother.

Madison sighed and rubbed her eyes.

It was a start.

CHAPTER 32

Any man worth his salt knew fishing had medicinal qualities that couldn't be quantified. Better than anything that
came out of a bottle. Casting a line into the crystal-clear, blue-
green waters of Tetrault Lake on a brilliant sunny day caused
wounds to begin to heal, even when a person didn't want to let
go of the punishing pain.

Andy settled onto a log embedded into the sandy shore-
line and rummaged through the shiny, fluttery lures in the kit
he'd purchased at the bait shop on Highway 37 on their way
out of Eureka. He paused to watch Johnny argue with Derrick
over whether a Panther Martin lure with its blue-silver pattern
would snag a trout before the younger boy's Fish Creek spinner.

Logan, the middle child, always eager to spur them on, suggested a contest to see who caught the first trout and who
caught the most. The first winner handed off his duties to clear
the table, load and unload the dishwasher, and take out the
trash for a week. All chores assigned to the kid who caught the
most fish would be divided between the two losers for a week.

"You had the right idea." Henry squatted next to Andy and
worked to untangle the six-pound line on his small reel. "Even
if you didn't have the guts to go solo with them."

"I don't know what you're talking about."

"You wanted to do penance by spending time with John's sons, but you weren't sure you could handle it alone." Henry yanked on the line, which only served to knot it further. "That's why you invited me."

Henry wasn't far from the truth. When he walked into the house after his boss decided to close the shop and go hunting with his retired buddies, Andy had been nearly faint with relief.

"I invited you because I haven't seen you since the funeral." Andy chose a small lure he hoped had the necessary qualities to interest a largemouth bass. Or any of the numerous trout that lived in this small lake four miles northwest of Eureka. "And I needed your buggy."

Henry settled back on his haunches and laughed. "They got a kick out of riding in a buggy, didn't they?"

"It was gut to see them laugh."

"Rough going at the house?"

"Jah. Madison doesn't blame me, but they do."

"They're young. They have a hard time seeing death the way we do."

They weren't Plain, Henry meant to say, but Andy was, and he still had trouble closing his eyes at night when John's empty face reappeared in his brain. His head lolled. Blood dripped from his nose and the corner of his mouth.

How could a man be giving advice one minute and be dead the next? Where was God's plan in that?

"I can see the gerbil going round and round on the wheel in your head." Henry grabbed the lures and picked a spinner for his now detangled line. "You look troubled, my friend."

"Trying to find Gott's plan in all this."

"You mean John's death *and* your troubles with Christine?"

Andy had managed a three-sentence summation of the situation in St. Ignatius at Henry's insistence on the ride out to the lake. "We're not to worry. We're not to fear. That's faith. Is mine so rinky-dink that I throw my hands in the air and fall to my knees, questioning God's sovereignty?"

"I see a man still putting one foot in front of the other." Henry paused in his trial-and-error practice flicks of the wrist. "I don't see a man who has given up."

"I held a dead friend in my arms."

"That would shake any man."

Andy stood. Henry did the same. Together they trudged to the water's edge. The smell of decaying leaves and mud scented the air like sweet perfume. Andy inhaled. His shoulders relaxed. The lap of the water against the shore provided background music. Bullfrogs chorused. Nature had its own kind of healing medicine. His hand tightened on the rod.

Christine's words about the Kootenai and their spiritual connection to nature came back to him. *"I didn't recognize the connection we have to nature. We take that for granted. The Natives don't. They see themselves as part of nature. Their spirituality—what we would call faith—is intertwined with animals and trees and plants and birds. It made me see all those things differently. We're knitted together with nature, but we don't acknowledge it or give nature her due."*

Giving nature "her" due meant giving God his. God created the heavens and the earth, the plants and the trees, the wild animals, the livestock, the birds, and the fish, and every creature in the sea. That's where Andy parted ways with Raymond. And it's what he should have said to Christine. What he would say whether she decided to come back to him or go her own way.

"'My soul, wait thou only upon God; for my expectation is from him.'" Henry whispered the words so softly, they sounded like a gentle breeze in Andy's ears. "'He only is my rock and my salvation: he is my defense; I shall not be moved.' Psalm 62:5–6."

"Now you are a scholar of the Bible?"

"Nee. I was married once."

Andy stopped midcast. He allowed his arm to slowly fall. "You never mentioned it."

"No point in it. She died in a buggy accident in Munfordville, near where I'm from, only months after we married. Like you, I came for a new start."

"Not like me. The woman I cared for chose another."

"Anyway, I, too, questioned God's plan. My bishop told me if my faith was based on my ability to understand, I either had to understand everything—which isn't going to happen—or be tormented by my anxiety when I couldn't understand."

"Those are my only two options?"

Not much of a scriptural pep talk.

"Peace is found in trusting Gott. That's what faith is. Trusting even when you don't understand. He's in control of the chaos. It doesn't have to make sense to us. It does to Him."

Andy cast his line with the flick of his wrist. "I talked to Noah. I'm not sure it helped, but it was worth a try."

"I didn't even think of it. Instead, I considered giving up my faith. I lay on the bed I shared with Vivian and stared at the ceiling for days and nights. The bishop came to me. He grabbed my arm and jerked me upright. He said enough is enough. Get up and start again."

"And you did."

"Finally, but I'm saying instead of giving up, you went to

see Christine. You came here and got these boys. You're on the right track."

Wood ducks squawked in the distance. Ospreys huddled together on the distant shore. Blue jays jabbered. A Cooper's hawk dipped close to the water, then soared away. "Maybe."

"For sure."

"I caught one. I caught one." Derrick tugged his line back. It bulged in the middle.

"Reel him in. Come on, buddy, you can do it!" Johnny rushed to help his little brother. Logan jumped up from his perch on a fallen trunk. Together he and Johnny cheered Derrick on until he landed a medium-sized cutthroat trout.

"Nice." Henry helped hook it onto the line they'd fixed for this purpose. "I bet he weighs at least four pounds. That's some good eats."

"I got the first one!" Derrick danced a jig around his brothers. "No cleanup for me. One whole week."

"Lucky dog." Logan picked up his rod. "Just remember, you'll be doing my chores for a week when I catch the most total fish."

After that they all concentrated on fishing. After all, that was the point. To let go of the anxieties, the difficulties, the grief, if only for a few hours. The next fish went to Johnny, a small rainbow trout. After that they could've been the disciples fishing on the Sea of Galilee after Jesus gave them a helping hand. They caught eight trout, one after the other, and two largemouth bass. All eating sized.

"Let's fire up the Coleman and grill these babies." Johnny high-fived Logan, who pivoted and fist-bumped Derrick. All three had sun-kissed freckles on their noses and grins that produced sizable dimples. They looked so much like John—

except for the dimples, which came from Madison. "Did you bring chips and dip? I'm starving."

Fishing did tend to produce hunger. All that fresh air and exuberance.

"Help me get the cooler and the stove from the buggy." Andy started up the incline toward the parking lot. The boys trailed after him while Henry stayed firmly planted with his line in the water. He'd caught the smallest number of fish—a measly two rainbow trout. "Your mom contributed a big package of those circus animal cookies with the sprinkles on them. I like those—"

Madison's blue Traverse pulled in next to the buggy and stopped. Why would she drive all the way to the lake? It didn't have to be bad news. Maybe she changed her mind and wanted to fish. Andy charged ahead. No need to speculate. She shoved open her door and waved.

"What's up? Is everything okay?"

"Sheriff Brody called. He knows Henry is staying at the house." She smiled. Seeing her smile was the icing on the cake of an afternoon on the lake with her three boys. "You can go home." Her smile wavered. "I mean, you can get back into Kootenai to start rebuilding. The evacuation is lifted."

Andy halted. He let his head hang for a few seconds. *Danki, Gott. One step at a time. One foot in front of the other.*

"Does that mean we have to go right now?" Derrick kicked at the gravel with a dirty sneaker. "We can't grill the fish?"

"No way." Andy opened his eyes and grinned. "We're celebrating. You should join us, Madison. We have enough trout for an entire Plain family."

"I'd love to." She pointed her thumb toward the SUV. "I was

hoping you'd say that. I brought Ben & Jerry's ice cream to celebrate—all the boys' favorite flavors."

The hooting and hollering of John's boys followed Andy down the incline as he went to tell Henry the good news. It sounded like a hallelujah chorus.

CHAPTER 33

St. Ignatius, Montana

Christine mopped in time to the *chug-a-chug-a-chug* music provided by the wringer washing machine in the laundry room next to Aunt Lucy's kitchen. The lovely scent of bleach and clothes soap tickled her nose. Juliette would call it aromatherapy especially designed to help her clean-freak friend relax. The muscles in Christine's shoulders did seem to respond to the combination of scents and sounds and the mopping motion. They served as her best medicine rolled into one.

The lump in her throat refused to dissolve, no matter how hard she scrubbed the countertops in the kitchen or how thoroughly she wiped the baseboards in the living room on her hands and knees. According to Jasper, Andy had left the bed-and-breakfast. Her cousin didn't know if he went back to Lewistown or on to Eureka. And she had no way to find out. Uncle Fergie forbade her to leave the house, except for church. She didn't dare ask to go to the store to use the phone.

Although . . . the other unspoken exception was courting with Andy. Her muscles turned to mush every time she relived that moment Andy kissed her with such gentleness by the pond. His face as he said those words "meet in the middle."

How could she take care of her unfinished business while confined to this house and its yard?

Christine stuffed the mop in the bucket with more force than necessary. She went to the refrigerator and removed a covered tub containing some largemouth bass Jasper had brought in after an impromptu early morning fishing trip. Tonight's supper. She planned to bread it in a spicy panko and pan-fry it. That the rank smell of fresh fish didn't bother her spoke volumes. Raymond would be proud. She chopped off the heads, slit the bodies open, and removed the guts.

Danki, Gott, for this bounty of food. Raymond's ancestors hunted and fished for food. Not for sport, but to provide for their families. There was honor in their hunting. She leaned into the work. The fish still stank. But she had changed. If only she could tell him how the time spent with him had changed her.

She laid the glistening fillets on a clean plate and covered them with plastic wrap. The guts went into the trash. She would take it out to the barrel between trips to hang the laundry. The scent of a fresh round of cleanser on the countertop cheered her. When all else failed, cleaning kept a body occupied.

The *chug-a-chug-a-chug* stopped. Christine went to work wringing out the clothes into the rinse sink. The machine did all the work, but her body ached. The tension returned tenfold. Andy was right. She couldn't live with her feet in two different worlds. She loved—yes, loved—talking to Raymond. She loved spending time with him. She loved the way he loved the natural world.

But she didn't love him—not like that. She was not a biblical scholar, by any means, but some things she understood.

Scripture said if anyone doesn't love his brother whom he has seen, he cannot love God whom he has not seen. She loved Gramma, and she'd only met her once. Tonya might require more work, but she was fascinating. She would be worth getting to know. The whirlwind of emotion she felt when she saw Raymond had more to do with the fire, the evacuation, and the first heady taste of freedom in the world that came because of them. She'd have to be dense not to see that.

Gott, help me.

Three simple words were all she could muster. She snatched up a basket, heavy with wet dresses, and marched out to the backyard clothesline. There she inhaled the smell of autumn and wrestled with one of Aunt Lucy's voluminous dresses. The breeze caught it so the wet material flapped in her face like a slap.

"Okay, Gott, I get it." She pinned the dress with two wooden clothespins to the rope line. "I have a brain the size of a peanut, but I'm not completely stupid."

What exactly did she get?

That she needed to return to her roots, to cleaning houses and taking care of babies and planting vegetables and canning fruit? That was her people's connection to God's creation.

There was more than one way to peel an apple.

Only then would she know how to clean up her messy life.

A shrill honk made her jump and drop her cousin's lilac dress in the grass. She grabbed it and turned toward the road. A dusty white van pulled into Uncle Fergie's gravel-and-dirt driveway that led to the barn where he housed his buggies and horses.

The front passenger door opened. Father emerged. A second later, the middle door slid open. Mother.

For the first time in weeks, the enormous boulders of uncertainty and insecurity on Christine's shoulders teetered. She shrugged. They fell away with a silent thud. "Daed! Mudder!" She dropped the dress in the basket and scurried toward the gate. Mother beat her to it. She shoved the gate open and held out her arms. The hug felt like heaven.

Mother's arms dropped, and she took a step back. Her forehead furled, and she shook her head. "You look tired, Dochder, and thin."

"It's only been three weeks."

"Busy ones, apparently." Her father approached at a more dignified pace. "According to Fergie."

"I'm so sorry. You didn't need to come all the way back because of me."

"We did." Father's fierce growl accompanied his frown. "Fergie's concerns are real, there's no doubt in my mind. He wouldn't have called us otherwise."

"I know. I only meant to say, I've been staying home, cleaning and cooking and watching the babies."

She had no choice because Andy had left and Raymond had made no attempt to contact her since their trip to the medicine tree. Something had happened at the tree. Something they didn't want to talk about with a stranger. Since then, complete and utter silence had reigned.

"After Fergie's bishop got involved—"

"Let's go inside and talk there." Mother took Christine's arm. "I'm glad to see you, Dochder."

She stopped short of saying she'd missed Christine, but everything about her reddened eyes and watery smile said as much. Christine hooked her arm through Mother's, and together they trudged into the house, Father a few steps ahead.

There she busied herself making coffee and cutting pieces of her fresh-baked cherry pie for them. She asked about the rest of the family. Mother answered while Father sipped his coffee and stewed in the chair across from her. Everyone was fine. The children liked Kansas. They liked playing with their cousins. They'd settled in at the new school, and they liked their new teacher. She wasn't Mercy, but she would do.

"Enough chitchat." Father interrupted Mother's detailed description of the birthday party they'd given for Grandma. "How could you stray so far from everything we've taught you? Sneaking out to travel across the country with an Indian."

His tone and the words stung. Christine took a breath and said the first thing that came to mind. "He's a Native."

Not the right response. "I don't care what you call him. He's not Plain, and you're not sixteen and on your rumspringa. We left you here with Fergie because we believed—wrongly—that you would be no trouble to them. We thought you would be getting married soon. What of Andy? How could you treat him so poorly?"

The torrent of words poured over her, scalding hot and blistering in their disgust for her behavior. She opened her mouth and stuttered worse than Esther Marie. "I just, I-I-I wanted—"

"This isn't about what you want." Father smacked his hand on the pine table. His mug shuddered and coffee spilled down the side. Grimacing, he sopped it up with a dish towel. "It's about what's right, what's decent, and what's acceptable. What has happened to your faith and your obedience to the Ordnung?"

"I didn't think—"

"Nee, you didn't."

"Ben." Mother slid her hand over his. "Give the girl a chance to speak."

"I don't need her excuses," he growled. "We've come to take her home."

"Nee." Shame mingled with fear and rebellion. After all she'd done and all the repercussions, she still rebelled. How could that be? Had she not learned her lesson? Her rebellious soul wanted to be in the only home she'd ever known—Kootenai. Her portion would be a punishment that took her away from her friends and from Andy, the man she loved. "I'm sorry. I don't want to leave Montana. It's my home."

"It's not about what you want. It's about what's best for you." Father tugged his hand from Mother's. He stood and paced the floor like a caged mountain lion. "You can't be trusted to make gut decisions. You still need your parents' supervision. This does not make me happy. I've failed as a parent."

"You'll like Haven." Mother picked at remnants of the pie-crust with her fork. "They have a goodly sized group of young people your age. They have singings regularly. It's a bigger group than we have here."

Translation: more single men of marrying age. "I'm not interested in singings. Andy and I are trying to work things out. He will return to Kootenai. So will my friends Nora, Mercy, and Juliette."

"Juliette was never a gut influence." Father tossed aside her feelings like so much garbage. "Why would Andy bother with you after what you've done?"

"He's trying . . ."

Mother's slight shake of the head reminded Christine of her mother's advice during her teenage years. *"Never argue with Daed when he's angry. Wait to talk to him when he has cooled off."*

"I'm sorry, Daed, Mudder. Truly I am." The quiver in her voice gave her away. She swallowed tears and cleared her throat. "I never meant to shame you. I only wanted to learn more about St. Ignatius's history. It seemed harmless."

"Maybe at first, but when you started sneaking around to spend entire days alone with a man—an Indian—you knew. Maybe you lied to yourself about it, but you knew what you were doing went against everything you've been taught."

Father was right. She'd always known that, but she'd weighed ignorance of the world against being able to see how her faith and beliefs held up when compared to those of people like Raymond. Father would never understand that. He preferred to put his head down and his shoulder into the task of living up to the cornerstones of their faith—obedience, humility, and Gelassenheit—dying to self.

"I promise to do better."

"You will because you'll be in Haven—"

A door slammed somewhere in the recesses of the house. A few seconds later Uncle Fergie trotted into the kitchen. Aunt Lucy followed close behind. Their faces creased in broad smiles.

"You're here. That was a quick trip." Fergie clapped Father on the back while Lucy went to Mother. The two sisters hugged long and hard. "I was hoping you would be. I have news. My friend in Eureka called. The evacuation has been lifted. People can return to Kootenai. I thought you'd want to know."

"We can go home." Christine stood so quickly her chair fell over with a bang. "Please, let's go home."

"Kansas is our home now." Father shook his finger at her. "It's your home."

"Ben, let's take some time and think about this." Mudder rose from the table and went to him. Her placid face filled with such love Christine couldn't look away. "Shouldn't we make a trip to Kootenai to see the condition of our property? We have furniture to pick up, and we need to prepare it for sale, anyway. Shouldn't we help the people who have been our neighbors for the last twenty years to rebuild?"

Daed stood very still, as if mesmerized by his wife's voice. No one else moved or spoke. Finally, he drew a breath and nodded. "I'll pray about it." His gaze wandered to Christine. "No promises."

Prayer was good. It allowed for a sliver of hope to remain.

CHAPTER 34

ARLEE, MONTANA

Little fanfare accompanied the burial of Sadie Runabout. Gramma wanted a plain pine box and a hole in the ground next to the one that held Great-Grandpa Runabout in the Jocko Valley Cemetery. That's what they gave her after a service at the Arlee Community Center.

The sun broke through woolly clouds, making Raymond squint. His eyes burned from unshed tears. His clenched jaw ached. Not even the northerly autumn breeze cooled his face. It rustled the leaves on the faded plastic flower arrangements left on simple graves in rows beyond a small white church.

Gramma had never gone back to church after those years at the Mission school. What would Christine say about that? Did Gramma burn in hell because she rejected the white man's Savior? Did it matter that white men caused her disbelief?

He shrugged off his unease and focused on the mountains in the distance. They beckoned. *Come away from that sad little place.* Heat in the middle of his chest throbbed and spread. He wanted to rip off the black jacket he wore over a long-sleeved white shirt and blue jeans. He edged away from the throngs of tribal members who'd gathered for the burial. Later they would have food and stories at Velda's, where they would play cards and reminiscence about a much-respected elder who'd gone on to the spirit world after a long, honorable life.

His stomach heaved at the idea of food. He gritted his teeth and picked up his pace toward the road that held a long line of cars, including the Volvo. He'd run it through a car wash in Gramma's honor and discovered that one of the windows leaked.

"Raymond. Wait."

One of his brothers called. He turned back to see Vic striding toward him. The middle child, the stoic one, the most aboriginal in looks. Nothing of his mother could be seen in his face, so he must have the attributes of an unknown father. As kids they'd never talked about their fathers. How could that be? Like it was a taboo topic. Raymond drew a line in the dirt with the toe of his good boot while he waited for Vic to speak.

"Are you going back to Velda's?"

"I don't think so." Raymond cast about for an excuse but could find none that would be deemed acceptable. "My stomach is a wreck. I might go home."

Not a lie. His stomach had been messed up since his visit to Swan Lake. It lurched at the idea of going home to his solitary one-bedroom, one-bath apartment over a garage on a dead-end street in Arlee, but time spent with a bunch of people rehashing Gramma's life did nothing to make it feel better.

"Me and Janie are going back tomorrow. Our bereavement leave will be up." Vic jerked his head toward his wife, a pretty dark-haired Native with a voluptuous body and light-green eyes. She had propped herself against their Jeep Cherokee with the dazed look of a person who'd talked to too many strangers in one twenty-four-hour stretch. "It's a long drive and her stomach has been bothering her too."

A goofy grin on his face belied his words and their meeting spot in the middle of a graveyard. Raymond studied him. "What aren't you telling me, little brother?"

"We're expecting. It's early. That's why we haven't told anybody." The goofy grin stretched across his face, then disappeared. "I was hoping Gramma would stick around long enough to meet her grandson."

"It's a boy?" Raymond asked as he folded Vic's skinny body into a hug. The guy never gained weight. He was three inches taller than Raymond but weighed less. "Congratulations."

"I don't know. Just a feeling." Vic let go and backed away. "Anyway, I'm reupping when my contract's up."

"I thought you were coming home." Raymond's disappointment came as a surprise. Vic hadn't been a part of his life in a long time. Not since high school when they played football together and worked at the grocery store at the same time. "You said you would use the GI bill to get your degree."

"Not with a baby on the way." Vic shrugged. "Besides, there's nothing on the rez for us. Down there, no one really knows we're Native Americans. I think they probably figure we're Mexicans. It's kind of nice. Although Latinos don't always get treated great, either."

"With a name like Old Fox, I doubt it. Only if you don't say something."

"Nothing to say." He nodded at Janie, who made a *let's go* gesture. "She probably has to pee. She does that a lot."

Raymond hugged him a second time. "I wish you could stay longer. We could go fishing or something."

"You should ask Tony. He's the fisherman in the family." Vic nodded toward the cluster of people around their younger brother. Tony seemed to be telling a story. They were smiling.

Some whopper about Gramma and her parenting methods seemed likely. "He's doing good. Did he tell you he and Sheila are getting married?"

Sheila was an Arapaho originally from Wyoming. They met at a powwow in Oklahoma during Tony's wanderings after high school. She was friendly. Kind of bossy, but Tony didn't seem to mind. Tony was the easygoing brother. He looked nothing like them or Mom. Short, round, high cheekbones, long nose, wide mouth, big hands, big feet. No athletic abilities, but a mathematical brain that could do physics problems in his head. He must've gotten that from his dad too. "He didn't tell me. I'm glad for him."

"That leaves you."

"That leaves me."

"Gotta go." Vic stuck his hands in the pockets of his gray dress pants and turned toward his waiting wife. "Come visit sometime. Don't be a stranger, bro."

"Hey, Vic." Raymond called before his brother reached the car. Vic turned back, his keys jiggling in one hand. "How come we never talked about our dads?"

"Nothing to talk about. No-good deadbeats who bailed out on Mom."

That was one story. Not the one Cap Dawson told. "Did Mom tell you your dad bailed?"

Vic walked back toward Raymond. Janie threw up her hands and began to pace around the Jeep. "No. She died before I was old enough to wonder or ask. Why are you asking now?"

"I just wondered why we never talked to each other about it. Seems weird. And why didn't you ever try to find your dad after Mom died?"

"Did you try to find yours?"

Not until a few days ago. "Not as a kid."

"And now?"

Vic was quick on the draw. Raymond sketched the events of the last few days. His brother's hewn features sharpened. His ochre eyes flamed. "Wow." He stared at his dusty ostrich-skin cowboy boots. "I guess Gramma and Velda were always enough for me. They were so . . . bigger than life. The two of them made up for six men. I never felt like I lacked for anything. Did you?"

"Not really."

"So why now?"

Good question. "You better go. Janie looks like she's about to bust a blood vessel."

Vic glanced back, waved, and grinned. "She'll live."

"Did you know my dad was white?"

Vic's bushy eyebrows rose and fell. "I guess I did. I dunno. Does it matter?"

That was so like his brother. A full-blooded Kootenai who had no feel for his indigenous brothers and sisters. No interest in tribal history, the Kootenai language, or customs. Just a guy. It must be so restful.

"I guess not."

Vic smacked Raymond's shoulder with his fist. "Gramma was a fine old lady, wasn't she?"

"I'll miss her."

"Me too." He ran his hand through unruly black curls. Also from his father. Maybe they could sketch drawings of the fathers by the characteristics they inherited that didn't come from their mother. "Like I said, come visit us. Nothing says you can't leave the rez now and then."

"Yeah."

Vic's square chin jutted out. "By the way, Tonya Charlo is staring at you."

She'd kept her distance during the service at the community center. Her mom said hello and patted his shoulder. Her dad sat as far from her mom as possible in the tiny gym. "No she's not."

"Yes, she is."

"Whatever."

"Get a life, dude."

He had one, just not one Vic would understand.

Janie waved as they drove away.

He waved as he walked to the Volvo.

He couldn't talk to Tonya. Not yet.

She would know that. She knew everything.

CHAPTER 35

The silent landscape was unnerving. Christine tilted her head, trying to hear something. Anything. No birds twittered. No crickets sang. No dogs barked. The stench of devastation hung in the air. A layer of white, gray, and black ash softened the thud of their footsteps as they approached their home. The Mast house stood, a squat, sturdy reminder that they had fared better than some of their neighbors, but the barn, the lean-to, the shed, and even the chicken coop had suffered a fiery death.

The drive along Wilderness Road squelched any desire for conversation. Stands of blackened toothpicks dotted the mountains where once-beautiful trees had stood. The stench of burnt wood and rubber still hung in the air. A person could only take in so much at one time. Christine's joy at Father's decision to allow this trip home before heading to Kansas dissipated in the high mountain air. She stared at her dirty sneakers while Mother and Father stood side by side studying the miracle of their untouched home in the midst of so much devastation.

"We'll need to clean up this mess before we put it up for sale." Father's voice held steely determination seasoned with mild sadness. "We can't expect a buyer to take it like this. I'll rent a truck to take the rest of the furniture. Thanks be to Gott that we still have it to move. It'll save us having to buy more in Haven."

"Why do we have to sell at all?" Hating the whine in her voice, Christine still couldn't quell the outburst. She ignored her mother's arched eyebrows and quick frown. "Come back to stay, Daed. The whole family can rebuild the outbuildings together. I'll get more houses to clean. Zeke will work at the furniture store with you. Delilah can go back to work at the store or take over teaching when Mercy finally makes up her mind to marry Caleb. It'll be like it was before, only better."

She would be safe from those influences they feared in St. Ignatius. Leaving without saying goodbye to Raymond had broken her heart. She didn't even have time to write a note for Esther Marie to deliver. If anyone would understand, Raymond would. He, too, straddled a line and found it untenable. Half Native, half white, he wandered lost somewhere in between. She would learn to confine herself to the world in which she'd been born and raised. Where she would someday die.

To her surprise Daed didn't rebuke her. Instead, the sadness spread across his face and lined his mouth and eyes. "I know this is hard for you. It was harder for me than I expected, leaving this place. But it's what's best for the family. We're doing better there. You'll see."

"Let's go inside." Mudder reached for Christine's hand. "It'll take a lot of cleaning to get the smell of smoke out of the house. We'll want it to be spick-and-span for the new family who lives here. Knowing you, you'll have it shipshape in no time."

They were trying to be kind, which made it all the harder not to cry.

She accepted Mother's hand and walked with her into the house. Memories greeted her. Abigail, then Maisie's birth in Mother and Father's bedroom. Birthday celebrations at the big table with carrot cake and homemade vanilla ice cream. Giggling under the covers with Delilah as they struggled to understand why boys were so strange yet so beguiling. Father and Zeke playing checkers by the fireplace. Mother teaching her to make sourdough bread from the starter.

Hundreds of memories had been sewn together into a beautiful crazy quilt that made them family.

Tears welled in Mother's eyes. The memories crowded her too. Christine squeezed her hand. "I'll get the supplies from the wagon." That would give Mudder time to collect herself. "We'll need lots of bleach, buckets, and scrub brushes. Daed will have to paint."

Outside Father stood talking to Juliette Knowles's father, who leaned against his Suburban. No doubt they were discussing plans to rebuild the Knowles's house. The Plain community—not just from West Kootenai, but from every district in northwest Montana—would pitch in.

That meant Nora and Mercy would be here. To have their friendly chatter again would be a blessing, even if it was only for a short time before Daed exiled her to Kansas.

With a big ache in her chest where her heart should be, Christine waved at the men and trudged to the buggy. She tugged at a box filled with cleaning supplies. Tears threatened. *Don't you dare.* She swiped at her face with the back of her hand. *Our house still stands. We have another one in Haven. We're safe. Gott is gut. You have no reason to cry like a big bopli.*

The squeak of buggy wheels and the whinny of a horse made her look up.

Andy.

Danki, Gott.

He pulled in next to their buggy and climbed down. *"Guder mariye."*

"Guder mariye." She managed a stiff smile to match his. "Have you started on your cabin yet?"

"I'll be over in a minute," he called to the other men. Her dad's frown dissipated. "I'll carry in these heavy boxes first."

The box wasn't that heavy. An excuse to talk to her? Christine ducked her head and moved aside. Maybe the meeting in the middle had begun.

Please, Gott.

Yet neither of them spoke on the short walk to the house. He stalked through the living room to the kitchen and plunked down the box. "It's not too bad in here. Smoke damage and the smell are really the only damage. You'll have to paint the walls, I reckon."

"Andy—"

"The men are gathering to make a plan. We'll start with Leland's house. The word has already gone out to St. Ignatius, Libby, Lewistown, and the other districts. My brothers will be here next week. I reckon Fergie and his brood will be here sooner."

"Andy!"

"What?"

"Did you . . . take care of your business?"

"Did you?"

"I didn't get a chance."

Disappointment flitted across his face. "Do you still—?"

Mother traipsed into the room. She stopped when she saw Andy. "Gut to see you. I was sorry to hear about John."

"He was a gut freind."

They commiserated over the fire and discussed the rebuilding plans while Christine busied herself unpacking the cleaning supplies and filling the buckets with soapy water.

"Christine, give Andy some of those brownies you made while I pack up the rest of the kinner's clothes." She trotted away without giving Christine a chance to answer.

The retort "Andy doesn't want my brownies. He doesn't trust me" danced on the tip of her tongue. She wrangled the words to the ground and cut him two large chunks of frosted brownies.

"I can't eat all that."

"Maybe their sweetness will remind you of something."

Like the sweet memory of the kisses they'd shared or the dreams they'd once held dear.

"Me?" He ducked his head and sighed. "I can think of nothing else. Meeting in the middle means leaving behind certain things. Are you prepared to do that?"

"I had hoped to say my goodbyes, but if that doesn't happen, then I'll have to live with it."

"So you're ready to commit to your faith, to your family, and to me?"

"I already did that. It's possible to learn more about the world and, in doing so, strengthen your own beliefs. It's important for two people who love each other also to trust each other."

"I'm trying, but you can imagine how hard trust is for a person like me who has been treated badly by someone who claimed to love me." His hoarse voice dropped to a whisper. "I have to know for certain that you'll not change your mind and decide to seek after this man and his beliefs."

"Look at all the time you spent with John and then with his

family. Does that mean you want to leave our faith and become like them? Baptists?"

"Nee, of course not." He rubbed his forehead and then let his hand drop. "John was my friend. His wife and children are still my friends."

"Raymond is a friend. He shared his world with me. Nothing more, but nothing less either. It was a precious gift. Like John's gift to you."

"It's different." More forehead rubbing followed the shuffling of his big feet. "I know it might not seem fair, but it is different."

"Because I'm a woman."

"Jah. You're a woman. He's a man. As much as you flaunt the rules, you know better. He's not even a Plain man."

He was right. She'd known from that first day when they went to The People's Center that she shouldn't. Raymond wouldn't understand. Nor would the rest of the world—even the Christian world, but she did. *"Be not conformed to this world: but be ye transformed by the renewing of your mind, that ye may prove what is that good, and acceptable, and perfect, will of God."*

"I'm sorry, Andy, I truly am. I want you to trust me. You can trust me."

"I'm trying." He swiveled and headed through the door. A second later he returned and swooped up the brownies. "Danki." He whirled and retreated once again.

"You're welcome." Her yell echoed in the kitchen where she'd learned to make elk stew, pie, and bread. "There's plenty more where those came from."

Funny how words could say one thing and tone something completely different.

Sometimes when they were courting, she and Andy would return to the house and sit in the kitchen after their buggy ride. They'd grin at each other as they whispered over iced tea and her brownies. They liked the idea of being in the house alone while everyone slept.

The last thing she wanted to do was hurt this man. But she had hurt him. His fear of trusting her held merit. Christine plopped into the closest chair and laid her forehead on her clasped hands. *Gott, forgive me. Please help me understand what is right, what is gut. I love Andy. I care about Raymond and his people. Can I not do both?*

Lay your worries and fears at My feet, child. I will do the work according to My perfect plan. Not you.

The voice echoed in the nearly empty room. As loud and as strong as Father's when he disciplined the boys.

"Gott?"

Be still and know that I am God.

Raymond found his Creator in the Douglas firs and the red foxes and the mountain lions. Hers made His thoughts known among the bleach bottles, cleansers, and sponges in a smoke-damaged kitchen.

Could He be the same God?

"By the way." Andy strode into the kitchen yet again. He had frosting on his upper lip. For some reason it made him seem young and, despite all her efforts to see him to the contrary, endearing. "I plan to buy this place from your daed. I'll set up the sawmill on this property. I'll live and work here."

Once again he strode from the room.

He planned to return to Kootenai to stay. She breathed. "So why're you telling me all this?" Her words bounced around a kitchen empty of their intended target. "What does that have to do with me?"

Could it be that having the man she loved live in the house she loved reflected just how God's plans were always bigger than any she could imagine or hope for? That Andy had chosen to trust her? That he'd laid his fears and worries at God's feet? That God was working in them, just as He worked in Raymond and his people?

"What's all the yelling about?" Mother stuck her head through the door. "A fraa bows to her mann's wishes."

"I'm not a fraa."

A knowing grin spread across Mother's face. "Not yet, but from the sound of things, soon."

From her lips to God's ears.

CHAPTER 36

St. Ignatius, Montana

Sh-sh-she's gone." Esther Marie's forlorn expression communicated more than her stuttered words.

Raymond stuck his fists in his khaki work pants. He had no excuse to stop by Valley Grocery Store anymore. He had no need of horseradish cheddar cheese. Those trips to the cabin to eat supper with Gramma were no more. With time the hole her death left in his life would shrink, but today it gaped like the Grand Canyon. His excuse to come here had been a good one. Christine deserved to know of his great-grandmother's passing. She'd want to know he'd found his father and planned to see him again. They had unfinished business.

"Gone where?" He took the roast beef, swiss cheese, and spicy mustard on rye sandwich from Esther Marie. "I'll take a bag of barbecue chips too."

"Her parents came and got-t-t-t her." Esther Marie held out the bag of chips. "They went-t-t to K-k-kootenai. Then K-k-kansas."

To Kansas. Then she'd left for good. Not for good. For bad. He had another hole to fill. He'd known Christine just shy of a month. How could there be a chasm this size already?

"She didn't leave a note?" In other words, she didn't say goodbye? "Nothing?"

"No t-t-time." Esther shrugged skinny shoulders. She grabbed a rag and wiped at a spotless counter. "Not me either."

"I'm sorry. You liked her, too, didn't you?"

She nodded. "She didn't mind the st-st-stutter. She didn't finish my sentences."

"I can see why you'd appreciate that." Raymond studied her pale-blue eyes. They were red rimmed. Her nose was red and her white, freckled skin tear-streaked. A woman with a speech impediment who dealt with customers all day long had a great deal of courage. "Have a good life, Esther Marie. You deserve it."

She blushed crimson. "You t-too."

"I'll tell Christine you miss her."

"Th-th-thank you. You're-re-re going to K-K-Kootenai?"

"Yes." He lingered at the counter. "Did you ever go to a speech therapist?"

She nodded. "It d-d-d-idn't help."

"Don't give up. They're always coming up with new treatments in medicine. I'll bring you some information the next time I come."

"You'll come back?"

Three perfectly clear words. "I will. I like the potato salad, and I get good service."

She smiled and nodded.

"Thanks for the sandwich."

Raymond saluted her with the plastic-wrapped goodness and headed to his car. He would come back to this store. The Amish offered something the cookie-cutter grocery store didn't—good food, a quirky collection of homemade rocking chairs, bulk materials, suspenders, hats, cookbooks, and employees who smiled when they helped their customers. Life could use more real people connections and fewer generic exchanges. Less social media.

Fewer computers.

One of the many things he learned from time spent with Christine. He'd wrapped his life around computer screens and software programs when what he really wanted was to be with people, to connect with people and the earth.

He had to tell her that. Then he would do what he was meant to do. Study people, not machines.

With his search for his father and Gramma's death, he'd missed too much work to take off for Kootenai immediately. Instead, he spent the next two days nose to the grindstone at S&K Technology. He liked his work. He liked his coworkers, but his work offered no connections to the real world, no soul. No spirit. Computers offered access to virtual worlds beyond the horizon, but these worlds no longer interested him.

Friday night he dug through his contacts and called Tonya's number. Her voice suggested the caller would have better luck next time but to leave a message in case she felt like calling back. He hung up without obeying her command. A twisted tongue kept him from telling a machine he had a hole in his heart and would the woman on the other end be willing to fill it?

Tonya would laugh at this. She would say she knew he would call and hang up. She knew he still had that unfinished business. She knew he had one more trip to make to the mountains.

Saturday morning he arose before dawn and drove the three and a half hours from Arlee to West Kootenai. In his entire life he'd never been farther north than Kalispell.

When the blackened landscape came into view, Raymond pulled over. The granola bar and coffee he'd consumed for breakfast roiled and threatened to come back up. He hopped from the car, leaned over, hands on knees, and concentrated on not vomiting. Fire had always been part of the natural plan. A thunderbolt of lightning ignited this conflagration. He breathed in and out and murmured an apology for his weakness.

If it hit him this hard, how much harder it must've been for Christine and her community, with their lack of understanding of the Creator's ways. They'd lived here for a few years—not centuries—but long enough to feel a connection.

Time to seek her out. Still murmuring in his Native language, he drove the remaining distance into Kootenai. A stop at the tiny store on the edge of the community resulted in directions to the home of a man named Lyle Knowles. The first build belonged to his family.

The whole town had turned out and then some. Nearly two dozen picnic tables were arranged in an open field near a cement basement and foundation of a good-sized house. The wood frame had been partially erected. An army of men wearing tool belts swarmed the structure. Pounding punctuated good-natured yelling back and forth.

Women surrounded tables laden with sandwiches, bushel baskets of apples, oranges, and peaches, pasta salads, pickles, chips, cookies, cakes, and pies. Many of them wore long dresses, aprons, and prayer coverings. Even though they came in all shapes and sizes, Raymond had difficulty telling them apart.

There she was. Christine stood near a row of Igloos on a table at the edge of the feeding area. A smile on her face, she filled a water bottle while talking to a long-haired blonde woman in jeans and a T-shirt. The woman threw her head back and laughed. Christine shook her finger at her friend.

The friend strolled away in purple cowboy boots.

If her parents saw him with Christine, she'd be in trouble. Sneaking around might cause even greater problems. It certainly had in the past.

"Here we go," he said to no one in particular. "Do what you came to do."

That last part he directed to himself.

Dozens of pairs of eyes turned his direction as he marched across the barren yard toward Christine. She hadn't noticed him yet. "Christine."

She glanced up just as an Amish man with the most vivid green eyes Raymond had ever seen stepped into his path. "You must be Raymond."

"I am."

"I'm Andy Lambright." The man shoved his straw hat back on his head. "It's time we had a talk."

Christine started toward them. Andy shook his head at her. She opened her mouth. He shook his head a second time. Her gaze shifted to Raymond. Her eyes spoke an apology, but she said nothing and ceased to move as if her black sneakers were encased in the cement used for the house's foundation.

"I came to share some news with Christine. It's personal." Raymond tempered the words with kindness drawn from a well of understanding. This was the special friend—the man who loved Christine. She was deeply lovable and deserving of such adoration. "It won't take long."

Andy's eyes darkened. The forest green turned dusky as if night had fallen in the forest. "Christine has returned to her home and her friends. She realizes she shouldn't have become so involved with outsiders. It violates our basic tenets."

"Okay. Let's talk." Raymond spun around and stalked toward the road in worn Reeboks. Andy matched his steps in dirty work boots. Even in the crisp October air, Raymond's shirt felt damp on his back. The soft breeze no longer cooled him. "Let me start."

"Fine."

"I never meant any disrespect for your community." Raymond threaded his way through stacks of lumber and dumpsters filled with debris until he reached asphalt. He stopped and faced Andy. "Christine thirsted for knowledge. She wanted to know about my people. She gave me a chance to know about your people."

Rubbing absently at a smudge of dirt on the back of his hand, Andy stared at Raymond. "You didn't learn much then. Planting gardens, taking care of our families, cooking, cleaning—that's the knowledge our women need. They don't need exposure to your world."

"Christine's not a housewife-in-waiting. She's an intelligent woman capable of making her own decisions. What harm does learning about another culture do?"

Raymond stopped.

He clamped his mouth shut. People wouldn't agree with many of his people's cultural mores either. Engaging Andy in an argument would serve no purpose. Long-standing beliefs didn't change on the strength of one conversation, but by relationships that evolved over time, like drops of water shaping boulders on the banks of a river. "Don't answer that. I respect your belief system. I understand your traditional view of male-female roles. The Kootenai people have their own, although ours is a more matriarchal society. I came to tell Christine that my great-grandmother died. She met her. She would want to know."

Andy's hands dropped. His gaze softened. "I'm sorry for your loss." His tone shifted to the awkward one men adopted when confronted unexpectedly by emotion. "It's been a hard time for all of us."

"There is something else I need to tell her. Something personal."

"Tell her or ask her?" The distrust returned as quickly as it had fled.

Raymond's temples began to throb. "Look, personal means personal. It concerns my dad. She'll know what it's about."

Empathy flitted across the man's face. Some struggles were clearly universal. Coming to terms with parents took many paths, but almost everyone related to the feelings associated with making that journey.

"I'll send her over."

Just like that. Christine's special friend had emotional maturity to spare. "Thank you."

"Then you'll go?"

"Then I'll say goodbye. I'm headed to Missoula to study ancient peoples at the university. I'll not be in these parts again. This truly *is* goodbye."

The battle raged on Andy's face. His gaze lingered on Raymond for several seconds. He shifted and straightened. "She'll be well cared for among family and friends. It's where she belongs."

"You mean with you. She belongs with you."

His gaze came up. "Both. You know it."

"She's special."

"Plain people do not aspire to be special." Andy backed away as if he loathed to turn his back on the enemy. "But your point is taken."

"You're a lucky man."

"We don't believe in luck." He whirled and walked away. "I am blessed."

The words danced on the air.

To be so blessed.

. . .

The path from the man who had intruded willy-nilly into their lives to Christine was a straight one. His head clear for the first time in weeks, Andy took his time walking toward her. He guarded his feelings and gathered his words. No one had a right to judge the Plain ways. Nor did he have the right to judge Raymond Old Fox. The man's intentions, however good, were not proper.

If he were honest—and he had to be because God knew his heart—Andy would admit to Christine that his actions had less to do with her eternal salvation and more with his own jealousy. Regardless of their discussions in the last few weeks, he loved her. Or because of his love, he argued with her instead of telling her his true feelings.

He didn't see those feelings in Raymond's eyes. Raymond liked Christine. She interested him. She might even arouse feelings in him. But he chose to see her as a friend he would let go for her good. It took an honorable man to do that.

Aware of knowing gazes and curious minds, Andy stopped so a picnic table stood between Christine and him. He picked up a cup and handed it to her. "He is a gut man."

"He is."

"I'm sorry I've let past experience get in the way of trusting you for who you are."

"I gave you far too many reasons to worry. I'm also sorry." She glanced toward the road and Raymond, but she didn't move. "We've both grown and changed, but I like to think it's been for the better. We will be better together than apart. I have never felt anything so strongly."

"I love you." The words slipped out in front of the whole world. "I always have. I always will."

A smile broke through the clouds. Her glance strayed to her father who stared, a frown on his craggy face. "You had to say that here with everyone around?" Her voice dropped to a whisper. "Shouldn't a statement like that be followed by a kiss?"

"It should. But being forced to wait for something so special causes it to be all the more pleasing and enjoyable."

"Is that right?" Her smile widened. "I love you too."

"Raymond has come to tell you something. You should go to him."

"Danki for letting me talk to him." Her smile disappeared. "I'll never see him again after today."

"He said as much. He has come a long way and he has news. Go before I change my mind."

"Gramma." Concern, followed by sadness, flitted across her face. She nodded. "I have to go to him. To be continued."

"To be continued." Andy watched her trot across what had once been the Knowles's front yard. She picked up speed as she went. She wanted to face Raymond's bad news head-on, and she wanted to offer her friend comfort. That made her a kind, good woman. Andy should be pleased at that.

God had blessed him with a loving woman. He couldn't wait to make her his bride.

Danki, Gott. He whispered a prayer and went to talk to Christine's dad before he stampeded his daughter and her visitor.

CHAPTER 37

WEST KOOTENAI, MONTANA

Only sheer willpower had prevented Christine's legs from declaring mutiny and running straight to the spot on the road where Andy and Raymond stood talking only minutes earlier. Now she rushed because joy awaited her once this conversation was complete. The chapter with Raymond would end. She would miss him. But a new chapter in her life had begun.

The fire changed her, changed Andy, and changed their community. As much as they jabbed at each other, they knew the moment he walked into the Mast house and announced he planned to buy it, he'd staked his claim and she'd accepted it. The events of the past several weeks grew them into people who could say that they loved each other aloud, no holds barred.

He still had to ask her to marry him, but she didn't doubt that he would. He couldn't do it until she cleared this final hurdle. Raymond Old Fox had come for her. She needed to complete her business with this good, kind man who'd taught her so much. Andy would never understand, but he would accept her hike into an alien world, and they would go on.

She could no longer let anything come between them. The restless desire for something more had left her like a fever that dissipated.

Raymond had returned to the car. His face weary, he leaned against the dirty bumper and examined something on the ground with great interest.

"Raymond, is Gramma all right?"

"She died." His hand dropped and he straightened. His face crumpled. His shoulders slumped. "We buried her earlier in the week."

Gramma was gone. That one afternoon spent riding in a car with her would never be forgotten. Her face—a road map of a long, fruitful life—would remain etched on Christine's memory. She'd had one day with Gramma, and that experience would leave a hole as if there should have been more. How much bigger that hole must be for Raymond.

His head down, he studied the ground, waiting for her response. He needed a hug. Anyone in her right mind could see that. Christine's arms ached to provide it. Her parents would say men and women could not be friends. The elders would counsel her that she must not enjoy the company of non-Plain men. Or any men who were not her family or soon-to-be husband.

How could this feeling—so like what she felt for her brothers—be wrong? She swallowed her own tears and breathed through the ache in her throat. "I'm so sorry." Before her entire Plain community and many others, she squeezed his hand. "She rests in peace now."

"You don't believe that." His lopsided smile softened the cynicism in his voice. "She was a heathen, as I am."

"I'll never stop praying for you."

"It's the pinnacle of arrogance to think your beliefs are the way, the truth, and light."

"I only know what I believe."

His gaze went over her shoulder to all those who pretended to work but instead watched and whispered. "Even after everything we talked about?"

"You opened my eyes to the beauty of the world around me. I'm so thankful for that." Every time she saw a blue heron or smelled the mustiness of wet leaves and dirt on a riverbank, she would think of him. Every time it rained or the wind blew or the water lapped along the shorelines of the lake, she would think of him. "That is a great gift."

"You made me examine what I believe and what's important in my life." He patted his old green car. "I left my laptop at home. I filled out the application to attend the university next semester. I'll study archaeology. That is a great gift, and I'm thankful for it."

Those beautiful eyes were so sad even though he spoke happy, hopeful words. He still had many miles to go before he found his contentment. Hers waited for her only steps away. "You're on the right track then."

"I am. I also found my dad. He's a guide for an outfitter company at Swan Lake." He ducked his head. "You have so much family, and I thought I should be more in touch with what I have."

"You're right. You should." They had both made progress. Because of the fire, their lives had touched for a brief few weeks. Part of God's plan? The bishop would say no. So would Andy. But those were human perspectives. No one knew for sure how God's plan unfolded. Only He knew. "Will you see him again?"

"We might go fishing."

"That's a good start."

"It looks like you have a good start here." He nodded toward the beginnings of a new house for the Knowles. "Are you and Andy getting married?"

"He hasn't asked yet, but I think he will." Heat curled up her neck and around her cheeks. Not a topic she ever imagined discussing with a man like Raymond. Yet she would tell a brother. "It might be soon."

"He seems like a good man, and it's obvious he loves you. Good for you, Christine." The sadness gone from his smooth face, he tugged car keys from his pocket. "I should go. You have work to do. And I have to get back to my life."

"Goodbye, Raymond Old Fox."

"Have a good life."

"I will." Christine walked around the car with him. She waited until he got in and rolled down the window. "Clean out your car before you decide to take Tonya on a date. Even girls who aren't germophobes like me prefer a man with a clean car or buggy, as the case may be."

He grinned. "Thanks for the tip. I'll take it under advisement."

"You do that."

He stuck his hand out the window and waved as he drove away. Christine watched until the car became a speck and then disappeared. Sadness for his loss washed over her, but Gramma's days were done. What happened to her now was in God's hands. They would both have to be satisfied with the knowledge that God's ways were perfect and, at the same time, unknowable.

A steady stream of delight filled the void—delight at having known this man and peeked into his world. His trip here to tell her about Gramma and his dad reflected his feelings. Their time together had been important. Now it was over.

She turned and walked back to the picnic tables. Andy, to his credit, waited. He didn't rush her. He refilled his paper cup. Her father had gone back to work. As had the bishop. There would be private discussions later, no doubt, but right now work was more important.

"He's gone for gut." She grabbed the full trash bag from its can and tied off the top, then set it aside so she could replace the bag. "Danki for letting me talk to him and for explaining to Daed. I know he doesn't understand. The elders don't understand. But it's done now. Raymond won't be back."

Andy glanced around. He crumpled his cup and tossed it into the fresh bag. "I know I've had my own struggles. It's only been a month, but so much has happened." He picked up a hammer and laid it flat on the palm of his big hand. "I keep reminding myself that we're honed by our struggles. Iron on iron. I don't like it. I suppose that's human. I wish I were a better man."

In this world there would be trouble. It surely didn't end here, but facing those troubles with Andy, God between them, meant she had no reason to fear. "You are a better man. I've seen your changes with my own eyes. I hope I can do as well. I feel like Gott must be so disappointed in me sometimes. Often."

"I reckon He must be used to it by now. We'll do better, but we'll never be perfect."

His lopsided smile made Christine's heart do that crazy drumroll. Heat toasted her cheeks. She picked up the trash bag. "I better get back to work. Everyone is watching us. I should help Mudder make more sandwiches."

"They all have their own troubles to tend to." He took the bag from her. "I'll drop this at the dumpster."

"I can do that."

"I don't mind. I need to stretch my legs."

He needed to think. That's what Andy did.

"Have you seen the girls? I need to talk to them." All three had their own struggles with men in this season of their lives. At least Christine wasn't the only one. They might not have the answers, but they could commiserate. ASAP. "Do you think Daed will want me to go to Kansas until we . . . I mean, until you . . .?"

The heat on her skin now a boil, she stopped and threw up her hands. "You know what I mean."

"He doesn't plan to return for at least another week, maybe two. He told me so this morning. He wants to help his neighbors, as does your mudder." Andy's words, coupled with the way his knowing gaze burned through her, grew hope from a spindly seedling to a stout oak. His smile widened. "We have time. Mercy had her own visitor—the smoke jumper. Caleb's fit to be tied. Juliette took a walk with her deputy. I haven't seen Nora. You have time to huddle with your friends."

Christine took the time to watch him walk toward the dumpsters. Everything about his muscle-bound frame, his walk, his broad shoulders, the shaggy blond hair peeking from under his hat mesmerized her. With a shake of her head, she grinned to herself. *You have work to do, missy. And friends who need you. And news to share.*

He loves me. And I love him.

She couldn't wait to see what came next.

CHAPTER 38

The tumult of emotion on Mercy's face when she turned, her hand in Caleb's, to face family and friends, brought tears to Christine's eyes. A burst of applause punctuated a ceremony filled with somber reminders of the sacredness of their profound, unbreakable vows. Joy permeated those bonds too. Caleb's friends pulled him from the arms of his bride—most likely for a round of foolish pranks. They'd bring him back in time to take his place at the corner table for his first meal with his new wife.

Mercy was the first in their tight-knit group to marry. One minute they learned to make peanut butter cookies together, the next they helped set up for a wedding feast. With a quick look to make sure no one noticed, Christine dried her face on her sleeve and threaded her way through the crowd that threatened to burst the seams of Noah Miller's home, to offer her congratulations. The bishop's willingness to host the service in his house had allowed the couple to marry despite having lost their homes to the fire.

"I can't believe it." She wrapped her arms around Mercy's tall figure. "You're a fraa."

"Me neither." Mercy's tremulous, dimpled smile grew. She dabbed at her hazel eyes with a crumpled handkerchief. Her chestnut hair carefully tucked under her ironed kapp, she looked beautiful in the dark-blue wedding dress she'd sewn herself. "Danki for all your help getting the food and tables ready. Not having our own home made it seem almost impossible to make this happen."

"This is what we do." Christine tugged her friend back to allow their fathers and the other men to pass. They needed to remove benches and add more tables to the living room where the simple service had occurred. Thanks to cooperative autumn weather, more tables were ready in Noah's front yard. "We wouldn't let a small thing like a wildfire keep us from having a wedding."

"Brace yourself—here comes Juliette."

Dressed in a beautiful antique-white lace dress with demure long sleeves and collar, their English friend had her hair pinned up in a bun, with long curling blonde tendrils resting on her neck. Of course, she wore her signature purple cowboy boots. Engaged to her deputy and newly committed to her Savior, Juliette would always be a unique, beautiful friend.

"Hey, Mrs. Hostetler, how's married life treating you?" Juliette swooped in with hugs for both of them. "Where's Nora? We need an ASAP to discuss exactly when Christine and Nora will join us in the ranks of one-man women."

"She rushed from the house the second the ceremony ended." No reason to tell her friends that the tears on Nora's face didn't look like happy ones. Christine sought an excuse that wouldn't be a lie. Something was going on with their friend, and it didn't look good. "She probably had to finish laying out the plates on the tables outside."

Arms entwined, they two-stepped toward the kitchen where an industrious cluster of women would be busy plating venison sausage, elk steaks, mashed potatoes, gravy, corn bread, green beans, and cherry fruit salad.

At the kitchen door Christine glanced back one last time in hopes of finding Nora. Life changed from one breath to the next. Mercy and Juliette looked so happy. Moreover, they looked as if they knew exactly what they wanted in life. They'd found their contentment.

Andy bent over and slid chairs into the tables near the floor-to-ceiling windows in the living room. He straightened. Their gazes collided. His eyebrows rose and fell. A tiny shrug followed. He cocked his head toward the door, edged that direction, and a second later disappeared through it.

"I'm right behind you, girls." Christine disengaged from the other women. "I need to . . . do something."

Several women looked up at Juliette's knowing snort. "Sorry—had a tickle in my nose." She giggled and squeezed Christine's arm. "It's a wedding. Love is in the air. Go hunt down your man and tell him you're ready."

"I'm just going to the bathroom."

"Sure, sure. Don't hurry back." Juliette grabbed an enormous peanut butter–chocolate chip cookie and handed it to Mercy. "Eat, Mrs. Hostetler. It'll hold you over until the feast. I know you were too nervous to eat beforehand, and you have to keep your strength up."

Christine left them bickering over whether Mercy should eat a cookie when a multitude of food dishes awaited her during the wedding meal. With all the stealth she could muster, Christine sidestepped her father talking to Henry in the living room. Her mother and Delilah were busy in the kitchen. The kids played outside in the brilliant autumn sun.

No sign of Andy in the front yard. Or near the corral. She found him in the barn admiring a beautiful saddle Noah had made. The bishop's trade as a leather worker brought cowboys from around the state to his doorstep seeking his creations. Andy turned when she shut the door. She halted in the shaft of light radiating from a narrow window in the loft. "It is a gut day. Mercy and Caleb will be happy in the home he's building for them."

"Gott willing." Andy brushed hay from his jacket sleeve. He seemed to look everywhere but directly at her.

"I like the smell of a barn." She edged closer. "Don't you?"

"I do." He seemed determined not to help this conversation along.

"Have you decided when you'll set up the sawmill? Or where?"

"Not yet."

"Andy Lambright. You wanted me to follow you out here, didn't you? Why?"

He cleared his throat. "Now that you're here, I find the words have flown out the window." Smiling, he met her gaze. "How's that for a fanciful turn of phrase?"

"Gut. Almost poetic." She smiled back. "But I don't need fanciful words. Plain words do fine. A Plain man even better."

"That's gut. Because that is all I have to offer."

"And all I need." Her voice shook despite the assurance that wrapped itself around her shoulders, its multicolored threads woven together by the experiences of the last several weeks. Loss, uncertainty, gain, new people who came and went, growth—each bright color shimmering in the present-day sun. "I don't know why we had to go through these things, but we did. We made it and here we are."

"I don't know either." Andy eased to within arm's reach. His gaze traced her face. His smile widened. "The only thing I know for sure is that there will be more travails in the future. Gott will be there to walk me and you through them. That's how it works."

"I was just thinking the same thing." Christine took two more steps. Andy did the same. They met in the middle, like two people who'd crossed a long bridge from opposite sides. His hands slid up her arms, across her shoulders, to her cheeks. His fingers were warm and calloused. She shivered and lifted her head to stare into those beautiful green eyes. "I'm so glad it works that way."

"Me too."

He nuzzled his chin in her hair. Then he did what she'd hoped for all along. He lowered his head, and his lips met hers. A gentle, sweet kiss that grew and grew. Palms of her hands flat against his chest, Christine closed her eyes and leaned into a future filled with such touches. A tiny fire nestled in the center of her heart crackled and grew. The flames leaped higher and higher. Heat warmed her head to toe. Breath left her body.

Christine stumbled back a step. She opened her eyes. Her hands went to her cheeks. "Ach, you know you have my heart. All of it. Always."

"Danki for giving it to me. I promise to never drop it or lose it." Andy grabbed her hands and drew her back into the tight circle of his embrace. "Marry me, Christine. Promise to never leave me. To always love me and only me."

"Jah. I will marry you." Christine laid her head on his chest and counted the thrum of his heart. "I'll love only you. I will never leave you."

Andy cupped her face in his hands and dropped kisses on her cheeks. "I love you. I can't wait to marry you."

"I love you." She whispered the words, but her heart shouted them for all the world to hear. "I can't wait to be your fraa."

His lips found hers again. The nicker of a horse, the smell of hay and manure, and bits of dust swirling in the rays of sun flickering through the narrow cracks between the wooden slats created the stage from which this memory would forever play.

It might seem like the first day, but it was, in fact, one of many leading up to that moment when life finally came into focus. Forests, rivers, medicine trees, bridges, waterfalls, traveling far from home—these had simply been a prelude. What seemed like adventure before had simply been rehearsal. The real adventure began this day with this man.

"Let's not say anything to the deacon today." Andy's fingers touched her kapp and lingered on the silky strands on her neck. Every stroke made it harder to breathe. "Today is Mercy and Caleb's day."

"Agreed. Tomorrow, then."

"Tomorrow, then." He grinned. "That doesn't mean we can't have another kiss, does it?"

"Just one?"

"Or two or three."

The squeak of the barn door gave them just enough notice to allow a few inches to grow between them. "You guys! There's plenty of time for that later." Juliette stuck her head through the door. "Mercy and Caleb are seated at the thingamajig—the *eck.*" She correctly pronounced the word for corner table. "It's time to start celebrating."

The kisses would have to wait. But not for long. Their celebration and their lives together were just beginning.

CHAPTER 39

Three Months Later
Missoula, Montana

Setting changed the way a person looked. Or maybe it changed his perspective. Raymond eased his way between tables where students applied themselves to laptop keyboards, iPads, smartphones, and occasionally the old-fashioned smell of ink-and-paper books that brought them to the University of Montana library.

Tonya sat alone at a table near the window. She could be any MU student, not a Native fresh off the rez. A pen stuck behind one ear, she chewed on her lower lip and wound her finger through a lock of her loose hair. She wore blue-rimmed glasses. Raymond had never seen her adorned with glasses. She became a beautiful woman all the more alluring, because her cocoa-colored eyes were sheathed by lenses. The rust-colored cable-knit sweater dipped in the front. A little chilly for January weather, but it made for a nice view. Again, perspective.

She didn't look up until he sat in the chair closest to her—all the better to see her.

"Hey."

"Hey."

She removed the glasses. "You came. Welcome to the Maureen and Mike Mansfield Library."

Ignoring her foray into the dulcet tones of a tour guide, Raymond took the glasses from her slim fingers and returned them to her nose gently. "I told you I would."

"I knew you would."

"Don't give me that." Raymond rolled his eyes. "You said you would have to come for me."

With a lazy smile she leaned in and kissed him, a long, lingering kiss. Her scent of sandalwood enveloped him. She straightened and went back to her laptop. "I told you I would come for you."

After a few seconds the fog cleared and Raymond was able to think—albeit not clearly. "I enrolled in the College of Humanities and Science archaeology program."

"Good."

"Don't you want to know how I found you?"

"You talked to my mom."

The woman had superpowers.

"She texted me as soon as you hung up with her. Then my roommate texted me to say you stopped by the apartment. Why didn't you just call me?"

"I wanted to show up. I wanted to show you I could."

"You're so cute when you're earnest."

"I'm glad you think so." Astounded, actually. "I'm sharing an apartment with Jeff Bear Don't Walk."

"That should be fun. He's more of a computer nerd than you are."

"He's studious, which is what I need." And the two-bedroom apartment was within Raymond's price range—cheap to cheaper. "I'm not sure I'm ready for this—academically."

"Baby, you've been ready for this for years. Even Gramma knew it. She just wanted you to herself a little longer."

Did she just call him *baby*? Raymond fanned himself with his financial report. "You think so?"

"I know so." Tonya smiled. Raymond fanned harder. Her finely etched eyebrows rose and fell. "I also know Gramma would be happy for you. She held on too long. She knew it. She wanted you to spread your wings. She knew if she'd let go sooner, you would've learned what you needed to know and come back to the rez bigger and stronger and bolder."

The lump that always filled his throat when he thought of Gramma didn't appear. "My dad and I went fishing in the fall."

"I know."

"You did not."

"Believe what you want to. I find out things. You know the grapevine at the rez is infallible." She tossed her sleek mane of hair over her shoulder for punctuation. "Is he still a white supremacist?"

"Do you think I would go fishing with the Aryan Brotherhood?"

"He's your dad and you needed to know him."

"He's kind of a sad guy. He drinks and smokes and sits staring at the lake a lot. But when he gets out on the water, he's different. He loves the outdoors. He loves nature. He's connected."

"Which is how he and your mom connected. It makes sense." Her phone squawked. She stuck it in her backpack without looking at it. "That and fast cars, fast horses, and fast lives."

"It's like he never figured out how to get on with his life."

"You won't make that mistake." She touched his cheek with one finger and then traced his jawline. "You know when to slow down and stare at the stars."

"Will you stare at them with me?"

The question slipped out and stood between them, naked and vulnerable.

Her smile blew through him like a gusty spring wind bringing rebirth, renewal, and possibilities too numerous to comprehend. "Count on it."

He pulled his chair closer to the table and laid his class schedule on it. "I can't decide whether my subspecialty should be straight archaeology or cultural anthropology."

"Really?"

"What do you mean?"

"You spent several weeks last year studying the Amish culture up close and personal. It's a slam dunk." She swiveled the laptop toward him. The archaeological program's website appeared. "Read the first paragraph for me."

"Sociocultural anthropologists explore how people in different places live and understand the world around them. They want to know what people think is important and the rules they make about how they would interact with one another. Even within one country or society, people may disagree about how they speak, dress, eat, or treat each other. Anthropologists want to listen to all voices and viewpoints—"

"You get the gist of it. Describes you to a T, Mr. Sociocultural Anthropologist."

"Did you know this university is located in the aboriginal territories of Salish and Kalispell people? I thought I wanted to dig around in the ground and find artifacts that revealed new information about our indigenous cultures." The memory of Christine's eager face as she walked through The People's Center bubbled to the surface. "I'm not sure who was being studied—me or her."

"You had a mutually beneficial exchange of information."

"I thought I might take some religion classes. You can't get a degree in religion right now, but they offer a bunch of courses. Did you know you can take classes in Hinduism and Buddhism here?"

Again with the eyebrows. This time they stayed up. After a few seconds of deliberation, Tonya nodded. Apparently a decision had been reached. "The point of higher education is to learn all you can about everything, even if it's learning for learning's sake. College is the only time we might get to do that. We figure out what we can use and what we can't."

This gorgeous fount of wisdom had kissed him. What made her more exciting—her brains or her looks? Hard to say. Tonya was a package deal. What would it take to get her to kiss him again? "What about us? Are we having a beneficial exchange of information?"

Tonya swooped in for another kiss, this one harder and deeper. She broke away far too soon. "More like an exchange of spit."

He shook his head, trying to clear it. His ears rang and his heart did jumping jacks. "You're a romantic gal, aren't you?"

"Gal?" She giggled.

"Shhh!"

Her eyes widened. Raymond craned his neck and swiveled. The librarian, a tall redhead with *come-hither* blue eyes, not much older than Raymond, kept the words to a whisper despite her glare. "Go outside if you can't keep the noise and the PDA to a minimum. Please."

"Yes, ma'am," they chorused in unison.

Tonya shrugged on her down jacket, scarf, and cap. Taking her time, she gathered up her books and stuck them in a faded denim backpack. Raymond followed her to the elevator. With equal deliberation she sauntered into it, pushed the button for the first floor, leaned against the wall, and studied her shiny blunt-cut nails. Raymond studied her. Together they strolled from the five-story building. Finally, to break the silence and not because it really mattered as long as she allowed him to go with her, he asked, "Where are we going?"

"Someplace where you're not ogling the librarian." Tonya adjusted the backpack, which looked like it weighed thirty or forty pounds, on her shoulders and then slid her hand through the crook of Raymond's arm. Snowflakes floated through the frigid air. They landed on her nose and eyelashes, sparkling like frosted jewels. "Or is that an existential question? Do any of us really know where we're going?"

"No ogling. Got it." He would never deny that the love of all women added joy to his life, but for this woman he would rein in his obvious enjoyment of the opposite sex. Raymond eyed the wide sidewalk, slick with rain that had frozen and turned to ice. He squeezed between two workers who spread salt and scraped the cement with shovels. The journey could be fraught with obstacles and falls. "I don't know where I'm going, but I hope it's with you."

"Honey, the fun is in the journey, not the destination."

Had she called him *honey*?

Contentment, awash in the possibility of adventures he couldn't begin to imagine, filled him.

Together, the white puffs of their breaths mingling, they set out to find their future.

ACKNOWLEDGMENTS

I n my journey as a writer of Amish romances, I never expected to learn as much as I have about such a myriad of topics. Writing *A Long Bridge Home* was no exception. In fact, it took me to such unexpected and delightful places. My husband and I spent a week driving through northwestern Montana. We visited West Kootenai, Libby, Rexford, Eureka, Kalispell, Glacier National Park, Arlee, Pablo, Polson, and St. Ignatius in the space of six days. It was a whirlwind trip that left me with great memories of a beautiful state.

I'm so thankful for the people who generously shared their knowledge and expertise with me along the way. The writing of *A Long Bridge Home* would not have been possible without the generous assistance of Jordan Stasso, the education coordinator at The People's Center in Pablo. Jordan spent almost two hours giving us a private tour of the center's exhibits and explaining the history and culture of the Kootenai tribe to my husband and me. He'd spent the previous evening until the early morning hours drumming at the Arlee Fourth of July powwow, so he was tired, but his enthusiasm for sharing his tribe's history didn't waver. He didn't shy away from answering delicate questions or shirk on time because he was eager to get back to the powwow. I did a great deal of reading about the Flathead Reservation, Kootenai history and culture, but nothing could compare to the interview I did with Jordan, who lives in the midst of it all and who is shaped by that history. Much of what he told us about his personal experiences as a Native Indian growing up in Montana colors Raymond Old Fox's character. Any mistakes or misinterpretations of the tribal experiences are all mine and, of course, greatly a figment of my overactive non-Native imagination.

As always my thanks to the entire team at HarperCollins Christian Publishing, but especially my editor Becky Monds for her enthusiasm and unerring eye for story. I've said it before about my line editor, but it bears repeating: Julee Schwarzburg, your patience for my lackadaisical approach to the *Chicago Manual of Style* deserves an award or a week's vacation in the Bahamas.

To my husband, Tim, I owe a debt of gratitude for his patience, sense of humor, and willingness to pilot the ship. We put one thousand miles on a rental car in six days, and he never complained. He did all the driving and turned a work trip into a couple's retreat filled with good food and lots of laughs—even when my choice of four hotels in seven nights left something to be desired. He was always there to speak up when my introverted nature kept me from starting a conversation. Driving through such gorgeous scenery with someone who appreciated it as much as I did will remain a sterling memory forever. Thank you and love always.

Last but by no means least, thank you to my readers who keep coming back for more. Your kind support is treasured more than you will ever know.

God bless and keep you.

Discussion Questions

1. Andy's parents urge him to tell Christine about his past relationship and how it ended. Do you think Christine had a right to know? Why? Have you been open with loved ones about past relationships even if it was a hard conversation? Why or why not?

2. It is common for missionaries to visit other countries and cultures to spread Christianity. What do you think of the methods employed by the Jesuits as described from the Native American Indian's perspective as told in this story? Do you think the details would be remembered differently by those who were involved in the evangelizing? What does this tell you about how history is remembered and recorded?

3. Christine has a difficult time reconciling Raymond's spiritual beliefs with her faith. She knows that he is a good person, but she also believes he is lost without Jesus' saving grace. Does she have a responsibility to try to change his mind? Have you ever been in a similar situation with a good friend who is a nonbeliever or member of a different faith? How did you handle it?

4. What do you say to people who believe that there is more than one way to heaven? What does the Bible say about good works and getting to heaven? Do people who are "good" or "nice" go to heaven?

5. Andy is torn between returning to Kootenai to have his own life and bowing to his father's wishes that he settle in Lewistown. Do you think he has a familial responsibility to stay? Why or why not?

6. The Amish believe in purity before marriage and that marriage is a permanent bond. This is no longer a commonly held belief in the secular world. What does the Bible say about premarital sex, marriage, and divorce? Is it hard to live up to those virtues in today's society? Why or why not?

7. The difficulty of forgiveness runs through *A Long Bridge Home*. Do you think Raymond should forgive the Jesuits for their treatment of his ancestors? How do you think they would react, knowing their actions have resulted in some Native American Indians choosing not to worship in Christian churches?

8. Andy has trouble forgiving his brother for "stealing" his special friend and marrying her. Could you forgive a sibling for such a painful, egregious action? Should you?

9. How did you feel about some of the beliefs espoused by Raymond and his great-grandmother regarding shamans, visions, and spirits occupying animals? How should Christians react to beliefs so different from their own?

ABOUT THE AUTHOR

K elly Irvin is the bestselling author of the Every Amish Season and Amish of Bee County series. *The Beekeeper's Son* received a starred review from *Publishers Weekly*, who called it a "beautifully woven masterpiece." The two-time Carol Award finalist is a former newspaper reporter and retired public relations professional. Kelly lives in Texas with her husband, photographer Tim Irvin. They have two children, three grandchildren, and two cats. In her spare time, she likes to read books by her favorite authors.

Visit her online at KellyIrvin.com
Instagram: @kelly_irvin
Facebook: @Kelly.Irvin.Author
Twitter: @Kelly_S_Irvin

10812236

80052194

800 5212194

800 52 12914

$ 79.63